Greta & Valdin

Rebecca K Reilly

HUTCHINSON
HEINEMANN

1 3 5 7 9 10 8 6 4 2

Hutchinson Heinemann
20 Vauxhall Bridge Road
London SW1V 2SA

Hutchinson Heinemann is part of the Penguin Random House group of companies
whose addresses can be found at global.penguinrandomhouse.com.

Penguin
Random House
UK

First published in New Zealand by Te Herenga Waka University Press in 2021
First published in the UK by Hutchinson Heinemann in 2024

www.penguin.co.uk

A CIP catalogue record for this book is available from the British Library.

ISBN: 9781529154191

Typeset in 12.19/14.3pt Bembo Book MT Pro by Jouve (UK), Milton Keynes
Printed and bound in Great Britain by Clays Ltd, Elcograf S.p.A.

The authorised representative in the EEA is Penguin Random House Ireland,
Morrison Chambers, 32 Nassau Street, Dublin D02 YH68

Penguin Random House is committed to a sustainable future
for our business, our readers and our planet. This book is made
from Forest Stewardship Council® certified paper.

Greta
&
Valdin

This book is set in BASKERVILLE. John
Baskerville of Birmingham formed his
ideas of letter-design during his
early career as a writing-master
and engraver of inscriptions.
He retired in middle age,
set up a press of his
own and produced
his first book
in 1757.

To the unknown man

Characters

Greta Svava Valdinova Vladisavljevic is Valdin's sister
Valdin Valdinovich Vladisavljevic is Greta's brother
Valdin Vladisavljevic, only called *Linsh*, is their father
Beatrice, mostly called *Betty*, is their mother
Lavrenti Vladisavljevic, frequently called *Casper*, is their older
   brother
Greta Gregers, in certain contexts called *the other Greta*, is their
   sister-in-law
Tang is their seventeen-year-old nephew
Freya is their six-year-old niece
Anthon Vladisavljevic, usually called *Thony*, is their uncle
Giuseppe Alonso, often called *Gep*, is their uncle's husband
Xabier Alonso is their uncle's husband's brother and that's it
Geneviève is their mother's best friend
Cosmo is the closest they have to a cousin
Lavrenti Vladisavljevic, always called *Vlad*, is their grandfather
Fereshteh, *Rashmika* and *Elliot* are friends of *Greta*
Vyacheslav, known as *Slava*, is a friend of *Valdin*
Holly is someone who works at the university
Ell is a PhD student in biology at the university

Sender

V

I come back to the apartment and find the worst thing in the world. A yellow postcard has been shoved between the door and its frame. This is not a postcard that says something like *I wish you were here with me on the Costa del Sol*, or, *Why didn't you tell me the Camino de Santiago is full of slow-moving retirees*. This is a postcard that says *CARD TO CALL*. It means that someone has arrived at my apartment with a package after driving through the narrow city streets, probably double-parking, and walking up six flights of stairs, and then, seeing as I wasn't there, because it was the middle of the day on a Wednesday and I do have some semblance of a life, has taken the package away again. Now I will have to go through the stress of locating this product in whatever mystery location it happens to be. I hope it's not Penrose because I don't have a car.

I pull the card out and while I'm thinking of a way that I could pass this burden on to someone else, it occurs to me that I haven't ordered anything. Maybe Greta ordered something? She orders a lot of books online and then shouts at me when they arrive. She shouts that she knows it's unethical to buy books from big conglomerates but it's the government's fault that she can't afford to be an ethical consumer because they took away allowances for postgraduate students in 2012. That's her official statement but I know she just doesn't like the girl who works at the bookshop near our house.

Greta and I were at our uncle's birthday recently and she had too many Bacardi and lemonades and announced that the girl who works in the bookshop near our house thinks she's better than everyone because she works in a bookshop and has a stupid nightingale tattoo and, well, Greta has also read Oscar Wilde so this girl can fuck right off. I said I think the people at the bookshop are fine, and she told me to go and fuck the Happy Prince with them then. I don't like them enough to suggest we have an orgy with a fictional French statue. Not at this stage, anyway. When I turn the card over and read it properly, I see that it isn't for Greta. It says *VALADDIN VLADISAV J* in big Sharpie letters. This isn't how I usually spell my name, but I can't prove beyond reasonable doubt that they meant someone else. I painstakingly enter the twelve-digit reference code into the courier website. The package is at the depot on Victoria Street West, which isn't far away, but it's hot and I want to go inside. I walk back down all the stairs, groaning. I want to sit on my nice new turquoise couch, drink the sparkling apple juice that's in the fridge and read my book of Spanish poems. I don't like reading about pain and trauma, I have the Al Jazeera app for that. And at the moment, for personal reasons, I don't like reading things about people being in love with each other either. Greta studies comparative literature and I can hear her exclaiming things in her room all the time, like, 'Oh, God, this man's just bloody jumped out the window because of hyperinflation!' 'Oh, Jesus Christ, everyone's got cholera because the warning posters are all in Italian!' A book about the beauty of the desert and sea and mountains and other Spanish landscape features avoids such things, for the most part.

I don't let myself consider going back inside as I leave the apartment building. I have to follow through with everything I plan to do. If I don't, I feel as if I've upset the natural order of things. Sometimes when I think things aren't going quite as I would like them to, I burst into tears or throw up. It's so bad, it's so embarrassing. I can't handle people cancelling plans with me. This happens, of course; plans change all the time. I wish I could be chill about things like that; I wish I could receive a message about not wanting to go and see the new remake of *Pet Sematary* because it's actually supposed to be really bad, but I can't. I just say that I don't mind but I do, and I go down to Event Cinemas Queen Street by myself because if I don't I'll throw up in my just-cleaned bathroom sink. Having OCD is so stupid. I wish I had something cool, like double joints or purple eyes. I feel as if the pathways in other people's brains are like well-maintained Department of Conservation hiking trails, while mine are modelled on the dodgiest slides at Waiwera Thermal Resort after it was shut down.

There are a lot of teenagers hanging around the fountain in Ellen Melville Square, their hands in the water in the January heat. Kids who go to the fancy city school with subjects like media design instead of uniforms. I went to a state school that was famous for its championship-winning sports teams and infamous for stealing promising athletes from other schools. None of this had anything to do with me. Greta wasn't involved with any sports either, except for a brief stint as a tennis player that was mainly to do with a short story she'd read about people playing tennis in the 1940s and wanting to wear a white skirt. Our older brother Casper was involved with sports inso- far as he wanted to report the school to the media over the sudden influx of boys on the rugby team who looked about twenty-one and all claimed to be transfer students from Fox- ton, but our mum strongly suggested that he keep his head down and get enough credits to pass without creating a media circus in our front yard.

I didn't cause any problems. I didn't say a single word to any- one the whole time I was at school, which was troubling to my parents, but the teachers didn't really have time to worry about it. Then my parents didn't have time to worry about it either, because Casper impregnated someone and ran away to Moscow. I was good at things, still. First in physics, first in maths, first in history. I yearned to learn French though. I wanted to wear a beret and meet a mysterious man late at night in a Parisian park. My ideas of what was sexy and what happened under cover of darkness due to conditions of homophobic oppression hadn't been fully developed at that stage.

The footpath on High Street is narrow, and I keep swerving around the bags of rubbish outside the shops and stepping off the kerb to let other people pass. I'm wearing jeans and white sneakers, a bad choice, because now I'm worrying about them getting dirty and it's way too hot. People smoke shisha all day and night on this part of the street, the raspberry smoke clouds linger in the dense humidity. It must be nearly 30 degrees. I've never smoked shisha, it's too much of a public statement. The men sit with their legs very wide apart and these jeans are new and too tight to do that. I prefer to sit with my legs crossed, anyway. On Victoria Street I start to worry about what the package might be. Maybe an official letter in a flat cardboard packet. I could technically become a Russian citizen – maybe they've sent me a letter saying I have to go there and serve in the army. God, wouldn't that be just the worst? What does their uniform look like? I look good in green, but I don't want to kill anyone. Or get up early. And my heart tells me their uniform might be navy. What else could the package be? I wait at the diagonal crossing outside Farmers and I have a bad and confusing feeling that might be more than just the heat.

Why would he have sent me anything? He's been gone physically for more than a year now and recently he'd all but evaporated from my mind as well. Why did I have to think of him again? I feel the folded Card to Call in my jeans pocket and think about him having touched it too, which doesn't even make sense, and I hate myself for it. Why would he have sent me anything? Why would he want anything to do with me? He was the one who broke up with me, that day in June, it was raining, I had come home early because I thought we could get a table somewhere nice if we went right then.

Xabi. God. I try not to think his name or say it out loud, using choice words like *someone I knew* and *this guy I went out with*. Those phrases always fool the listener. They make Xabi sound like a guy I met at the clubs and went for brunch with a few times before realising I just liked açai bowls and didn't like him at all. It was not like that. I loved him in a way I've never been able to love another person. When I was with him, it felt like nothing else mattered and I would be fine forever. That sounds stupid, but it's how I felt. I think that's how he felt too. I wasn't living in a fantasy of my own creation, my friends weren't at Food Alley drinking Black Russians and talking about how dumb I was for thinking I loved someone ridiculous, someone with a chest tattoo and a bejewelled vape, the kind of person who would leave you for someone they met at the trap club night you didn't want to go to because it seemed like cultural appropriation and it didn't start until midnight.

People liked us together, even though he was older than me. He was conscious of that; he wasn't one of those guys who makes a habit of dating younger men. He didn't make a habit of dating anyone, really. That made me feel special, but maybe in retrospect it was a red flag. He was used to being alone. He always felt like he was in the way. Things went wrong when I started feeling bad all the time, crying every morning before work. I didn't know what the problem was. No one wants to go to work; you just have to. Xabi thought it was his fault and went to live on a ranch in Argentina by himself. I don't resent him for doing that. I was so deep inside how bad I felt that I wasn't able to articulate what the problem was to anyone, not even to myself. I just really wanted him to love me and I was upset that I had become so deeply unlovable. Then it turned out that I just didn't want to be a physicist, despite having studied to be one for eight years, but he was gone by the time I figured that out.

Sometimes I think I can regain control by doing everything right, but the things I think I need to do don't make any sense. It's like being extremely superstitious but also hating yourself. When I don't do things right and I check Al Jazeera, I think everything is my fault. The war rages on in Yemen because I didn't close the freezer properly. The Amazon burns because I bought socks from the Korean stand in the arcade that were too small. People own five properties while other people sleep in cars because I dropped my phone and it cracked. I know it sounds self-centred. It's a horrible way to feel and I wish I felt some other way. I walk up the hill past the Sky Tower, and if it falls over today it won't be my fault. I'm going to pick up the package right now.

I can tell things are not going to be easy when I enter the post depot. There is a queue and the woman running the show looks as if she was once an excellent shot-putter. A man in front of me wearing a mismatched basketball uniform and Nike slides is holding a Malaysian passport, driver's licence, and what looks like a power bill. Jesus Christ, it's like trying to buy a gun in here. Or apply for a library card.

The guy at the front of the line hasn't got his Card to Call or a photo ID, but he does have cargo shorts and too many keys. He's shouting about how he's an electrician. None of that matters here, no one wants to hear his sob story. The argument rages on for several tense minutes, and the man leaves with nothing, pushing past me and muttering. This makes me feel like I'm a part of the show. I'm Miss Brill in the Katherine Mansfield story 'Miss Brill'. She thinks she's observing everyone in a park in

France, but it turns out everyone's looking at her and thinking about how she's a miserable old bitch. No, I don't want to be her at all.

'NEXT.'

The basketball man throws down all his forms of ID. The post depot woman is sizing him up; is this man going to get his package today? She takes pity on him and he thanks her profusely. He rips his package open. It's an HDMI cable.

I step forward. The counter is grey with a peeling laminate top and multiple taped-down notices about ID requirements. There are three wires strung across the front of the window, I guess to stop you from jumping over and grabbing your package in frustration. I'm too tall; I peer at the woman between the wires. Her name badge says *LORETTA*.

'How can I help you today, sir?' Loretta asks.

'Hello, I'd like to pick up a package,' I say, in what I hope is a bright and friendly voice.

She looks at me like this is the dumbest fucking thing anyone's ever said to her. She has her hair gelled back in the tightest bun. I've put gel in my hair before, but I looked creepy and scared myself. I looked like Bela Lugosi.

'Do you have a Card to Call?'

'Yes, I do.'

'Well, where is it?'

I put it on the counter and Loretta picks it up in disbelief. 'This is your name? Your name is Valaddin? Like Aladdin?'

'No, that's not my name, my name is Valdin.'

'Valdin Valaddin?'

'No, Valdin Vladisavljevic.'

She looks at me like I'm joking. I like my name, but I kind of wish I was joking right now.

'Why does this say Valaddin then?'

'I'm not sure, I guess the courier spelt it wrong,' I say, and then feel guilty about it. I'm reluctant to blame anyone but myself.

She shakes her head and goes over to the computer. 'Spell it.'

'Um, V-A-L, like Valerie Adams, D-I-N.'

She raises an eyebrow, 'B-I-N, like chuck it in the bin?'

'No, D, like . . . eternal damnation.'

'Oh, yep. And your last name.'

'Do you just want to look at my licence?'

'Don't have my glasses.' She stares impatiently at the computer screen.

'V-L-A-D, like Glad Wrap, but with a V for . . . Vortex Mega Howler. Then I-S, like . . .' I can't say Islamic State, that's not a good example. 'Like isthmus. A-V, like an AV library; L-J, like LJ Hooker—'

'The real estate company?'

'Yeah.'

'Then what?'

'E-V-I-C. Echo, Victor, Indigo, Charlie.' I forgot I knew the real phonetic alphabet.

She does some more typing. 'You from Slovakia?'

'Oh, um, nah, I'm Māori. My dad's, um, Russian, though.'

She raises an eyebrow again. 'Your package is here, I'll just go get it.'

I've been so distracted that I forgot how worried I am. My heart rate rises as Loretta shuffles off and searches in some bins behind her. Who's sending me something, and why? I hope Xabi hasn't sent me anything for my birthday. Why would he want to do that? And my birthday isn't until next month anyway.

Loretta comes back with a thick brown envelope, scans a barcode on it, and hands it to me under the bottom wire.

'There you go, Valdin, now you just sign there and then have a good day, okay.'

'You have a good day too, Loretta.'

'Oh, I will,' she says, confidently.

I take the package outside and I feel like my ribs are going to burst apart. I walk down the concrete steps and stand in a small car park next to a wall of red post-office boxes. The package feels like a book. I have a sudden horrible image of Xabi having sent me back a book of mine that got mixed up with his things. The book was called *Summerhouse, Later* and it was very special to me, but I don't ever want to see it again. I don't want to see it back here with a handwritten note saying something like *V – found your book while I was sorting through things. Hope you're well, X.* I don't want to see that.

I tear the side off the envelope and slide the contents out. It is a book. It is a book called *Dead Sea Fungi: Fungal Life in the Dead Sea*. What a stupid, stupid title. There is a note tucked into the cover.

Dear Prof. Vladisavljevic,

Thank you so much for your recent lecture at our research facility, it was greatly enjoyed by all and very informative regarding the recent developments in your region.

We hope to see you in Oman again soon,

Dr Hissah Asfour

This isn't for me; this is for my dad. My dad has the same name as me. They must have used the university database, we're both in there. No one's sent me anything. I don't know why I thought they would.

Lanyards

G

I think maybe I hate the university as an institution and question my involvement with it as both a staff member and a student, but nothing matters when I'm on the fifth floor of the library, touching the books and looking out at the harbour and the islands in the Hauraki Gulf. I like looking in the backs of the books and seeing how long they've been sitting on these shelves, sometimes fifty years. Everything that's happened in the world in the last fifty years, and these books were right here. Apart from, maybe, a few sojourns in someone's flat, or going along on someone's holiday to the Motueka Top 10 Holiday Park where they didn't even read the book because they were, like, too busy kayaking in Tasman Bay or whatever.

The reason I'm so happy is I'm in love. I think about whispering this to a copy of *Anton Chekhov: The Voice of Twilight Russia* but I don't want to embarrass myself. I'm in love with a fellow English tutor. I only refer to her as my co-worker, so that my feelings remain a mystery. If I say something like, 'My co-worker and I were having an ice cream at Island Gelato Company last night,' and someone replies saying something like, 'Oh, right, yeah, Holly said,' I act surprised. Maybe that's her name, how would I know? We're just co-workers.

I indulge myself in a fantasy about Holly inviting me to her family Christmas in Napier, where the National Aquarium is. I imagine her parents are on a first-name basis with all the penguins who live there. Holly will say, 'This is Greta Vladis-avljevic,' because she knows what my name is and she isn't afraid to say it, and in this fantasy she knows how to say it properly as well. There won't be any holly, a Christmas plant in other places, which I will point out for some seasonal humour. Everyone will want to pull a cracker with me, even the dog. I assume they have a dog. And a deck. A big deck. We'll all wear paper hats and they won't slide off or slip down over our eyes.

My own family will hardly notice I've gone to have Christmas somewhere else. My brother V will be busy bossing everyone around, hiding the presents in case we open them *wrong* somehow, and changing into a second outfit like it's his televised wedding reception. While waiting for V to get ready my dad will drink too much plum brandy and start speaking Russian exclusively, telling my mum she's as beautiful and knowledgeable as Sofia Kovalevskaya, the first woman to get a PhD in maths.

Holly doesn't drink plum brandy, she drinks whisky. I've never in my life thought, You know what, I might just have a whisky. Holly walks around at parties, whisky glass in hand, laughing, nodding. She knows a lot of people and they all want to talk to her. Boys like to talk to her about books and politics. Boys never talk to me about those things, even though my thesis is on Cold War Russian and English novels. They just ask me who I'm there with. I walk around at parties wondering where the recycling is.

I always hope that at the end of these parties Holly might ask me to come back to her house, but she never does. Maybe she wants to keep things professional. Maybe I shouldn't be thinking so much about kissing my co-worker. Maybe I shouldn't be looking at my co-worker's bum when she helps my supervisor plug in a computer screen. I try very hard not to look at Holly's Instagram photos of her with her ex, from when she did her master's in the UK. I know nothing about this woman except that she's blonde, but I assume she's called Natasha and they used to sit in little dark cafés talking about Proust. I imagine, if I met her, she would think I was very sweet and say that she could never grow long hair like mine.

Sometimes when I ask Holly how she is, she says, 'Better now you're here,' and I feel like I might open my mouth and all of my organs will come out onto the library floor. No one would look up from their laptops, because they all know how it feels to be in love too. One of these moments occurs presently, when I'm looking in the back of a book that was last checked out in 1978, and she messages me: *Hey, are you still at uni, can you help me with something?*

I feel proud, to be needed to do something. Like at school when a teacher asks for two strong boys, how it must feel to be one of the selected strong boys. I straighten my dress as I walk across Symonds Street to go and meet her. Holly dresses like Hannah Gadsby and I dress like someone whose boyfriend is late to meet them at the French Film Festival. She's leaning on the railing of the ramp to the arts building, looking at her phone. She's wearing a long-sleeved white shirt and navy suit pants with black Docs. Not really a summer look. It will be months before the leaves come off the big oak trees that line this part of the street.

'Hey, thanks for coming,' she says, as I stand as casually as I can. 'It shouldn't take too long.'

'Oh, it's no problem, I wasn't doing anything,' I say.

Touching books is not really what you can refer to as doing something. She runs her fingers through her hair as we walk through the automatic doors into the building. She has short hair that goes into a point and reminds me of an illustration of a shark in a book I liked as a child. I wonder if she ever thinks about my hair, and what illustrations it reminds her of. I wonder if she remembers the time we lay on the floor of the PhD common room, after everyone else had gone home, listening to the same song over and over again.

We go in the elevator and I still don't know what we're doing. She presses the button for the fourth floor and stands with her hands in her pockets, looking nervous.

'What are you doing tonight?' she asks.

'Oh, I'm not sure,' I say, trying to present myself as somewhere between too busy to spend time with her and not having any friends or social life at all. 'I'm going to Wellington tomorrow, I don't know if you remember.'

'Yeah, right, your mum's down there, isn't she?'

'Yes, she's there for a couple of weeks running a summer theatre programme. I'm going down with her friend Geneviève who has a very . . . bold attitude, so I don't know how that's going to go.'

Holly laughs and shakes her head. There's something about her that makes me feel like every time we're together is the first time we've ever met. Things never become more comfortable. She lets me get out of the elevator first. We walk down the corridor and stop at the English department PhD office, where she leans down to unlock the door with a key on a navy university lanyard. There are two kinds of people in this world, lanyard and non-lanyard people. Holly is a lanyard person. She has the confidence to pull it off. She holds the door open for me. That's another thing I can't pull off. When I hold a door for someone, ten people end up going through, thinking it's my job. Asking where the toilets are.

Holly stands in front of two stacks of poster board with her hands on her hips. 'How are we going to do this?' she asks.

'How are we going to do what?' I ask. It comes out a bit bewildered and suggestive.

'I have to carry these down to the gallery on Shortland Street. Didn't I say?'

'Oh.' She definitely did not say that. 'How far away is that, 850 metres?'

'I'm not sure how many metres, Greta.'

I pick up half the boards straight away. They're A1 and they're heavy as fuck. I have long arms, but they're quite similar to twigs in terms of breadth.

Holly surveys me. 'Are they too heavy? Should I get someone else?'

'No! This is fine. Not a problem at all.'

She picks up the other boards with minimal effort. She has a much more suitable physique for doing things like this. I'm quite good at origami. Should I bring that up? Maybe later. I open the door with my knee and we trundle back to the elevator. I press the button for the ground floor with my knee as well.

Holly laughs. 'Are you trying to show me your dexterity?'

'No. I don't need to prove anything to the likes of you.'

'That's true. I have seen you open a bottle of pre-mixed gin and tonic on the side of a bus shelter.'

I pause. Then I say, 'I'm also very good at origami.'

'Go on, then,' she says, looking down at the boards. We're standing close together in the elevator. Our elbows are touching.

'I can't do it right now, I need Zen.'

'Are you saying I'm not Zen?'

I shake my head slightly. 'You are absolutely not Zen. You're ruckus.'

'I'm *ruckus*?'

'Someone in my stage one tutorial said that,' I say. 'He said Chaucer was ruckus.'

We step out of the elevator on the first floor and walk through the foyer, past the German receptionist who's always hated me, and through the courtyard. I used to meet my dad after school here on Wednesdays. He would call it his standing Wednesday 3:30 to make me feel important. He would get sushi and coffee; I had hot chips and a blue Powerade. There weren't a lot of options back then. Now there are tacos and crêpes and all sorts, sold from inside painted shipping containers. Maybe Holly and I can get crêpes after this. We could go to the Kāpiti Store and get ice cream. I love ice cream. A couple of weeks ago we went to all four of my top Auckland CBD ice-cream locations in one day. My favourite is the blueberry, lime and sake flavour from inside the Ferry Building, even though the girls there always roll their eyes at each other if you take a long time to choose. Holly often chooses a bad flavour like rum and raisin or black sesame, but I don't hold that against her.

We come up to the crossing opposite the High Court, and no one's pressed the button.

'Do you want to use your knee for that too?' Holly asks.

'No.' I flick my hair over my shoulder, coyly. She raises one eyebrow and presses the button with her elbow, without dropping the boards and without breaking eye contact with me.

When my parents were away after New Year's with my uncle and his husband, Holly came over and fixed my bike. We didn't end up riding to Mission Bay; instead we sat on the driveway and I got sunburnt because we talked until it got dark. I took off my clothes in the upstairs bathroom and looked at the lines on my back. I felt like I was wearing our conversation.

We walk past Old Government House and the patch of grass where they put up a marquee and serve orange juice and sparkling wine at graduation events. V was upset at his graduation and kept saying it was because he didn't want to wear the hat. That's a thing he does whenever he has a big problem, like not wanting to be a scientist – he imagines all of his issues are the fault of a single object. Everything is the hat's fault. He's not crying because he misses his ex, it's because the corner of his bed is too close to the wall.

'Are you okay?' Holly asks as I adjust my fingers on the boards.

'Yeah, I'm fine.' She smiles at me and I smile back. 'Sorry for making you into my Hire a Hubby.'

'No, no. It's great exercise. My arms are going to be so jacked after this.'

She smiles again and shakes her head at me. 'I would have done two trips but I'm in such a rush, I'm so nervous about meeting Sonja's friends tonight. It's weird having a girlfriend again after so long, having to go through all this meeting-the-friends, meeting-the-family stuff. I haven't done all of this since, you know, the disaster in Portsmouth. It feels different with Sonja, though. I know it's only been, what, a couple of months? Do you remember?'

'No.' I have never heard of this Sonja before in my life. I maintain a steady grip on the boards as I walk across Princes Street and down the hill of Shortland Street.

'How long do you think it will take me to get to the hospital? I'm supposed to meet her there at five when she gets off.'

'What does she do there? Phlebotomy?'

'No, Gre. You always guess such funny things,' she says. 'She's a mental health nurse. I swear we've talked about this.'

'No, we haven't.'

'I feel like I haven't thought about anything except her for weeks.'

I want to throw the boards on the ground, but I don't, I grip them tighter and tighter, so tight that white patches form around my cuticles. I can't breathe properly and I suck in as much air as I can without arousing suspicion, wishing I could suck back in every dumb misguided thing I've said and thought back into my body, pushing them all deeper and deeper until they never existed.

'Where did you meet?' I ask.

'The usual way.'

'Oh, so at a cocktail bar?'

She's looking at me like I've lost my mind. 'No, on Tinder.'

Whenever I go on Tinder it's all single mums keen to experiment and straight couples looking for an *extra pair of hands*. A nurse! Nurses are the heroes of our society! Russian literature students are definitely not! She swears we've talked about this!

'Do you think I look okay?' she asks. 'I just want her friends to like me.'

'Why wouldn't they like you? You're fine.'

I'm melting into the footpath. I can see the gallery, our end point, but it's so far away. I'll be dead by the time we get there. Someone will have to call my mum to get a spade and scrape the puddle that used to be me into a bucket. She'll throw me on her gardenias, and they'll die too. The neighbours will ask what became of the pretty white flowers and their glossy green leaves and where did the pit of smoking ash come from, and my mum will say, 'Do you remember my daughter, Greta? She's dead. I swear we've talked about this.'

'Thanks, mate,' Holly says. 'You always make me feel better.'

I try to shrug, but it's hard when emotionally I'm dead and physically my arms are about to drop off.

'You'd really like Sonja. She's a good person – you know, she cares about real things that matter. She's not worrying about the kind of shit we worry about. She doesn't waste her life complaining that *Das Kapital* has been grossly misinterpreted by Anglophone scholars. We don't argue about whether John Stuart Mill's dad was gay with all his academic friends.'

They were definitely gay, all of John Stuart Mill's dad's

friends were gay, one of them lived in Montpellier for God's sake, they were going for *walks* all the time, talking about *Herodotus*. They were sending each other *letters* about how they didn't want to be in the *war*. If that's not gay, I don't know what is.

'She's hot too,' Holly says in a low voice, like we're just a couple of bros having a smoke around the back of the pub, leaning on a fucking Subaru or whatever it is men do. 'She's Slovakian.'

I want to kick the cover off the manhole I'm walking over and fall into it. I bet Sonja's last name is something good that fits on forms, like Jovich or Bobkov. I imagine her on the phone, being hot, saying, 'Yes, that's right, B-O-B, K-O-V.' She's never once been prone on her kitchen floor while shouting at some poor person at Studylink, 'No, V for Victor, L for lanyards, A for . . . aneurysm, D for . . . a didactic approach – hang on, only eleven more letters – I for Icarus, S for Susan Sarandon—'

'Cool. Hot? Nice,' I say, like I'm advertising ice blocks.

'Yeah, I don't know what she's doing with me.'

I don't know what I'm doing with you, Holly, I think. I should be on a beach somewhere with people bringing me drinks and telling me that I'm hot too and that the things I like talking about are scintillating and not a waste of my life at all.

She unlocks the front door of the gallery with a swipe card. I don't look at her. I put the boards down heavily in the foyer and fold my arms.

'What are these for anyway?' I ask.

'They're for a competition where people make posters about their thesis topic.'

I think about making a big sparkly poster about my thesis, with Mikhail Gorbachev's face made out of rhinestones and glitter. I don't tell Holly, because I guess she would think that was stupid. Outside she stands in front of me with her hands in her pockets. I don't unfold my arms.

'I'd better get going to the hospital, then. Which way are you going?'

'The opposite way.'

'Oh,' she says, nodding. 'Well, thanks for your help. I'll see you soon.'

'Yes. Maybe.'

'Maybe?' She looks at me right in my eyes and smiles like nothing is wrong. 'You're a mysterious woman, Greta.'

We say goodbye and I turn around and start walking down the hill. I don't know where I'm going, but I don't turn back. She can't ever know that I'm crying.

Desks

V

I hate the feeling of the book that isn't for me. It burns as hot in my hands as the sun across my face so I decide to get rid of it as soon as possible. I walk back up, down, up Victoria Street the way I came, then I keep going up the steep path to the university. I take the worst route possible because I don't want to see anyone I used to work with and have to listen to the concern in their voices when they ask me how I am these days. In a small country, in a small field like physics, you can't just make out like you got a similar job somewhere else and that's why you quit. Everyone will know you had a breakdown. You will have to live with the memory of deleting your email account and of figuring out how to change your phone number so no one can contact you while you're sitting on the floor of your parents' basement watching your fortieth episode of *Say Yes to the Dress*. I decide not to think about that anymore.

There aren't many people around at the university because it's summer, mainly people doing extra papers and people who work at the radio station, so I don't run into anyone. No one asks me if I'm okay or if I know where I'm going in this building, because it's obvious what I'm here for. I'm here to see one of the most well-regarded yet infamous people at the School of Biological Sciences, to whom I also happen to bear a striking resemblance.

I knock on the door and my dad says, 'Come in,' in an authoritative, professional tone, because he doesn't know it's me. Not someone who respects him as an expert in the symbiotic relationship between crustaceans and gram-negative bacteria, but rather someone who respects him as the person who taught them how to set the VCR to record *McDonald's Young Entertainers* in 1997.

He looks up from what he's doing. 'V, what are you doing here?' he asks. He has a printed-out crossword puzzle from the *New York Times* in front of him on his desk. It's always strange seeing him in his work environment and his work clothes, today tan chinos and a forest-green shirt, usually thinking about something serious. 'Has something terrible happened?'

I shake my head. 'No. Not that I know of. This got delivered to me by mistake. Why are you standing up doing that?'

'Haven't you heard of standing desks?' he says, taking the package. 'They're all the rage, everyone stands up all the time these days.'

'I don't think you're supposed to just stand up in front of a regular desk.'

I put my hands in my pockets and look around the small room, imagining what it must be like to see my dad from the perspective of the students and colleagues he interacts with all day. Nervous about their dissertation meeting, excited about . . . fungi, I don't know. There's a picture of a clown pinned on the wall with the caption: *Hello Papa Linsh, are you afraid of clowns? I'm not. By Freya, age 6.* Freya is my niece. There's a photo of all of us too outside a restaurant a few years ago. I have my mouth open, Casper has his eyes shut and Greta's looking in the opposite direction, but my mum looks good. Not really happy to be there, though. It was probably because the restaurant was in Ponsonby. She hates being around people who believe themselves to be the upper echelons. My dad took the photo, and I guess decided it was the perfect choice to print out and hang on his wall. I wonder what happened to the sage silk shirt I'm wearing in it.

'*Dead Sea Fungi: Fungal Life in the Dead Sea*. A creative title, huh?' he says, having opened the envelope and inspected the note in the front cover of the book. 'Oh, it's from Hissah. They were so nice to me in Oman, I will have to send them something back. Thank you.'

'What for?'

'Bringing this over to me. You could have just left it until we next saw each other.'

I shrug. 'It's okay, I just wanted to get rid of it.'

He looks up at me sharply and I realise this phrasing delivered a bit more subtext than I would have liked. 'Why?'

I look around again. Out the window, someone in green overalls appears to be hosing down a roof.

'Oh, I just. I don't know,' I say. 'I had to go and pick it up at the depot and I thought it might be someone returning a book I lent them a long time ago.'

'Who would return a book via the post rather than use it as an excuse to meet up for coffee and gossip?'

The person hosing hasn't thought their plan out very well and the water is running straight back down the roof onto them. 'I don't know. Xabi, maybe.'

'Ah,' says my dad, and I don't look at him in case he feels sorry for me. 'Do you need the book back? I can ask Thony, if you would like.'

'No,' I say, in what I hope is a breezy, indifferent tone. I don't love thinking about the fact that other members of my family are still in contact with Xabi. I don't want to go into why that is right now. 'I can just buy a new copy.'

'Look at you, buying books like you're going to singlehandedly save the local book industry.' He leans on the back of the chair he's standing behind at his desk. 'Work's going okay then?'

'Yeah. It's fine.'

'Do you think you'll ever get to film something in Oman? I

think you would like it; you can see turtles on the beach there. I know you like how the turtle's spine curves inside its shell.'

'I don't know if that's on the cards at the moment. I got in trouble about the episode we filmed in Matamata, with the tourism board. Because of what I said about the hobbits.'

He shakes his head. 'Oh, Valdin. The hobbits are national treasures.'

'You don't have to tell me. I was CC'd into many emails.'

He looks down at the crossword on his desk. I wish I had my own desk. I guess if I had stayed being a physicist, I could have had my own desk. Now I work in a shared space with a break-out room. I don't know what I would do with a desk – I guess I could get one and put it in the middle of the living room and just sit at it. Greta would be annoyed. She would think I had made a communal area all about myself.

'How's Slava?' my dad asks, out of nowhere. Slava is my Russian friend. He works in marketing and keeps me up to date with all the latest gay slang and celebrity feuds, whether I want him to or not.

'He's fine. I saw him the other day. He said he was going to start drinking more frappés as a power move and I didn't know what that meant.'

'Is there anything going on there?'

'What? No, he's my friend. I wouldn't want to go out with him, he would make me go to wineries and the sorts of cafés where the waiters are too friendly and they're selling pieces of bread and calling them freedom loaves.'

He shrugs. 'I thought you might be a bit lonely.'

'I'm not,' I say, but I don't know how true this is. I hadn't really considered it until I got the stupid Card to Call.

'What about Greta?' he asks.

I raise my eyebrows. 'I'm not so desperate that I'm going to start an incestuous relationship with my sister.'

'I meant is she seeing anyone.'

'Oh. There's this woman who hangs around our house a lot. Greta does an unnatural laugh when she's there, so she's probably in love with her. I don't trust her though. She's always explaining things that Gre definitely already knows.'

'Like what?'

I think about it. 'Like how to use the ice-cube setting on the fridge. It's our fridge. Greta knows how to make ice, she's always drinking caipirinhas and watching Brazilian soap operas. She won't watch my show, she said it would be weird to look at me through a public lens. Anyway, I don't trust this woman. She was doing this speech the other day about why Michelangelo painted the Sistine Chapel. And she was wearing a blazer in the middle of summer. She reminded me of one of those teachers who acts really fun and laid back for the first couple of weeks and then gives you a low grade because they don't like your attitude.'

'So you don't think it will work out between the blazered woman and your sister?'

'I couldn't say. Greta does seem to have a particular interest in people who tell her things she already knows.'

'I've noticed. Valdin, I was worried when you came in here. I thought something bad had happened.'

'Like what?'

'Anything could have happened. Something serious, for you to show up here in person.' He pauses and then says, 'Maybe your brother had an accident at work and lost his hand.'

'How would he do that? He's a visual art lecturer not a mill operator. He's not going to lose his hand setting up a Power-Point.' I'm relieved that he hasn't brought up the last time I came to see him unexpectedly. That time, I had quit my job and was crying and asking if I could move back home. Maybe I had presented some melodramatic ideas about how I was destined to live a life of poverty and abject misery. 'Besides, Casper wouldn't call me in an emergency, he'd call Mum. I'll let you know if Greta gets bored to death by a lecture about how our rubbish collection works by one of her love interests.'

Someone knocks on the door. My dad says 'Come in' again, in the same professional voice.

'Sorry to interrupt.' A person with a shiny bob and a button-up shirt pokes her head around the door, as if I might be someone serious and my dad wasn't just doing a crossword. 'I was just wondering if you knew where Erik was?'

'Yes,' he says, looking concerned. 'He had a dental emergency, his crown broke and he had to leave early. Is everything okay? Does someone need help in the lab?'

When my dad says *crown* it doesn't sound quite right, or rather, it doesn't sound the way I say it or the people in a local advertisement for Crown forklifts say it. He's lived here for a long time, since he was a teenager, but there are some words that always sound vaguely Russian when he says them. It's strange to think that there was a time when he didn't speak English at all, and a time when he must have had a strong accent. People weren't filming themselves so much in those days, there are no known records. I suppose, in that way, the phenomenon of my father with a different voice doesn't exist.

'Oh no, it's fine. It was just a supervision. A supervisor meeting,' the person corrects herself. She isn't from here either, she sounds like – maybe Sean Connery playing the part of a mouse.

'Ah, I'm sure he'll be disappointed to have missed you. I'll let him know that you came by when I check on him.'

She thanks him and looks at me and nods her head before closing the door again, as if to signal that I can now get back to my vital business. I don't really want to, though. I didn't think bringing the book here through and now I've exposed too many of my underlying emotions and feelings about Xabi.

My dad looks seriously at me. 'Come for dinner with me.'

I shake my head. 'I'm not that lonely; it was an overstatement. Because of the heat.'

He shrugs. 'I am, though. Your mother's been away for a while now.'

'Why didn't you want to go and see her with Greta and Geneviève this weekend?'

'Oh, I don't want to intrude. She'll be back soon enough.' He straightens the book on the desk, almost too carefully. 'Why don't we go somewhere nice in Newmarket? We can invite Thony as well. And what about Greta?'

'She'll be fine, she's never lonely.'

He furrows his eyebrows then nods. 'Okay, let's hit the town.'

The Hill

G

I've solicited a woman. I'm Wellington Greta now, and she solicits women. I've put on a dark purple lipstick. I'm wearing the new lavender cord jacket my mum bought because I was cold. She didn't believe I'd forgotten my jacket, but she didn't know how much I'd been crying while packing. This woman is not part of Auckland Greta's usual repertoire; her profile just said *I'm depressed and frigid* with a tongue-poking-out emoji. Auckland Greta is usually entranced by people who say they like books and films and things, and look where that's got me. It's time to shake things up.

I'm supposed to meet the woman in the suburb of Brooklyn and go to an after-party for a play. Obviously, I haven't seen the play, but it was called *elicitations* and looked like it involved a lot of audience participation and throwing flour around. And I think that all sounds great and not anxiety-inducing or a situation to avoid at all costs because I am not a stick-in-the-mud anymore. I'm a fun, cool person who goes to parties where they don't know anyone, in Wellington, where people pronounce the letter T so sharply that any offers of water sound like a threat. I had prepared this whole speech for Geneviève when she questioned me about leaving the hotel at 10pm to go and meet a stranger from the internet, but then she just said, 'Okay, have fun.' My mum would have questioned my motives more, but she's staying somewhere else, with some friend of hers. She felt bad that there wasn't room for me to stay there too, but I didn't want to stay on the coast. I like to be in the city, where the action is.

I walk from Courtenay Place to Victoria Street to wait for the number 7 bus. The town aspect of this town is quite different from my own town on a Saturday night. There's just 50 metres of people really going for it and that's it. In Auckland the concept of town is spread thinly over some kilometres. I suppose it's like a Helen Frankenthaler painting as opposed to the Mark Rothko style they have here, if you want to use abstract expressionism as an analogy. I feel like I'm in a movie. Like *Trainspotting*. Or one of those reality shows that takes a behind-the-scenes look at the lives of bouncers in northern England.

I rub my legs to try and warm up. Most skirts are short on me, but this one is intentionally so. I hope the woman I'm going to meet doesn't hate me. What's the worst thing someone could reasonably ask me to do at a party? Maybe heroin. *Don't you even want some heroin? Sorry, I have an early flight. Otherwise, wow, yeah, that would have been . . . primo.* I don't go inside the bus shelter, because three people are smoking in there. Maybe the people at the party will think I'm more fun if I smell like smoke, though.

The bus comes and I tag on as if I'm from here and I'm going to Brooklyn for a normal reason, like I live there or a close personal friend of mine lives there. Not because I'm going to meet some woman who after tonight I'll probably never see hide nor hair of ever again. I shouldn't say things like *hide nor hair* when I get to the party. The old Greta, in love with any person who said they'd read a book, she would have said that. The new Greta says *dope* and *lit*.

The bus has bright fluorescent lighting. I sit on a fern-patterned seat and feel crazed. What if someone sits next to me and I don't even go to the party, instead I go to this new person's house and smoke weed and watch an absurdist sketch show, the kind that has lots of men and gross stuff happening, except I don't frown and say I hate it, instead I say, 'Woah, crack-up!' What if I bring this person to the party, and the woman says, 'Wow! What a power move, bringing a second date to your first date,' and then everyone at the party stops to look at me and compliment me on how bold I am? Yes, yes, yes. I'm never going to be sad again. Am I drunk? Gen kept ordering drinks for me at dinner. Older people like to make up for having no idea what's going on by splashing cash around. I didn't even know there was such a thing as an absinthe cocktail.

The hill to Brooklyn is unnecessarily steep. It would be easy to become fit in this city; everything seems inconveniently placed and the bus routes make no sense. I have a strong interest in urban planning because I used to live in Germany. My friends probably expected me to come back from Europe insufferable, talking about drinking $5 bottles of wine while looking out over a fortress at sunset but no, all I came back with were my thoughts about how we could improve the bus network.

The other three people on the bus start looking in their pockets and shuffling around. This must be the place where everyone gets off. I tag off and say thank you to the driver in a confident voice.

The bus people walk down the road in a line and stop at a set of traffic lights where there are shops. There's a hairdresser with a blackboard sign out, inviting me to have a cut and colour with senior stylist Sarah for the new customer price of $180. I look at the sign to impress the bus people, as if I don't get a $28 haircut every six months and feel like I'm the Queen of Sheba.

The woman is not at the Brooklyn shops as agreed. I don't message her right away, so I don't seem too eager. I stand in front of a closed fish-and-chip shop for approximately thirty seconds and then message: *hey I'm at the shops now*. Suitably casual. I wonder if this is a friends thing or if she wants to do kissing and more. I don't know who in their right mind is using dating apps to look for new friends, but apparently a lot of people are. This is why you have to swipe on the profiles that say things like *I'm a gay horny bitch* or *Full-time lesbian, part-time barista*. My 'Depressed and frigid' could go either way. It's quite depressing being one of the queer people sometimes. It's a good idea to start off saying you're frigid so no one expects too much.

I go into a liquor store and do some browsing to use up time. Maybe a nice pinot noir, maybe a cheeky cab sav. There's a white guy about my age working here and he doesn't look at me. Not many people are in the right demographic to be looking at me in this city – lots of blue-haired teens, lots of old people with reusable bags. In Auckland, men are looking at me every day, shouting from cars that they would be interested in getting to know me and my oral services better. Not in those words; in other words. They aren't great orators like I am.

I would like to buy one bottle of pre-mixed gin and tonic, but they only have four-packs. I buy a four-pack. The guy checks my ID for a really long time, as if I would have gone with 'Greta Svava Valdinova Vladisavljevic' if I had been in the market for an inconspicuous fake ID. I try to glare but my face smiles of its own volition, probably because of sexism.

After twenty minutes, I've inspected each and every storefront. None of them have really spoken to me except for the giant photograph on the side of the chemist of a clearly Slavic family enjoying some advice from a pharmacist. I'm cold. And now I miss my granddad. I decide I have to call the girl, which is an unpleasant situation to be in. I used to work in a call centre so I'm used to calling people I don't want to talk to, but that doesn't make me feel better. She doesn't pick up. Maybe it's loud at the party and she can't hear her phone. Maybe she's on too much heroin already. I should have asked for the address so I could go on my own. At this stage any option would be preferable to standing in front of a Ray White and looking at property options in the Brooklyn and Happy Valley area. I wonder if I'm going to tell V about this incident when I get home. If this happened to him, he'd make it into a two-hour story where he made me role-play as one of the characters, probably him, while he drank a cocktail and narrated. He doesn't always tell me things, though. That's his prerogative as an older sibling.

It's been one hour, now. It's ten past eleven. I should have got the woman to add me on Messenger so I could at least see if she was seeing my messages and ignoring them. I've already given her my number, because it's a new bit I've been doing. It makes me feel cool and like I'm in the past. But I'm not, I'm in the present wandering up and down aimlessly in a dark suburb.

I call her again and she doesn't pick up, so I call her a third time. I think of a meme I saw that said, *Double text? I'll quadruple text you buzz buzz it's me again bitch*. Honestly, what the fuck is she doing? Did she die? Did she throw her phone out the window? This is ridiculous. She asked me if I wanted to come to the party, she should be acting appropriately as a host! I could message my friends to complain about it, but they'd probably just tell me to go back to the hotel. Clearly, I should go back to the hotel, I don't need anyone to tell me that, fuck off.

I press the button for the pedestrian light on the deserted street, and cross when it turns green. Well, here I am on the other side of the street. I call a fourth time. No answer. I look at my reflection in an Indian takeaway and, honestly, I look fresh to death. I look like a true party girl who loves to have fun and never brings up things like fracking or the Arab Spring. I drink one of my bottles of gin and tonic, still looking at my reflection. I look at my phone with its zero notifications. Fuck. This is my first time being stood up and I don't know what to do. Wellington Greta is not going well. To add insult to injury, the buses have stopped. It's not even that late. How is the guy from the liquor store supposed to get home? He probably has a motorbike. He won't give me a ride, because he does not like me. I start walking down the hill. I feel very small, like the hill is not really made for people to walk down, only horses and intrepid mountaineers. Not deflated girls in short skirts. I see a bin but it's not a recycling bin, so I close my eyes when I put the glass bottle inside. A bus drives past. *Not in Service*. If I were in a small town the driver would offer me a lift down the hill. I wonder if my lipstick still looks good. My mum's grandmother wore lipstick every day of her life, and one time stopped her car on a one-lane bridge because a man was following her car too closely. I could be confrontational too, if I had the addresses of the people I wanted to confront.

I walk around the biggest corner I've ever seen and past the High Commission of Malaysia. I don't know why that's all the way up here. Maybe the diplomats wanted to recreate the feeling of walking up the stairs to the Batu Caves or to the top of Mount Kinabalu. I know how they feel. I too long for the comforts of home, of late-night buses and effective streetlights, and I've only been gone two days.

I come to a sign that suggests I could walk down a dark, gravelly forest path to get to the City Centre. This seems like a dangerous option, I think as I walk down the forest path. This is an interesting choice I've made. No one else appears to be in the forest, so I start singing 'Uninvited' by Alanis Morrisette from the *City of Angels* soundtrack. People like to point out that that movie is a remake of *Der Himmel über Berlin*. They're not very similar, though. I don't like Berlin very much, but I would probably move there if a woman told me I should. What are women up to, what are they doing to me? Maybe I need to be in a remake of *What Women Want*, in which I find out what women want. I feel like crying, but I can't even be bothered to do that anymore.

Where's the path gone? Fuck. I turn around in a circle. Which direction did I come from? Why aren't there lights? I start going what I think is the right way but I end up walking into a bush.

Stupid . . . New Zealand tree ferns. I pull leaves out of my hair. It seems to get darker and darker and I really don't know where I am. I look at the map, but it doesn't know where I am either. Fuck, fuck. Maybe I'll have to call my mum to come and rescue me. I open Find My Friends and I see little dots in places I can expect – V is at Wine Cellar on K Road; three of my friends are at a flat in Kingsland; my mum is nowhere near me at Evans Bay, where her friend's house is. There is a dot near me. A dot labelled *MP* is moving slowly up the hill. Oh, Jesus. I send a message. *Hey are you walking up Brooklyn Rd ha ha*. A tick appears immediately, and I feel seen for the first time all night.

Yeah . . . why . . . ?

I feel triumphant. *Can you come and get me? I'm lost in the forest ha ha ha.*

I add all these *ha ha*s so it seems like I'm having a good laugh in the forest and I haven't been stood up on my journey to enlightenment after having my heart broken two days ago.

What? Which forest? Do you mean the bush track in central park?

I hope it's not called that. I think it would be very cringe for New Zealand to have a park called Central Park, Brooklyn.

I'm not sure, can you check find my friends?

Um yep. What are you doing down there?

Exploring.

Nvm, I'm coming now. Don't move.

I stand as still as I can. Here I am, perfectly calm, under the forest canopy, about to be rescued. A voice shouts out, 'Greta?'

'Who is it!' I call, and laugh at my own joke.

'It's me, the Westpac Rescue Helicopter come to save you from a city park.'

It's Matthew. He looks better than he did back in the day, when I was running in different circles. Straight circles. He looks down at the top of my head and says, 'You have leaves in your hair.'

'That's on purpose,' I say, as I try and rake them out.

'What are you doing down here?'

'I love nature.'

'I mean in the city.'

'My mum's doing a summer theatre workshop with at-risk youths. But I just came for the weekend, I'm going back tomorrow. What are you doing here?'

'I live here,' he says, walking ahead of me with his phone torch on. 'You know I live here.'

Matthew was my boyfriend once. We lived together in a falling-down villa near Western Springs with three other people, who left pots full of spaghetti everywhere and thought bathrooms were self-cleaning. He's wearing tan chinos and a blue button-down shirt, which is nice in a kind of gross I'm-a-public-servant way. Which he isn't, but he has the vibe. I probably still look hot, even though I'm now a lost helpless person.

'I meant in this forest.'

'Well, I was walking home from town because the last bus was cancelled and my friends didn't want to stay at the bar anymore, and then my ex messaged me out of nowhere saying that she needed rescuing from a park. How did that really happen?'

'Someone on Tinder invited me to a party and said they would meet me at the shops, but they didn't.'

'How long did you wait?'

'An hour and a half.' I hold out one of my last two bottles to him and we open them. He puts the lid in his pocket. 'Cheers.'

We clink the bottles together and he looks at me in the eyes. 'You have to do this, right, or Germans think something bad will happen.'

'Yeah, you'll be cursed with bad sex for seven years.'

'Well, we've done enough of that.'

I frown at him and he leads me out of the forest, still drinking from the bottle.

'Who stood you up?' he asks.

'Some kind of actress, it was a cast party for some show that was on.'

'It wasn't *elicitations*, was it?'

'Maybe. Did you see it?'

'Yeah, you would have hated it. I don't know why they had to throw so much flour at the audience.'

'Why did you go?'

'What else was I going to do, stay home scraping condensation off my windows?'

I don't say anything. It seems like there might be lights in the distance so maybe we won't die tonight in the forest. If we do, there will be a news article about it and people will argue in the comments about whether it was our own fault or somehow the prime minister's. V will hate it if I die. He'll have to get a new flatmate who doesn't blindly accept all his habits because they grew up with them.

'Do you not like it here?' I ask Matthew.

'Oh, I don't know,' he shrugs. 'People here are nicer, they have more time for you, you know. At home everyone's so exhausted from their bad jobs and bad commutes and the rent's so expensive they don't have money to go out anyway. But it can be claustrophobic, without the other like, 1.2 million people I'm used to. And I get so homesick when I see people at home are eating at New Flavour with bare arms.'

I think of myself enjoying some crispy beans and black pepper beef at New Flavour last week with bare arms. I don't have a long commute or a busy job but I'm very reliant on V subsidising my rent, and I cried every day I was doing honours because if I didn't get an A average then I wouldn't get the scholarship to do a master's, and the government doesn't fund postgrad anymore. 'Are you going to come back?'

'I have to finish my master's first; they don't have politics, philosophy and economics at Auckland. Then I don't know, I might go to London for a bit.'

I wrinkle my nose. 'London's boring. You should move to Bucharest – it's like Berlin but cheaper.'

'You hate Berlin. You say it's full of everyone who's too insufferable to stay in Melbourne.'

'Those people haven't found out about Bucharest yet.'

'Why don't you move there then? You can speak Romanian.'

'Sort of. No, I'm also doing my MA. In comp lit. And I'm a tutor.'

'In German?'

'No, Russian and English. It's much easier reading Russian, even though I like the books less.'

'That seems like a bad idea. You should have done what you were interested in.'

I glare at the back of his head but I don't say anything. 'I'm already lost and heartbroken, you don't need to rub salt in the wound.'

'Heartbroken?' He turns round to look at me and his silly floppy hair flops in his face. He holds it back. 'Surely that's an exaggeration. You never even met this girl.'

'No, there was another girl. Who turned out to be seeing someone else, and she never said.'

'Ouch,' he says, and suddenly we're back on the road. There are bright floodlights over a tennis court. I feel like we're a part of things again.

'It's okay. I might actually hate her after all.'

He laughs. 'How did you get that so wrong?'

'I thought we had a special connection, but I think maybe she had just read one of those art of conversation books and was performing it on me so I would help her with things at uni.'

'Does she read a lot of self-help books?'

'No, she was always reading books that had won awards and

stuff. Old classics and things touted as new classics. I think . . . I think she thought I hadn't read anything, because I hadn't read the same things she had.'

'She sounds like a dickhead.' He shakes his head. 'She sounds like me. Did your family hate her?'

'V made a lot of faces whenever she came over.'

We walk past a tall social-housing block with grimy windows, which scares me at first, and then I feel annoyed at the council for not maintaining it properly.

'I can't really make a comment, because I don't know her,' Matthew says. 'But I wouldn't be surprised if she was trying to impress you all the time and wasn't good at it and gave up and went on to someone else. I know how that feels.'

'Were you trying to impress me?'

'Well, obviously I wasn't doing a very good job of it.'

'You were. I just didn't know you were trying.'

We go past a hotel with mirrored windows and I sneak a look at myself to see if I still look hot or fully dishevelled. I hate those windows, because I like looking at myself but you never know who's on the other side.

'I used to be so pretentious. I still feel bad about that Christmas when I kept talking to Casper about *Slaughterhouse-Five*.'

'It's his fault for having read it in the first place. If you haven't read the book people are talking about you can just barbecue the Christmas halloumi in peace. Do your family still do that weird game with the balloons at Christmas?'

'I don't think you're in a position to say that other people's families are weird.'

I still don't really know where we are, but then we reappear outside a McDonald's I recognise on a funny diagonal street where everyone seems to walk in front of buses.

Matthew stops. 'Do you want to eat something?'

'Yeah, I could go for an ice cream.'

The McDonald's is full of young people having a very big night. When we get our turn on the touch screen, I order a plain cone and Matthew orders a McFlurry. Extravagant. It's chaotic in here. The workers shout order numbers and command people to have a good night as they throw paper bags full of burgers and chips at them. I like the loud, hectic type of customer service, the type that's viewed as being beneath office work or greasing people up on the phone. It's not like it even pays different. I would know – I used to sell tickets at the rugby, and I did so much shouting. I loved it.

We clear a mountain of debris off a table so we can sit down with our ice creams.

'I want to know more about your failed relationship,' Matthew says.

'Why?' One good thing about Wellington is that you can have an ice cream without it instantly melting all over you and the floor.

'Because I deleted my dating apps and I want to live vicariously through your drama.'

This seems rude, but I still tell him all about Holly. The wedding she invited me to at the last minute, all the prawns we ate, the hair touching, *Gravity's Rainbow*, the time I called her because I fell down the stairs by the art gallery and needed her to cover my tutorial but she said she needed time to process her ex's new job as a lecturer at Goldsmiths, the sage ice cream I mistakenly bought in an attempt to be daring. Matthew twirls his plastic spoon. I hope he isn't going to say the whole thing was my fault. When we were together, I always felt like he was trying to teach me a lesson, when all I wanted in my life was for someone to listen to my complaints and say, 'Wow, that's terrible!'

'I can't believe she spent so much time with you and told you every intimate detail of her life, even that gross foot fungus thing, and never mentioned she had a new girlfriend. She took you to her friend's wedding, not her girlfriend, and you slept in the same bed?'

It seems bad when he puts it like that. 'What do you think I did wrong?' I ask.

'What do you mean?' He holds his spoon with a Malteser balanced on it.

'You must think I'm partially to blame.'

He smiles. 'You, Greta, live your life hoping something exciting will happen every day. You could have asked her what was going on, you're a good communicator. But you didn't, because you didn't want to be told it was nothing, for the mystery to be over.' He shrugs. I fold up the little piece of paper my ice cream was wrapped in.

'I wouldn't do something like that. I'm a good, normal person.'

'No, you aren't. That would be boring.'

When we're finished, he walks with me all the way back to the Museum Hotel. It's not called that anymore, but I like that name better. I tell him I can walk by myself, that these aren't the mean streets I'm used to, but he doesn't mind. When we get to the hotel, I try to shake hands with him, but he hugs me, and I don't mind.

'Sorry I used to tell you Jack Kerouac was a genius, Gre.'

'Sorry you had to come and rescue me. Do you want me to order you a ride?'

He steps back and shakes his head, puts his hands in his pockets. 'No, I want to walk. Let me know when things get better for you.'

He walks off into the dark, back towards Brooklyn, back up the hill.

Glitter

V

When I come out of the downstairs bathroom in my parents' house, I stop and stand for a while. The voices of my dad and his brother are echoing down the hallway. I like being around them, even though they switch between Russian, Romanian and English when they're together and I can't keep up. I get tired of trying so I start speaking Russian in my New Zealand accent and my dad doesn't like it. I'm the worst one; Greta loves languages and thinks talking about linguistics is interesting to everyone. Casper is very into cultural heritage and is also, to be honest, kind of try-hard. And he lived in Moscow for five years, whatever.

There's a photo collage with a thin black frame hanging in the corridor with a photo of Casper and me in the top left corner. It's my first day of high school and my legs are too thin in my school shorts. Casper looks heavily influenced by a burned CD he had, labelled *Indie Rock Hits '04*. By the end of that year I had grown 6 inches and convinced my parents to get broadband so I could download a pirated file of *Brokeback Mountain*. Casper had become a dad. I feel strange looking at the photo. One of the other photos is of Greta as a small child wearing a fake beard and holding an old bone. I don't know what that was about at all.

In the kitchen, my dad and Thony are arguing about something, but I don't remember what *înşelător* means. I think of a time Xabi forgot the word *towels* and called them *toallas*, like koalas. He told me there weren't any in the airing cupboard and

I said they were probably outside in a gum tree. He was embarrassed. In Ireland, airing cupboards are called hot presses. Greta and I found this out from a TV series that had about a thousand more sex scenes than were necessary to watch together as siblings. Luckily Greta knew a lot of words that are different in other Anglophone countries for us to talk about. I had no idea Australians call a hot dog on a stick a *Dagwood dog*. In Wales, *togs* are rugby boots. Ridiculous.

Thony and my dad stop talking when they see me. My dad clears his throat and takes a glass bottle out of the fridge, filling up three glasses with something that's fizzing with mint leaves floating on top. 'There you are,' Thony says, putting his arm around me as I come and stand next to him at the counter. He looks like a more normal version of my dad; they have the same nose and the same eyes but Thony is half a foot shorter and doesn't dress like he was once in an art pop band in the late eighties. He wears a lot of linen, turtlenecks and cashmere, I guess so that people know he's a gay European photographer without him having to explain. He also talks about normal things, like new cafés that have opened, and interior design, which is nice because my dad and siblings once had a three-hour argument about what really happened to the family of Tsar Nikolas II that fateful night in 1918. My mum ate the whole plum clafoutis she'd made us for dessert by herself in the kitchen.

'V, I heard you need a book back from Xabi, do you want me to ask him for it?' Thony asks, looking at me like I've lost something much more sentimental than a book, like a locket containing a cutting of my first child's hair or my grandmother's wedding ring. I wish I'd never told my dad about the stupid book.

I shake my head. 'No, it's fine.' I don't add anything else because I want the conversation to end before Thony reveals any information about what Xabi's been up to.

'It's no problem, I can ask Giuseppe tomorrow.'

'No,' I say again.

Giuseppe is Thony's husband. Xabi is Giuseppe's brother. I know that it's weird, that's why it's better not to think about it too much. I don't have to think about it much now that Xabi is far away in Argentina, but sometimes I have to see Giuseppe and he looks at me in a way I don't like either, like we both know something that no one else does. We probably do, but none of those things — those quirks, those scars and those anecdotes — concern me anymore.

Thony nods, and I drink all of whatever the drink is. It's at least 40 per cent rum. They start talking about someone Thony ran into that they both went to school with, someone called Richard Brooker, who is now a very important banker. I look around the kitchen and dining room, the framed maps on the wall and the big wooden table with the six chairs we used to need every night, and think about how empty it seems without my mum. It doesn't feel quite right being here without her. Maybe I should have gone to Wellington. She asked me to come, and I said no because I had expected a dramatic and exciting change to happen in my life in the three weeks since Greta booked her ticket.

My phone vibrates in my pocket. Slava wants me to come into town. It's almost ten, and I don't know if it's a good idea. I'm twenty-nine, I should be posting a photo of work drinks at quarter past five and then going home two hours later sloshed out of my mind in a Corporate Cab. I feel disappointed that things haven't turned out like I imagined when I was a teenager. I blame the global financial crisis.

'Who's that?' my dad asks.

'Slava wants me to come into town,' I say without looking up at him. 'I don't know if I want to go out now though.'

'You could ask him to come here.'

V

I'm not going to do that. Slava thinks it's funny to flirt with my dad and I do not like it. He also does it all in Russian and I don't always understand the connotations of what he's saying. I don't think my dad does either, but that's because he's straight.

'You should go,' Thony says, touching my arm again. 'It might make you feel better.'

'It wouldn't even be possible for me to feel better than I do right now,' I say, which is overkill, and they both look at me like I've lost it. I look at my phone again. I message Slava that I'm coming.

There comes a time of night when it becomes okay to sit on the ground, even away from parks and boulders and other natural sitting spots. Slava and I are sitting on the kerb outside St Kevin's Arcade. We are men without a plan. We have a third friend, Chris, but he texted *fuck no!* when Slava asked if he wanted to come to Family tonight. He would have fit in, everyone there was straight too. Chris lives with his girlfriend now, so they have to do a lot of things like try out new recipes and talk about going for a run. There used to be a whole group of friends on a Saturday night, but one's moved to London and the other two had a baby and bought a house in Hamilton. You have to find a true baller to acquire children with if you want to stay in Auckland these days. This is one of the things I don't like about being an age by which you could once have expected to feel established but not anymore. At least I know myself and what I'm all about.

'Should we go to Wine Cellar?' I ask Slava. He's rubbing glitter off his forearm. People were throwing a lot of glitter around in Saloon Bar, but we left when someone started one of the worst karaoke performances of 'Back to Black' I've heard so far.

'No. You always run into some intellectual friend of yours there and start talking about something I don't care about.'

'When has that ever happened?' I rest my head on my shoulder and look at him. He's straightening the cuffs of his jeans now.

'The time I was upset because Leo was fucking someone else and when I came back from the toilet you were talking to that glasses girl with the fringe about Sartre. It was boring.'

'We were talking about Satya, the restaurant on Mount Eden Road.'

'Whatever, I was emotional.'

'That guy was called Liam, not Leo. You've heavily romanticised this situation.'

'You're a shitty friend.'

'No, I'm not.'

He's rubbing his hair now, looking for more glitter. Slava is naturally blonde, which is an unimaginable way of being to me. He's one of the few Russians I know outside my family. He was born in St Petersburg and he doesn't have any family here; he came as an exchange student when he was sixteen and didn't go home. Maybe his issues with his parents are why he's always coming on to my dad.

'Yes, you are. All the guys flirt with you when we go out because you're tall,' he says, wiping glitter off his nose. He has fine features, like an elegant bird.

'That's not true.'

'I should warn them you've got a bizarre personality.'

'They realise pretty quickly on their own. What do you want to do now?'

We watch a group of boys lining up for one of the clubs that plays Pasifika music. They must be eighteen or twenty, all in white shirts, dark jeans, shiny leather shoes. I wonder what it looks like inside. Greta has a friend at uni who took her to the Tongan bar on Dominion Road. She said it was fuckin' boss and she sang 'Mysterious Girl'. One of the boys has an expired ID: 'Aw, come on, uce, don't be a sad cu—guy.'

'I don't know. Should we go to Eagle?' Slava asks.

'We're too young to go in there.' He's evening out his socks now. He has white socks with Nike swooshes. He doesn't understand why I don't care about brands.

'You like old men, we can pick up a couple of bears, maybe they'll take us back to their fancy apartment and give us coke.'

'Slava, I don't want to have sex with an old man for drugs.'

'Is that not why you were going out with your old Spanish man?'

I elbow him. 'No. That was different.'

He sighs. 'I can't understand how it's possible to love someone who remembers a time without computers.'

'You went out with that guy who was twenty and didn't know that flip phones were real. I don't know. It was weird, the first time I met Xabi. We were all at this restaurant, one of those restaurants where people get oysters on ice and take photos of them, with my uncle because Xabi had just arrived from Spain. I came alone from work and I nearly walked into him, he was on the phone outside. He said sorry, I didn't say anything – it was when I didn't talk in public. But we looked at each other, and it was strange. I just felt like something was going to happen. When everyone was at the table, my uncle introduced him to me and we shook hands, he didn't mention that we'd just seen each other. That made me feel like . . . it wasn't just me.'

'When was this?'

'Three years ago, I guess.'

Behind us there's a loud group of people in their forties and fifties sitting outside Verona. They're talking to a man in an old tracksuit with a long beard and I don't know if he lives on the street here or if he's their friend. Maybe both, of course.

'Did you never meet before?' He moves closer. It isn't cold, it's 20 degrees still. Neither of us has a jacket. I'm in a white

T-shirt with rolled-up sleeves and Slava's wearing a striped short-sleeved button-up in shades of pink and yellow.

'No. His brother lives here obviously, with Thony, but he lived in Spain. He used to live here a long time ago.'

'I always thought you'd known him your whole life.'

I'm surprised. 'Don't you think that would be weird? I wouldn't be okay with it. He definitely wouldn't be. He was very concerned about the age difference.'

'I think it's fine. My sister's husband is a lot older,' he says. 'A lot of girls back at home have older husbands. My parents thought it was good for her to have someone with money and an apartment. A good job. Things are different here, though. People are judgemental in different ways. What did your parents think?'

'I was speaking in public for the first time. My parents had never seen me able to talk in shops or do things like present at a physics conference or shout for the bus driver to open the back door. So, I don't think they cared that it happened when I started dating someone who they considered a friend. Haven't we talked about this?'

I can't remember why this has never come up before. Slava and I have known each other for five years. We met at a house party and he was very excited to meet someone else Russian, even though being Russian is one of my many identities I don't entirely fit in with.

'I was mad at you. We weren't speaking.'

'Oh, right.' Why Slava stopped talking to me is one of the many things I don't like thinking about.

'It was stupid when you couldn't talk. We would talk so much in your old apartment and then as soon as we went out, I had to talk to all the taxi drivers and bartenders and the people who worked at the kebab shop.'

'I knew it was stupid, I just couldn't do it. Thank you, for still being my friend even when I was terrible.'

'You should be grateful every day of your life.'

'Maybe I can go out with someone who buys you drugs next time.'

He leans his head on my shoulder. 'I can buy my own drugs. I work in marketing.' I look down at him, his knee touching mine on the side of the road. 'So how did your parents meet Xabi? Were they friends with him and Giuseppe at uni?'

'No, Thony and Giuseppe met each other in Rome when they were eighteen. Thony was on holiday and I think Giuseppe was working there. Their grandmother is Italian. Xabi was studying here and didn't really know anyone so Thony gave him my dad's number. Thony wasn't out then. He told my dad that Giuseppe was his friend from a travelling youth choir.'

'That's romantic, that your uncle's been with the same guy since he was eighteen.'

When I breathe in, I can smell his hair. He smells expensive. Like an Aēsop store, sage and bergamot.

'No, they broke up at the end of the summer. I don't really know how they ended up together again. There are pockets of time where no one likes to talk about what went on. Bad things happened. I don't think Giuseppe and Xabi have a great relationship as brothers; Xabi got so mad that he went back to Spain and stayed there until, you know, he was here again.'

'I'm sorry he left you.'

'It's okay. I was in a bad place. I felt so shit all the time. I couldn't explain that it was because I'd studied for eight years to do something I didn't want to do, not because of him. It was good that everyone thought I was having a breakdown over my boyfriend leaving me, though, and not because I . . . didn't feel right in my job that was paying me 90K. I'm good now, better than I've ever been.'

People are walking past screaming. Their friends run across the road in front of an Uber. They laugh when they're together again outside the liquor store and the place that sells special rolled ice creams. One of the girls hugs her cardigan over her dress. It doesn't fit quite right and is falling down at the front. *Oh my god, Marty, you nearly fuckin' died. Your mum would have lost her shit.*

'I like you better now,' Slava says. 'You talk less about maths and get me into more media parties. Is there anything happening tonight?'

'There is, but I don't want to go. My sister went on a date with a MediaWorks guy and burned that bridge for me.'

He touches the inside of my hand with his delicate fingers. 'She's away, isn't she?'

'Yes.'

'Can I come over? I don't want to go back to Ellerslie.'

'You shouldn't have moved there then.'

'V.'

'Fine.' My breath moves his hair slightly. 'But just tonight. I don't want you to get mad and not talk to me for months.'

He looks up again, close to me. 'We'll see.'

Sorted

G

'Do you know where your children are?' Geneviève asks my mum, tapping aggressively at her phone screen with one finger. We're in the café at Te Papa and it's very bright for someone who spent last night mountaineering and drinking pre-mixed gin and tonics. There's a slow-moving queue of elderly people off a tour bus, and a child behind us screaming for a hot chocolate with two marshmallows.

'Greta's here at the table with us,' my mum replies, frowning into her cup of berry tea. I don't think it's what she ordered.

'What about all those other ones, though?'

I'm glad to see my mum again, because Geneviève can be a bit much when there's no one else around for her to divert her energy to. I don't know if she's always been like this, or if she's one of those older women who's become sick and tired of the rules of society and feels beaten down by the patriarchy to the extent that they start shouting in a museum gallery about all the artists they used to know in the 1980s and what types of drugs they had and how good they were at kissing. I had an art teacher at school who said the best thing about going to the galleries in Paris is you can touch all the paintings. 'You can touch a Picasso,' he said. 'You can just go right up and touch them all.' Maybe all artists are terribly behaved in galleries. I asked my mum once what Geneviève was like when they were younger, and she sighed and said she didn't want to talk about it.

'I don't know,' my mum says to Geneviève. 'V messaged me he was having dinner with Linsh, and Casper said he had a lot on at work, so I don't think they could have gone far.' My mum tucks a strand of hair behind her ear. How does she look so good with her hair in a bun on top of her head? I never do.

'Oh, so you know what they're doing all the time, then. Do you ever feel like you've done something wrong by them?'

'What do you mean?'

Geneviève's looking in her bag for her glasses now. She's given it a good go, holding the phone a metre away from her face.

'To end up with these clingy sons and a lesbian daughter.'

'Hey,' I protest feebly. I've already answered enough of Geneviève's questions about sexuality and gender this weekend. She told me if she decides to be a man later on in life, she will change her name to Bob Hawke. I didn't tell her that was already the name of an Australian prime minister. Sometimes people have the same name as each other.

'I like my clingy sons and lesbian daughter,' my mum says, putting down the cup of tea and looking to the end of the queue. There are about twenty-seven elderly people queuing, staring vacantly into the distance.

Geneviève groans at her phone. 'How do I get this man to stop texting me?'

'What man? Do you have a new man in your life, Gen?'

'No, this same old man, Giuseppe Alonso, who keeps wanting to know where our son is. He's thirty years old, he can do as he likes.'

'Do you not know where Cosmo is?'

'No. Why would I?' Geneviève puts her phone down and cuts her ginger slice in half.

'When did you last hear from him?'

'A month ago, maybe. He was in Paris. He had been in a new play.'

'And where is he now?'

'Well, no one knows where he is now, this is the issue. According to Giuseppe. He thinks he was upset about something and went somewhere else.'

'So you don't even know what country he's in?' My mum looks concerned and twists her wedding ring around on her finger. If I went missing in a foreign country, my mum would probably be worried enough to do something about it. I wonder where Cosmo is. I like him a lot. He's a calm, gentle and thoughtful person. These adjectives sound like something I would write in an undergrad language exam after reading a short text about the friendship of Pierre and Emile or whatever, but he is honestly like that. He hardly ever comes back to New Zealand, though. He has a French passport. My dad said he could get me a Moldovan passport because he 'knows a guy', but I wasn't sure I needed that kind of international bureaucratic drama in my life. Geneviève's phone starts ringing and she turns it face-down on the table.

'You should answer; he'll be worried,' my mum says, leaning back and folding her arms. I wonder if that's true. I've never seen Giuseppe worried about anything before, but I guess all people are worried sometimes. He's a confident Spanish businessman who has a fancy car and is married to my uncle. I don't really know how he ended up having a son with Geneviève. I think if I asked her about it she would give me more detail than I would care to hear.

I screw the top back on my $5 bottle of Coke and look at my mum in her navy-and-white striped shirt and red silk scarf. She's very confident as well, in a quiet, assertive way. I wish I could be like that. She would never end up walking around in the dark like a sad ghost no one wanted to go on a date with. I wonder what she would have said to Holly if she had been led on like me. She probably wouldn't have covered any of her tutorials or looked at photos of her foot in a medical capacity in the first place.

'Betty!'

My mum looks over, surprised, and I turn round as well.

Three older women are waving and making their way over to us in a buzz of drapey black cardigans and long carved bone earrings. 'Who are those women?' I ask.

'You shouldn't assume people's genders; they might be hasbians,' Geneviève says, continuing to eat her ginger slice. My mum stands up, so I stand up too, and all three of the women are kissing my mum on the cheek and kissing me on the cheek, which I'm bad at, and I nearly go the wrong way and knock my Coke onto the concrete floor.

One of the women is holding my hands. 'Is this your kōtiro, Betty? It's a shame we didn't get to meet you yesterday down the beach.'

My mum looks blank for a second. 'Ah, yes, this is my daughter, Greta. She's not an early-morning-walk type.'

'You know who you look like?' the woman says to me, looking right into my eyes. 'Hiria Hine Te Huia.'

One of the other women makes an approving noise. 'The spitting image. How tall is that dad of yours, Greta?'

I look at my mum, who's looking at the floor and not being helpful at all. 'Um, 6 foot 5, I think.'

'Really? He didn't look that tall, I would have guessed 6 foot 2 at the most,' she says.

'He's always, um, bending over and stuff,' I say. I have no idea who these people are or why they're in a position to debate me on how tall my dad is.

'Your parents make a lovely couple, anyway. And you must be so proud of your brother,' the woman holding my hands says.

'Oh, yeah, I guess so,' I say, wondering why exactly I should be proud of V. Maybe they saw the episode of his show where he said Waikato was objectively the worst region in New

Zealand and thought it was about time someone came out and said it.

'That money's going to go so far for those rangatahi.' She nods seriously and then they all nod, all three of them, all looking at me in their black outfits. I feel like I'm in a strange version of the witches scene in *Macbeth* where everyone's Māori and I have even less of an idea of what's going on than Macbeth himself did. What youth is V giving money to? I guess he sometimes takes our nephew to the movies, but how would these women know about that? Then again, they seem to know a lot already.

'Yes, we're very proud of Casper,' my mum says suddenly, as if awakening from a trance. Oh right, my other brother. The one who lobbied the government for money for Māori teenagers to get proper careers advice. Both my brothers have appeared on TV shouting about something they don't like, be it the massive advantage that Pākehā students have coming into higher education, or Hobbiton. 'Um, Gre, this is Pātia, Te Paea and Tūī. They work with the Arts Council.'

I'm surprised that these are the women's names. All of my mum's relatives have names like Eksodus and Angel B. When I was nine, Angel B had a Von Dutch hat and told me her one piece of advice was to marry rich and not get stuck living in a shithole. She married a personal trainer and they go on runs around the Whangārei Basin. I don't know what happened to Eksodus; he once called V a pussy for being fifteen and not knowing how to drive. We didn't see him much after that. I guess he was busy driving around somewhere.

'Casper, that's your boy's name,' the woman called Pātia says. 'I knew it was some cartoon thing, but I was thinking it was Scooby.'

'Oh.' My mum is blushing slightly, which she almost never does. 'It's just his nickname.'

Casper's real first name is Lavrenti, after my dad's dad, but he only goes by it when he's in Moscow. When my mum took him back to Aotea when he was born, her father said, 'Holy hell, this baby's so white you should call him Casper the fucking ghost!' My dad told me about that. He was so inspired by this interaction that he's been calling my brother Casper ever since. Everything I know about my mum's father comes from my dad. She doesn't talk about him; he died a few months before V was born.

I wonder if my mum is embarrassed because these women think she named her firstborn child after a cartoon character, or because she didn't give any of us Māori names. Would a different name have improved my life, or would people have been more openly racist towards me? Once, at school, I got called to the dean's office because I didn't show up to a careers meeting for Māori students, and they assumed I'd been wagging. It turned out my form teacher thought it was a mistake and threw the letter about it in the bin. I was just in maths trying to measure stupid triangles the whole time, when I could have been learning about joining the army or becoming a security guard. Everyone else came back to class with a keychain that said *NZ POLICE*. My life would be different if I didn't lose my keys all the time.

Earlier, upstairs in the gallery, I looked at a painting that I didn't like, a painting of a dark-skinned woman with golden hair, which the little plaque described as a *racially mixed goddess*. The same as me and the opposite of me, with my pale skin and black hair. Not a goddess at all, just a normal racially mixed mortal woman. I didn't tell Geneviève that the painting made me feel bad, because I didn't know if she would understand. I couldn't move on to the next painting, because an elderly woman and a person who might have been an exchange student were in front of it. 'There used to be a lot of problems with the Mow-ris and the Europeans, what with the Treaty and all that,' she told him in a loud, clear voice. 'But that's all sorted now, except for the fisheries.' The painting they were looking at was about Pacific migration in the seventies. The student was nodding. Why would you question someone's knowledge of the country they claimed to be from? I didn't know what to do, so I went to a different section and looked at a picture of a man standing in front of the Canterbury Plains. He reminded me of V's friend Slava, who he pretends he doesn't sleep with when he's sad.

'It was so nice to see you again, Betty,' the woman named Te Paea says. 'Inanahi, nōnāianei, and maybe āpōpō as well.' They all laugh and my mum smiles and nods even though I'm not sure if she knows what those words mean. I don't.

Geneviève sighs and shows me her phone. 'My only son is not dead,' she says. On the screen are five all-caps messages saying the same thing: *CALL YOUR FATHER NOW!!*, and the reply at the bottom, a single *k*.

Plants (I)

V

Greta has come back from Wellington wearing a pale blue pant-suit. She's standing in front of the mirror in our living room, analysing herself. I'm reading a magazine about how to look after plants. We have a lot of plants in the apartment, but I'm not sure if any of them are the ones mentioned in the magazine. It's from another country where they have different plants and you need to do different things to look after them, because the weather is different. We have 90 per cent humidity here today, which is good for calatheas.

I know Greta's about to say something to me. I turn the page of the magazine. A San Pedro cactus would be a nice thing to have. A really tall one. I would put it in the corner between the window and the couch. Plants that are already tall are expensive, so a lot of our plants are small at the moment. Maybe I could get a new boyfriend with a car to take me to the big garden centre out south where the tall plants are cheaper. But what if I put all the work into getting a boyfriend with a car who wants to drive me around, and then it turns out he's one of those guys who gets all funny if you get soil in his back seat? What if he's one of those guys who wants to know where you are all the time? What if he runs a meme page and I don't think it's funny? Maybe my mum will take me to the garden centre. She likes plants. She might go halves with me on a tall cactus.

'Does this pantsuit make me look really butch?'

I look at Greta with her long, wavy hair, glitter eyeshadow and lace camisole. She smells strongly of a new perfume she got at whatever Kirkcaldie & Stains is called now. I close the magazine. 'No.'

'What did you do while I was gone?'

I look across the room, where I can see my scarf neatly folded on the end of my bed through the open door.

'Nothing. What did you do while you were away?'

'Oh, nothing,' she says, and pulls a small piece of leaf out of her hair.

Sabbatical

G

I'm in the toilets of the very poorly lit Bluestone Room and I'm on a straight date with a man. How did this happen to me? I swiped through all the available women in three minutes and got jealous of my more sexually flexible friends and the hours and hours of swiping they had left, so I decided to give men another go. I can't really tell if I find people attractive or not by looking at their pictures, so I just swiped right on any guy who had a cat. I try not to look at my reflection in the mirror. I don't know who this woman is. Greta, you idiot. What the fuck are you doing. If you wanted to meet some cats you could go and walk around in the suburbs. The cats in the pictures probably don't even belong to the men, they're just using them for attention. God. I can't believe this bar puts cucumber in gin.

When I come back into the bar, the man is still sitting there with his beer that I paid for in a moment of frivolity.

'Oh, you're still here!' I say, for a bit of a joke. He frowns. Men are so sensitive.

'How are we going?' he asks, drinking some of the $9 beer.

'How is this date going? Oh, I don't know, seven out of ten?' I think seven is the right number to say. Eight sounds too keen, six sounds rude. It's definitely better than the last straight date I went on, with a man from the South Island. I told an anecdote about when I went to Nelson and for the first time in my life I saw an older white lady out on the road directing traffic around a diversion and enjoying herself as if it were a hobby. I thought that was very exotic. She had a Marian Keyes book sticking out of her bag. My date didn't respond well. Maybe he thought I was fetishising his culture. I also said that everyone at the media company opposite my old call centre office was a dickhead, and it turned out he was one of them. I would still rate that date a seven out of ten, just to be polite.

'No, why would I ask you *how this date is going*?' the current date says. 'I meant how are we going in the cricket.' He gestures at the multiple screens around the pub, all showing the same game at Eden Park. I give a cursory performative look at what's happening. I can't see anything. I didn't wear my glasses here because I wanted him to think I was hot. I watch a bunch of blurs walk around on a big green circle.

'Seems all good,' I say. He shakes his head again. He seems annoyed that I assumed he'd be interested in a mid-date progress report. I consider announcing that I'm from a family of scientists, but then he might want to talk about what kind of science they do. I'm not very good at explaining it, beyond my dad gets way too excited about squid, and V is the only person I've ever met who understands black holes.

I look at the cricket again. 'Bring back Daniel Vettori.'

'What?' He looks confused and leans in closer to me.

'I'm just saying some sports stuff to, um, get into the sports spirit. You just have to say the right words and then people assume that you know what you're talking about. Ah, bad call, ref, should've punted it over, that's a penalty for sure, yellow card, golden duck, obstruction, Zinzan.' I trace a square in the air with my fingers like I'm calling for the video ref. He nods politely. He's a polite guy. He tried to buy me popcorn at the movies. I had wanted an ice cream but that was more expensive, so I just said no a bit too loudly.

The date keeps drinking his beer and I have a look at him. He is one of the white men. I made some jokes about that earlier and he seemed sort of okay with it. He lives in Ponsonby in a house owned by a relative of his. I made a joke about him being a land baron and he was less okay with that. I'm not sure I think he's sexy. He doesn't look like the men I think are hot – Adrien Brody and young Stalin – but he is in the same oeuvre as the nerdy but fairly socially capable men who have liked me in the past. They like me because I'm smart and then they don't like me because I don't really care about facts and logic, I just like having a good time. They're also often posh and don't understand my working-class ideals. My parents are fairly middle class these days, but they don't take it for granted.

'Mambo No. 5' comes on over the speakers, and I plan the next little bit of conversation in my head. I will say that this is a great song, and did you know that Lou Bega is from Germany? No, the date will say, that's a great fact. I will say yes, Boney M. are from Germany as well. My favourite Boney M. song is 'Daddy Cool'; there's a great scene where a girl dances to it in the 1980 film *Moscow Does Not Believe in Tears*. He'll probably say his favourite is 'Mary's Boy Child', which is boring, but I'll forgive him. Then I can talk a bit about my dad's life in the Soviet Union, which will make me seem interesting by extension.

The date leans right over to me. 'Is this music annoying you? I don't know why bars always have to play music.'

'What?' This isn't part of my conversation plan.

'I don't really like music,' he says. 'It hurts my ears.' He looks in my eyes, and smiles kind of sheepishly. Aha. Doesn't like music. That's fine. It would be strange if we had everything in common. Opposites attract. That's a great song by Paula Abdul. I love music a lot. The ladies at my call centre job didn't believe I was Māori too until I said I made Matthew sing 'Cheryl Moana Marie' when I was sad. I'm not sure Pākehā are going around singing to make themselves feel better. Once I went to one of their funerals and no one sang anything. They put that woman in the ground, had some tiny sandwiches and went home.

G

I look at the date's eyes. He has nice grey eyes – he sort of reminds me of a koi. I laugh so I don't have to think about how he doesn't like music and lean forward in case he wants to look at my boobs. Maybe we could talk about them. I've had three of these horrible cucumber gins and I'm running out of conversation topics. I feel like I have to win the date somehow, like I have to convince this man that I'm desirable. And he's not so bad; he hasn't asked me if I like being pissed on yet.

'I think the bar might be closing,' he says, adjusting his glasses and watching the bartender put the chairs up. 'Where would you like to go now?'

'Um, I'm not sure.' I stand up and look under the table for my bag, forgetting that I didn't bring one. It's hard to stand up again and I regret the three gins.

We walk out of the bar and into the street. The streets around this part of town are all narrow alleys and smell like rubbish, especially in this heat. A line of people younger than us are outside a club playing K-pop with flashing lights and a smoke machine.

'Well, we aren't going in there,' he says, snorting.

'We could go to karaoke,' I suggest. 'I know a good place with tambourines.'

He laughs, but it's not a joke. I feel like singing 'At Seventeen' by Janis Ian.

We walk until we get to the big crossing, the one where the big Santa used to live on the Farmers building at Christmas. I miss how he used to wink and beckon. It felt like the city wasn't so sexually repressed back then.

The date is standing close to me. 'We could go to the casino and play blackjack,' I suggest. He shakes his head. He thinks I'm being quirky. When my granddad comes to visit, who everyone calls Vlad even though it isn't his real name, we always go to the casino and play blackjack and eat at the buffet. It's a lot of fun. I think Vlad's coming to New Zealand in November; he isn't conducting any Christmas or New Year's concerts this year. Maybe it's a bad sign that I'm on a date wishing I was hanging out with my granddad.

The date looks at me in a way that I think is supposed to be alluring. 'You'd be most welcome to come over, Greta.'

I stop thinking about my granddad and look at him. Have I succeeded sexually? Is this what I wanted?

I find myself nodding. 'Okay, I will come to your house. In Ponsonby.' I turn around and start marching up Victoria Street. It's now or never. That's a great song by Elvis Presley. The date trots after me. It's a steep street but I have powerful legs. My ancestor walked from Hastings to Kawakawa with some guy and that's what, 650 kilometres? He had kidnapped her though, I think. Don't fact-check me on that. Fuck. I want to go on a trip to Hastings. I could go to Splash Planet. If I want to experience the wonders of Hawke's Bay, I will need to avoid Napier, so I don't run into Holly's dumb parents and their dumb dog. Sonja's been to Napier to stay with them. I saw an Instagram Story about it by mistake and I couldn't make it stop because I had cake batter on my hands.

We walk past the lobby of the Best Western Hotel, the convenience store, the funny dark restaurants that I've never seen anyone eat in. We wait for the lights at Albert Street and I look at the headlines on the tatty newspaper signs outside a dairy. Kiwis are suffering because of tax, apparently. Kiwis are suffering because some Kiwis aren't being taxed enough, I think. Is tax a good conversation topic? Maybe if my date turns out to be a raging socialist, I'll be more interested in having sex with him.

'Do you have an opinion on tax?'

'Ha-ha,' he says. 'Greta, you know that I'm a tax lawyer by trade.'

'I thought you said you worked at the library.'

'That's purely sabbatical,' he says, waving a hand dismiss-ively. 'Tax is the field of law where you can really be creative.'

He looks deep into my eyes and touches my waist. Suddenly I wish I was wearing sunglasses, even though it's midnight. I look up at the Sky Tower as if it's the Madonna. Please save me, beautiful stucco icon of the City of Sails. I think of my South Island date. He said no matter where you are in Auckland, you can always see the Sky Tower. Then he made a large flourishing gesture and we couldn't see it at all. That was a good joke. Then he ghosted me.

It's quieter when we get past the TVNZ building. There aren't as many lads around trying to chat up backpackers from France and Brazil. This is all fine. I can definitely go back to this man's house and have sex with him. That's what people do. And I'm one of the people. If it goes badly, I'll find an e-scooter on the ground and zoom all the way back home. I just have to not think about the point at dinner when he pronounced 'Taupō' the bad way.

'What's your stance on strategic board games?'

I stop walking. I have a huge pain behind my eyes all of a sudden.

'Are you okay?'

'Yeah,' I say. I lean against a lamppost in what I hope is a cas-ual way. 'Maybe, um, maybe the satay I had at the food court earlier had . . . gone off.'

He nods. 'Your energy levels do appear to be waning.'

'And the other thing is, I forgot that I'm going to this brome-liad show in the morning and you have to get there really early if you want to get a good one. This isn't a lie.'

He looks disappointed and takes his phone out. 'You did talk a lot about bromeliads over dinner.' Why has he got his phone out? Is he going to call the police on me? 'What's your bus number?'

I don't need to catch a bus; I live in town. Did I not say that? '22N,' I find myself saying.

'Oh, shit, that's coming in two minutes back at the top of the hill.'

'I'd better run up there then,' I say and start running. He runs along next to me. Oh, Gre. This is what happens when you lie. This is the first moment in our short, shared life where we've had the same objective, which is for me to get on a bus to Avondale via St Lukes, where I don't live. My first boyfriend lived on that bus route; his flatmate would always put the *Born in the USA* record on in the middle of the night and we would sing along in his bed. The bed smelled like CK One and didn't have matching pillowcases. I wish I could go back to that now. I wish we were singing 'I'm on Fire'. That's the last track on side one; we'd have to wait for the flatmate to turn the record over after that. I like 'Streets of Philadelphia' the best, but that's not on the album. It's just on the *Philadelphia* soundtrack.

The bus is pulling up in front of us and I'm really convinced that I need to get on it. I'm Alfred Ill in the Friedrich Dürrenmatt play: *Get on the train, get on the train!* There are people lined up for the bus, someone's trying to pay cash, so I am going to make it. The lights are bright, which makes me feel even more drunk and insane.

'Well, goodbye then,' I say, and I try to shake his hand because I got really into it when I was living in Germany. He hugs me, though. Then he kisses me, on the neck. The bus driver is annoyed.

'Greta,' the date calls out to me after I tag on. I look at him, standing there on the street.

'Yeah?'

'Have fun at the bromeliad show.'

He waves and walks off into the night. I take the bus three stops and get off at the university. Then I walk back to the city through the empty park, singing 'The River'.

Fruit Bowl

V

It's time for a new chapter and a new me. I'm not going to be worrying about men anymore, I'm going to be focused on my career, like a woman in a movie from the 1990s. I get up early and put on some black trousers with a pleat that I haven't worn before, and a navy turtleneck T-shirt. I consider asking Greta if she wants to join me in my new life and go out for breakfast, but I assume she doesn't want to as I heard her come in after midnight and for some reason start listening to Paula Abdul.

When I walk through the city, the streets are quiet and the only people around are tourists going down to the ferry terminal and young families with prams going to an event at the art gallery. There are new flowers being planted in the park and I smile at people I walk past, so they know that I'm a Sunday-morning person too. I walk up Symonds Street, over the bridge and past the turn-off to Grafton, wondering how long I should walk before I stop at a café and enjoy my breakfast as an independent person. Then I see someone I know and haven't seen for a very long time.

The person I know stops wheeling his bike when we meet each other on the footpath, and smiles. 'V, I haven't seen you in so long.'

'Yeah, no, I haven't seen you either,' I say. What a barbaric thing to say. Of course I haven't seen him if he hasn't seen me. Now it sounds like I'm some sort of failed spy.

He smiles again. 'I heard you'd become a comedian.'

'Oh, yeah,' I say with my hand in my hair. 'Sort of, I guess.'

'What happened at the physics lab? I heard you were doing big things.'

'I was, well, I was doing medium-sized things but it, um, it wasn't for me.'

'What wasn't?'

'The physical world.'

He laughs. I wasn't trying to make him laugh. This is why I'm a better comedian than a physicist; I had to try very hard at that every day. Now I just live my life and try not to die, and people seem amused enough by that to pay me for it.

'What about you, Ben?' I ask, saying his name so he knows I remember it. 'I thought you were living in Chemnitz.'

'Oh, I was; I was there for seven years, at the lab at TU Chemnitz. It was good, you know, except for the neo-Nazis, but I always missed home. Even when you're living in a cheap apartment with central heating and eating Egyptian strawberries in the middle of winter, it doesn't feel as good as being here. Then I heard about a job opening up here and . . .' He shrugs.

'And you've brought the cycling lifestyle back with you.'

He smiles down at his bike. 'Yeah. I forgot how dangerous it is here.'

'It's not so bad, once you accept that you're a part of New Zealand's most hated minority.'

'I also forgot how funny you were.'

Ben looks at me for a second with his shiny light brown hair and his neat white teeth, and I remember how I used to feel when I was younger and he would come round after school to study with Casper or stay over in the weekend. I would hang around in the kitchen, picking things up from the fruit bowl and putting them down again, inspired by a DKNY ad of people holding apples alluringly. *Be delicious*, it said. I would open and close the fridge until it beeped, and Casper would shout at me to choose a yoghurt or fuck off. I hope Ben doesn't remember any of that.

'Have you seen Casper? Sorry, I don't know how long you've been back.'

'Only since Christmas. I have seen him, I had dinner at his house. I definitely got more than I bargained for.'

'What happened?'

'I hadn't seen Freya since she was a baby and—'

'Oh, God, what did she ask you?'

I love my niece, but she tends to ask the kinds of questions you might ask yourself at 2am after a particularly hard day.

'The standard how old are you, what's your job, are you married, do you have kids. Then it quickly turned into this discussion about why I don't go to church, where my ancestors come from, and she asked me if I'd ever shot a gun. And if I owned a talking horse whether I'd make it sleep outside.'

'Would you?'

He runs his hand through his hair. 'I would feel bad, but I live in one of those divided villas and I don't think a horse would fit through the doors.'

I smile.

'It was nice to see Casper so happy,' he continues. 'With his wife and kids and house and people appreciating his desire to achieve social justice a lot more than the administration did at our school.'

'Oh, yeah, don't get him started on the rangatahi.'

'It's cool, it makes me wish I was doing something more beneficial for the world.'

'Don't you develop new medicines?'

'Yeah, I do, I forgot. How stupid; that's the main thing I do.'

He laughs awkwardly and looks at the ground, and I feel bad that I made him feel stupid. Ben is not at all stupid. He was the dux of our school. I remember because my mum came to the prizegiving; his own parents went on a business trip to Singapore. They were always over there. Ben had a Singapore Airlines tag on his backpack that I would look at whenever Casper made me walk home slightly behind them.

'How are your parents?' I ask.

'Oh, you know. They bought a house in Tauranga, "for the lifestyle". They call me to talk about the economy, that sort of thing. Hey, V, are you still really into Eurovision?'

I bite my lip and feign ignorance. I don't think it should be allowed for anyone to remember me as I was before maybe, like, two years ago. For their sake. Lovely Ben should not have to remember me as a teen Eurovision fanatic who threw out the batteries for the remote so no one could even try to change the channel, and then screamed because I couldn't turn the volume up. These days I'm much more dignified.

'I thought of you every year it was on anyway,' he says. I feel increasingly embarrassed. He looks down and I look down too, worrying he's thinking my shoes are as cringe as I am. Who goes out for breakfast alone wearing white leather sneakers? 'We should go for coffee sometime.'

We should go for coffee sometime is definitely code for when you want to end a conversation with someone and never see them again. People at my work say it all the time.

'Right,' I say.

'I'll let you get on your way; sorry, I'm holding you up,' he says, still smiling, his shiny hair the colour of non-volcanic sand.

'It was good to see you,' I say, not quite able to look him in the eye.

'It was good to see you, too.'

I keep walking until I get to one of my favourite cafés, all full of normal morning people not humiliating themselves, then I walk into the liquor store next door, where I stand in the beer fridge until the man from behind the counter comes to check that I haven't died.

Waves

G

On Sunday I lie on my old bed at my parents' house being sad. I said I'd come and see them, but I'm a shell of a woman after my date and have just been lying down the whole time. With the door open so they know we're still spending time together. I'm wearing a big grey jumper and some beige linen pants I'm not sure about. I'm not wearing anything underneath the jumper, because I thought it was sexy, but that turned out to be a stupid idea because it's a hot day and now I can't take it off. It's nearly the end of summer. I look at the harsh sandal tan lines on my feet. My foot looks like a tapir, actually. I'm inspecting my foot more closely when my dad walks past.

'Hey, Dad?'

He walks backwards into the open doorway. 'Yes, Greta?' He's wearing black jeans and a black T-shirt and carrying one of those flexible washing baskets that every person in the whole country has.

'Do you think my foot looks like a tapir?'

'Ah, in what sense?'

A thing about my dad is that he takes every question seriously, and to be honest I don't know how positive the effects of this have been on me as an adult. 'In terms of colour.'

He looks at it from the doorway. 'An adult Malaysian tapir? A little bit, I think. It could be improved if you only wore swimming pool sandals next summer, to get the correct ratio.'

'Slides.'

'Hmm. They're better for people with flat feet. You have a

high arch; you'd better stick with the Birkenstocks.' He nods and keeps walking.

'Wait, Dad.'

I sit up properly and he walks back into the doorway again.

'Yes, Greta?'

'Can I ask you something?'

'Always.'

'Have you ever asked a woman to come back to your house?'

He looks surprised. 'Not recently, no. I don't think your mother would appreciate that. It would be inappropriate. Unless we'd discussed it beforehand.'

'I meant in the past. When you were a young man out on the town.'

'I don't know if I ever was a young man out on the town as such, but I know what you mean. Yes, I have in the past asked a woman to stay over at my house.'

'And what phrase did you use?'

He thinks. 'It's hard to recall. It was a different era; we all thought plastic was great.'

'Would you say something like . . . "You'd be most welcome to come over"?'

He tenses his grip on the washing basket. 'God, no, that's awful.'

My dad has a tattoo of the Carpathian Mountains on the inside of his arm. I don't think my date had any tattoos, but I guess I didn't end up seeing most of his body.

'You wouldn't, then?'

'No. Jesus, that sounds like something you'd say to someone at the end of a funeral. "You'd be most welcome to come back to our house; my wife has made enough brisket for everyone." '

This is very embarrassing. Even my dad is cooler than my date. My dad the sea fungus analyst. I put my face in my lap.

'I don't know, Gre. I would probably try and keep it casual, maybe something like "Do you want to come over?", "You can stay if you want", something that makes it seem optional.' He looks thoughtful. 'Once, your mother was looking at the bus timetable at my flat, and I said she didn't have to do that, if she didn't want to.'

'What did she say?' I pull my knees up to my chest and rest my chin on them. I like to hear my parents talk about each other.

'She said she didn't want to sleep on my couch, and I said I didn't want that either.'

'Wait, why would she sleep on your couch? Were you known to be a popular couch-surfing host?'

'No.' He puts down the washing basket. 'That came later. I'm not sure where to start; this is embarrassing.'

'You're never embarrassed.'

'That's not true. Um, I think this particular episode started around the end of May; I had just turned twenty-one. I had begun my postgraduate studies in biology. I was in Xabi's ute. You might remember him from your brother's ongoing anguish.'

'How long had you known Mum for?'

'Three years.'

'What?'

'Ah, yes.' He raises his hands. 'This is one of the embarrassments. I'd known her for three years; I liked her so much but she kept seeing other people because she was popular and socially capable. Then Xabi confronted me.'

'Did he know you liked her?'

'No. He asked if I hated her. They were good friends; they'd even been on holiday in Italy with his family. But he said he could stop inviting her round, if it upset me. Then I realised I had probably been a little harsh in feigning disinterest to keep my feelings private. I told him I didn't hate her, I was in love with her. As it were.'

'You were in love with her?'

'I mean.' He pauses. 'I didn't think there was any point beating around the bush anymore. I had considered it for three years.'

'And then what happened?'

'He said that he thought she liked me too, even though she was with someone else at the time. So, when she took out the bus timetable that weekend, I thought I might as well ask her to stay longer. We'd never talked alone before that. Oh, except—' He shakes his head and closes his eyes for a second. 'Apparently I put my head in her lap and told her about my sad childhood once at a party, but I don't remember that.'

'Why did you like her so much?'

He smiles. 'Have you met her? I don't know. She made me feel stupid all the time and I liked that. She brought all our plants back to life. She took a wētā outside when I was apprehensive about it. The only bad part was how nervous she made me feel. I never looked directly at her. I tried not to laugh at any of her jokes, which was difficult. I thought a lot about her strangling me with her hair. Everyone would applaud and say I deserved it.'

'Dad.'

'It's my story, Greta; you asked for it. She was always very lovely to me; she remembered things I liked; if we went to a Chinese restaurant she would say, "Oh, let's get the crispy beans, for Linsh. Did you see Sparkling Duet is on special at Foodtown?" That sort of thing.'

'And you were just rude and didn't look at her?'

'Yeah, I was really rude. Except one time I made a great joke about Bismarck and she laughed, and I laughed, and it was like we were in our own private world. We weren't though, we were in one of her boyfriends' cars and he wasn't that happy about it.'

'Otto von Bismarck, the Prussian Chancellor of the German Empire?'

'Yes, he created the first welfare state in modern history. The joke wasn't to do with that, though, it was something to do with the Crimean War and "cry me a river".'

'I can't believe this is how I came to be.'

'Ah, it could be worse. My parents met as drunk teenagers on a train and had their passports stolen and got stuck in the Moldavian SSR.'

'Dad, that's very dark and mysterious. Sparkling Duet isn't even a good drink, that's why it's always on special. This doesn't make sense. So – Mum is really nice to you, you're acting all nasty for some reason, but you love her, and you assume she doesn't love you back?'

'I thought she felt sorry for me. I wasn't very confident. She kept going out with other people.'

'But she was only doing that because you were pretending you hated her.'

'Yes. That's what happened. For three years. Then I asked her if she wanted to stay over at my house and not on my couch.'

'And she did?'

'Yes. She folded up the bus timetable and snapped her handbag closed. I didn't know what to do, I just went to my room and she followed me.'

'Oh, and like, that was it?'

'No, I was still me. I wasn't pulling a lot of smooth moves. We took our shoes off, she lay on my bed with her arms crossed stiffly as if dead, and said, "So this is what it's like to be you." That might have been racist, because I'm from the vampire region of the world. Then I said I was sorry about how I had acted. That I didn't hate her.'

'What did she say?'

'She knew. She said that when I wasn't ignoring her I used a special voice, as if we knew about something no one else did. And, as I said, I had got very drunk after exams and put my head in her lap and performed a monologue in Romanian, which she clearly didn't understand, except at the end I grabbed her wrist and said, "There's no way of knowing."'

'She knew, and she just let you be weird anyway.'

'Yes. She asked me how I felt. I said I thought she was an upstanding citizen and that she would go on to do great things.'

'I can't believe at the beginning of this story I was concerned it was going to be too sexual.'

'Yes, well. She didn't like that. Then I said, "No, Beatrice, you're so beautiful and so special that I don't know how to describe it except—" Do you want to hear my speech? I think I still remember it.'

I nod, my head still on my knees.

'Okay,' he says and looks past me, at the garden out the window. ' "I saw the sea for the first time when I was nine years old. We went to Odesa, in Ukraine. And I was transfixed. I stood on the beach, right at the water's edge, amongst all the sunburnt Ukrainians, and I just stared out at the sea. I had never seen anything so expansive, so powerful that it could kill you, if it wanted to. And it went right to Turkey, which wasn't even Europe anymore, and that was everything I knew. I had seen a documentary that said that only 5 per cent of the ocean had been explored. It was like another universe, that we knew nothing about, right there in front of us. And I knew that I would feel the unimaginable force of that unknown world forever. And that's how I feel about you," I said.'

He stands still in the doorway with the washing at his feet. I don't know what to say. No one's ever said anything like that to me before. Matthew said my essay about *Death in Venice* was objectively fine. Holly said I have blue eyes, but I don't. The date said I had some strong opinions about kebabs. I wonder if people are having beautiful things said to them all the time, and I've just gone wrong somewhere.

'What brought this on?' my dad asks. 'Did someone tell you you'd be most welcome to come over?'

'Yes. Someone did.'

He scrunches up his face. 'You didn't go, did you?'

I shake my head. 'No. Nearly. Then I said I had to go to a bromeliad show in the morning.'

'Ah, and now your mother is at the bromeliad show alone and you're lying down feeling sorry for yourself because your quest for love has reached another impasse.'

'At the time I thought being on a date with this guy was like being on a date with my dad, but he was a lot less cool than you. Even if you didn't tell Mum you liked her for three years and then . . . told her she was an upstanding citizen.'

He nods. 'We're all strange, romantic, emotional people in this family.'

'Do you think that's a good thing?'

'Yes. Ah. Except one time, we were having dinner when you were all kids. Casper and V were both crying because of some injustice that had happened at school, and I thought in that moment, How have I managed to raise two such wonderful and sensitive boys?, and I just really wished we could go outside and . . . burn something. I would like it if just one time, my sons would stop talking about how terrible everything is long enough to drink a beer and watch ice hockey with me.'

'Does Codru have a game today?' Codru is my dad's favourite Moldovan ice hockey team. Their games aren't broadcast anywhere; someone films them on their phone and uploads them to Facebook. My dad loves it. I have no idea why he supports them; they represent an area near Chişinău, which is nowhere near where he's from in the north. He refers to people from Chişinău as city slickers. There's a really terrifying

Soviet-era circus building with an enormous iron crest of head-less clowns there. And a mall called MallDova.

'No, but Bucharest is playing Galati.'

'I thought Bucharest had two teams.'

He smiles. 'Yes, you remembered. Rangers are playing.'

'Is the commentary going to be in English?'

'I would say almost certainly not.'

I groan.

'You can understand Romanian. I know you can.'

I groan again. 'Fine.'

He clicks his heels together and picks up the basket. 'I think we have a box of Tui downstairs. We can answer trivia questions. Did you message this man today to say you don't want to see him again?'

'No. I asked him what he was up to and he replied saying, *Sorry, Greta, I don't feel a Spark with you.* With a capital S.'

'Like the phone company. Wow. That's a low blow. I think we have a bag of chips as well. Come down whenever you're ready; you'd be most welcome to.'

I groan and he keeps walking down the hallway.

Facade

V

The houses in this suburb are too big, too grand, and the trees
are too tall and imported. People have gates with keypads to
protect themselves from each other. Expensive dogs yap
through the black iron bars as you walk by, letting you know
you aren't supposed to be there. I always walk a bit more hastily
than I usually do here, just in case the police come and take me
away. Māori male, approx. thirty years, thin build, seen enjoying the shade of a colonial tree. Witnesses include a $3,000
Pomeranian and ten high-tech home security systems. I run my
hand along the green and white of the azaleas as I walk up Thony's driveway. Thony and Giuseppe don't have a gate. Their
house is much more modern than the nineties mini-mansions
and restored villas neighbouring it. It's a raised concrete slab
with lots of windows, split-level with polished wooden floors
and glass balustrades. I ring the doorbell. Thony is surprised
when he opens the door.

'V, what are you doing here?'

Maybe the dogs were right, and I'm not supposed to be here
after all.

'You asked me to come over; you said your laptop and your
phone weren't syncing properly. When we were having dinner
with my dad.'

'Oh, I'm sorry, I don't remember that at all. But, uh, come
in.' He opens the door properly and I go inside, partially feeling
like I shouldn't. 'I would have got more dressed up.'

He's wearing a grey cashmere sweater despite it being

February, and tan linen trousers and those felt clogs that people in Ikea catalogues have. The house is much classier than houses in Ikea catalogues. There's real art hanging from the off-white walls, and it looks more like a gallery than a place where people actually live. The painting that Thony most wants is not here, though. Geneviève painted it and she wanted to gift it to him, but when she called her agent it had been sold to someone else. It's of women swimming together in Greece, their hands joining them together in a circle in a deep blue sea. A sea much bluer than ours here, which is mostly grey and sometimes green.

'Where's Gep?' I ask.

'Ah, he went to Jakarta.' He rubs the back of his head, where he still has a surgical scar.

'Are you okay?'

'Yeah, I'm fine.' He stops and looks at me. 'V, you don't want any weed, do you?'

'Uh, no, I can't smoke. Because of my lungs.'

'Right, right, of course. I'll get you an Aperol Spritz.' I don't argue, despite this not really feeling like the right time for a fruity spritzer. I notice that there are three records and an ash-tray lying in the middle of the living-room floor. All the windows and doors to the deck are open. I sit on the brown leather couch, glad I'm not wearing shorts so I don't get stuck to it. I want to know why Gep's gone to Indonesia all of a sudden, but I feel unsure about asking.

Thony comes in and puts the lurid orange drink carefully on a coaster on the coffee table in front of me and inspects his records on the floor.

'Do you want to listen to Laura Branigan, Whitney Houston, or Gloria Estefan?'

'Uh, I'm not sure.'

He waves his hand at me. 'I know you only listen to sad men

prancing around in singlets. Did you know wearing singlets used to be for people who liked having fun? Being gay used to be fun. And illegal and dangerous. Now it's just about being romantic and sad.'

He puts one of the records on and sits down on the other couch, his hands resting on his knees like he's in a school sports photo.

'Did you ever have a dream, Valdin? Of what your life would turn out like?'

I look at the coffee table. There's a photo journal on it, but it's not the kind that would publish the photos Thony takes. He takes photos of actors sharing their homes for the first time, embracing their bodies, perfume ads, that kind of thing.

'I think I just try and take each day as it comes.'

'That's because your generation knows better than to have dreams. When I was fifteen my dreams were to go to the West and attend a beach hop.'

'What's a beach hop?'

'I saw one in a movie, all these attractive young Americans dancing on a beach and drinking out of coconuts. We didn't have many good movies in our town, we just watched whatever someone found somewhere in a basement under the library.' At this point he lies down on the couch, which seems to be the exact same length as he is. 'Have you been in love before? Did you love Xabi?'

'Ah, yeah. I guess so.' I poke at the jute rug on the floor with my sneaker. I don't want to recall a montage of times I told Xabi I loved him, but I do anyway.

He nods. 'I know how it feels. Do you miss him?'

'Yeah.' My voice doesn't quite come out how I want it to, but Thony is oblivious.

'Gep misses him a lot, too.' He sighs. 'And he's always worrying about Cosmo.'

'What's going on with Cosmo?'

'Something happened and he left Paris, but we don't know where he went or what happened. He hardly replies and when he does, he says he's fine and don't worry, but Gep worries anyway. He had an argument with Geneviève about it; her thoughts are if he says he's fine, he's fine. But Gep used to disappear like that when something was wrong, so he knows he's not fine. I feel like a spare part. I love Cosmo, but I'm always aware I'm his extra parent. The two he has are already enough to deal with. One of my other dreams was to have my own baby.'

'Why didn't you? Was it too complicated?'

'I can't. Because of the drugs they had me on when I was sick. Things were more difficult then, and we already had Cosmo half the time anyway. It wasn't something that mattered to anyone except me. It's okay. I have many other fortunate things in my life. It's not environmentally conscious anyway, to go around reproducing.'

I look over at him. He's still lying flat on the couch looking up at the ceiling. 'I'm sorry, Thony; I didn't know about that.'

'I don't know if I've told anyone else before. Some things we talk about all the time and some things we never talk about. Sometimes your dream comes true and it doesn't feel like you thought it would. I was so afraid.'

'When you were sick?' I pick up the Aperol Spritz and drink some of it because I feel like I should. I'm the only person in the family besides Thony who's ever been seriously ill, so he doesn't mind talking to me about it. My dad and Casper tend towards hand-wringing.

'No, when I found out that we were coming to the West. When I was fifteen. Linsh was fourteen. I thought that if we ever got to leave, it would be because whoever in Moscow said that we could; Brezhnev would have made a deal for us to go on holiday for being such good Soviets. Maybe it would be deemed good for international friendship. And we could take a trip to London or Berlin and buy jeans and eat burgers and then we'd come back. I didn't think we were going to be defectors. My life is so comfortable now that when I hear about people leaving North Korea, I feel so sorry for them and their struggle, and then I remember we did that. Even though we don't talk about it, we did that too.'

'What are you talking about?'

It's only at this point in my life that I realise that my imagined reconstruction of my dad's coming to New Zealand is completely illogical. The scenes of my grandfather Vlad going to a travel agent and buying the plane tickets, the feeling of the new visa arriving in the mail, the nostalgic packing up of the house in the small Moldovan town, the smiles and tears at the goodbye party – these are all things I've made up. No one told me any of these things, I just assumed this was how it must have happened. But none of it would have been possible.

'I still remember the day very clearly. It was November. It was snowing for the first time that winter; I had made the fire and I was sitting by it. Linsh was on the phone to a boy from school, they made plans to see a movie in the library basement the next day, a monster movie. When he hung up, Vlad told us we needed to pack one suitcase each and get in the car. We could tell from his voice that it was serious and that we weren't coming back. We never expected that our own father would be one of those traitors you would read about in the news and that he would make us be traitors with him.'

'Was there a specific reason he wanted to leave?'

He pauses. 'I remember Linsh said he wouldn't get in the car until he knew why. He was always like that; he needed an explanation for everything or he wouldn't do it. Vlad was blunt about it, he just said, "You can't stay here." I knew he meant me. Linsh had made trouble at school and in youth group, questioning things that we weren't supposed to question, but I knew it was me who people had been talking about. I knew what would happen to me if they found out it was true. And Vlad knew too. I couldn't look at him, I was so ashamed.'

I feel one of the worst sinking feelings I've ever felt and cross my legs anxiously. 'Did Dad know?'

'I don't know if he knew. He didn't always know what people were saying around town; he was more interested in reading and petitioning the council. But he didn't argue. We got in the car and drove six hours to Kyiv in our old white Lada. Going over the internal border to Ukraine was fine, Vlad did it all the time because he played in an orchestra there. He was the first chair violin.'

'Why did you live in Moldova then?'

'I'm not sure what Vlad's reasons were. He thought we were safe there, I think. He never really told us how he felt about anything. We fought in the car. Linsh wanted Vlad to tell us the whole plan and he wouldn't. I thought we should trust him. I'm a trusting person. When we got to Kyiv it was about three in the morning. We stopped in a supermarket car park; other people from the orchestra were there. They were all part of it. And Vlad was the leader, we realised. It was a fake tour.'

'What?'

'This was one of the reasons you could leave temporarily – to spread the joy of Soviet culture and heritage. Vlad had planned a whole sham orchestra tour. There were posters, itineraries, hotel confirmation letters, a commemorative record they had pressed. That's when it started to make sense. Vlad had been making us practise these pieces for months – Tchaikovsky, Stravinsky, Borodin. The border guards would suspect that we were fleeing and not let us go if it looked like Vlad was bringing his sons on his work trip for no good reason. So we had to act like we were part of the orchestra too. He and Linsh were always arguing about why he wanted him to play viola and not piano. There wouldn't be a piano in the KGB office if we were forced to prove ourselves, whereas the viola fit in the car.'

I feel cold, as if I too have been standing in the Ukrainian car park in the middle of the night in the snow.

'Then we flew to Moscow.' He stops, and I wonder if that's where the story ends. It can't be, surely. 'Valdin, I'm embarrassed that I've been smoking drugs and now I'm telling you all my secrets when you just came to fix my computer. I should be paying a psychologist to listen to me.'

'That's okay. I want to know. I feel bad that I didn't know, that I never thought to ask.'

'I don't want you to feel bad. You're very special to me.' He sits up and pushes a piece of hair behind his ear. 'So I had never been to Moscow before. Linsh had never been to Russia at all, but I always went to Sochi in the summer to stay with our mother. Linsh stayed home and checked the trains were running on time. Did he ever tell you that?'

'I've heard about the trains.'

This is a sore point for my dad. I know when I'm having a hard time, he thinks about how he would watch the trains every summer and that it's his fault I'm like this. I wonder for a second which option is preferable, to dream of having a child and it never happening, like with Thony, or, like my dad, to have a child who reminds you of the worst parts of yourself. My dad never talks about his mother.

'It wasn't his fault that he didn't want to come to Sochi,' Thony says. 'He was too afraid to go away for a whole summer. He didn't remember our mother at all; she was a stranger to him. She wrote to him twice a year, but he never opened the letters. I always went through his things when he was out. He had some very risqué literature.'

'Gross – like eighties Soviet porn magazines?'

'Oh, no, of course not. Books about women finding themselves.'

'Like going to India and learning how to cook?'

He shakes his head. 'No, masturbating. Vlad was nervous in Moscow. We were there for three days; we had to pick up our documents. Linsh wanted to ride the metro all day and all night, but Vlad thought people would think we were planning a bomb attack. Then Linsh wanted to go to the Museum of Cosmonautics, but Vlad said we had somewhere else to go. He was very serious and wouldn't explain. We went out to a residential area. I remember we walked up a lot of stairs, and then Vlad knocked on a door, and an older man opened it. We went inside and no one said anything. Linsh and I sat on a piano stool, and Vlad and the man stayed standing. Then the man started shouting. "How could you do this, Lavrenti? You just go to school one day and never come back – I thought you were dead." We didn't know he had a father, we thought he was dead. We didn't know his name wasn't actually Vlad, either.'

'Where was his mother?'

'She was gone. That was what happened, Vlad's mother left Moscow for Germany and Vlad tried to follow her. When he was fifteen he met our mother in the national junior orchestra and she agreed to run away with him. They went south by train because they heard it was easier that way, but they only got as far as the Romanian border when they had their money and passports stolen, so they stayed in Moldova. They used different names, pretended they were eighteen, got jobs in the town. Three years later our mother couldn't take it anymore and left, but Vlad was too proud to take us back to Moscow. That's what his dad said. Vlad had called him once and said he had two sons and that his girlfriend had left him, and then he'd hung up before his dad could say anything back. Vlad had sent back pictures of us every year; they were displayed on a cabinet in the apartment. We learned all of this through an hour of them shouting.' He puts his head in his hands and sighs. 'Maybe I shouldn't be telling you this. I don't want Linsh to be unhappy with me.'

'It's your story too, though,' I say. I can't process all this information quickly enough to decide if I feel sorry for my dad or if I resent him for never having told me any of this.

'He was so scared. Linsh was. I just wanted to hug him and tell him it was all okay, we could go to the space museum and learn all about Yuri Gagarin. He's never really let me feel like I was his big brother, but I did then. I would have given all my money to buy him a stupid piece of space rock and then ride around on the metro all day. After the arguing was over, we had tea and Vlad got Linsh to play chess. He won. Vlad's father was pleased. Vlad told him we were going to the West and he needed a document. His father just nodded and went and got it and he gave us each a hundred roubles before we left. The next day we flew to Hong Kong, and the day after that we were here. Vlad didn't tell us until we were in Hong Kong, that we were coming to New Zealand. I had never heard of it. Linsh told me there were a lot of beaches and someone called John Walker had won a running event at the Montréal Olympics. Then he was annoyed I didn't get his little joke because my English was so bad. I was just hopeful about my beach hop. When we got here, Vlad told the border police we were Russian refugees, and showed them the document he'd got from his father showing that his mother was Jewish. This was news to us as well, but what wasn't.'

'Then what happened?'

He shrugs. 'We got in. Vlad had a contact who had done the same thing, so she came and picked us up and showed us around. He had an audition lined up with the orchestra here, and then suddenly we had a new house and a new life, and we just never told anyone we were refugees. It seemed easier not to. People had no concept of where we were from or what our lives had been like anyway.'

'What about your mother?' I feel strange about the idea of having a grandmother out in the world somewhere, especially the idea of not being able to recognise her if I saw her. I wonder if she knows about me.

'She still lives in Sochi. She's a professor at the university. Russian and English literature.'

'That's what Greta studies.'

He stands up and goes to turn the record over. 'You should tell her.'

I nod and I know I should, but like so many generations before me, I don't.

Opener

G

I'm at a party with Rashmika, Fereshteh and our friend, a white man called Elliot. No one in my family can remember that he's called that. They call him Greg. We're late to the party because we had to wait for Rashmika to finish recording a rap in her new studio. Her mum wasn't pleased that her spare room has been turned into a recording studio, or that Rashmika's rap was about cancelling people by shooting them in the dick, but she gave Elliot and me two glasses of water each and showed us Rashmika's degree certificate while we waited. Then we had to drive all the way to Greenlane, because Fereshteh has a new boyfriend and that's where he lives. The traffic wasn't too bad, because it's Good Friday. Rashmika shouted, 'Not my holiday!' out the car window at every closed liquor store we drove past.

The party is exactly how I expected – full of people who look like they drive old Subarus and know someone who has an art exhibition coming up. There are pink fairy lights and a loud song is playing about beating that pussy good. We mainly stay together as a group, occasionally talking to people we used to know more than we do now, listening to what they're getting up to these days. People are working at wine delivery call centres, people are thinking about going back to uni, people are moving to Berlin. I don't tell them they should move to Bucharest instead because I don't know them like that. I talk to a guy who studied visual art at AUT. Casper was his favourite tutor. He's wearing an open denim shirt and a white singlet with a long gold earring. He thinks he might go back to uni. I say,

'Oh, wow,' a lot until he has to go and talk to someone who's just moved back from Berlin.

Rashmika appears from somewhere and grabs my arm. 'Greta, there's a girl in the toilet who's your type.'

What is my type? I briefly reflect on every girl I've ever liked. The girl who transferred to my school from a private school, who vaped a lot and had a lip piercing and bleached hair. The girl at the Model United Nations: glamorous black dress, fez, very shrill during a rebuttal speech about outsourcing labour. A lanky girl in my European 100 tutorial: big nose, cheeks like a squirrel, did not know shit about the French Revolution but kept bringing it up anyway. A very beautiful and bored Korean Air flight attendant who spilled wine on the woman next to me.

'What's my type? Wait, what do you mean, in the toilet?'

'Yeah, I walked in on her. I opened the door without knocking. She said sorry to me and I looked at her and thought, This girl . . . is Greta's type. So I winked at her. Then I closed the door.'

'You winked at her?'

She doesn't say anything, she just winks at me too. Fereshteh is trying to open a bottle of tonic. This new boyfriend of hers opens it for her and she looks at him like he's the true hero of our times. I can't remember his name; I think it might be William. I respect Fereshteh's choice, but we don't need another white man in our group whose name people have to remember, it's confusing enough as it is. It's not that crowded in here, but they stand face to face with their forearms pressed together anyway, staring into each other's eyes.

'Where are you going to pour that?' I ask.

Fereshteh looks around. 'Oh no, I didn't think of that. We need cups.'

'Pour it in my mouth,' Rashmika says. I frown at her and

look around. Elliot seems to have disappeared. Maybe he's winking at people in the toilet as well. Fereshteh and the white guy are making out.

'I'll go and look,' I say, to no one. Rashmika's joined in with some people dancing to 'God's Plan'. I leave the living room and walk down the corridor. The kitchen is typical of a flat like this: too many cupboards with thin wooden doors painted bright blue, a yellowing stove that might have been there since the seventies. The floor is black-and-white tiled lino with pieces missing. Through the window I can see people drinking and rolling cigarettes in the backyard. They are probably calling them durries. I imagine this house is horrendously damp in the winter and is probably worth around $2 million.

I close a cupboard door and there's a girl there. She has a shiny dark bob and is wearing a navy shirt with dots and navy trousers with the cuffs rolled up. She also has dots on her face. Freckles, those are called.

'Are you looking for cups too?' I ask.

'No,' she says. 'I'm looking for a bottle opener.'

She doesn't say 'bottle opener' in the normal way. She sounds like Shrek. I put my hand out and she gives me her bottle of cucumber-and-lime cider. I open it on the edge of the Formica bench.

She laughs. 'Oh, thank you so much. Don't judge me on the flavour; it was cheap.'

'It's very much not a problem,' I say. Why did I say this? Maybe this is all a sign that I need to stop drinking. 'Do you live here at this house?'

Of course she doesn't live here – she doesn't know where anything is.

'No, my housemate used to go out with someone who does, though. They're trying to act like they're cool with seeing each other again in a casual setting. Do you live here?'

Of course I don't live here – I don't know where anything is. 'I don't live here; I live somewhere else. In one of the other houses or dwellings in the city.'

She nods. 'That's a real coincidence: I live in one of the other houses or dwellings in the city as well.'

I smile at her with my teeth. She's smiling too, but she keeps her teeth hidden. Playing it cool, I see. What can I do that's cool? I hang my hand off one of the cupboard handles above my head, but this causes it to open and I nearly fall over. Cups. Here are some cups. They're tall and metal and probably for making milkshakes, but they will do. Now that I have the cups I don't need to be here anymore, but I'm still looking at the girl.

'Do you want to give me your phone number?' I hear myself asking.

She's surprised. 'My phone number? You don't want to follow each other on Instagram or add me on LinkedIn or anything?'

'No, I don't want to investigate your history or forge a business connection with you. That would be very forward.'

'Well, okay then.' She opens a couple of drawers until she finds a Sharpie and carefully writes her phone number up the inside of my arm.

'Thank you very much,' I say. With that, I stack up the metal cups and go back to the living room. I hold my arm up to Rashmika and wink.

Beautiful People

V

We're standing around a high wooden table in the domestic terminal. The other people from work seem really surprised that I haven't been to Queenstown before.

'Are you sure you haven't? Not even when you were a kid?' Kayleigh asks with her face scrunched up. She's a production assistant who wears her red hair piled on top of her head.

'No, I definitely haven't.' I smile when I reply. I want everyone to like me. I can't for a second imagine my parents taking us on an expensive holiday involving flights and tourist activities, especially not to a ski resort where people go to be cold on purpose. We used to drive to rundown cabins vaguely near beaches. When I was a teenager I would sometimes accompany my dad on work trips, but that usually involved me walking around Cairns or Puerto Princesa by myself. I didn't bungy jump or go to an escape room.

Simon the producer sends us all the final itinerary and shooting schedule via Bluetooth, because we're zero waste now. I scroll through it and it's all pretty standard, although there's an interview with the owner of a golf course that I don't remember discussing in the production meeting. The amount of money the show operates on has increased recently, and with this I've noticed a bit of a hierarchy emerge and a few more decisions being made without consulting me. I don't mind; I know I'm not in charge and I'm lucky I even have a job, but sometimes I think that I could have been better prepared for the work I'm expected to do.

People are talking about whether we'll be able to get a decent coffee when we're down there. 'All right, folks,' Simon says, clapping his hands. 'First off, I just want to thank everyone for their mahi on this project, which I think is the first of big things to come. And thanks so much for committing to filming over Easter weekend; we really appreciate the sacrifices everyone's made to get this done. I just want to acknowledge Mia, who postponed her trip to Raro for this, and everyone who put in the extra hours last night. If we keep focused and stick to the schedule as tightly as we possibly can, we might even have time for a few beers when we're down there.' Everyone makes noises of agreement, and Simon turns towards me. 'V, did you want to say anything quickly?'

I blink, trying to remember why I might need to say something. 'Um, no, I don't think there was anything else?'

'Oh, I just meant like a quick karakia before we get on the plane.'

Everyone looks at me. They look serious and warmly accepting of my beliefs. I can't even think of one karakia. I think of a school camp where we had to sing, 'Thank you, Lord, for giving us food,' to the *Superman* theme tune. In a panic, I think whether it would be appropriate to sing a song by the Māori and Pasifika reggae band Herbs.

'Oh, if someone else wants to, that's fine,' I say, taking my glasses off the table because I've remembered having something that's touched your head on a surface where you eat is against my own cultural practice.

'I can step in,' Bailey, the production manager, says. She has a sharply trimmed bob and round glasses and is wearing a yellow dress with boots, and a lanyard. Everyone looks down respectfully as she recites a karakia beginning, 'Nau mai e ngā hua,' which I'm pretty sure is about food, not travelling. Then I doubt myself. I look around for another brown face, someone who might relate to how I'm feeling, but I don't see anyone except a security guard way on the other side of the terminal.

In Russian culture you need to sit down for a minute before you leave on a trip somewhere. I feel like sitting down now, but we're already rushing off through security.

'Have you never been to Queenstown because you always go to your family bach for the holidays?' Kayleigh asks me, wheeling her carry-on suitcase as we walk.

'Yes, we have a house right on Papamoa Beach,' I say, because it's easier.

Expectations

G

I find myself in my parents' backyard, trimming a hedge with my mother. I don't remember agreeing to this, but here I am with pruning shears in my hand and leaves and bits of twig all over the ground. I don't even remember if I tagged off the bus or not.

'Greta, what's going on?'

'Huh? Where?' I look around but there's no one here except my mum, who has her hands on her hips and is looking at me as if I might be a deeply troubled young woman. She's wearing a green dress I haven't seen before, with wide straps and a square neckline. She isn't one of those mums who puts on leggings and an old T-shirt to do the gardening. Or one of those old women who wears special gardening capri pants and a bucket hat, who shouts about what a lovely day it is to everyone who walks past. And special gardening shoes, rubber clogs with a floral print. Where do you even get things like that?

'There must be something going on somewhere, because you aren't paying attention to what's happening here.'

'Sorry. What were you saying?'

She sighs. 'I was just trying to tell you that I'm sorry we can't have dinner with you tonight anymore, because of our trip to the Whitsundays.'

'What? Since when are you going to the Whitsundays? Are you renewing your vows?'

'No. Greta, that's why I asked you if you wanted to come over this morning instead. I've been talking about it the whole time. How did you miss that?'

I feel bad and start trimming enthusiastically to make up for it. 'So why are you going there then?'

'Your dad got a call from the lab there last night. They think they've discovered something exciting.'

'A fungus?'

'No, something proper. An anemone, I think. They want him to look at it. I have some comps for a late show tonight at the Waterfront Theatre, if you want them.'

'What show is it?'

'I can't remember the name. It's a new play; one of those old companies has brought some young director in and is trying to market it as a refreshing take on today's society. I don't think he's that young, though, and he's probably one of the board members' sons.' She looks at me to check if I'm paying attention. It must be hard for my mum, that we're always either talking about ourselves and our latest opinions on hot-button issues or not paying attention. Even when V didn't talk, he still seemed very loud. 'I mean, it could be refreshing. But I'm sorry we can't take you to dinner tonight. I know you wanted to go to that new restaurant, and you wanted me to pay for it.'

'That's okay.' I look at the flowers on the hedge we're trimming. There's no winter here, really. There's always sun and yellowy peach flowers with dark, shiny leaves. I rub one of the leaves and it's so smooth. I decide to leave it on its branch. 'I have a date tonight, anyway.'

'Oh,' my mum says, trimming away. 'Is this someone you've been seeing for a while?'

It would be typical of me to meet someone and not mention it for months. I don't like to publicly announce my feelings for anyone because I'm always unsure about how much I really like them once we're together. This has caused issues in the past. People want your mum to like them. I'm pretty sure V tells Mum when he thinks he saw a hot guy waiting for a lunch order in St Kevin's Arcade, so she gets enough information already.

'No, we just met last night.'

'Oh.' She doesn't prompt me, because she knows I'll let it all out anyway. Once I get started, I don't stop. I sigh. 'I'm nervous.'

'Why? Have you changed your mind about them?'

'No. Just, like, what if it goes really well and we get married or have a civil union party in a non-denominational community hall and stay together forever. What if I have to reshape my future expectations to include this new person.'

'Well. That sounds terrible.'

'I don't want V to be mad with me.'

'Why would he be mad about that? Are you not planning to let him give an emotional speech at your proposed civil union ceremony with someone you just met last night?'

'He likes being single together. It means he doesn't have to worry about it.'

'Oh, Valdin.' She stops pruning and steps back from the hedge, looking worried. I frown. I don't want to talk about V and all his emotional issues, I want to talk about me.

'Maybe I'm being presumptuous; maybe we won't end up having a civil union at all. Maybe we won't ever even have an argument about whether or not we should leave the city and move to a lifestyle block. At least not before V comes back.'

'He's coming back on Wednesday, Greta. Who is this person? What about them has convinced you that you need to start considering how your brother might feel about your marriage to them?'

'Nothing. I don't know anything about her. I know her phone number because I can't rub it off my arm. I have some idea of what she looks like, but this might be a false memory because we only talked for a few minutes. She has a very good voice. It reminded me of one of those races where you roll cheese down a hill, but if all the cheese had melted and it was running into my ears.'

'Okay,' she says. 'What does she know about you?'

'Nothing! I guess she knows what I look like and what my voice sounds like too, but I don't know what she thinks about it.' Or whether she thinks it sounds like cheese. 'I don't even think I told her what my name is. Oh no, I did, when I called her, I said, "Hello, this is Greta Vladisavljevic, we met last night in an old villa on Murdoch Road." I don't know why I said all that; I got all nervous and turned into Dad.'

'You and Linsh have always been similar. He asked out a girl he saw on the street once. They saw the movie *Risky Business*.'

I stop my pruning work and stand with one hand on my hip, dangling the shears from my other hand. 'He told me that he didn't ask you out for three years.'

'That was a complex situation.'

'He said you were seeing someone else at the same time.'

'Yes, I was.'

'Who was that?'

'What do you mean, who was that? Why do you think it would be someone you know? Do you think I'm going to say, "Oh, it was your old form teacher, Mr Horrocks," and you'll say you knew it, that sly old dog?'

'Well, I didn't think of that until you said it. Mr Horrocks *was* a bit of a sly dog though; sometimes he would go for a smoke with the Year 13s at the bottom of the cricket pitch. What was he like then, this unnamed man? Did he let teenagers borrow his lighter?'

'He was a lot of things.' She is taking the pruning of the hedge very seriously and not looking at me.

'Could you give a list of adjectives?'

'Um, tall, dark hair, green eyes. Broad shoulders.'

'Not a sexy police report – what was his personality like?'

She stops and thinks about it, which is nice because she's often quick to say she doesn't have to tell me anything. 'He was very charismatic. I met him on holiday. I didn't think I was going to like him at first, because he seemed a bit overconfident. He could talk to anyone, but it made me feel special that he wanted me most. Everything had changed so quickly for me. No one ever liked me that much on the island; people thought I was above my station, you know, because I got an A Bursary when I was sixteen and moved to Auckland. People said a lot of things about me. Then it was all so different, I came here, and people were interested in what I had to say, what I thought about things. They invited me to nuclear-free protests and on holiday. And men liked me; they didn't say I was a frigid bitch or anything.'

'You thought this man seemed cocky but then he didn't call you a frigid bitch, so you were into it?'

'That's a bad summary. He was a great guy; he had many desirable personal qualities and he was very good at dancing. There were issues, though. He didn't really live anywhere. He had all these different apartments in different cities, but he didn't really live in any of them. He didn't seem to have any stuff. He would work until after midnight and the only things in the apartment would be me and the flowers he bought me. I started to feel like we were just something pretty to look at, after everything else. It was an exciting, international life, but I couldn't live like that.'

'Hmm,' I say. I don't think my mum has ever shared anything personal like this with me before. 'Is that why you started liking Dad? Because he was more reliable?'

'I was interested in Linsh before I even met this other man. I just wanted Linsh to say how he felt, which took him years to do. I don't want you to think that I'm just with your dad because he's reliable. I don't want you to think I'm some sad old woman who settled for the first dependable man she met.'

'I don't think that.' I look at her in her new dress and her make-up done even though we're just working outside, and wonder how anyone could think that.

'I love Linsh so much. I loved the other man too, but I could never envision a life where we would be happy together. So when he asked me to marry him, I had to say no.'

'What?'

'Yes, I had gone to Istanbul to see him when he asked, and I said no. I told him I wanted to go home and he said he did too, but I don't know where he meant by that. Maybe he didn't know either. Then he rang the airline and bought a ticket for me and I came straight back to Linsh. It was the middle of the night, but he was awake; he was reading this conspiracy theory book about what happened to the dinosaurs.'

'Was he happy to see you?'

'We were both very happy to see each other.'

'And what happened to the other guy?'

'Oh, he's around.'

'What do you mean? He's here in Auckland?'

'I don't know, Greta. He might be away. A lot of people go away for Easter.'

'How do you know that? Do you keep tabs on him?'

She turns towards me with the secateurs open in one hand. 'Our time as lovers is disproportionate to the time we've spent as friends.'

I know she isn't going to say anything else about it, and I don't make her. The secateurs she's holding are much bigger than the shears she gave me. I wonder what else I don't know.

Vienna Calling

V

After the shoot, everyone pats me on the back and tells me I did well, despite what happened. They talk to each other and not really me about *starting a conversation* and *bringing these voices to the front*. I say I don't want to come for a drink, and trail off thinking of an excuse, but I don't think they hear me anyway. I start walking back to the hotel. I want to buy a bath bomb to cheer myself up, but the nearest Lush is in Dunedin. Fifty-two hours' walk away. I try not to make eye contact with the tourists, domestic or otherwise, and all of their tourist things, which make me feel so wholeheartedly disconnected from the place itself. The town filled with adventure attractions and cloned restaurants from the city makes me feel as if I'm in one of the simulation games I used to play, only without Greta in the background telling Mum how many minutes it's been since I let her have a turn.

I buy a big container of Radox Muscle Soothe bath salts that says it contains herbal extracts and essential oils. I can't tell which ones by smelling it. Maybe eucalyptus. The girl at the counter asks me if I pulled something kayaking, and for some reason I say yes. I don't feel I can tell her the truth: that there was an incident at work, that I recently found out my dad is a refugee, that I'm afraid that no one will ever love me.

Back at the hotel, I realise the bath is way too small for me to fit in, so I pour the bath salts into the bottom of the shower instead. It works okay. I do two Sudokus to try and calm my brain down. I complete some maths problems from a website that generates them. I drink a litre of cranberry juice. I consider messaging Slava, then think better of it. I download Grindr. I delete Grindr. I download Tinder. A lot of people are looking for a threesome on their Easter weekend away. I don't imagine they want to cheer up a surprisingly tall man with very little muscle definition and a lot of talent in calculus. I search *maths* on Pornhub but it's all just people having sex with their tutors and one video about solving derivatives that doesn't appear to be sexual at all. I watch it while I eat the mini Easter eggs the hotel left on the pillow.

The incident today makes me think of the pūrākau that Casper tells my niece Freya and that my mum used to very occasionally tell me when I was small. She called them legends. My dad used to tell Russian folk tales as well, but they were always terrifying and about people being stolen by swans or eaten by Baba Yaga. What makes the pūrākau good is the smooth blending of truth and fiction, and the special feeling you get when your ancestors get a mention. I guess I don't really know anything about my Russian ancestors. I think for a second and check the time. Eight. I pick up my phone.

'Hallo, hier ist Vladimir.'

'Vlad, it's Valdin. Um, guten Morgen.'

'Oh, V, I'm sorry, is this a new number?'

'Ah, yeah, fairly new. How are you? Where are you?'

I can't tell where he is exactly, but it sounds like it's in public somewhere. I imagine the people of Vienna beginning their days, looking for signs of spring, becoming enraged if the U-Bahn comes more than a minute late. Vlad will be wearing something nice, a camel coat and a tartan scarf, brown leather shoes.

'I'm in a Kaffeehaus looking over some programme notes for a meeting later. Don't worry, it's not too formal here, I can talk. Where are you calling from?'

V

'A hotel in Queenstown. For work.'

'Oh, how's work going?'

'Ah . . . it's okay. How about yours?'

'Ahhh,' he laughs. 'I think I speak in the same tone as you. There are always directors who think they know better and accountants with a bottom line. I've brought additional negotiation issues on myself by being the only person here who speaks Romanian; there's supposed to be this special Christmas concert and—'

'You aren't coming to us for Christmas this year?'

'Oh, I definitely am, I don't care what anyone says. I'll come down in November; I'm too old to put myself through these winters anymore.'

'Are you thinking of retiring?'

'One day. I just don't know which one yet.'

I imagine this happening, discussing whether it's unseasonably warm for November, school students walking past wearing Roman sandals, someone suggesting we get the barbecue out. In the fantasy, I'm the one who brings Vlad back from the airport, even though I don't think this would happen; I don't have a car. I feel comforted by the promise of an eventual November, sitting on the carpet with my back against the base of the hotel bed, rolling the foil Easter egg wrapper between my fingers.

'Vlad,' I say, not sure where to begin. I don't call my grandfather something sweet like *Papa* or *Yeye* like other people, but by the name he gave himself when he ran away from home at age fifteen and needed to get a job. 'I was talking to Thony and—'

'He isn't sick, is he?'

'No, no, he's fine. Well, he seemed like he had some stuff going on, but he wasn't sick.'

Vlad sighs. 'Ah, right. That would be too much, if he was sick on top of everything else he's dealing with.'

I contemplate prying but decide against it. There are too

many other things I want to know at the moment. 'He told me about how you came to New Zealand. With the sham tour and everything. I hadn't heard that story before.'

'Oh. That's an interesting choice of Anthon's, to tell you all of that now.'

'I wish I knew before. I mean, I wish my dad had told me.'

He sighs again. 'Yes, that probably would have been the right thing to do. But we don't always make the best choices.'

'How did you know you were making the right decision then?'

'I don't think that I did. I had made a lot of bad decisions up to that point, really. Then all of a sudden, I was thirty with two teenage boys who only had me and each other to rely on. And that was my fault, that we were so isolated. I could have taken them to be nearer to my father or their mother, but I didn't because of my own issues with them.' He pauses, and I can hear a smile in his voice. 'These people here at the Kaffee-haus are really getting an earful today, huh.'

'I'm sorry, we don't have to talk about this. I've just been having a hard day.'

'No, it will add some interest into their morning. Yes, so I knew I had to stop being this dramatic, emotional young man, living in this ridiculous old thatched house in the middle of nowhere, and do something to give my sons a better life. I didn't think I could take them back to Moscow, because they would get in trouble there too.'

'Thony said people had been talking about him in town.'

'Yes. That was too much. I didn't mind people not trusting me because I was Russian, and I was always being called down to the school because of your father's desire to question every-thing they were taught. I don't think I handled the situation with the teacher best way, either.'

'Did you threaten the teacher?'

'No. No, she was a very nice woman. From Kolomyya. A beautiful town, complicated history. Sorry, what was your question?'

I can't remember for a second myself. 'Um, if people knew that Thony was gay.'

'Oh. They didn't know for sure, but they knew he wasn't like the other boys in town. All his friends were girls, he spent all his money on magazines, he was always talking about the Moscow Olympics opening ceremony. I knew. Even though he cut out an ad for a mechanic and stuck it to his wall. He had a picture of a football team as well, but he didn't know who they were. I was from the city; I knew these kinds of things went on. I loved my son. Some of the boys started trying to force him to go with them on a wild boar hunt. Then I knew we had to leave, before someone hurt him.'

'Weren't you scared, though? I don't know if I could do it.'

'Of course. But I knew that's what I had to do. And I knew we had the out, that I could declare refugee status on grounds of religious persecution, even though no one knew I was Jewish aside from my father. I knew someone from the orchestra who had managed to get to New Zealand and I wanted to be as far away as possible, even though it was hard. We couldn't buy the food we were used to, no one understood us, we all had people we missed.'

I wipe my eye with the back of my hand. 'Like my dad's teacher.'

He laughs. 'There are public servants in every country.'

'Well, thank you, anyway. I'm very lucky, to have the life I have.'

'You would have done the same thing. I know you would have.'

I nod, even though he can't see me and I'm not sure if I believe in myself as much as he does. 'What do you think about dating apps? Should I try and find a Queenstown local for the night?'

'I've never used an app for that, and I think I do okay.'

'Yeah, you just go down to the council and pretend you need to file a building permit or whatever.'

He laughs again. 'Yes, I just visit the Amt and ask to be re-zoned.'

'Thank you for talking to me. I feel better now, I think.'

'I'm glad I could help you. You should call more often, even if you don't have questions about my dark past.'

'I will. I miss you.'

'I miss you too. Now go and live your free life and feel indebted to me for every moment of it.'

After I hang up the phone, I go and stand outside on the balcony in the dark, looking at the lights across the lake and thinking about the people being lit up by them. I think that my time of being a dramatic, emotional young man is coming to an end, and I'm okay with that.

Enthusiasts

G

The city isn't as busy as it usually is; maybe my mum's secret ex and everyone else's secret ex are all away for Easter like she said. There are a few more strung-out-looking evangelical types, shouting into microphones that it's time we accept God into our hearts and denounce our sinful ways, but it's nothing I can't handle. I don't think anything could ruin my mood, because I really like my date, despite the fact that I do not know what her name is.

I like the way she says my name, with a rolled R. I like her walk; she has a strong walk, which matches her square body. I keep thinking of more and more things to talk about, and she's responded positively to all of my conversation topics. Her favourite Boney M. song is 'Rasputin'. Her favourite Christmas movie is either *Gremlins* or *Elf*. The place she'd least like to go to on holiday is South Sudan. I'd thought you could see pyramids older than the Egyptian ones there, but I looked it up and that turned out to be in the north of Sudan. She didn't mind that I was wrong, and said she'd have to check them out. Then she paid for my gin with lemon and our Salmonella Dub pizza at Kiwi Music Bar, because she'd found out I was a tutor at the university.

'What do you do during the day?' I ask, remembering I forgot to get that information, not wanting to assume she has a job because some people don't.

'I'm a PhD student, in biology. I study nitrogen signalling in plants,' she says.

'Oh, do you know my dad? He doesn't work with plants but he's in the biology department; his name is Linsh Vladisavljevic.'

She smiles and shakes her head. 'Everyone knows Linsh Vladisavljevic.'

'How do you know how to say it properly?'

'He uploaded a pronunciation guide to the intranet and encouraged anyone else whose name was ever mispronounced to do the same.'

'Of course he did.' I think how I would write how to say our name phonetically. *Vla* like blah, with a V. *Dis* like a Paradiso ice cream. *Sav* like Saab, with a V. *Ljev* like Lyev Skynight, the character from *Magic: The Gathering*. *Vic* like rhymes with bitch.

'I couldn't believe it, when you said your whole name to me on the phone this morning. I thought you must be related, from the name and the . . . unabashed confidence. I have an email thread between him and the maintenance office printed out above my desk. *Re: The Leak*. Are your parents together? What's your mum like?'

We stop and wait for the bridge to go down so we can cross to Queen's Wharf and the theatre where the play is. Someone jets past on their boat with *Key Largo* written on the back of it. I don't know how it got here, through the Panama Canal, I guess. I think to ask my date what her favourite Beach Boys song is later.

'My parents are together. My mum is a fairly mysterious woman who is Māori and from Great Barrier Island. She used to be a director for TV ads, but now she works mainly in youth theatre. She always looks nice and sometimes it makes me jealous.'

She laughs. 'My mum mainly goes about in gumboots and woollen jumpers and repeats back misremembered news articles from the BBC to everyone she meets.'

'How long has it been since you moved away?'

'Ah, eight years. I left as soon as I turned eighteen. I moved to Edinburgh to go to uni, and then I moved here last year. Do you live with your parents?'

'No, I live with my brother but he's away at the moment.'

'Older or younger?'

'Older. I have two brothers and they're both older than me. V, my brother I live with, is five years older than me and he used to be an astrophysicist and now he hosts a travel show where he goes to different places and spins a wheel to find out what budget he's going to get, and then tries to have the most fun in twenty-four hours on that budget. All of his ideas are ludicrous, so he's perfect for it.'

'Your brother's the guy who got given $900 to spend a day in Matamata and refused to go to Hobbiton?'

'That's him. My other brother is much more normal. Oh, but here's the thing – he has a wife and her name is also Greta. I don't know why she couldn't have some other name.'

'Is she a big rival of yours, this other Greta?'

We sit down on a bench outside the theatre. There's still time before the show starts. I don't know why we don't go inside and sit in the bar, but I'm glad we don't. There are all sorts of people in this part of town who look like they have very different lives from me. They've got fake tans and highlights, shiny high heels and pointy dress shoes. Some of them are talking about the boats that are berthed here, because boats and mooring costs are things that they know about.

'No, the other Greta is a very nice person. She works at the Auckland office of a big publishing company and they always have lots of drama. She spends the rest of her time trying to convince my niece to sit still.'

'I didn't realise you were Aunty Greta.'

I beam. 'Yes, I am. My niece is Freya, she's six and she's the boldest person I know. Sometimes she sends me emails that are just a close-up picture of her face with the subject line *HELLO GRETA*. My nephew is called Tang and he's seventeen. He doesn't email me.'

'How do you have a nephew who's seventeen?'

'Well! My brother Casper is ten years older than me and he was a teen dad. Oh, the theatrics that were had. Casper already liked the other Greta when they were at school together, but for no reason he thought that she liked someone else, so he got sad and drank too many RTDs at a party and then ended up having a baby with a girl he didn't know the name of.'

'Oh, Jesus,' she says looking out at the boats and the boat people as well. Maybe boat enthusiasts would be a better name for them.

'It was some classic straight people nonsense. He had no idea until a couple of days before Tang was born. A friend of the girl's texted him because she thought it was wrong that they weren't going to tell him. Tang's mother was a private-school girl and her parents wanted to cover it up, move to Australia and pretend it never happened. It was like a TV movie. My parents wanted to raise the baby but . . . How long have you been in New Zealand? Have you heard about racism?'

'Yes, I've heard about racism. I know a bit about this country; I didn't just read an article written by an American who's never been here and get on the next plane.' She tilts her head to the side and her hair falls in a shiny circle around her face. It looks like it's made of brown and gold light.

'Well, I can be honest with you then. Racism came into play. The private-school girl's family thought that the baby was Casper's fault, that this was the kind of thing Māori boys were always up to, getting good girls pregnant and messing up their futures. They said it would be best for the baby to go to a good home. Oh, they'd also heard from someone about how V was a selective mute and accused my parents of having abused him.'

'Greta, that's awful,' she says, frowning.

'It was quite awful. Everything was a big mess. Everyone in our house was always shouting and slamming doors, that's the main thing I remember. Casper had been offered a place at a selective uni in Moscow and my dad was really upset, he didn't want him to go.'

'Is your dad from there?'

'No, but my granddad is. My dad hates Moscow, he won't go there. I don't know what happened; maybe he saw a puppet there.'

'What?'

'My dad is terrified of puppets. My granddad took him to this famous puppet theatre in Bălţi, near where he grew up, and he screamed so much he had to be carried out. Oh, God, I don't know why I said that – don't tell anyone at the lab.' Something about her face makes me want to share every piece of information I've accumulated over the last twenty-five years with her, even my dad's puppet-related trauma.

'I promise I won't. What happened with the baby?'

'He was living with an older woman, in what was supposed to be a temporary arrangement, and then she died.'

'Oh my God, are you serious?'

'Yeah, Tang was at kindy, he was four. Casper's details were on his file for some reason. This wasn't something we knew about, but the police picked him up and dropped him off at our parents' house. Tang lied to the police and said he usually saw his dad in the weekends, and they didn't think anything of it.' I shrug. 'The whole thing was wild. Then Casper came back from Moscow and told Tang he would never leave him again. There was a bit of a court case, which I don't know that much about. It was hard, having Tang come to live with us so suddenly. There were six of us in one house and we didn't know anything about him. Casper gave him a Snickers and he had an allergic reaction. He cried silently all the way through *The Wizard of Oz* because he was hor-ribly afraid of scarecrows. He would probably be embarrassed that I told you that. He's a cool teen now; he cares about the issues and sends me TikToks.'

'So things worked out in the end?'

I nod. Some people walk past us into the theatre complaining loudly about how far they had to walk from the car park in their high-heeled boots. 'Casper stopped poisoning his child, got back together with other Greta, and now they all live together in a white house in Epsom with a white fence. Do you have any siblings?'

'I have a younger brother but it's . . . just normal, he lives in Glasgow and does social media for a shipping company.'

'That's cool, you could make so many memes about the boats. You could start a rivalry between different shipping routes.'

She smiles down at her lap. 'You're great. Greta, is this a date?'

She doesn't look up at me, she keeps looking down. I don't know why I wasn't clear that it was a date when I asked her on the phone, since I was so clear about what my name is. 'Um, yes. I hope you didn't think this was a job interview. We aren't looking for new hires until the third quarter.'

She turns to face me, leaning on the back of the bench, hold-ing her head up with her hand. 'That's a real shame, I've made a PowerPoint about the skills I can bring to the team and everything.'

I look at her eyes and they're an unusual colour; not brown or green but in between somewhere, like a marble I used to have that I hid in my drawer, as if anyone wanted to steal it. What is it like to have freckles, to live your life with a constellation across your nose every day? I wonder if she knows the constellations of the southern skies. I wonder what she thinks of my face, if she thinks I'm pretty.

I lean on the back of the bench too. 'What's your favourite Beach Boys song?'

She doesn't tell me. She puts her hand on the side of my face and then we have a nice kiss. It's not over quickly. I start to think that a bench at the Viaduct in front of a woman in a fluoro-pink tunic dress and black pleather leggings yelling into her phone for Mark to tell Sharon she's already picked up the tickets is maybe not the best place to make out.

'Do you want to come over?' I ask.

'What was the synopsis of the play again?'

'Magz and Krumper are two millennials trying to make their way in the cut-throat world of telemarketing.'

'How far away is your house?'

'One point five kilometres.'

'What if I tell you my favourite Beach Boys song is "Sloop John B"?'

I put my hand on her knee. 'Well, then I won't be inviting you out again, but you can still come over this one time.'

'Are you sure this is a good idea?' she asks, stroking the back of my hand. 'To ask someone back to your house without knowing what their name is?'

My face feels very hot. 'What is your name, please?'

She grins. 'It's Elizabeth Alexandra Livingstone. But please never call me that.'

Miss Photogenic

V

I'm hiding out in the kitchen pretending to use the SodaStream to fizz up some water and I'm so on edge I don't wait for any hellos or how are yous when she picks up the phone.

'Mother, it's me, Valdin Vladisavljevic.'

'Mother? Why are you calling me Mother? You're making me feel like I'm an old drag queen in a silver bodysuit, maybe smoking a cigarette in a club in New York City.'

'That sounds cool, but I don't have time for this fantasy; there's a woman in my house.'

'You're the one who said your sister could live with you.'

'An additional woman.'

'What do you want me to do about it, come round and ask her to leave?'

I push the button on the SodaStream a few times impatiently. 'Mum, can you stop sassing me for a second and listen to my story?'

'I think you could be telling it a bit better.'

'I changed my flight to last night because I . . . wanted to, so I got home really late, Greta's door was open and the light was on, so I went over and shouted to her, "Zdravstvuyte!" Then she started screaming and yelling at me to get out, and I was so surprised that I walked back out the door again and went and sat in Esquires for two hours.'

'What, the coffee shop? How late are they open?'

'They're open till one.'

'I had no idea they were open that late. Who would want an eggs benedict at one in the morning?'

'Me, when I've just walked in on my sister and some woman and she's screaming at me to get out!' I hiss into the phone, crouching slightly as if that's going to hide me from view.

'Why didn't you just go into your own room and shut the door?'

'I don't know! I'm lucky I didn't see more. I wasn't wearing my glasses.'

'Valdin. Wear your glasses or get contacts.'

'I won't touch my eyes, that's disgusting.'

'I'm sure you've touched a lot worse.'

'Ugh! Mum!' I can hear her laughing at me and I don't know why she's in such a positive but largely unsympathetic mood. 'I hate wearing my glasses on planes. I can't relax and my face gets all oily. It's offensive that they don't make pore strips big enough for my nose. It's antisemitic.'

'Stop going to that shop that's for young Korean women. Or get a clay mask. Didn't I get you one in Vietnam?'

'Yes, that was very kind, thank you. Did you know Greta was seeing anyone?'

'I did know she had a date, actually.'

I look over at Greta's closed door. 'She's still here. The woman. I can hear them laughing. They're watching Miss New Zealand 1973.'

'How do you know that?'

'I'd know it anywhere. It's a hallmark of broadcasting. A cinematic gem. I can't believe Greta's watching it with someone else. I can't stop its joy from being spread, I guess.'

'Greta was worried about you.'

'Why?' I unscrew the bottle from the machine and decide to

pour some ginger-and-lime syrup in it for a treat. Plain sparkling water is disgusting.

'She thought you would be lonely if she found someone new.'

'No, I – I never even considered that. I'm fine.'

'It's okay if you aren't, mate.'

I feel special hearing that; usually only Casper gets to be called mate, and then I feel embarrassed for seeking validation from my mother.

'I am fine. I haven't been doing anything weird. I bought some Easy-Off Bam, but it was part of a planned cleaning event, not in a frenzy or anything.'

'Have you been seeing anyone, or talking to anyone, or . . . ? Whatever vague expression you like to use. I don't know because Greta doesn't ring me up if you have.'

'No, I'm very busy. I deleted the apps. I don't do that anymore.'

'Okay. How was Queenstown?'

'Oh, baffling. Bizarre. Not of this world. I don't want to talk about it.'

'I look forward to seeing the end product, then.'

I drink a little bit of my concoction from the bottle and it tastes good, but I don't feel refreshed. 'Mum, do you need me to come over right now?'

'Why would I need you to come over right now? Do you think I might be trapped somehow and I've just let you tell me about your problems first anyway, as if that's the kind of sacrifice I would want to make as a mother?'

'I don't know. No.'

She sighs. 'I'll come and pick you up. I want to go to Plant Barn.'

'Okay, I just need to really quickly steam my pores.'

'Fine. I'll see you in half an hour.'

V

I hesitate for a second. 'I love you, Mum.'

'I know. Bye.'

I put my phone down on the bench. I can hear Greta laughing again. I feel like shouting out that Miss Otago wins, but I don't.

Peach

G

I sit with my hand straight up in the air until a waiter gives me the nod across the crowded restaurant and I feel the hot anticipation of what's about to happen.

'What do you think of Wilson?' Fereshteh asks, refolding the menu.

'Who the fuck is Wilson?' Rashmika isn't looking at her, she's looking behind her at a large hanging picture of a cowboy.

'The guy I brought to the party. Why don't you ever pay attention to my life? Greta, did you remember we want extra Taiwan sausage?'

I nod, trying to keep the order in my head until the waiter comes over with his notepad, flicking his hair. 'Yep?' he says.

'Could we get eight chicken breast, eight pork belly, eight beef brisket, eight potato, ten Taiwan sausage, two eggplant, four tofu, two Tsingtao, one Coke Zero, and one peach ice mash juice?'

'How spicy?'

'Medium,' I say, folding the menu triumphantly.

'What about the lamb?' Fereshteh asks.

Elliot shakes his head. 'The lamb isn't cost-effective.'

The waiter nods and goes to ring up our total.

'Are you sure that guy's name was Wilson?' Rashmika asks. 'I thought it was Winston.'

'Of course his name wasn't *Winston*; I should know, I'm the one going out with him.'

'Was he named after the volleyball in *Cast Away*?'

'I think he was born before that; I don't know when it came out.'

'It came out in 2001,' I say. 'My dad took me. He was supposed to take me to *102 Dalmatians*, but he thought it looked uninspired.'

'I hope Wilson wasn't born after 2001,' Elliot says.

'I think it would be cool if you were going out with someone who was born after 2001 and named after a volleyball,' Rashmika says. 'You do you, babes.'

Fereshteh groans. 'I'm not doing that. I don't even think I like him, anyway.'

'I can show a photo of you at the end of my English 121 tutorial, see if you get any takers.'

'Rashmika, shut up. Change the subject.'

Rashmika laughs as the drinks arrive at the table and she cracks open her Tsingtao. 'What did you think of *Cast Away* then, Gre?'

'I don't really remember. We saw it at like ten in the morning. It wasn't long before I started school and I used to have Wednesdays out with my dad when he wasn't working.'

'Before I started school, I hung out with this old woman who owned a liquor store,' Rashmika says. 'She called me Naughty Rashy and we would go to Pak'nSave and buy, like, forty bags of chips to sell at the liquor store.'

'Where was your mum?' Fereshteh asks, opening her can of Coke Zero carefully. She's just had her nails done.

'She was working at DEKA. She worked in the lingerie department at DEKA when we first came to New Zealand because her accounting degree wasn't recognised here, then it shut down and she worked at the counter at Rendells. Then it shut down, so she worked at the post office and studied to get her accounting certificate at night. Which is lucky, because that post office shut down. Did your parents ever work at DEKA, Elliot?'

He rolls his eyes. 'No, they didn't. They met working at KPMG, because their accounting degrees were recognised by the white-privilege state. As you know.'

'Yeah,' Rashmika says. 'I just wanted to make you say it.'

'You mum's so proud of you,' Elliot says. 'She showed me and Greta your degree certificate the other night, you know.'

Rashmika freezes. 'No, she didn't.'

'Yeah, she did,' I say, mixing my peach ice mash juice with my straw. 'She showed us your degree certificate and then told us not to buy you any Rupi Kaur books for your birthday because you do not like her. And then she gave us two glasses of water, each. Which we drank in silence while you recorded your provocative raps in the background.'

Fereshteh laughs so much she nearly chokes on her Coke Zero.

'Oh, shut the fuck up,' Rashmika says to her. 'Your parents are always trying to give us a whole plate of raisins every time we come over. They must spend hours emptying those little red boxes onto a plate to impress us.'

'Raisins! When have my parents ever given you a *whole plate of raisins*! And if they did, why wouldn't they just buy them in a bag!' Fereshteh laughs and laughs. 'Maybe things would have turned out better with Wilson if my parents had shown him my degree certificate.'

'What's that got to do with anything?' says Rashmika. 'I don't want to fuck Greta.'

Fereshteh shrugs. We all know that I was not the only person there that day in Rashmika's mum's kitchen, having her achievements shown off to me. Elliot drinks his Tsingtao.

Rashmika frowns. 'Greta's taken now, anyway. I set her up with that toilet woman and now they're in love.'

'Oh,' I say, focusing on my straw, wishing I hadn't been thrown under the bus because the other topic was too sensitive. 'I don't know if I would say that.'

'That girl with the Shrek voice?' Fereshteh reaches over and grabs my wrist with her pointy maroon nails. 'Did you see her again?' Her eyes are wide like . . . big plates of raisins.

'Yeah, sort of.' I turn around and look at the chefs turning the skewers on the charcoal grill that stretches across the back wall. 'Do you think we ordered enough Taiwan sausage?'

'We ordered ten skewers, it's enough! What happened with the girl!'

'We had an agreeable meeting.'

'Don't be like that, Greta!' Fereshteh's nails are digging deeper into my wrist.

Rashmika puts her bottle down heavily on the table. 'Just say if you had sex or not so we can all concentrate properly when the food gets here and burn our mouths the way the creator intended.'

I wrinkle my nose. 'We didn't the first time; she came to my house after our date and we made out a lot but that was it.'

'Oh,' Fereshteh says, relinquishing her grip on me.

'And then what happened the second time?' Elliot asks.

'Well, then we did; like, we were, and then my brother came home from his work trip a night early and was shouting in Russian, and I hadn't closed the door because he wasn't supposed to be there, so I yelled at him to get out, but she thought I was yelling at her to get out of me, so she yanked her hand out and V ran out the door with his bag still on, and then it turns out he went and sat in Esquires until 1am and had a gateau.'

Everyone looks at me in an astonished silence while the waiter unloads the forty-six skewers onto the rectangular plate in the middle of our table.

'Are you going to see her again?' Fereshteh asks.

'Oh yeah, I'm going to see her again.'

Rashmika groans. 'Now everyone's going to remember this story, and not my good one about how I was part of an illegal chip-selling syndicate.'

I smile and start loading skewers onto my own plate. 'Sort out your own sexcapades then, Naughty Rashy.'

Rumbo + Dinska

V

My dad never gets annoyed or flustered, unless there's an organisational mishap, so I'm surprised to see him stand up from the table with a red patch forming up his neck in the middle of dinner. I bet Greta wants to evaporate. She has brought her new love interest to meet our parents. She even has lipstick on, even though we're just at our parents' house. Greta is always a little bit dressed up so it's hard to tell when she's making a special effort, but lipstick is a dead giveaway. The love interest might be dressed up as well – she has a new haircut – but it's harder for me to tell, since I haven't known her since the day she was born.

Everything was going well with the dinner. No one brought up colonisation or euthanasia or the Springbok Tour. It's because Casper's not here. He probably would have brought up all of those things, but he had to go to the other Greta's dad's sixty-fifth birthday. Greta's dad didn't want to make a big deal of it because he's a very quiet and serious German man, but they couldn't very well leave him at home so they could come and interrogate Gre's new girlfriend. It was probably the right choice; I don't know if Ell is ready for Freya.

The food part of the dinner was particularly successful; we've had a nice rare roast beef, nice roast potatoes and sprouts and a nice merlot. But now I've brought up Rumbo and my dad has got mad and is standing up shouting at me.

'Valdin, he's a real person! Rumbo is a real person! I am not making it up, I am not embellishing the story for dramatic effect, Rumbo was a very violent child who once hit the teacher with a hockey stick and fought off a wolf with a burning branch and started a forest fire, and he was my best friend!'

I lean back in my chair overly casually, knowing that I'm being a dick about this, and I should stop. 'If he's real, why does Thony never talk about him?'

'Because Thony's an idiot and he doesn't know what a good story is! His favourite movie is *La Dolce Vita*, for fuck's sake!'

Greta probably didn't expect Dad to swear so dramatically within the first hour of Ell being here, but it's too late. She probably also wasn't expecting the swearing, if it did happen, to be about Italian cinema, but he does have a lot of contempt for it.

'That's what he says, but I'm pretty sure his real favourite movie is *Miss Congeniality,* or *Speed 2.*'

Greta is looking up at my dad through squinted eyes, as if trying to view an eclipse without suffering retina damage. My mum is not happy. 'Linsh, sit down.'

He doesn't sit down. He moves his chair back and leaves the room.

My mum sighs. 'I'm sorry, Ell, he's not usually like this. You could stop being so antagonistic, Valdin.'

'I've reached a point in my life where I need Dad to admit that Rumbo isn't real.'

'Why don't you think he's real?' Ell asks.

'Um,' says Greta, tucking her hair behind her ears. She might have to get up and stop us from brawling in a minute. 'All my dad's stories about him are so preposterous that V and Casper decided he wasn't real and have insisted that Dad was lying every time he said anything about him.'

I wonder what I would do if my dad tried to fight me. No one in our family has had a physical fight before, unless you count a revolutionary game called Worm War 3 that involved a sleeping bag, stairs and wrestling. It faced a quick ban, passed under urgency, after my parents had to be called home from the theatre because all three of us ended up trapped with our arms and legs stuck through the bannister. We screamed until a neighbour came over. That was the first time Casper had been allowed to be in charge.

'Do you think he's real though?' Ell looks at Greta in a way I understand to mean that she'll side with her no matter what she says.

'I don't know. I want him to be real, even though his list of misdeeds is absolutely barbaric. Especially the time he wore a red suit and covered his face in coal and broke into people's houses to scare them on New Year's morning. Do you think he's real, Mum?'

She rolls a serviette in her hand. 'I believe he's real. It would be very unlike Linsh to lie. There have been times when I've thought he probably should lie to you and he hasn't.'

'When did you first hear about him?' Ell asks her.

'Within the first year we were together. Before Casper was born. The first story he told me was the one where they found a dead bird at the side of the road when they were walking home from school, and then later someone found a dead bird baked into a loaf of bread from the bakery. Linsh knew that Rumbo must have been the one responsible, but he didn't know how he did it. The most unbelievable aspect of the Rumbo saga, I thought, is why Rumbo would choose to be friends with Linsh. Surely there must have been children who were more willing to break rules and carry out revolting plots than Linsh, a very anxious goody-good.'

'I'm going to tell Dad you said that,' I say.

She shrugs. 'He knows.'

'I always thought Rumbo liked Dad because he was different from the other kids. He would never judge him or try to fight him for the crown of town prankster, he just let it all wash over him.' It seems like Greta's degree in analysing fictional literature has finally come in handy. 'I always thought that Rumbo was dead, though.'

'What!' I exclaim. 'That was never a part of any of the stories.'

'I know, but I can't imagine a world where he's still alive today. Maybe I've seen too many nineties films for children where someone's acting out because they know they don't have much longer to live and want to make every moment count. Something like that.'

'You think Rumbo put a dead bird in a loaf of bread because he didn't have long to live?'

'I don't know. He could have died after Dad moved to New Zealand. I just don't think he's alive now. He's never come across as being particularly healthy.'

I sigh. 'Mum, do you think I upset Dad too much? Should I go and talk to him?'

She shakes her head. 'No, he's coming up with a plan. I can tell he's not upstairs sulking because the stairs have been creaking.'

'Do you think he's standing on the other side of the door, ready to jump out and shout that none of us ever take him seriously?'

'I don't know what his plan will entail.' She pours herself another glass of wine. I pour myself one too. What a ridiculous situation to be in. Ell had probably been worried that this was going to be awkward because she and Greta are gay, not because of this fucking Soviet Union Rumbo backstory coming to a thrilling crescendo right here at this dinner table. I eat another sprout.

Then my dad reappears, open laptop balanced on his arm, a glass of wine in his hand. 'Rumbo is real,' he says, as if this is the final word on the discussion.

'How old was he when he died?' Greta asks.

'Rumbo is not dead, Greta, he lives on to this day, working for an international trucking company, transporting goods between Chișinău and Bucharest, and also to Hungary and Czechia, and so on.'

'You're making this up.'

'I am not making this up.' He turns his laptop around to face us, displaying the Facebook profile of one Andru Rusnac, a bald man with a red tracksuit jacket zipped up to his chin.

'That could be literally anyone in Eastern Europe. He's not even called Rumbo.'

He glares at me because he knows I'm right. This is a completely unsubstantiated claim. He must have forgotten that I'm a scientist and I know a thing or two about facts and logic. He puts his glass of wine on the table and turns the laptop around and starts typing, still standing up.

'Linsh,' my mum says, 'maybe this could be an ongoing project for you, trying to prove to Valdin that you had a friend when you were younger. Something you could work on after dinner, when everyone's gone home and maybe I've gone out.'

He doesn't answer her. We all have some more wine.

'Ell, how long have you been in New Zealand?' my mum asks. I can't believe she's carrying on with the meet and greet, despite my dad feverishly typing and clicking, holding the laptop with one hand.

'Ehm, just since last October, actually. I wasn't expecting to; I'd been living in Edinburgh since I left school and I was working on my PhD up at the uni there when my supervisor left suddenly and I—'

'Everyone stop talking,' my dad says, and I think my mum might kill him. He has his ear pressed to the laptop keyboard, which is insane. He turns the volume up. 'Allo?'

'Allo, Dinska!'

The voice of a man who has smoked hundreds of thousands of cigarettes and may be driving a truck on an EU-funded bypass at this very moment fills my parents' kitchen and dining area. He starts speaking very quickly in what might be Ukrainian. My dad is nodding even though it's a voice call.

'Rumbo, ty rozmovlyayesh anhliys'koyu?'

'Tak, yes, I'm speaking English all the time. I'm driving Chișinău–Praha . . . four times a week.'

I feel shown up by Rumbo that he can probably speak four languages and I can usually speak English and barely enough Russian to be able to order blinis. Greta frowns. 'That's like 1,500 kilometres. Driving Chișinău to Prague would take seventeen hours at least.'

Dad waves her away as if everyone's spending sixty-eight hours a week driving. 'That's a lot of travelling, do you not have a wife?'

'Ah, a wife in every city!' He cackles, then adds, 'I'm divorced.'

'That must be nice,' says my mum.

'Dinska, you remember Martina Borisnova Yevtushenko?'

He thinks. 'Ah, yes, I think so. With the . . . unusual voice.'

'In 2014 she's leaving me for rich Romanian man from Iași. There's an airport there with many flights to Kipr.'

'Cyprus,' Greta tells Ell.

'I'm maybe moving to Cluj-Napoca,' the man thought to be Rumbo continues. 'Big entertainment industry.'

'Ha, interesting,' my dad says, nodding again. I briefly picture Rumbo hosting a show where you have to scale an obstacle course and then stuff birds into loaves of bread. 'Look, the reason why I'm calling you is because my son doesn't believe the things that happened in Lipcani, when we were children. He's, um, gorodskoy pizhon, he doesn't understand.'

'Ah, previous times. Things are very different from now. What's the name of your son?'

'Valdin.'

Rumbo laughs. 'Stupid name.'

'Yes, my wife named him.'

'Oh, for fuck's sake, Linsh,' my mum says, pouring a third glass of wine.

'Do you have only one son?' Rumbo asks.

'No, I have two, and one daughter.'

'Hmm. Very lucky. I have three sons but no daughter. You should always remember, Dinska, you're very lucky to have a girl. My sons are always . . . believing they can become famous on the internet. Doing parkour. A girl would have better ideas.'

'I know how lucky I am, don't worry. Um, what do you remember about the old times? What was your happiest memory?'

Rumbo sighs. 'There were good times and hard times. I remember that I was a very bad child, making many pranks, scaring everyone with masks and coal on my face, taking money from children to fight someone else's pig. Then I'm very sad because I'm not allowed to visit the, ah, leather factory. For school excursion. But my happiest memory' – he laughs – 'is when it was snowing and I told you that someone from secret police is chasing us, you have to take my backpack with chicken I stole, the memory of you running across the ice with the chicken screaming in the bag.'

My dad smiles. 'I forgot about that.'

'How is Thosha? Does he have a wife?'

'Huh? Oh, Thony? Um, he . . .' He looks across at me, like I'm a gay advisory board for all occasions. I shrug and shake my head. 'He works in the entertainment industry,' my dad says.

'Hmm, maybe I will call him as well.'

My dad laughs. 'Yes, that could be a good idea, give Thony a call. Rumbo, thank you so much for talking to me. Have a good trip to Prague.'

'Yes, I will buy many cakes, trdelník. It's nice to talk to you, Dinska. I hope your son doesn't think you're a liar anymore. Do pobachennya!'

'Do pobachennya! I hope you . . . find a new wife soon.'

Rumbo laughs again, and Dad ends the call. He puts the laptop down on the cabinet behind him, sits back at the table and resumes eating his roast beef. My mum is a picture of disbelief.

'Ell, are you a PhD student in biology at the university?' he asks.

'Ehm, yes, I am,' she says, pushing her hair back.

'We've spoken before, haven't we? Is Erik your supervisor?'

'Yes, he is.'

My dad puts his cutlery down very carefully and folds his hands in front of his plate. 'Please never tell him that I did this.'

Lunch Essays

G

Rashmika and I are walking through the university complaining about a stupid lecture we've been to. We have to go to the lectures for the classes we tutor, which isn't usually a problem, but this lecture was a guest lecture and it was terrible.

'If that guy hated the traffic here so much, he should have gone back to LA,' Rashmika says as we walk across the street, around the colourful plastic things that are meant to stop people parking or smoking or something, and past the library. 'I don't know why the course convenor thought the students needed an American perspective on New Zealand literature anyway. He didn't even give a perspective, it was just a speech about how we aren't as progressive as we think we are when it comes to, like, electric buses.'

'I think maybe the course is just bad,' I say, and take a drink from my can of Mountain Dew. 'It's kind of a trick that it has contemporary in the name and the most recent book on the reading list is from 1978.'

'At least we're still getting paid. I don't know how long that's going to last, though.'

We walk under the stone archway, where there's a line of people queued up for the Hare Krishna lunch. Ell's sitting by herself on a bench.

'Hello,' I say, feeling my heart jump into my throat because I wasn't expecting to see her.

'Hello!' she says, brushing pie crumbs off her lap.

'Sup, E,' Rashmika says. She's wearing rimless purple

sunglasses and baby pink flares and her vibe hasn't matched anyone else's all day. I wonder if Ell likes my new lip gloss or if it
all rubbed off on my Mountain Dew can. Rashmika sits down
on the bench and there isn't enough room for me, so I sit on the
grass, carefully, because I'm wearing quite a short skirt.

'I'm just waiting for a couple of people from my lab; they're
in the line,' Ell says, gesturing. The line has about fifty people
in it. I open the packet of my spinach and feta roll from Munchy
Mart and Rashmika takes out a Tupperware container with rice
and saag aloo in it.

'Having a good day?' she asks Ell.

'Not too bad, we've just been watching presentations all day.'

'About plants?'

'Well, not about plants themselves, more about the processes
behind the plants' ability to keep producing the chemicals they
need to survive in artificial or constructed environments.'

'We've just had some American guy try and take us down a
notch about how good our public transport is,' Rashmika says
with her mouth full.

'What class was that?'

'Contemporary New Zealand Literature.'

I smile up at Ell. She's wearing an outfit I haven't seen before,
with pants and a satin shirt both in a kind of rust colour. She
looks good, like a Communist statue. I showed her pictures of
all my favourite statues over the weekend and she responded
very well. I wonder if this new look is an extension of that.

'Greta.'

I look behind me and it's my dad. He's holding a cardboard
filing box and standing with a man with a very friendly round
face.

'Sup, Dr L,' Rashmika says.

'Ah, sup . . . master's candidate R,' he says. 'This is my col-
league, Erik.'

Erik smiles at all of us. 'Hello, Ell, Greta, master's candidate R.'

We all say hello and I wonder if Erik knows that my dad told our whole family about his new kitten. Erik's phone starts ringing.

'Um, Ell,' my dad says, glancing at Erik, who's taking the call, 'I just wanted to apologise for my theatrics the other night. I really should have waited until maybe the fourth or fifth time you came round before I did anything like that.'

'Oh, it's fine, I had a great time,' Ell says, confidently, but slightly red.

'Was Mum mad when we went home?' I ask.

'Oh, furious. She hasn't been so perturbed by my actions since I told Casper he should drive without a licence to go and get me an ice cream from McDonald's.'

'When was that?'

'He was fourteen, so it was a while ago. It was Christmas, I had become excitable after having too many of my father's duty-free liqueurs. Ah, anyway, I just wanted to ask if you would let me take you two to lunch sometime to make up for it.'

'You don't have to do that,' Ell says.

'It's a free lunch,' Rashmika says, still eating her own.

'Okay then, great.' Ell nods, and I'm already thinking about what my ideal lunch would be. Not a Mountain Dew and a dry spinach roll if my dad is paying.

'Wonderful,' he says.

'Linsh, we'd better get going,' Erik says, smiling and pointing to his watch.

'Ah, we have to go to a budget meeting, which I'm sure will be fantastic and we'll all feel very valued coming out of it. Enjoy your lunch.' He nods and taps his heels together and they go striding off. My dad looks way too tall out of context, without his tall family and house where everything is high up.

'You're lucky,' Rashmika says to Ell. 'Gre's family aren't usually huge fans of the people she wants to bone.'

'Bone is so gross, don't say that,' I say. 'My family just get overexcited when they meet someone because I have one brother who's pretty much had the same girlfriend since high school and one who went out with an old friend of my parents' like he's a member of the oligarchy.' I poke at Ell's shoe with my foot. 'Casper wants us to come for dinner, by the way.'

'Wow, I'm getting wined and dined all over the place,' she says, looking down at me because I'm still on the ground.

'He doesn't usually have wine, but he might offer you a beer if he likes you.'

A shadow falls over me and Rashmika frowns and puts down her Tupperware. 'Good afternoon,' she says.

I crane my neck upwards and see the upside-down face of Holly.

'Gre, I was just wondering if you could do me a favour,' she says, in her bespectacled, blazered, lanyarded manner.

'What is it?'

She unclasps her leather satchel and takes out a stack of papers. 'I was just wondering if you could mark these essays for 102. I've just got a bit too much on my plate right now.'

'Oh, with your dissertation?'

'Yeah, and a few other things. Do you mind?' She holds the papers out to me, not many, maybe ten essays, and I hesitate and then take them.

'Yeah, it's fine. I think most people in our class are going to hand in late anyway.'

'Great,' she says, pushing her hair back from her face. 'You tutored that course last year, didn't you?'

'Yeah, and I thought I'd moved on,' I say.

She laughs. 'Well, thanks. I'm back from Pauanui on Tuesday so maybe we could catch up and get a drink then, go over things.'

G

'Um, yeah, okay, I guess so.' I run my hand over the pages and then put them in my tote bag.

'I'll message you about it,' she says, looking at her phone. 'Thanks, Greta, you're a true beauty. I've got to go and meet some people. Ciao. Bye, Rashmika.'

'Nice to see you,' Rashmika says to Holly's retreating back.

'Who was that?' Ell asks.

'Someone who's not getting invited to lunch or dinner,' Rashmika mutters.

Anuncio

V

From when I was twenty-one until I was twenty-eight, I worked in a university lab. That's a long time to work in one place, and every day at the lab was by and large the same – we sat at the same desks, worked on the same projects and most people even ate the same lunch. Now when I say I'm going into work, I go into an office that has things like break-out rooms and collab spaces. There are all sorts of different desks – standing desks, big tables, stools far too low for me to sit on. People eat different lunches every day. I don't talk much about the lab in this office; it's too foreign to the people here. It's like when my dad tells a story that relies on the listener understanding the concept of local informants, or when my mum tells a story where you really have to hold seafood in a high regard to get it. The lab is a different part of my life. Sometimes I miss it. I miss my best science friend, Chris, who's Ngāpuhi from Kerikeri so he can appreciate a good story about seafood.

Today in the office there's a particular tension in the air. It feels like something is going on. Maybe the hot barista everyone likes is rostered on, or someone's suggested going to the new craft beer place after work. On Fridays, we used to go for drinks at the university club to spy on people from other labs. My favourite beer is the working man's drink, Lion Red. My mother would disown me if I started drinking a beer from the South Island like Speights. She would tell me to go and be the pride of the south on my own time.

'Hello, hello,' Emma says to me, spinning around in her chair as I take off my coat. She's my favourite person at the office. Maybe things would have been better in Queenstown if she'd been there; she's not afraid to speak up when something weird happens. It's probably because she's Australian.

'Hello,' I say, draping my tan scarf on the back of a chair. 'What's going on?'

She points to the glass-walled meeting room where Simon and Bailey seem to be on a conference call. 'They want to see you.'

Simon pokes his head around the door. 'Hey, V, meeting here in five.'

I have a feeling of foreboding. I wonder if I'm being let go, because of what happened. Simon gives me a thumbs-up and goes back to the call.

I take my water bottle out of my bag and go to the water-cooler to fill it up. Greta has had several terrible office jobs, and she says that visiting the watercooler is one of the very few freedoms one has at a bad job. It's one of the only things you can do that isn't strictly work-related and not get into trouble. 'What about going to the toilet?' I asked. 'You can't get into trouble for doing that.'

'No,' she said, 'no one can see you in there. If no one can see you, you're probably doing something bad.' With the watercooler, things are transparent. I feel lucky to have never had a job where you weren't allowed to piss when you needed to, and then I think urination is a human right and not something that I should be feeling grateful for.

Simon waves me over into the meeting room and I close the door as gently as I can. I wish this potential firing wasn't taking place in a glass room, but I suppose that's late-stage capitalism for you.

'V, take a seat. How are you?'

I take one of the wheeled chairs from around the table, realise it's too low, and have to try to adjust it while appearing calm and ready to open a dialogue. 'Yeah, good, thank you.' Bailey is still on a phone call, and has her chair turned away from us. Today she's wearing an ankle-length khaki pleated skirt and a cream blouse with a round collar. Red lipstick.

'You probably know why I've called you in here. I just wanted to grab you for a quick word before we make the announcement.' He smiles and drinks from a glass bottle of cold brew as he talks to me. He's wearing a beanie.

'Ah, right,' I say. He seems to be smiling a bit too much to be firing me, but maybe that's just the way things are these days.

'It really is all down to you that this is going ahead, and I wanted to thank you for that. We showed some of the footage from Queenstown in the meeting with the sponsors and they loved it; I don't think we would have got the deal with the airline if anyone else had been hosting. You're so talented; I have no idea how it is that you . . . come up with the things you do, but just know that we're so grateful that you've come on board.'

'Oh,' I say. I'm trying to imagine in what world what happened at the golf course was good and not uniquely horrible. 'Thank you, it's nice to hear that.'

Bailey hangs up the phone and looks at her watch. 'Simon, it's ten now – should we get everyone in?'

'Yeah, sure,' he says, and pats my shoulder on the way past to call everyone into the meeting room.

There aren't enough chairs for the other twelve or so people in the office, so some people wheel their own ones in. Simon checks to see that everyone's here, and Mike, an editor, shuts the door. I haven't said everyone's name but please imagine that there are twelve people in this meeting room, and they all look like they work for a small media company and enjoy talking about coffee and how cold it is. Simon is standing at the head of the table.

'Welcome, everyone. Hope it wasn't too hard getting out of bed this morning. What was the temperature, 8 degrees?'

'It was below zero in Dunedin,' says Mike. Some people start murmuring. They've heard about other temperatures in other places as well.

Simon puts his hands together. 'Okay, so you all probably know by now why I've called you in here. Yes, we have secured the sponsorship with the airline, and yes, we have got the go-ahead from management this morning, so we will be shooting in Argentina from the tenth.' Everyone turns round and starts talking and Simon laughs. 'Yeah, we know what a short turn-around time that is, but we've got all the passports we need on file – thanks, guys, for getting that sorted – and the tickets are being booked today. We'll be in Buenos Aires for three days, then on to Patagonia, and then back up to Salta; we're wanting to get three episodes out of this. We will be away for twelve days in total, then straight on to post—'

I don't know what temperature it is in Buenos Aires because I never look, I never let myself imagine what it would be like to be there, I just focus on what it feels like to be here, where my life is, on my island, Te Ika-a-Māui, and I don't worry about what anyone else is doing on their island, América del Sur, and what they might see when they wake up, whether it's someone else or just the wall, if they still like cutting up fruit for breakfast and eating it from a bowl with a spoon, leaning on the kitchen counter and scrolling through the news, if they have anyone to tell if they see any-thing interesting, what they see when they look out the window to check the weather – another building, people talking on the street, traffic arguing with itself, empty land as far as the eye can see, a suburban neighbour hurrying their kids into the car – I don't wonder how many days the house is left in a rush, the bowl in the sink, the chopping board on the bench, who the meetings are with and whether they start on time, if they're in glass meeting rooms like this one and what colour the chairs are, whether they're bright green and the walls are white, if the room is too hot and a woman called Anita uncrosses her legs and opens a window, I don't think about whether they eat lunch alone in a plaza in the city, a green salad with chicken and almonds, it's supposed to be healthy, then maybe a KitKat, before another meeting, this one more casual, a walk around a new exhibition being set up at the gallery, then a café, just a black coffee and an alfajor, a glass of water, I don't think about how the other person must feel talking to them, looking at them when they smile and noticing their front teeth overlap very slightly, wondering if it would be appropriate to ask them what they're doing later, oh but they can't tonight, there's a film to go to and thankfully it won't be dubbed, a birthday dinner at a restaurant where it's hard to get a reservation, or a date at a bar, if you could really call it a date, it's been so long now that it's a comfortable part of both of their lives, one of their favourite parts, resting their arms on each other, questioning if things are becoming too routine and ordering a pisco sour, laughing about that, or maybe the other person is away right now, and they miss them, they go home alone on the train and as it thunders along the tracks the way it does so many times a day, they take out their phone to send a message, *I miss you and I love you*, that's something they might say to this person, but not to me because they don't love me anymore and they don't think about me and that's why I stay on my own island and never think about them either. Not when I have good news and want to share it with someone, not when I turn my face away from another man in the night, not when I reach my hand out in the morning and no one's there and all I see is the wall.

'Sorry, I just have to fill this up,' I say, standing up with my bottle, and everyone nods because water is an acceptable thing to want. It's transparent.

Plants (II)

G

I'm reading a magazine about how to look after plants. My back is to the window; some sunshine is still coming through the clouds and warming my back, despite the rain. I wonder what plant I would be, if I were a plant. Maybe something with big leaves that droop sulkily if not provided with the exact right amount of water and light. Maybe something with intent to take over, with long, creeping tendrils sneaking their way up a bannister. I love to be high up somewhere and see that a plant has taken over down below. There's something like that at the university – a window you can look out of and see that a big monstera has taken control over a negative space between buildings, a space there's no access to and is therefore of no use to humans. I feel like that could be my final evolution.

V has entered the apartment while I've been thinking about this, but he hasn't said, 'Hello, Greta, how has your day been?' or anything polite like that. He seems completely vexed and perturbed by something. I watch him in his navy coat and undone scarf, standing in front of the door with his keys still in his hand. There are flecks of rain on his glasses. I wonder if he's going to tell me what's happened, or just go into his room and shut the door and put on Sufjan Stevens. Sometimes he doesn't think that I could be of any assistance because he thinks I'm too young to understand anything.

'Greta.'

I wait behind the magazine.

'Greta, I have to go to Buenos Aires.'

'Why is that?'

'For work, we got sponsorship from an airline and now I have to go to Buenos Aires in two weeks.'

'Did you tell Xabi that you're going to be there?'

He looks at me. He's still standing in front of the door, perfectly still with his arms slightly out as if he's waiting to be crucified.

'No. Do you think I have to? Is that the right thing to do?'

'You don't *have* to do anything. But I don't know. He'd feel bad if he found out that you came to his city and didn't tell him. Worse than if you'd been upfront about it.'

'Why would he find out I'd been there? From a local informant?'

'No. V, your show is on TV.'

'Oh. Yes. Right. Greta, what if he's dead?'

'What? He isn't dead. We would know if he were dead.'

'What if you know that he's dead and no one's told me because they're afraid that this is going to be the one thing that sends me over the edge and I'll never be able to function in society again.'

I sigh and close the magazine. 'Xabi isn't dead. No one cares to spare your feelings so much that they would concoct an elaborate plan to cover up that Xabi is dead. Also, he's quite prominent in his field, so someone would probably start a hashtag to mourn him.'

'I muted every word I could think of that had anything to do with him, including *art*, *man*, *Catalonian independence* and *bisexual*. Greta.'

'Yes?'

He pauses for a second, still not having moved. 'I'm still in love with him.'

'Okay,' I say, as if I've never heard him crying listening to 'I'm Not in Love' by 10cc.

'I think I'm just going to have to call him,' he says, and walks right back out the door.

'All right, goodbye,' I say, to no one. If it had been me, I would have just sent him an email.

Crème de Menthe

V

I stand in the corridor in the engineering building of the university. It's taken me three days to make this call. I've been overthinking it, testing out different locations around the city, on the bus so I could cut the conversation whenever I wanted by announcing that I had to get off the bus, under the motorway bypass so I could act like I couldn't hear if I heard anything I didn't like, down by the harbour so I could stare across the sea with a nostalgic glint in my eye. But then I had to come into uni to meet someone, and then I thought I could have lunch with my dad or Greta, but I didn't, I came here to this building. I watch the traffic moving slowly over the tangle of bypasses between me and the Domain. It doesn't seem there are so many trees when you're over there, under them, trying to find a car park.

I get my phone out. I don't look directly at the names as I scroll through my contacts. It's dialling, it's ringing. I put the phone up to my ear and lean against the wall.

What's he doing? It's night there. Maybe he's at a dark wine bar with some woman. Maybe they're laughing, maybe she's very funny. Maybe she's tired and he has money and he's not mean. Maybe they're eating empanadas. Maybe they're at a bar that has free corn chips. Oh, no more for me, thanks; I don't like chips very much. Go on, eat some more. Let's have another drink; I'll have crème de menthe. Great, I'll have a gin fizz.

The phone stops ringing.

'¿Dígame?'

'Hi. It's, um, it's me.'

'Val?'

He doesn't sound like he's at a wine bar with free corn chips. He doesn't sound like he's anywhere.

'Yeah.'

'Are you okay? Has something happened?'

'Yeah, yeah, no, everything's fine. It's just, um, I felt like I should let you know that I'm coming to Buenos Aires in two weeks.'

'What for?'

'For work. I'm filming a show, that's what I do now. We're going all over the place, but we'll be in BA for a few days when we arrive.'

'Oh yes, yes, I know that's what you do now.'

I pause. 'How do you know that?'

'I, ah, I saw. People were posting about it. Where will you stay?' He sounds strange, he sounds flustered. Maybe there is a woman there with him and she's just being really quiet, and he's embarrassed that his ex has called him announcing that he's coming into town, just when he was about to, I don't know, probably have the best sex of his life or something. Probably propose to this woman and have two kids and, I don't know, probably buy a horse trailer and ride horses around together in the countryside and it's always great weather.

'I don't know where we're staying yet, there's a person who organises that type of thing.'

'Oh yes, of course. Um, so do you want me to come into the city and see you?'

'Um, yeah, yeah, I don't know. Um, I could come out and see you.'

Very smooth, Valdin. Yeah, I can come and visit you on your horse ranch with your beautiful Latina wife who doesn't like chips and probably has a long Spanish name that I can't say properly. Let me just throw up on myself in this corridor first.

'I'll drive in and meet you; just let me know where you're staying. Do you have any free days, do you know?'

'Yeah, the first day after I arrive, the eleventh.'

'Okay, great, I'll come and pick you up.'

I can't do this. I can't have sangria on the porch with him and Esmerelda and spend the whole time trying not to notice them playfully touching hands and averting my eyes from her enormous natural breasts.

'Xabi?'

'Yeah?'

'Where are you?'

'I'm just in the house.'

'Who are you with?'

'No one, it's late.'

'Oh.'

'Where are you, Val?'

'In the engineering building at the university.'

'What are you doing there?'

'I'm not sure, I thought it might be quiet. I was going to see if my dad or Gre were around.'

'How is Greta?'

'She's good. We've been living in an apartment together. She's got a new girlfriend.'

'Oh yeah, what's her name?' He sounds genuinely interested, which makes me feel sick.

'Ell.'

'Like A-L?'

'No, E-L-L. I think. I don't think it's E-L-L-E, she doesn't look like one of those.'

'What is she like?'

'She's from Scotland; she's really smart and . . . practical. Funny. She survived a dinner with my parents when my dad was in one of his moods, so I think she'll probably be around for a while. I think Gre loves her; she always listens to what she's saying. She never listens to me.'

'Of course she listens to you.'

I feel a sharp feeling in my eyes and my throat feels dry. Fuck. I just want him to take me and hug me and tell me that everything's going to be fine and I don't need to take the bins out because he's already done it. We can watch *The Bachelor* because he wanted to find out what was going to happen anyway. And maybe we can go to Cuba like I've always wanted to since I was fifteen and I thought smoking was cool, even though I never did it, I would probably get lung cancer and die if I did, that's the kind of luck I have. But none of this is happening. I'm by myself in a white corridor. I think it's white; the lighting isn't very good. It might be yellow. Or grey. Or even a very pale blue. Xabi has green eyes.

'Val? Are you okay?'

'Yeah, yeah, I'm fine.'

'It's okay if you don't want to see me. I understand.'

'No, I do. I do. Do you want to see me?' I hear my voice cracking and I hope he can't hear it too.

'Yeah, I do. Um. It's really nice to hear your voice.'

'Yeah.'

What if a nineteen-year-old sees me crying in the corridor on their way to a compulsory tutorial that they're already five minutes late to? Why is this tutor crying? Did he get a horrible class review because he doesn't know shit about – I don't know what I look like I could be a tutor of – anthropology? People were always crying when I was a postgrad, but only in the special postgraduate areas designed for crying and printing out hundred-page documents. Not me though; I wasn't crying. I didn't start crying until after I graduated.

'Valdin, are you sure you're okay?'

He sounds like he cares, which makes me feel even more sick.

'Yes. Hey, Xab, I think I have to go now.'

'Okay. Let me know where I should meet you, when you know.'

'Yes, I will.'

'Thanks for calling me.'

'Yes. Okay, bye.'

'Bye, Val. I'll see you soon.'

'Yes, bye.'

Other Greta

G

It's around five o'clock when Ell and I get to Casper and the other Greta's house. It's been raining and the sky is a brilliant orange colour, reflected in puddles on the freshly resealed road. The house is in Epsom. It seems very unlike my brother to buy a house in an area best known as a hotspot for right-wing plotting, but it isn't far away from our parents' house. To get the money for the deposit he stopped doing his usual university art-teaching job, obviously, and for two years he worked for Thony's husband, Giuseppe, and walked around wearing suits. I'm not sure exactly what Giuseppe's job is because he doesn't like to talk about it, but I'm pretty sure he's a CEO or shipping magnate. V said Casper sold his soul to the capitalist overlords, and Casper hit him in the face with a spatula covered in pancake mix. My dad thinks he designed a workforce rostering app. My mum said, 'Why can't you three ever talk to each other? I'm not an information helpdesk.'

The house is really pretty, anyway. It's white and made of weatherboards with a triangular roof and a fenced front yard. There are hydrangeas growing next to the front steps, wet from the rain. I think about pulling off a bunch for Ell. I don't know what she'd think if I started tearing apart a plant in front of her. I don't know if she's nervous to meet my older brother. She never seems nervous about anything, but I did for whatever reason give her Casper's complete personal history on our first date, so she probably feels like she knows a bit much.

He opens the door in a hurry, standing as if his hands are wet.

'Oh, Gre, thank God you're here. Hello, you must be Ell. I'm Lavrenti Valdinovich Vladisavljevic. Casper. Sorry, my hands are wet.'

'Hello, it's nice to meet you,' Ell says, now unsure what to do with her hands either. Casper is wearing a good navy jumper with a Nordic print and I wonder where he got it. Something is happening, though. He's gone all frantic-looking.

'Is there something happening?' I ask.

'Ah, Greta's in Mission Bay and someone backed in so close to her that she can't get the car out, so she tried to wave down a cyclist to help, but they didn't see and rode into her. She wants me to come and back the car out for her.' He smiles at Ell. 'The other Greta. I know that it's weird that I married a woman with the same name as my sister; I'm sorry.'

'I believe in you to back a car out of a tight spot; you're the best person at driving manoeuvres I know,' I say.

'That's not the problem,' he says. 'Greta's hurt her hand, so someone needs to drive her car back and someone needs to stay here with Freya. I had to pick her up sick from school and I think if I take her in the car she's going to vomit everywhere.'

An indignant squawk comes from somewhere in the house. 'Dad!'

'Look, I know a thing or two about vomit, Freya,' he shouts. 'Sorry, she's in a bad mood because she had to miss Pippins. Do you know what Pippins is? It's like Brownies but for younger girls, singing songs and glitter pens and things.'

'Oh yes,' says Ell. 'We call it Rainbows. I was a Rainbow.'

I look at her. This is not something I can imagine at all. 'I can stay here with Freya,' she says.

I make a face at her. I'm not sure if she knows what she's getting herself into.

'Are you sure?' asks Casper. 'I don't want to assume you don't mind looking after a child just because you're a woman. Sorry, I shouldn't assume what people's genders are.'

'Oh, I'm . . . woman-adjacent. I hope that isn't a problem,' she says, gesturing towards me, perhaps to remind him that his sister is a queer person.

'No!' Casper says, too loudly. 'Um, the more the merrier. Ah, we all hated Greta's ex-boyfriend, so.'

'Cas.'

'What,' he says, walking ahead of us into the living room, wiping his hands on his jeans. 'If I wanted to know about the life and times of Kurt Vonnegut, I would enrol in a first-year English paper.'

Freya is lying flat on the couch in a hooded dressing gown. Casper sits on the arm of the couch.

'Freya, this is Ell. She's going to stay with you while I go and help Mum with her car, isn't that nice? She was a Pippin too, except in Scotland they're called Rainbows.'

Freya doesn't move. 'Is she a professional babysitter?'

'You know very well she isn't a professional babysitter. Sit up properly, please; say hello. Take your hood off.'

She sits up begrudgingly and pulls her hood back so that it's balanced on the back of her head. 'Hello.' She turns back to Casper. 'How long will it take you to come back?'

'It shouldn't be more than forty-five minutes.'

'When's Tang coming home?'

'I'm not sure. I asked him to be back by six.'

'Why does he get to do whatever he wants? Just because he's old. Not fair.'

Casper considers the question. 'He gets more leeway to do what he wants because we've built a trusting relationship. He's demonstrated that he's able to be responsible for himself, making appropriate and reasonable decisions about how he spends his time.'

'And I haven't?'

'Not yet. You don't have the motor skills. You can't look and walk at the same time.'

'Does motor skills mean driving a car?'

'No, it means the control you have over your body and – sorry, mate, we can talk about it later. Your mother is standing at the side of the road somewhere waiting. Are you going to be okay?'

'Yes.'

'Okay.' He turns to Ell. 'I think she'll be fine, but just call us if she's sick again. Um, if she asks you anything you don't want to answer, just say no. We're . . . working on it.'

She nods slowly and he stands up and takes his keys out of his pocket. 'Okay, see you soon. Remember what I said about being appropriate. Love you.'

I squeeze Ell's wrist, not sure if we'll still be together by the time I get back. She'll probably text me within the first ten minutes, saying, *Sorry Greta, this isn't working out. We did have a Spark but then your niece asked me a lot of invasive questions and I think I had better just leave the country forever.*

'How are you?' Casper asks, looking over his shoulder to back the car down the driveway. The car is full of stuff, like a not particularly aesthetic vanitas. I move an NCEA Level 3 history textbook and an ice-cream container with a tennis ball in it so I can put my feet down. 'Ell seems cool.'

'She is cool. I hope Freya doesn't say anything too weird to her.'

He shakes his head. 'I can't guarantee that. My friend Ben came over a few months ago and it really felt like she was implying that if he didn't want to be in a relationship with a horse then he didn't really respect all living beings. Now she's even worse because she's found out about sex. I've told her you can't ask people straight out about that kind of thing, and now she keeps asking people if they ever hold hands and sleep in the same bed.'

'Did you give her the talk?'

'You're not supposed to do that anymore. It's meant to be . . . an ongoing dialogue. Tang is really not into that though; I feel like he's trying to avoid me in case I spring another conversation about consent on him.' He groans as we drive around the mountain, where the houses are huge and historic and students from the boys' school are still sloping down the road with their backpacks on. 'I don't know.'

'What?'

'I'm having a hard time with Tang and I feel guilty about it.'

'Has he done something?'

'No.' He sighs. 'He's such a good kid all the time and I can't accept that he's seventeen and he doesn't want to tell me everything that's going on with him anymore. And I feel bad when I'm put out because he won't tell me who he's hanging out with or where he's going, because I know what I was like when I was that age.'

'You shouted at Dad a lot and then moved to Russia by yourself.'

'Yeah, exactly. I was a real piece of shit. He would have done anything for me, you know; he would have spent so much money on lawyers to get Tang back with us and take leave to look after him, and I was going around shouting that no one understood me and listening to alternative rock hits too loudly. You must have hated me.'

I shrug. 'I thought if you left I would get more turns on the computer. V probably had more feelings about it.'

'How is he?'

I sigh and lean my head against the car window. 'You don't want to know.'

'Of course I do.'

Casper is driving a back way so that we don't have to go

down Broadway, and I see streets I've never seen before, despite living here almost my whole life.

'Did he tell you he's going to Argentina?'

'. . . No. Did he tell Xabi?'

'Yeah, he's going to see him. He rang him, for some reason, and then came home and said he was fine, but then he went in the bathroom and didn't come out for a very long time. I had to go and use the toilet at the hotel round the corner.'

'Do you think he's okay?'

'Yeah, he's been good for ages. He's bad at admitting that he's having a hard time because he's afraid everyone will worry about him.'

'It's hard. It's hard not to be overbearing.'

It's starting to get dark now and the lights are coming on in the houses we drive past. It's familiar to be driving with Casper again. He was the one who taught me how to drive. He said that Dad had tried to teach him, but he went into the mechanics of movement and speed too much, as well as not knowing all the English words for car parts, and Mum didn't tell him when he was doing something wrong because she thought he would figure it out. He just booked the test and gave it a go, but he thought I deserved better instruction.

'Mum told me about her other man recently.'

'What?' He turns his head quickly to look at me.

'From before Dad. Or at the same time as him, the details weren't very clear.'

'Oh, right,' he says, his eyes back on the road, less interested than I expected him to be.

'Did you know about that? I didn't know some other guy was trying to outwit, outplay, outlast Dad. Or that her and Dad were going behind the other man's back.'

'I don't think it was really like that. I don't know, I think there are a lot of things that we don't know about her.'

'Do you think that's bad?'

'No, I think everyone should be allowed to have secrets.' He shakes his head. 'Mum's had a hard life, she should be afforded some concessions.'

'What do you mean?'

He shakes his head again and doesn't say anything, his face bathed in red from a traffic light. We come out at the water, which is dark now with the city lights reflected on it. As we drive around the bays, I look at my reflection in the wing mirror.

'Cas, who's Hiria Hine Te Huia?'

'Why?'

'Some women we ran into in Wellington who knew Mum said I looked like her.'

We see the other Greta up ahead, standing at the side of the road with her hand wrapped in something, waving to us. Casper parks the car under a tree.

'She was our great-grandmother,' he says.

The other Greta is in good spirits by the time we arrive back at the house, having performed an animated recreation for us of how the cyclist rode into her at the side of the road. But when we come back into the living room, Freya is all curled up like a miserable porcupine and Ell has disappeared.

'Oh no, Freya, was ist los mit dir?' the other Greta asks, bending down in front of her in her black work trousers and navy blouse with white dots. She has her hair curled and lipstick on, something I can never understand how people who work in offices get up early enough to do. When I worked in an office, I never looked like I was supposed to be there.

'Nothing,' Freya says in the smallest voice I've ever heard her use. The other Greta makes a noise that doesn't exist in English and goes around opening all the windows.

'What did you do with Ell?' Casper asks, looking around. 'Oh fuck, the dinner.'

'The dinner's fine,' Ell says, coming out of the kitchen holding a tea towel. Tang is behind her, wearing his school uniform which he's much too tall for and rubbing his eye.

'Fuck, I'm so sorry, I forgot all about the food in the oven,' Casper says.

'Dad,' says Freya, looking up at him mournfully.

Casper groans. 'It's okay to swear if you've made someone you've only just met cook your dinner – I don't care what your teacher says.'

I look at Ell and Tang. They look entirely suspicious and perhaps trauma-bonded.

'Kei te pai, mate?' Casper asks Tang.

'I'm fine,' he says, sounding a lot like V – a big liar.

'That's good,' Casper says, and goes to set the table.

I look at Ell with my best questioning expression and she turns away. 'You must be Greta.'

'Ah!' the other Greta says, standing on the window seat to reach a particularly high window with a hook on a stick. She comes down and shakes Ell's hand. 'I'm Greta Gregers, but everyone in my husband's family calls me the other Greta.'

'Well, we should just give my Greta a new name,' Ell says. 'How do you feel about Ermyntrude?'

'I'm not sure about that.' I told Ell, very late one night, that as a child I wished that my name was Ermyntrude and that I lived on a houseboat in Volgograd, a place I had never been and knew nothing about.

Casper sets all the food on the table – a green salad with feta, a big tray of roast kūmara, yams and pumpkin, and a whole roast chicken with lemon and cayenne pepper. Tang slices up a loaf of dark rye bread and puts it in front of us with the enthusiasm of someone serving sausage rolls at a funeral.

'You aren't vegetarian, are you?' Casper asks Ell.

'No, no, I'm not.'

'You don't want to say a prayer, do you?' the other Greta asks her, sitting across from us.

She smiles. 'Erm, no thank you.'

'What was it like meeting my parents?' Casper asks, putting some food on a plate for Freya. 'Did they ask you too many questions like us?'

'Ah, it was nice. I like your parents.'

'Cas, Dad got in a fight with V about Rumbo and then, like, Facebook-called him at the table to prove he was real.'

Casper puts down the plate. 'No.'

'Yes, that's what happened.'

'Rumbo's not real.' He looks very serious, like when he's being interviewed on Māori TV about how the government isn't doing enough.

'He seemed quite real,' Ell says, taking a piece of bread.

'I just cannot believe that. What about all the shit with the wrestling of the pig?'

'It was true,' I inform him. 'Rumbo told us all.'

'I need to call Dad,' he says, standing up.

'Don't call him now!'

'I'm just getting a drink, Ermyntrude.' He goes over to the fridge. 'Does anyone want a beer?' Ell takes a beer and Tang shakes his head and doesn't say anything, pushing some spinach leaves around on his plate.

'I thought Dad was making up the stuff about Rumbo to prove a point about how we're so removed from the way he grew up that we would believe anything he said.'

'No, Rumbo was just a genuinely very out-there child. And now he's a truck driver.'

'I wish I was a truck driver. We had to have a meeting with a student today because he keeps submitting videos of himself wanking in the university toilets for all his project work.' He sighs. 'I think we all got our points across, but it would have been nicer to be out on the open road.'

'Yes, in my office we're having an ongoing argument about whether we should promote a book about how terrible young people are, just because it's Father's Day coming up.' Freya is slumped in her seat and the other Greta pokes her in the arm.

'Hast du noch kein Hunger? You're the quietest I've seen you since you arrived screaming into the world.'

'I thought you were feeling better,' Casper says. 'Tell Mum what happened at school.'

Freya looks sadly at her plate. 'I did a huge vom. I stopped playing Octopus and then I lay down on the ground and did a huge vom in the drain. Then Ms Patel took me to the office and asked me if she should call Mum or Dad, and I cried and said that my mum is a very busy business lady and my dad just hangs out with teens and tells them their paintings are good even when they aren't. Ms Patel thought that was really funny. Then Dad came and we went to Countdown and he made me sit in the car with an ice-cream container like I was a little dog.'

'You shouldn't leave dogs in the car,' says Tang, looking equally as sadly at his plate with a tear running down his cheek.

Freya bursts into tears.

'Tang, what's happened?' Casper asks quietly, but he doesn't reply; he just cries.

'I'm sorry,' he says, and Casper moves his chair to put his arm around him. 'I just had a bad day and I took it out on Freya.'

'Worse than your dad having to confront someone about their masturbation videos?' the other Greta asks, reaching for some paper towels.

He smiles weakly. 'Maybe not that bad.'

'You don't have to say if you don't want to,' Casper says.

I look at Ell, who obviously knows what happened, and she carefully looks away from me and takes some more kūmara.

'I'm sorry about all this, Ell,' the other Greta says, hugging Freya on her lap. 'You must think that every day with Greta's family is some kind of dinner theatre performance. Really, we are quite normal, and our children aren't usually so miserable.'

Casper frowns. 'The first time I brought you round to my parents' house I told everyone to act like regular people and V threw the remote out the window so no one could change the channel from Eurovision, and a squid had exploded on my dad at work.'

She sighs and smiles at him. 'Well, you just have to get used to it.'

Ell shrugs. 'It could happen.'

Analysis

V

There's some kind of commotion outside the apartment and I pretend it's the reason I can't sleep. Greta's awake and has music on. She's started listening to nineties pop playlists all the time. Edie Brickell, Suzanne Vega, the song 'Two Princes', which I thought was gay but turns out to be very hetero. Greta is always up very late. She read an article stating that many people in their early twenties experience a time shift which means they have trouble sleeping before 2am, which she brings up every time I point out that disordered sleep is associated with OCD.

'Greta?' I call out in the dark, lying still in my bed.

'What?' she shouts back from her room.

'What are you doing?'

'I was going to do some readings for class.'

'You won't be able to concentrate, there's a commotion outside.'

'Thanks for letting me know.'

'Will you come here?'

'Why?'

'I can't sleep.'

'Because you're worried about your trip tomorrow?'

'No. Because of the commotion.'

I hear her groan but several minutes later she appears in her mint-green dressing gown, smelling like the face cream I use when she's out.

'Can I turn the light on?'

'No.'

She sighs and sits on the bed next to me in the dark. I stay lying down and offer no hospitality.

'Do you want to talk about it?' she asks.

'No.'

She seems frustrated with me and leans against the headboard with her arms folded.

'What are you going to do while I'm away?'

'My life will carry on without you.'

'I know.'

'I'm going to an Iranian film night with Fereshteh. Her family friends approve of her having an Iranian friend.'

'You're Māori.'

'Yeah, I know, but they accept me. Fereshteh taught me some phrases and says I'm from Shiraz, which makes them all nod and say that explains it.'

'Is that unethical?'

'I don't think so. When I lived in Germany people were always disappointed in me for not being able to speak Turkish. They thought I had forgotten my roots.'

'You never forget your roots. How was Cas the other day?'

'He was good. He was a bit sad because Tang doesn't really need him anymore. Something's happening with him; Ell knows but she wouldn't tell me.'

'Shit, I wanted to see him before I went away but we couldn't figure out a time. What's going on with Ell?'

'With me and her? I think things are going pretty well.'

'No, with her and herself. Gre, I know a gay crisis when I see one. Her hair gets shorter every time I see her.'

She sighs. 'She's been experiencing a personal renaissance ever since she moved here. She has conservative parents who live on a farm in the Highlands so she moved to the city when she left school expecting that everything would come together, you know, in a gay way, and then it just didn't. She said there were a few people here and there but nothing really significant. Then her supervisor quit right before she was supposed to start her PhD, and no one else at her uni was specialising in her topic, so she ended up coming here, where her supervisor's trans and I'm walking around asking people of all genders to give me their phone numbers. Now she's loving life and she's cut her hair off and bought all these chinos and her parents won't talk to her.'

'Her parents won't talk to her?'

'No. She hasn't even told them about me. They already didn't want to talk to her just over what she looks like and her political opinions.'

'Does that put a strain on your relationship?'

'Um, not so far. She feels a bit guilty that my family is so nice to her and hers doesn't even want to know about me. It makes me feel guilty too. I feel like I'm showing off my almost too open, liberal family.'

'We have many personal faults as well.' I close my eyes for a second, but I still don't feel tired at all. 'When I first met Xabi, I assumed he was gay.'

'Isn't he?'

'He had never been with a guy before.'

'What did he identify as?'

'Nothing, he just avoided thinking about it. I think that's an issue with queer society. People still have trouble accepting anyone who isn't already in or aspiring to be in a same-sex relationship as a part of the community. Being queer is . . . it's in yourself, it doesn't always have to do with other people.'

'People always assume I'm bi.'

'Why? No one ever assumes I'm bi. Oh no, Greta.'

'What?' She turns to look at me. We haven't been looking at each other at all during this exchange, just up at the ceiling, like a therapy session. I'm the worst, dodgiest therapist, lying in my bed and not letting my clients turn the lights on.

'It's because of sexism, isn't it.'

'Yeah, it's just very hard to convince anyone that wanting to look pretty doesn't mean you want attention from men. And then people say it to me so much I think I am bi, and I go out with straight guys and feel like I'm suffocating.'

I exhale. 'I'm sorry.'

'I don't really feel like anything these days, just a beautiful husk filled with opinions about globalism and a strong desire to go out for dinner.'

'I'm exhausted just by being myself.'

'Did you ever come out to Mum and Dad?'

'I tried to. I told Mum in the car when she picked me up from school, and I cried and she said she frankly was not at all surprised, and I was disappointed because I wanted her to be really shocked so that I would have to convince her to accept me. She said she could make a special dinner instead, but when we got home Casper and Dad were shouting at each other and then there was the revelation about the baby. Mum and I ended up eating kebabs by ourselves in the kitchen. But she cracked open some champagne from somewhere and gave me the speech I wanted, about how it had taken her years to come around but she couldn't lose the love of her son just because of his passion for Adrien Brody's performance in *The Pianist*.'

'V, that's a wildly problematic crush. You shouldn't be objectifying victims of war.'

'I was thirteen. I didn't know what was going on.'

'He has a Dad vibe.'

'I like older men.'

'No, I mean specifically our dad.'

'Gross, why would you say that? Let me have my memories.' I side-eye her, suspicious that she's trying to put me off my favourite celeb crush so she can have it for herself. This is something she would do.

'I can't believe Mum gave you a coming-out speech. When she caught me with that private-school punk girl, she only told me not to let her pressure me into smoking.'

'You have to ask, if you want the speech.'

'V.'

'Yeah?'

'I won't judge you if you fuck Xabi as soon as you get to Argentina.'

'That's ridiculous. That's not why I'm going there.'

'Fine.'

We stay silent for a minute and I notice that the commotion has stopped. I don't want Greta to go away though, so I ask her to explain her thesis topic to me and then everyone else in her course's thesis topic and then I get her to rank them. I think this will bore me to sleep, but it doesn't; it's surprisingly interesting. I ask her to describe the narratives of different songs so I can guess the titles.

'A man who is very emotional about a photo album.'

'Nickelback, "Photograph".'

'No.'

'The Cure, "Pictures of You".'

'Yes. Someone's looking out the window of a plane and they're disgusted by the trivial lives of people in rural areas.'

' "The Big Country", Talking Heads.'

'Yes. Someone who goes through a break-up and they pray to swap bodies with their ex so they can take up their hobby of parkour.'

'What?'

'Vertical running.'

I look at her and she has her eyes closed. She's asleep. I lie quietly by myself. I used to watch Greta sleeping all the time, when she was born. I was good at it because I was so quiet. Dad told us in the car after school that we were going to have a sister.

Casper wouldn't stop crying. He said that Dad had lied and deceived him. He was going to move to South Korea and play Gameboy and never talk to us again. Dad said it didn't happen on purpose. At that time I had been at school for a month and I hadn't said a word to anyone. There were a lot of meetings about it. 'He doesn't seem unhappy,' they said. I would swing my legs off the brown plastic chair and look at the tiled floor. I wanted the baby the most. Everyone else was afraid because of what happened when I was born. I didn't remember that, though. I just wanted to name the baby Eevee, after my favourite Pokémon. We named the baby G.V. I would still say, 'Hello, Eevee,' when I stood very quietly in the doorway of her room, just watching her. I hope that you like me. I hope you want to be my friend.

I pull the blanket over Greta.

Prospects

G

I'm supposed to meet Ell and her science comrades for their Friday drinks, but I can't find the door to Old Government House, which is a university establishment that you can become a member of but only people from the science faculty ever do. Every interaction I've had so far today has made me feel as if I've come at it at the wrong angle, which I think is because I woke up facing the wrong way around and in V's bed instead of my own. I had a whole pep talk prepared for him before he went on his trip, but he was already gone when I woke up. I was going to tell him that he could get through anything and I'd be waiting for him as soon as he got back. It would have been very inspirational.

Two people come walking out of a door, talking about soil samples and not noticing me, so I duck through it before anyone asks to check my membership card. There are two big rooms filled with people talking around long wooden tables, and many of the people look the same so it's hard to tell which is the table I'm supposed to be joining. A lot of people are wearing a zip-up hoodie with a T-shirt and jeans and a lanyard and a lot of them are men. Then I see Ell. She's easily identifiable because she's in a teal satin shirt and rust-coloured cords and is waving at me to come over.

'This is my girlfriend, Greta,' she says, when I reach the table and while someone scrambles to get me a chair from somewhere. 'Nobody say anything rude to her about how she's an arts student or try and grease her up to get into her dad's good books.'

'Okay, we'll all act as neutrally as possible,' a man in a navy zip-up hoodie and a white T-shirt says. 'Hi, Greta, I'm Fahim and it's okay to meet you.'

'You seem fine,' I say, shaking his hand. Everyone else goes round and says their name and I know I can remember Sina, Min, Ashford and Ji-soek, but there's no way I'm going to remember Kieran.

'I hope Ell's nicer to you than she is to the people in the lab she supervised today,' Fahim says, and everyone laughs.

'Oh, I'm sorry I don't want to be responsible for the deaths of a whole lot of eighteen-year-olds because I want them to think I'm cool and not make them wear gloves.'

'I think we should print out the gloves reminder email and put it up next to the famous "The Leak" series,' Ji-soek says. He has a black hoodie but he isn't wearing it, it's over the back of his chair.

'Greta, what is it like to have Dr Linsh Vladisavljevic as your dad?' Fahim asks. 'If I'm allowed to ask that, Ell.'

'I'll allow it,' she says.

'I don't know,' I say. 'One day I was born, and there he was. He never emails me, so maybe I can't relate to your experience of him, though.'

Ashford groans. 'I wish he wouldn't email me.'

'What did you do now?' Min asks. 'Did you leave the fridge open again?'

'No, I accidentally switched it off at the wall.'

'Ooh, he's going to do more than email you. He'll put up a sign.'

Ashford groans again and pulls his maroon hoodie over his face. 'A sign is pretty much the worst thing that can happen to you in our lab.'

'The worst thing that happens in ours is you get scheduled to present after Ell,' Min says. Everyone laughs again.

She rolls her eyes. 'I couldn't believe it, Fahim, when Erik told you that you could probably solve your issue of mixing up your samples by putting the labels *on them* instead of *next to* them, and you said that's a *cool tip* and you'd think about *giving it a go* next time.'

'And look, I will think about giving it a go next time, or at some point in the future.'

I smile to myself. I didn't know that Ell was the boss bitch of science and got ragged on for being try-hard by everyone.

'What is it that you study?' Ji-soek asks me.

'Oh, comparative literature. My thesis is about the difference in perceptions of Soviet-era communism between texts set in the USSR by Eastern bloc authors versus Western ones.'

'What's the answer?'

I smile. 'It's the same answer as every arts thesis. Poverty is bad, racism is bad, capitalism is not that great.'

He laughs. 'If every arts thesis is the same, why don't you come and be a scientist with us?'

I shrug. 'It seems boring.' This makes the whole table laugh and I squeeze Ell's knee under the table, so she thinks that I'm just doing a joke and that her nitrogen signalling is interesting to me. 'No, but I'm not very good at thinking in a scientific way. I like things that can't really be either right or wrong.'

'That's cool, I can respect that,' Fahim says and Ell rolls her eyes. 'When do you finish your master's? What do you want to do after that?'

'Next July,' I say. I don't have an answer to the second part of the question. My ears feel a bit hot. The Russian department at our university gets smaller every year and now it's just one guy teaching the stage 1 paper 'Introduction to Russian'. I think of a conversation he had with me about how he thought I had a strong future with my research and should do a PhD, but that I couldn't do it here because they don't have the resources. Where would I go? Could I live in Russia, as a queer person? An American university would be a good choice, he said. I didn't like that idea, and still don't. I think of everything I've read about America. I think of everything I've read about working in academia. I think of my only other work experience, at the call centre. 'I'm not sure what I want to do yet, maybe take a break.'

'Cool, cool,' he says. 'Ell, you're not going to boss us around like those first years when we go to the conference right? I want to go on the luge, and I will not be taking safety into consideration.'

'What's a luge?' she asks.

'It's like a go-kart you ride really fast down a hill – you'll love it,' Sina says and moves her eyebrows up and down.

'I don't want to be coerced into any outdoor pursuits.'

'When's the conference again?' I ask.

'In two weeks,' Ell says. 'You didn't have anything planned for us that weekend, did you?'

I shake my head. 'That's when V's coming back. I will need to be on hand to counsel him and probably bring drinks to his bedside while he recounts every bad thing that happened on his trip.'

She smiles. 'You don't know that. He might have a good time.'

'He always manages to get himself into some situation.'

Fahim stands up and says he'll get another two jugs, which everyone applauds, and Min goes to help him carry them. I don't think anyone in my department has ever offered to buy the whole table a round. Someone bought a French press for the common room but now you can only go in there if you're a full-time staff member.

'Did anyone ask Erik and Linsh if they wanted to come for a drink?' Sina asks.

'Yeah, I did, to try and make up for what happened with the

fridge,' Ashford says. 'But they were both going on a date.' He turns to me. 'Oh, like, not with each other; with their respective partners.'

I smile. 'It's okay, I'm not going to get confused into thinking that my parents are getting divorced because of one poorly constructed sentence.'

'Ooh, got burned by the arts student,' Sina says and flicks some water from the table at him. 'We always roast Linsh for being a wife guy, because one time he took a call from her in the middle of telling us off and said he loved her at the end.'

'What had we done that time?' Ashford asks.

'Bag of unlabelled fish heads in the freezer,' she says, swigging the last of her beer before Fahim and Min put the new jugs down on the table.

'Once he put a whole squid he found at the beach in our freezer,' I say. 'It fell out onto the floor when my brother was offering his school friends some ice cream.'

Everyone laughs at that. 'If that squid was unlabelled, he's going to have me to answer to,' says Fahim.

I look around and smile at all the scientists, and I only feel a little bit jealous of their prospects.

Returno

V

I have been awake for a very long time by the time I'm standing on the side of the road called Pellegrini, waiting. I stayed awake until it was time to walk to the stop for the SkyBus. I stayed awake on the plane watching the third or fourth seasons of sitcoms I hadn't seen before in the calming purple light that planes have these days. I stayed awake all night in the hotel watching YouTube videos of people reacting to things. I drank two bottles of water from the mini fridge because I was concerned that I might die. I ate an alfajor. I close my eyes standing on the street, while all the cars speed past on the wrong side of the road. I think about a meditation podcast I once listened to the first thirty seconds of before I felt embarrassed and turned it off.

When Xabi studied painting at university, about one thousand years ago, he used to drive around Auckland in a ute, which is what he drives again now when he pulls up to me on the side of the road. I open the door before the vehicle comes to a complete stop and sort of throw myself in. I do this because I didn't know if we should shake hands or hug or hongi or what when we see each other, and none of these things are possible in a moving car.

'Hi,' he says, very startled.

'Don't stop, there are a lot of traffic cops around,' I say.

He looks at me for a second. I don't look back at him until he turns away. He looks unnecessarily good. He has a nice haircut and he smells nice and I have a horrible suspicion that he has got into fitness. Maybe he has a new love who's a CrossFit trainer, like my relative Angel B's boyfriend. Or maybe he's trying to get revenge on me by showing up looking so good. I learned a lot about revenge dresses and revenge bodies when I was addicted to *Real Housewives*, but I didn't think that I would ever be on the receiving end of one.

'Where am I taking you? Do you just want to get coffee somewhere?' he asks.

I imagine myself crying in public in a busy café and a whole scenario where I try to run off to the bathroom to throw up but there's a passcode to get in.

'We can go and see your house; I'd still like to see it.'

'It's quite far out, is that okay?'

'Yeah, yeah, that's great.'

I lean my head against the cool glass of the window. It's about 12 degrees here, the same as it was at home, but I feel very hot.

'Are you okay, Val?'

'Yeah, I just didn't sleep on the plane.'

'Oh, okay. I'm sorry, I'll be quiet. It's really nice to see you, though.'

I keep leaning against the window and closing my eyes for a bit, trying not to think about anything.

Xabi has an interesting accent. He was born in a small town in Catalonia, where his father was from. His mother always wanted to move back to England, to be with her English father and Italian mother, which they eventually did. When he was eighteen, he moved to New Zealand by himself. Then seven years later, he didn't want to be there anymore and moved back to Spain. A lot of this has to do with his brother. They aren't very good at being in the same place.

The people here in Argentina speak a different version of Spanish from the one I've heard him speak before. Less *th*, more *sh*. I thought the man at the hotel check-in desk was speaking Italian. I wonder if Xabi puts on a different accent to fit in here, or if he just ploughs through, like when I went to California for a physics conference and no one had any idea what I was saying. When we get out of the city, there are cows standing around in fields. Cows have accents, I read that somewhere. I try not to think about asado.

In Barcelona, there's a small gallery especially for Xabi's work. He did not think he needed to have his own gallery, but the city council of Barcelona disagreed. I've never been to the gallery, but I wonder if there's a small photo of me there, maybe in the back of a book no one reads, with a caption saying *Portrait of the artist and an unknown friend*. Once, before we were together, we both went to a dinner where I couldn't say anything. I wanted to, so badly. It hurts, not being able to make your body do what you want it to. He drove me home afterwards. I feel like that again now.

'Like a Stone' is playing. Is this the kind of music he listens to now? I look at him out of the corner of my eye. He doesn't appear to be particularly getting into it. He looks like an olive farmer. Not a really old Cypriot man, but like an olive farmer in a movie. Stupid broad shoulders, stupid big tanned hands. I can't even fault his driving; he doesn't even get in the fast lane and then drive the speed limit and complain about everyone else trying to overtake. People are always surprised that I know how to drive. Not many city gays can.

I imagine that I have a device in my ear so I can understand what the cows are saying. They're telling me that I'm good at Spanish, even though I'm not really. I'm okay. Casper was annoyed with me when I was learning Spanish because he thought that I should go to night school and learn te reo. I don't think he understood that wanting to know what my boyfriend was saying on the phone was much more of a motivator for me than feeling disconnected from my own culture. Or at least an easier issue to confront. The cows would understand, if I told them. They'd nod their heads and say, 'We get it, V; it's not even on Duolingo. You take your time with your colonial trauma. It's fine. It's all fine.'

'Val?'

I wake up confused. No one ever calls me Val except Xabi. Then I open my eyes and Xabi is standing on a gravel driveway with the ute door open, looking at me. He reaches across to take my bag and goes up to the house. It's different from how I imagined; it's a box made of glass and wood. There are no other buildings around. There are trees though, lots of small trees and vines and bushes. What is this house doing here in the middle of nothing?

'Xabi?' I say as I follow him up the driveway.

'Yeah?'

'What is this house doing here?'

'I built it here.'

'Why?'

'Oh, I don't know. I didn't have much else on.'

In the house he puts his keys in a wooden fruit bowl on the kitchen counter and leaves my bag by the couch. There are pears in the bowl, a winter fruit. Everything in the house is nice, but it looks wrong somehow. The carpet is grey, the couch is grey, the walls are a light shade of grey. There's a large painting above the counter in abstract primary colours. We saw a similar painting once at the NGV and he said he didn't like it. What is he up to?

I take myself on a little tour of the house without asking. It's all the same – all grey and some white, some wood, but mainly grey. There's a small room with a single bed made up with a grey duvet and a matching wool blanket, with a vase of fresh flowers on the bedside table. It looks like a place people go to die. A hospice. A very nice hospice, but a hospice nonetheless.

'Do you sleep in this single bed?'

'No, I have a full-sized bed.'

I can see him down the hallway, leaning on the counter. I don't know why he let me go on this tour by myself.

'What are the flowers for?'

'I like flowers. You know I like flowers.'

I have no idea what he likes anymore, other than listening to the American rock supergroup Audioslave and going onto whatever the Argentinian equivalent of the Freedom furniture website is and filtering out everything that isn't grey. I don't feel like I want to see his bedroom, so I go into the bathroom and test the taps and look in all the drawers before going back to the kitchen. Xabi is slicing bread and has arranged some pastries filled with dulce de leche on a plate.

'Where did you get these from?'

'I bought them when we stopped at the bakery.'

'What?'

'I tried to wake you up. How much bread do you want?'

'Two pieces. This is a lot of food – what if I wasn't hungry?'

'You don't eat the food on planes, and I doubt you got up early and went out this morning. Ai,' he says and pushes the plate towards me.

Ai is Samoan. I got really into Samoan Language Week a couple of years ago and kept announcing things to him from a phrasebook for a long time after the week ended. I forgot about that. I guess he didn't. I dip my bread in oil.

'Did you plant all those trees outside?'

'Yeah, I wanted to plant an orchard and I was just doing it by myself but Thony said that, um, I had become a sad portrait of masculinity and I hired some gardeners. They know what they're doing more than I do.'

'Do they think you need a woman looking after you?'

He stops eating the pastry. 'Ah, yes.'

'What do you tell them?'

He shrugs. 'No quiero.'

'Can people understand your accent here?'

He swallows. 'Usually. I try and tone it down.'

'You don't think that Iberian Spanish is technically a purer form of Spanish and everyone else should bend to your ways?'

'God, no, Val. Of course not. I feel bad enough owning this land, I feel like I've colonised it. Even though apparently it had been on the market for nearly a decade.'

'Did you pay for it, or did you just pillage it?'

'What if I told you I had, that I turned up with some caballeros and a sword and conquered this land?'

I shrug. 'That might be a story I was interested in hearing.' The pastries are so good, almost annoyingly good. I eat a second one. 'Did you make that fruit bowl?'

'Why, is it crooked?'

'No. You did, didn't you?'

'Yeah, I did.'

'Who cut your hair?'

He touches it and looks at me like I think it's ugly. 'A Korean man. I didn't get his name, sorry. Do you not like it?'

'No, it's good.'

'That was one of your values, to only have Korean people cut your hair.'

'I've changed that now.'

'Have you? I did think that it seemed a bit racist.'

'I found out my favourite hairdresser is actually from Hong Kong.'

I can't tell if he's laughing at me as he takes my plate away and rinses it in the sink.

'Xabi, do you hate that painting on your wall?'

He turns to look at it and sighs. 'Yeah, I do hate that painting. Someone gave it to me, and I didn't know what else to do with it.'

'Who, a woman?'

'What woman? Why do you think my life is full of women all of a sudden?'

'I don't know.' I pick up a pear from the fruit bowl, which has been crafted flawlessly. 'How's Rosa?'

'Oh, I am a great cause of stress to her. She said that she would have quit being my agent a long time ago if it weren't for the money and the fact that she doesn't want to make anyone else endure what she has to.' He concentrates on putting things back in the fridge and pours me a glass of a fizzing lemon drink from a plain glass bottle. 'She was going to come over here and talk to me about my plan, but I said November would work better.'

'What's happening in November?'

'I thought maybe I could have thought of something to appease her by then.'

I drink the drink and it isn't mostly straight liquor like any drink ever poured for me by a member of my family. It tastes like a fancy Lift.

'Why haven't you been painting?'

'I don't know, I haven't really felt like it. What do you want to do this afternoon? Should I show you around outside? I think it might rain.' He stands in front of the window in his turtleneck and black jeans and Blundstone boots, and I look him up and down then quickly look down at my drink again.

'Xabi, your neck is bleeding.'

'Oh, shit.' He puts his hand to it and walks down the hallway to the bathroom.

I turn towards the doorway on my bar stool. 'Do you have any DVDs?'

'DVDs?' he calls over the sound of running water. 'Do people still watch those?'

'I don't know. I wanted to watch *Cocktail*.'

V

'You thought I might have a DVD of the movie *Cocktail*, the film about Tom Cruise working as a bartender to pay his way through business school?'

'Oh. No, that's not right. Maybe it's called *Cocktail Bar*.'

'What happens in it?'

'Robin Williams owns a drag bar in Miami.'

'That's *The Birdcage*.' He turns the tap off and comes back to the kitchen, no longer bleeding. 'I don't know why you want to watch that; it's about a man who has to hide that he's gay and Jewish to appease the conservative parents of his son's girlfriend.'

'Is it? I think I was eight when I saw it.'

'I'm sure we can find something to watch, if that's what you want to do.'

I nod and follow him into the living room, where I sit as far to one side of the couch as possible. I think that watching a movie is logically the best idea because I won't have to talk anymore, and the more tired I feel, the closer I feel to saying something weird. I think everything I've said up to this point has been pretty weird, but Xabi doesn't seem affected by any of the things I've said. I wonder how he feels about me being here. Other people's perceptions of me are very difficult for me to think about. Sometimes I forget I exist and that other people can see me, until someone asks me to move so they can get off the bus or I get recognised from my show.

Xabi must know I exist because we once got stuck in an elevator together. Being stuck in an elevator is the kind of thing people remember. It was raining that day too. We had run back into my old apartment building from the street, car tyres speeding through puddles. The man on the intercom had seemed mad at us when he said it would be an hour until we were rescued, as if we had really inconvenienced him by being stuck in an elevator. I wondered how often he was having to come and rescue people, and wouldn't the job be more suited to someone with a hero complex, someone who took on the rescuing with a solemn sense of responsibility and pride? Being told off by the elevator man made me feel a certain way. Xabi thought there might be a camera in the elevator. I said there definitely wasn't, but I didn't really know. I didn't think any-one would be reviewing the tapes unless there was a crime committed in the building, and anyway I didn't mind adding some interest to the investigation.

I wonder if Xabi remembers that, or just that we were stuck in the elevator in general. He probably knows I exist now because he's looking at me, asking me what I want to watch, and I'm pointing at something, yeah, that looks good, and my head feels very heavy and I want to ask him how much he remembers about the elevator but it's enough effort just to keep my eyes open and look at Eddie Murphy in *Coming to America*.

I wake up in the hospice room in the single bed, but I don't feel like I'm dying. I try to remember how I got here. I remember seeing the first ten minutes of the movie. Then Xabi had his hand on my arm and was asking if I wanted him to take me back to the city. No, I hadn't had enough time. I needed more time to figure things out, I couldn't just say goodbye and go to work and never see him again. 'Take me back in the morning, that will be easier,' I said, watching the credits roll, an image of James Earl Jones wearing a crown adorned with things that looked as if they'd been found in the sea. Detritus. That's a word that I'm never sure if I'm saying right. I think of Xabi standing in front of the window, his neck bleeding. I look at the lilacs on the bedside table. I love lilacs, but they don't grow where I live because it's too humid. I said that, I said that to Xabi when we were in Albania and we saw them everywhere. That was my favourite trip I've ever been on, the bunker museum with Albania's campaign against hippy tourists, Hox-ha's former residence opposite the only KFC in Tirana, watching kids trying to walk up the pyramid in the square. It was there, in the sun, that I squinted at Xabi because I'd forgot-ten my sunglasses and said, 'This is my favourite trip I've ever been on.'

I get up out of bed and walk down the hallway; I knock on his door. He's sitting on the bed with just the lamp on. He takes his glasses off and puts his book face-down open on the bedside table. The book is my book, *Summerhouse, Later*. He didn't for-get about it, he didn't forget about anything. He didn't forget my aversion to beards.

I sit on the bed in front of him. I'm only wearing my under-wear and a T-shirt, but I don't think that matters anymore. I don't think thinking matters anymore.

'Xabi, are you in love with me?'

He scans my face for a second. 'Yes.'

I lean forward and kiss him. For one moment everything feels right, like a gif that demonstrates how a key opens a lock, or how a boat travels through a system of locks to continue its journey up the Yangtze River.

Then he pulls away from me, 'Val, I have to tell you—'

'Don't.' I rest two fingers on his bottom lip. 'Don't tell me anything.'

He looks in my eyes and I don't want to look away for once. Who has green eyes? He pulls me close on top of him and I feel like I can't breathe but it doesn't matter.

'You can tell me no, of course.'

'No,' he says, taking my shirt off.

Tang

G

I love peach soju so much. It's Fereshteh's birthday and I've loved peach soju so much that I've forgotten how to speak English. Poor sad Ell is bizarrely monolingual and can't understand anything I'm saying on the walk home from the Korean BBQ and karaoke. I feel sympathetic as I turn around to complain about how slow she's walking. She can't help it that she can't keep up with my gallant stride and dextrous language abilities.

'Elspeth, beeil dich! Es tut mir leid, dass du keine langen Beine hast, aber wir haben noch viel zu tun. Die Saison hat erst begonnen. Zärtlich ist die Nacht.'

She doesn't walk any faster because she doesn't know what I'm saying, even though I speak very clearly. She looks tired. I've been doing a lot of antics. The karaoke bar is only 450 metres away from my house, but I dropped everyone off at their bus stops and made sure everyone got in their Zoomys okay. Then I just quickly had to run to Esquires to get a smoothie before they closed. There are a lot of people around on Victoria Street, waiting for the night bus, going to the casino. Some Brazilian ladies are looking at each other and laughing as some English lads try to convince them to go to another bar.

'Why are you in such a hurry? We aren't going anywhere else are we? It's going on two o'clock.' Elspeth looks at her analogue watch.

'Weil ich realisiert hab . . . um . . . In the karaoke I realised that you don't know anything. You hear a song about going on holiday to Hamilton and it means nothing to you. Today, tomorrow, you don't know, it could be anywhere. Which one's Bic, which one's Boh, Elspeth doesn't know.'

'You do know my name isn't Elspeth, right?'

'I'm just trying to help you.'

'Help me to what?'

I stop walking and turn around. 'I'm helping you be more Scottish.'

'Where have you got the idea that I'm not Scottish enough?'

I sigh. 'Everyone's saying it. It's the word on the street. They've all seen the memes; they've all seen "431 Scottish Tweets to Revive Your Cold Dead Soul". They just want you to be a bit less "Does anyone want that last naan?" and a bit more "The madness when yer with yer maw on the gear in Greggs and ye canny believe ye killed a wain fer takin' the last saussy roll."'

'Ah've no – Greta, if you'd met my mother you would know she's never come close to getting on the gear with anyone, in any bakery.'

I smile and cross the road. I hope she's looking at my exciting hip-to-waist ratio in my almost-spring look, featuring vinyl miniskirt and metallic top that I thought was too sexy when I first bought it at SaveMart five years ago. Now I'm into it. I can hear her hurrying after me. I should write a book about flirting. Outside the dairy, she puts her hands on my waist to stop me speeding off again. I look down at her. I'm wearing velvet platform shoes that are appropriate for very few occasions. I look at her and her square face and her middle parting and her stupid matching burgundy cord jacket and flares and I think it's all really good. I look up at the Sky Tower and I think it's winking at me.

'Elspeth, I think we should go home and kiss and maybe more.'

'I thought you might say that.'

'Why?'

'Something gave me that impression, between your duet of "Buttons" by the Pussycat Dolls when Rashmika was pretending to be Snoop Dogg and you were sitting on everyone's laps, and when you were lying on the table singing both the Kylie Minogue and Robbie Williams parts of "Kids" by yourself.'

'You didn't sing many songs.'

'I don't know your friends well enough to lie on a table. And besides, you weren't playing many of my favourite tunes.'

'What are those?'

'Oh, you know, my favourite Beach Boys song, "Kokomo", my favourite Beatles song, "Ob-La-Di, Ob-La-Da"—'

I smile with all my teeth and then I kiss her in a way that's probably 80 per cent more sexy than people would rate as publicly acceptable in an Auckland Council survey. I pull away to see if anyone's eyes have been burned out, but only one person seems to have noticed. Fuck. It's the man. The man is standing on the other side of the road with his mouth in a little O, limply holding hands with a, might I say, very plain-looking girl in a Kathmandu jacket and bootcut jeans, as if she's about to go and check on her horse.

'Why is that man looking at you?' Ell asks.

'I went on a date with him in the summer. I nearly went back to his house, but I couldn't stop thinking about how he said he didn't like music and nearly had a panic attack at the side of the street.'

She looks bemused. 'You, on a date with a man? Who doesn't like music? You, the person whose friends demonstrated the most rousing group performance of "S Club Party" I've seen in all my days?'

I recommence walking but I hold her hand this time, dragging her along the pavement. 'It was a very dark time in my life. A woman was mean to me and I thought I had been turned straight.'

184

'He is a bit of a dish,' she says over her shoulder.

I think Ell likes seeing me embarrassed. She's singing a regional interpretation of 'Our House', potentially titled 'Are Hoose', by the time we get to my building. After three attempts at keying in the right code, we run dangerously up the stairs, grabbing at each other. She backs me against the wall when we get to the top.

'Not here, you'll ruin my neighbours' perception that my brother and I are a nice young married couple from Tunisia.'

'Why is that a perception you want to uphold?'

'It's exciting for them. They're really boring, they only talk about the City Rail Link and whether the mail's come.'

She kisses my neck and I reconsider the narrative I need to present to the neighbours, until we hear a loud sniff down the corridor and turn around.

'Tang?'

My nephew is sitting against the wall next to our front door, looking crumpled, wearing a black leather jacket, possibly crying. We hurry over like teachers who have just seen someone ignore a dropped chip packet.

'I'm sorry,' he says croakily. 'I came to see V but he's away, I didn't know what else to do.'

'Why do you need to see V? Are you having a men's health issue?' I look down at him on the floor. 'Maybe you shouldn't wear such tight jeans.'

'Why don't you open the door, Gre,' Ell says with her hand on my arm. 'We can talk about gendered health problems inside.'

She helps him up from the floor and I open the door, surprising myself with only a brief search for the key. Tang sits stiffly on the couch. Ell hands him a box of tissues, then goes to make tea from the wide assortment that V bought during a crisis because someone made a joke about him not being a good host. Neither of us drinks tea.

Tang has turned into an adult while I wasn't looking. I know he's eighteen in November, and I've obviously noticed that he's well over six foot, but I didn't know that he was walking around town by himself at 2am wearing a leather jacket and skin-tight jeans. He's wearing a tight T-shirt and pointy black boots as well. He smells nice, like Mémoire by Gucci, a fragrance for all genders.

'Oh my God, Tang, are you having a gay crisis? I thought teens were all chill and pansexual these days and only old millennials like Ell freak out and cut all their hair off the first time they touch a boob at age twenty-six.'

'It was a bit more complicated than that.' She puts the cups of tea on the coffee table and sits next to Tang on the couch. I sit on a wicker chair, presiding over things.

'I broke up with Odette today,' he says, looking at Ell.

'That's probably for the best,' she says. I have never heard of Odette. Maybe Tang is straight, and I just assume everyone's confused about their sexuality because I'm not hip with the kids. Ell is holding her cup of PG Tips like she does this all the time. 'How did it go?'

'It was fine, I guess. We had breakfast this morning because she had a tennis competition all day. She kept talking about how her parents were away and touching my ankle with her foot. I was laughing, but I wasn't really laughing. It was as if I had forgotten what it felt like to experience joy. I ordered an extra crêpe so I could keep eating and I didn't have to talk. When we said goodbye, I patted her on the back like I was saying goodbye to my cousin at the airport.'

'You don't have a cousin. We're the first ever Māori family to not have cousins,' I interrupt. Ell looks at me and I ignore her and pick up one of the cups of tea.

'I was going to say uncle, but you've seen V at the airport. He becomes overwhelmed with emotion.'

Ell clears her throat. 'What happened with Odette?'

'I went to the tennis club and told her I didn't think it was going to work out. That I was sorry if I'd been misleading or if I seemed . . . disingenuous. She said I was honest to God the weirdest person she'd met in her life and that she should have listened to Aja and Daisy about me.'

I screw my face up. 'Who are these people? Why are all their names like that?'

'I don't know.' He shrugs. 'I mean, I know who they are, I was kind of going out with all of them, but I don't know why those are their names.'

'All of them at once?'

He sighs. He looks too exhausted for someone who was born the same year as Facebook came out. 'Yeah.'

I shake my head. 'I knew Casper should never have let you live in that rich-people suburb. Now you're in a polycule with a girl named Daisy and you know people who play tennis.'

'I went out with my friends to a gig tonight. I hadn't told them what happened with Odette. They didn't like her, anyway. I don't know, I just felt strange. I told them I was going home but I walked around by the waterfront for a while and then I thought I needed to talk to V, that he would know what to do. When I got here, I remembered he's away. I'm sorry, to impose on your evening like this.' He drinks some tea and then says quickly, 'I'm in love with someone else.'

'Who are you in love with?' I think for a second that teens are in love with all sorts of ridiculous people, then I remember that I thought I was in love with Holly in January of this year. 'Is it someone called Clementine whose parents own a vineyard?'

'No.' He puts the cup down. 'His name is Plan. Plamen Gajević.'

'His name is *Plan Gay*?'

'Well. That's not a nickname I've heard him use before. He's from Montenegro. We met when I went on the history trip to Austria and Hungary last year.'

I don't think he likes me being disparaging about his secret Plan. I'll probably be annoyed with myself tomorrow, but I'll leave that for sober me to think about.

'And then you went out with scores of rich girls because you were sexually confused?' I ask.

'Greta,' says Ell, raising her eyebrows at me.

'I'm not sexually confused. Don't you think sexuality is a fluid spectrum?'

I think of my years upon years of sexual confusion and feel very outdated, like I've gone into the library and asked where I might find the microfiche. Wtf, I think. I think about getting my phone out and messaging Rashmika, *Wtf, my seventeen-year-old nephew is coming out rn and he thinks it's nothing*. I don't know what to say to him. I've sunk right down on my chair and I can't sit up again. 'How did you end up with all the girlfriends if you love this Plan, then?'

'I haven't actually heard from him since the end of the trip. I don't know how he feels, if I meant anything to him like he did to me.' His voice cracks and he puts his hands over his face. 'I'm sorry.'

'Don't be sorry,' Ell says, squeezing his knee.

'I just think about him all the time and I keep saying yes to things I don't want to do because I feel so unfulfilled. I just . . . I think I might be a monogamist.' He says this as if this is the thing to come out as. I feel stressed. The modern world is too much for me. I feel like I'm George of the Jungle. 'I worry about him too, you know; he said it would be bad for him if anyone found out about us. I felt awful, I know I'm lucky to live here and have the family I have.'

I nod. I feel hopeless thinking about how Ell's parents don't talk to her. She says it's fine and they'll come around, but I don't think it is fine. My parents have never stopped talking to me. Not even when I was thirteen and called my dad a stupid bitch when he said the ugly shoes I had to wear in the school production of *The Mikado* didn't seem so bad. Thinking back, I should have been upset because the show is very racist.

'Why did you want to talk to V about this? I don't know if he could give any useful advice, he's been prancing around here wondering if he's still in love with his ex all year.'

'Oh, yeah, I know, I just . . .' he trails off and looks down at the tea. 'The more stressed I got about all of this, the more I've been doing things that maybe I shouldn't be doing. I started thinking that I needed to write in black pen all the time or something bad would happen. I was in class and my teacher asked me to write something on the board and I pretended I didn't know the answer because there was only a red pen, and I had this . . . horrible headache. I thought I could keep everything under control as long as I drank a can of Pepsi Max every day by 12:30. I kept a box in my locker at school and one under my bed, but one day I was in town for the university open day and I couldn't find any for sale and I threw up in a bin in front of everyone. I haven't been sleeping or eating that much. I think maybe this isn't a normal way to feel.'

'Did you tell your dad?'

He shakes his head. 'I can't. He'll be so upset. He always says I can talk to him about anything, but I can't because he thinks that if anything bad ever happens to me it's his fault. I don't . . . know how to navigate getting him to give me enough space and not leaving him out of significant things in my life. I thought V could help me figure out what to do, how to talk to him.'

He sits there looking miserable, my nephew who used to be impressed by Fruit Ninja on my phone and is now suddenly at least four people's ex-boyfriend.

I sit up properly and lean forward, propping my face up with my hands. 'Casper's my brother too; we can come up with a plan and talk to him together. V will be back soon enough. You can talk things through with him as well. What do you want to do about Plan?'

'I think I need to know how he feels but I should sort myself out a bit first.'

'Why haven't you been talking, if he means so much to you?'

He rests his head on the back of the couch. 'It was too much for me at the time. It felt ridiculous to think that we could be together. He was nearly eighteen and talking about going to uni in Germany and I still had a whole year of school left and I couldn't see there ever being an end to that. I feel like a different person since I met him. I feel like the world is a lot bigger and a lot smaller at the same time.'

'I'm here for you all the time,' I say. 'I don't think you're the weirdest person I've ever met even though you do sometimes talk like a philosophical narrator in an independent film. No matter what happens, I think it's important that you felt like you could love someone like that. It's special, to be able to love.'

He nods. 'Thank you.'

Ell pats him on the shoulder. 'Why don't you let your parents know that you're with us? Gre, do you think V would mind if he stayed in his room?'

'No, no, please go ahead.' I blink a few times. It's been a harsh and sudden transition to go from being a drunk karaoke person on the street to a responsible adult mentor. 'What happened when we came for dinner?'

'Oh.' He scrunches up his face. 'I was at Daisy's house and we had an argument about, like, the economy, and she said, "This is why Aja doesn't like you." I was feeling dramatic and walking around in the rain and replaying conversations I'd had with Plan and then when I got home, I opened the door and Freya said . . . What did she say exactly?'

Ell thinks. 'Freya had been interested in the idea that you were my girlfriend and how old you had to be to have a girlfriend. Then Tang opened the door and she said, "This is my brother, Tang, who's never had a girlfriend, maybe because no one likes him." '

He groans. 'Yeah, and then I said, "Shut the fuck up, Freya, you don't know my life." '

'That's very unlike you,' I say, recalling a time V said something similar and then for some reason threw his phone out the window. From the second floor. Casper had to climb on the roof and fish it out of the gutter.

'Yeah, I don't know where it came from. I felt bad. Ell was so good to me though, and we hadn't even met before. You're really lucky, Gre.'

'I know. I love her.'

Ell is looking at me in a new way. I haven't said that before.

I'm not very good at telling people how I feel. I don't know why I'm like that and I don't always love to think about all the tiny pieces of me that add up to make a whole person. I feel concerned that too many of the pieces have something a bit wrong with them, like a puzzle you get at an op shop on holiday when it's raining. Ell is good at noticing the things that are wrong with pieces; she's always looking at molecular structures and pointing out trouble spots.

I pick up the cups and go and put them in the kitchen. I imagine what it would be like if this were our kitchen, hers and mine, and then I feel bad about where that would leave V and put that thought away.

Talk Talk

V

We have to talk. Neither of us enjoys having a frank and open dialogue about how we feel and what our future plans are, which is how we ended up in this situation in the first place. We sit next to each other on the bed with our knees up, drinking out of coffee cups. My cup has more of the lemon drink from yesterday in it. I thought while I was admitting things I might as well come out and say I hate coffee. The wall opposite us is glass and we look out on a pastoral scene, by which I mean just grass. In the distance, a truck drives along the unsealed road.

'I don't know where to start,' he says. 'I wasn't expecting this to happen.' He gestures ambiguously when he says 'this', and I have to assume he means my physical self. 'I feel like there are things I should have told you before anything happened.'

'Do I need to get tested for herpes?'

He nearly spits his coffee back into the cup. 'No, I wasn't so overcome with lust that I neglected to tell you that I have herpes.'

'Could you have, though?'

'Do you mean am I seeing anyone?'

'Are you?'

He turns towards me and leans his head on the headboard.

'No. I could have said that yesterday; you wouldn't have needed to look in every drawer in my bathroom for clues.'

'I think hearing it directly would have been too much. Finding someone else's personal care products would be a subtle enough explanation. Maybe a mouthguard or sunblock for sensitive skin.'

'I was seeing someone last year, but it didn't work out.'

'What happened?' I ask, even though I don't really want to know the answer.

He exhales. 'Someone who perhaps doesn't know me as well as I thought they did set us up. I think I knew from the beginning that it wasn't a good match, but I sort of . . . let the current take me. People kept telling me they were worried about me, that I was too isolated, they knew I hadn't made any new work, and I thought if I went along with this relationship all of those issues would disappear. It wasn't my best plan. I feel guilty for even considering . . . using someone like that. But I think, in the end, she found me to be the most infuriating person she'd ever met.'

'You? You're so temperate.'

'Some people don't like that. There was an impression given that I was hiding something, that I wasn't being my real self. That the, um, masks would fall off at some point and I would be revealed. She's used to having her opinions taken seriously. She's a very popular artist and activist here. So she didn't like it when I didn't want to open up or go to a therapy group where you stand in a circle and scream. We had a fight about it and she kept saying I needed to take the first step and admit that the most fundamental aspect of my personality is that I'm repressed. That was too much for me. I got a bit loud.'

'You were loud? I don't think I've ever heard you shout at anyone except your brother.'

'We were in Brazil, everyone was shouting. It was bad timing actually. We had just arrived in São Paulo for a three-day arts festival and we had to be on a panel together. She made no attempt to hide her animosity towards me. God, Val, it was terrible. Everyone knew about it. It was streamed. Geneviève called me and cackled for ten minutes straight. After that I got drunk and went home with a waiter.'

'Since when do you drink?'

'That day I did.'

I adjust my sitting position. I don't know what to do with this information.

'What about you?' he asks.

'What do you mean?'

'I feel exposed. You've seen my poorly decorated house, you've heard about my failed romance. For some reason you could tell that I'm still in love with you, even though I thought I was being very subtle. You haven't told me anything except that you made a race-based assumption about your hairdresser and you didn't watch age-appropriate movies as a child. I at least want to know if the attractive and charming media executives I've imagined you with are real.'

I shake my head. 'No. Just, you know, Slava.'

He groans. 'No. You didn't. Valdin.'

'I was missing you and he kept touching my hands and implying there was no bus back to his new flat. He doesn't love me this time, it's fine. He forwarded me someone else's nudes the other day. In an email. It was shocking. I was in line at the supermarket and everyone was annoyed with me for not hurrying up because I was looking at naked pictures of a stranger, wondering why he was holding a cricket bat.' I look at him as he listens attentively to yet another of the four million nonsense anecdotes my life is comprised of. I want to touch him, but I'm scared of what he has to say to me. 'Xab, you aren't sick, are you?'

'No. I'm probably the healthiest I've ever been. I've been running, and I live too far out of the city to eat panchos every day. Um.' He doesn't take his eyes off me and says nothing for a moment. Then he says, 'I'm adopting a child.'

'What?'

'You don't have to say anything, I know it's a lot. After I came back from Brazil, I felt like I was missing something in my life, but I didn't think that it was the romantic love that other people were telling me it was. I was talking to Maria, she's my gardener, and she was telling me about the town she's from in Colombia, how many kids there are without parents, and I thought, You know, what the fuck am I doing with my life? Nothing. I could give someone a home. Even if I'm repressed and distant and have a terrible personality.'

'No, you don't.'

'I didn't know if it would happen. It took about a year of forms and money and travelling back and forth. It was the day after you called that I found out there's only a couple of things left to do before it's confirmed. I'm going to Medellín in two weeks.'

I look at the ceiling. My face feels hot and my eyes are stinging.

'I wasn't thinking about how you would feel,' he says quietly. 'I didn't think I was ever going to see you again. If I did, I would have probably played things a bit differently.'

'I have to be at my production meeting in two hours.'

'I know.' He sighs and moves to get up off the bed. 'I'll take you into the city now.'

'How long did you have the beard for before I came?'

He puts his hand up to his face. 'Six months. You would have hated it.'

I shake my head. 'I would have loved you anyway.'

Lemonade

G

Holly asks me to meet her at Shadows to give her back the essays I marked for her, and I don't know how I feel about it. I think if she had asked me to meet her at a bar in town, I would have said no because that would have felt inappropriate. The bar at the university that only really broke undergrads go to lands somewhere closer to being professional. I haven't told Ell about my meeting with Holly, or rather I haven't reminded her of it, since she was there when she propositioned me in the first place. Holly heavily implied that she'd never had any feelings towards me whatsoever, so I don't know why I still feel weird about meeting her like this. Rashmika offered to come with me, but I got the impression that she was only offering because she wanted to start some shit, and I wanted to avoid such a situation.

I get up the stairs to the dark and mostly empty bar. It's the middle of the day and there isn't any cause for celebration. Holly is already there, finishing off a drink and reading *Naked Lunch*. I hope she isn't drinking whisky. That would add too much to the mise-en-scène.

'Gre, welcome,' she says. I don't know if this is a joke or Holly now thinks that she owns Shadows.

'Thank you,' I say, sitting down at the laminate table.

'How are you?' she asks.

I consider how I really feel. A little bit lonely in the house by myself without V. He's been gone almost two weeks now. I hadn't realised how much I associated coming home with his dependable *being there*, until he wasn't anymore. Even though he

G

complains a lot and tells me about all the most boring things
that have happened to him and keeps all the juicy stuff for himself, it doesn't feel the same to open the door and know he's not
there and he's not going to be any time soon. I like it when Ell
and I have the house to ourselves, but she has her own place and
her own things to do a lot of the time. That's not the only issue:
I don't think my thesis is going as well as it could be because I'm
not sure I can see the point in doing it at the moment. I only
have $90, which probably isn't enough money to eat anything
except soup and half-price sushi if I get to the place just when
it's closing. I don't know which of these things to tell Holly.

'My brother's away at the moment and I feel a bit sad without him, just being in the house by myself,' I say. 'I'm sort of
worried about him as well; he hasn't responded to any of my
messages.'

'Ugh, men,' Holly says, finishing her drink. 'Do you know if
you're getting your hours cut?'

'What? No?'

'There was a department meeting this morning. They don't
want any tutors doing more than ten hours a week.'

I shrug. 'I only have ten hours anyway.'

'Do you think you might lose them?' She looks at me with
her glass in her hand and I notice that her hair looks different,
sort of too clean and sticking up, like when you stay at someone's house and accidentally see their dad just out of the shower.
'They might reallocate them to someone more senior.'

'I would assume I haven't been affected since no one's said
anything to me about it.'

'Still,' she says, and stands up. 'Do you want something? A
juice?'

'A juice? Do they sell juice here?' I look around at the dark
booths, where probably thousands of regional eighteen-year-
olds have had their first drunken pash in the big city with

197

someone they've just met, and wonder if anyone's ever ordered a juice here before. Maybe a vodka and cranberry because they'd heard their aunty order one at a wedding once. Holly is already at the bar and comes back with a short glass of something dark for herself and a lemonade for me.

'Sorry, they didn't have any juice in the fridge,' she says.

'Ah, that's okay. Thanks.' I take a sip and feel like a little girl out with her dad. Not my own dad, who gave me my first shot of vodka when I was nine. The government had decided civil unions were allowed, so after being together for fifteen years already Thony and Giuseppe got one. My mum said giving vodka shots to children did not constitute something that could be excused as a cultural activity.

'Thanks so much for the essays,' Holly says. 'I'm sure you did a really good job on them.'

'That's okay. Um, how are you? Are you feeling like you're under a lot of pressure still?'

She ponders my question. That's not a word I would usually think to use but she's literally holding a whisky on the rocks and staring wistfully out the window. 'I feel a lot better since my holiday. I think it's important to know when to say no to things and really give yourself a break. Just unplug yourself from technology and really consider what you want, what your goals are and how best to achieve them. The place we stayed was so good, too. Let me know if you're looking for somewhere to stay down there and I'll give you the link. Well, I'll get it from Sonja, she booked it all.'

My eyebrow twitches. I can't really see myself going on a holiday with my $90 and no car, but okay.

'Thank you, I'll let you know.'

She swills her drink in its glass. 'Who was that butch you and Rashmika were with the other day?'

This is a funny thing to say. Holly knows who that butch is.

She always looks at my posts and conspicuously doesn't like the ones where I'm with anyone else. 'She's my girlfriend. Ell Livingstone.'

'How long's that been going on for?'

'Four or five months.'

'Hmm,' she says. I feel like saying, 'What the fuck is that supposed to mean?' but I keep quiet and drink my lemonade. 'Is Rashmika getting her hours cut?'

'I don't know . . . Like I said, I hadn't heard anything about anyone getting their hours cut until you told me.'

She sighs. 'I wouldn't be surprised.'

I bite my lip. I would be surprised if anyone tried to take Rashmika's hours away. She's a widely sought after and popular tutor and she would definitely go public straight away if the university attempted to wrong her in any way.

'Are you getting your hours cut?' I ask.

'Oh, me? No. I don't think that would happen.' She looks in her brown leather satchel and hands me a book over the table. *Mrs Caliban*. I forgot I lent it to her. It's not even mine, it's my mum's. That was in the summer, a lifetime ago, when I was just loaning out books without a care in the world.

'What did you think?' I ask.

'It was a lot to get through, I didn't finish it,' she says. I turn the book over in my hands. It's about a hundred pages long. 'There was a receipt in the back so I left it in; I thought you might need it.'

'Thanks.' I flick through the pages and take out a receipt for a packet of picture hooks from Bunnings Lyall Bay.

$3.95. Very thoughtful of Holly, not to throw that out for me, just in case my mum wants to go back to Wellington and get a refund on some hooks. I turn the receipt over and in scrawled handwriting that doesn't belong to my mother it says *left phone at fish*. What could that mean? I wonder if it's a code, like there's a key hidden under a portrait of a fish talking on a phone somewhere. Maybe whoever wrote this had been interrupted in the midst of writing *left phone at fish market, can't believe it, second time this week, anyway, be back shortly and I suppose we'll be having fish for dinner again, ha ha.* I wouldn't be surprised if my dad left his phone inside a fish, but he has the loopy handwriting of someone who started out writing in Cyrillic.

'How's your thesis going, by the way?' Holly asks. 'How much have you done?'

'Oh, um, not that much. I still have ten months left to go, though.'

'Mm. Do you think maybe your topic isn't good?'

I open my mouth to argue, and then I look at her in her paisley shirt with her sticking-up hair and I feel so annoyed with her, but more than that, I feel annoyed with myself for coming to this meeting in the first place. And retroactively for all the positive feelings I've ever had about this person who obviously doesn't value me or my ideas or my time. I close my mouth and bite my lip.

'Holly, you know what, I actually have somewhere else I'm supposed to be.'

'Oh. Are you meeting your girlfriend?'

I stand up and push the chair in. 'No. Thank you for the lemonade.'

Desert

V

The shoot goes better than I expected. I feel less different from everyone when we're outside our home country. We seem more united as a group of people from New Zealand, none of whom can speak Spanish properly. We're out in the desert in Salta at the moment. I have never been to a desert before and I'm not used to how quickly the temperature drops when the sun sets. I have to wear a puffer jacket I borrowed off my dad. I'm an adult, I should buy my own. The sun is slowing down across the red cliffs streaked with white and the sky is all different shades of pink. A couple of people are filming some pick-up shots and everyone else is inside having a beer with the local crew. Emma comes outside to the concrete ledge where I'm sitting and holds out a litre bottle of beer and a cup.

'What's going on?' she asks.

'What do you mean?' I take the beer. I've probably had enough but it's already in my hand and I'm already pouring it.

She sits next to me. 'You've been a bit funny. I was wondering if it was because of what happened in Queenstown.' She looks over her shoulder, but there's no one there. Just the sound of people enjoying themselves inside. 'You know I don't think that was fine, the way that was handled. I can say something, if you want me to.'

'Oh. No. I mean, yeah, that was fucked, but you don't need to do anything about it. I'm just a bit distracted. About something else.'

'Oh, what is it?'

I haven't told anyone what happened with Xabi. I tell everyone every banal detail of my life and then as soon as things get difficult, I keep everything to myself. Emma looks at me in anticipation, her puffer vest zipped up and her blonde wavy hair tied up with a scrunchie.

'My ex lives here. I went to see him the day before production started.'

'What? Like some backpacker you hooked up with?'

'Ah, it was a bit more than that. We used to live together, and I thought we were going to be together until one of us died, probably him because he's old, but then I had a nervous breakdown and he ended up moving to this huge empty plot of land here and we hadn't talked since.'

'Fuck. Why didn't you say anything?'

'It seemed like a weird thing to bring up. I didn't want to tell everyone about my personal issues.'

'You could have told me though.'

'I'm a big idiot.'

'What happened when you went to see him?'

'Um.' I look down at the ground. I have my legs stretched out and my shoes are covered in dust. Ever since we came to the desert, we've all been covered in dust. 'I thought it would be different. I thought he'd have a comfortable life with a woman who wears chunky bead necklaces and it would be good closure for me to see that. When I got there, he was worrying that I thought a bowl he'd made himself out of wood was wonky, and he had bought my favourite flowers and got a haircut.'

'What did you do?'

'What do you think I did, I came and sat on his bed in my underwear in the middle of the night.'

She hits me on the arm. 'I can't believe you didn't tell me.'

'It was gross, we were confessing our love to each other and exchanging meaningful glances. It's complicated though – he wants to be a dad.'

'Like, he wants you to sub all the time?'

'No, oh my God, Emma. He's going through an adoption process.'

'Well, sometimes you use gay slang I don't understand! Wait, so he's getting a baby just by himself?' Her eyes are wide and I'm realising that it's weird that this happened to me while everyone else was hanging out in Buenos Aires taking photos of the obelisk.

'Not a baby. He's eight.'

'What are you going to do?'

'I don't know. I want to be with Xab, but I have no idea how it would work with a kid. I've never thought about becoming – what, a *stepdad*? I don't want to ruin a child's life when he's already had a difficult start. He'll need stability and routine, not me hanging around. Dad's friend who can't speak Spanish and who sleeps in Dad's bed. There's no way I think my feelings are more important than that.'

'Do you want to leave the person you love to raise a child alone?'

'Fuck.' I look up at the sky, which is getting darker now. The pinks are fading into moodier purples and blues and the last people outside are packing up their equipment. 'I don't know if I can commit to that. I would want my family around if I did as well. I don't think I could live here. I need to be in an English-speaking country to work in this industry as well. I don't know.'

'But you love him.'

'How much does love really matter in this economy?'

She pulls her knees up to her chest. 'What do you want, though?'

'I want more time to figure things out. He'd only just told me about this when he had to take me back for the meeting.'

'Don't come back with us, then. I can change your flight. Schedule your voiceovers for the end of the month. That would work with the timeline.'

'Really?'

'Yeah. Don't worry, I won't tell anyone why.' She looks over her shoulder again. 'This job isn't more important than your life. Just do what you need to do, and I'll sort it. But right now let's go inside before I freeze to death.'

I zip up my dad's jacket and feel very far away from everything.

After dinner at the lodge we're staying in, I sneak out of the big wood-panelled dining room. I can hear laughter echoing down the hall and footsteps on the terracotta tiles. Plates are being cleared and more beer is being collected from the cellar. I can hear people talking about me, but in a good way, not in a *We need to talk about V* way. I lean against the wall and put my phone up to my ear.

'Hello?'

'Hey. Hi. It's Valdin. Vladisavljevic.'

'Oh, that Valdin. Not the one I met the other night. He was really cute, taller than you, perfectly fluent in Spanish, tiny little nose—'

'Xabi.'

'How are you?'

'I'm good. How are you?' I put my foot up against the wall, like I'm a cowboy. I notice a framed picture of the Queen of the Netherlands on the wall opposite me.

'I'm not too bad.'

'I want to see you,' I say, as one of the main culprits who drank all the beer at dinner.

'That's interesting,' he says. Why is he being coy with me? I feel like my neck is getting red and I put my hand on it in case anyone walks past on their way to the toilet and sees right through me. I can hear Xabi walking around and I wonder what he's doing. What he's wearing.

'What are you wearing?' I ask.

He laughs. 'What am I wearing? Val, you're making me blush.'

I melt a bit when he says my name. 'Tell me what you're wearing though.'

A woman carrying a tray of plates walks past me and smiles to herself. My neck is definitely red now.

'I'm wearing jeans and a T-shirt – what are you wearing?'

I look down. 'Well, I'm also wearing jeans and a T-shirt.'

He laughs again. 'I guess these jeans are quite tight, if that helps. I don't know what you're trying to achieve here.'

'In what way are they tight?'

'Around the thighs. You know I have big thighs.'

'I do.' I remember having seen them. Having maybe gripped them at times. 'Where are you?'

'On the bed.'

'I've been there. Do you remember?'

'Of course I remember,' he says softly.

'Do you remember what I said?'

'Harder.'

I turn around quickly and press my forehead into the wall. I forgot I said that.

'I meant when I said that I loved you.'

He laughs. Laughing is not the reaction I wanted. 'That was pretty nice too.'

'That was pretty nice!'

'I can't give myself up too easily to you. It would be like in that movie you like, what's it called?'

'I like probably ten thousand movies,' I mutter to the wall. '*Twins. Junior. Kindergarten Cop. Hercules in New York.*'

'*Earth Girls Are Easy*. I don't want you to think you can get whatever you want from me just because you've crash-landed into my life again.'

I feel embarrassed. I don't think I can have whatever I want. I never have. 'I'm sorry, I don't want to disrupt your life.'

'I want to see you too.'

'You do?'

'Yeah, I was messing with you. I thought you wanted to have phone sex but now I'm not so sure. Where are you?'

'I was having dinner with everyone from work and now I'm standing in the corridor by the lodge kitchen.'

'Oh, so just in public then.'

'My friend who's the production manager said she could change my schedule around, so I don't have to fly back for two weeks. Do you want me to come back and see you? Or do you think that would make things unnecessarily complicated?'

'I'm not going to be here, I'm flying to Medellín this weekend.'

'Oh.' I feel embarrassed again, and not sure what I'm really trying to achieve.

'Do you want to come to Colombia? Or is that too intense? You wouldn't have to do anything; you could just hang out and do your own thing while I'm . . . tied up. I'm nervous and I would like it if you were with me, but I know it's a really awkward position to put you in, before we've . . . made any decisions.'

Emma walks past holding a beer bottle that's dripping with condensation. She waves her free hand around, which I understand to mean she's getting a paper towel and that I should come back to the table because we've got more beer now.

'I'll come with you.'

'Are you sure?'

'Yeah. I'll book the flights tonight. Do you want me to call you later, when I'm alone?'

V

'I'd like that. Hey, don't worry if you change your mind about coming, I'll understand.'

'I won't. I'll talk to you later.'

I look at the drips of water all across the tiles and breathe in and out a few times to transition from local lovesick pansy to fun media personality. I follow the drips inside and try to think of a good joke about Uruguay.

Cake

G

Today is the day that V is coming back, and I see it as an opportunity for a cultural reset for me personally. Things have not been going well for me. My not knowing what I want to do after I finish my master's has turned into an issue. I can't stop worrying about it. I stay up all night doing government careers aptitude tests that tell me I'm best suited to being an actor or playwright. The job opportunities are described as *poor* and the pay starts at *zero*. I can't retrain as a lawyer because I've nearly used up my lifetime limit on student loans. I can't be a viral internet sensation because I'm over twenty-five. I've eaten 400 pieces of sushi and nothing else. When V comes back, he can buy me hot chips and a Mexican Coke, and we can talk about his problems instead of mine. I want to see him so much, his stupid too-tall presence in our house built for normal-sized people. I think that's what's going to make me feel better.

I check my bank balance and I have $7.49. I use this to buy cream cheese, two bananas and two loose eggs from a superette I know that sells them like that. I need to buy milk as well. I can't afford a whole bottle, so I get a little UHT carton with a straw. I don't want to pay for a paper bag, so I shove all these things in the pockets of my coat. Except for the eggs, which I carry carefully in my hands all the way back to the apartment building, all the way up the stairs. Then I start making a cake. I love baking cakes. It's one of the things that I feel I'm truly good at and I like it when people eat all the slices and give me compliments. For a brief moment, I consider monetising this hobby, but then I can't conceive of being a small business owner. It would put me amongst the groups of people portrayed by the media in a positive light. It's probably easier if I stay as one of the people who everyone complains about because they've got no money, no land, no prospects and they never go to the dentist or buy serviettes.

I put the flour, sugar, baking soda, baking powder and salt into a plastic bowl. We don't have stainless steel, because V doesn't like the texture. I create a well in the middle and add the banana, which I've mashed up with a fork, and the milk, butter and eggs. I like cracking the eggs; I tap them once firmly against the bench and then pull the shells apart over the bowl, letting the yolk and white fall out in one motion. After it's all mixed together, I pour the batter evenly into a round cake tin and put it in the oven at 180. Then I set about cleaning the house. I vacuum, I mop, I wipe down surfaces. I shake the rug out the window, like I'm in a film that depicts the old country. I go into V's room and check the photos on my phone so that I'm sure everything's back to how it was before I went through his stuff. I smell the backs of my hands to make sure I smell like my hand cream and not his much more expensive one. V feels almost as uncomfortable about expensive things as I do, but this all goes out the window when it comes to skincare. I wipe down all the leaves of the plants, so they look shiny. I straighten the cushions on the couch.

When the smell of my cake starts to fill the kitchen, I open the oven door and test the cake with a bamboo skewer. It comes out clean. I leave the cake to cool on the bench while I check that the flight is on time, which it is. I wish I could go and pick V up, but the bus from the airport stops close to our house, so he'll be okay. I put on the album *Bridge Over Troubled Water*, and make sure to skip the first track, 'Bridge Over Troubled Water', because it's really just not a good song compared with the rest of them.

I mix the softened cream cheese with icing sugar and butter, and I ice the cake. It would be nice if it had a caramel layer as well, but caramel is difficult to make. The temperature needs to be just right, and then it's hard to clean the pot afterwards. I would go and buy a jar of dulce de leche, but I don't have any money now and V probably has some ridiculous romantic memory about it which he might cry over and pretend he's not crying. I put the cake on a nice plate and leave it in the middle of the table.

Then I start waiting. I read some articles about Paul Simon. I read about boarding schools for girls outside New York. I look up what Paris Hilton looks like these days. I send a screenshot of a bad article about yetis to Ell, but she hasn't been online for four hours. I look at photos of people I went to school with, some of whom have babies now and share memes about having a lot of laundry to do, and some of whom are fitness influencers. A lot of the other girls from my form class are lawyers and policy analysts, and doctoral researchers enjoying a summer picnic in a London park. I look at the cheese in one picture and I can almost taste it. I wish I could afford cheese. These girls have a whole assortment of cheeses and a bottle of sparkling rosé. What should we have for dinner? I'll let V choose. He will have missed something very specific. As long as he pays. He'll pay; he wouldn't let me starve. I watch a video about how to keep your hair blonde all summer. It's winter and my hair is black.

The plane will have landed by now. I look on Find My Friends, but V's phone has been off for a long time. I thought they would have had Wi-Fi on the plane, but maybe not. Maybe it wasn't working properly. I figure out how long it would take for the bus and then I add an extra half an hour in case he got held up at customs. He probably got held up at customs; they're going to hear 'South America' and start searching all your bags for drugs. I wonder if he got me a present. I don't want to get my hopes up in case he didn't, but that would be nice. Even just something from duty-free. Another half an hour passes, and another. I look out the window and watch the streetlights come on. Less families and groups of teenagers walk past, and there are more people dressed up, going out for dinner, probably going to shows and things. A middle-aged woman with a dark tan and a green sequinned dress laughs as she nearly loses her stiletto in a grating and holds on to a man's suit-jacketed arm while she pulls it out again. A guy goes past on a longboard, looking at his phone and vaping. The longboard has a light under it and it's interesting that he's partially concerned about safety. Another half an hour passes and the median age of the people on the street drops. People get louder and seem like they're having more fun. They sit under outdoor heaters, drinking glasses of wine and sharing polenta chips.

I look at my phone again. No messages. I look at Instagram and there's a new post from V's show's account which he made me follow. It's a picture of a group of white creatives, looking exhausted but hydrated at the airport. *We made it back to Aotearoa safe and sound, bar one [eye-roll emoji] [laughing emoji] get back soon, we need you!*

I look at my cake. I go into V's room, sit on his bed, open his top drawer, reach to the back and pull out a Ziploc bag of coins. I take a handful and go to buy myself a Wendy's value meal.

School

V

'You don't have to come,' Xabi says as he washes his face over the sink in our hotel in Medellín. I am lying on my single bed waiting for my phone to charge. I don't like this room, with its two separate single beds and their white sheets. The person at the desk felt bad about the single beds and tried to offer us two separate rooms, which I didn't want either. And my phone won't charge properly here. I think it's something to do with the voltage. But I don't really want to know what's happening outside the bubble I've created anyway. Too complicated, way too complicated. What am I supposed to say to anyone back at home?

'I won't come inside,' I say. 'I'll just come along for the walk and then I'll go and buy a new phone charger.'

On our way to the school, we don't acknowledge what we're doing or how complicated everything is becoming.

The streets on the way to the school are pretty, nicer than I expected. A lot greener than I expected. Almost every place I go in the world is nicer than I expect. Stupid Western media. I think the scariest place I've ever been to is London and people go there willingly all the time. I like the apartment buildings here; I look at all the plants on the balconies and wish we had places like this where I'm from. I look across at Xabi and imagine us living in one of the apartments together, having a favourite pizza place we order from, watering the plants on the balcony with a hose. Hoping the water doesn't drip down onto the neighbours. Oh, but it will dry quickly anyway. I guess this will never happen now, though.

Xabi is dressed professionally for his meeting, in a light blue button-up and the sort of trousers you have to wear to a job interview. I'm wearing my favourite white linen shirt, which I'm always worried is going to get stained somehow. I feel like I look especially like a travel show host in this shirt, but anyone walking past would probably assume that we were work colleagues on our lunch break. Socios de negocios, I learned. The hotel receptionist thought we were socios de negocios and Xabi didn't correct him. 'It's fine, don't worry about it,' I whispered in the elevator when he felt bad about it. We don't negotiate anything, except our feelings, which we stay up late to talk about every night and reach no conclusions.

When we get to the gate, Xabi squeezes my wrist, which is not really appropriate for our business relationship. I don't think I've ever seen him look so nervous.

'It's okay,' I say. 'You're just going to go in there, talk to the social worker and the teacher, hang out with him for a bit and then we'll get dinner.'

'It will be way too early to get dinner,' he says, rolling up his sleeves.

'Please respect my culture of not eating in the middle of the night.'

He looks worried. 'What if he hates me?'

'He didn't hate you the first two times you met, you said. You would get through it, anyway. You're a good person, Xab. You're not going to fuck up his life by being a part of it.'

'Okay,' he says, still frowning.

I look around. There are people about – someone getting a food delivery across the street, and a woman walking with two small children – so I extend my hand for a business handshake.

'I'll see you later,' I say as he shakes my hand reluctantly and disappears into the reception.

I get my phone out to look up where I can buy a charger and

it's almost run out of battery again. There are a few places called things like *Ktronix* and *Electronic Servicio Técnico* if I walk through the school and back onto the main road. I look around. Is it okay to take a shortcut through a school here, or will someone think I've got a gun and call the police? Then again, people are probably more used to people having guns here. I think school's finished for the day anyway.

The school has pretty big grounds for this area. It doesn't feel so different from my own school, except the buildings are made of brick and I can't see anyone being reprimanded for not having the backs of their Roman sandals pulled up. Xabi was conflicted about the school. He's been paying for it all year, having described the child's previous living situation as 'not ideal'. I don't know his name; Xabi never said, maybe in an attempt to keep me distanced from the situation. I think he was living in a group home, which I had never thought about as being a real thing. Group homes only existed in the memories of old men walking around a field with their hands in their pockets in local documentaries, the voiceover announcing that they're glad the borstal burned down. Xabi doesn't agree with private education or American-style curricula, but he agreed with the social worker that it was the best option they had while the paperwork was being sorted out. I don't know what will happen afterwards. Xabi said it was best to leave him in school until the end of the year, but he didn't say where they were going after that. I don't think he knows.

A group of kids are playing football in a dusty courtyard. Why there, when they could be playing on the field? I want to call out to them that they'll break a window playing like that, but I don't know how to say that in Spanish. Windows are ventanas, but I can only suggest that they open them, not refrain from smashing them.

The kids are taking the game seriously. There's eight of them and they're all tackling and running and diving after the ball. Every play they make creates a cloud of brown dust that rains back onto them. They kick the ball back and forth, back and forth, the fine particles of dust floating around them, and then they kick it towards a ninth kid, who doesn't seem to be as much a part of the game as existing near it. As the game wears on and the plays move closer and closer to him, he does nothing except occasionally brush some of the dust off the page of the book he's reading. I can see the title of the book, *Herejes de Dune*. I think it's the fifth *Dune* book. Is that what kids are into these days? Maybe there's a new cartoon version of it come out or something.

The game is increasing in aggression and the kids are shouting at each other over possession of the ball so I give the game a wide berth as I walk past. I don't want to get dust on my clean shirt. It was so hard to get the dust out of all my things when we left the desert. I check that I'm going the right way, and my phone only has 6 per cent battery left now. The afternoon is hot and I want to get a can of Coke and roll it on my neck. The last time I tried to do that, the man in the shop opened the can for me and I had to say thank you and drink it immediately. What if I—

There's a loud noise, and a dead silence. The kids stop playing. I stop walking. One of them is on the ground. *Dune* is on the ground. There's blood. The ball is rolling off silently into a corner.

I'm running. I'm on my knees by the time the dust clears, trying to see where the bleeding is coming from.

'Hey, hey, look at me, um, mírame. ¿Estás bien?'

He isn't okay. He manages to sit up and blood gushes from his nose, all over his hands, all down his shirt. He gasps and I don't know how to tell him what to do, so I pinch the bridge of his nose and hold his head forward. He looks up quickly at the other eight kids, who are standing as still as statues staring at him, and he squeezes his eyes shut. Go and get someone, you idiots, I think. I'm just a random tourist passer-by who now can't let go of this boy's nose.

'Necesitamos ayuda, por favor,' I say to the kids and they all look at each other before one runs off somewhere. I feel a tear running down the back of my hand and I wipe it away. 'It's okay, there's always a lot of blood when you get knocked in the head. It's just a shock. We'll get someone to take you inside and get you cleaned up, and then you can have a drink and lie down. Um . . .' I want to speak in a cool, calming tone, but I can't do that and speak Spanish at the same time. 'Te traeré una bebida, maybe.'

Xabi comes running outside. A woman with a long black plait and a pencil skirt runs behind him, very quickly for someone in high heels.

'¿Qué pasó?' Xabi asks, crouching in the dust, looking at me with blood all down my arms, on my trousers, all over my white shirt.

'He got knocked off the bench by the ball, I think.' I watch as my patient reaches out and holds Xabi's arm. The woman with the heels is shouting at the kids, I hear 'ventanas' and 'campo de fútbol', so I know we're on the same page.

He looks down at the small hand that doesn't reach all the way around his forearm, and says in a quiet voice, 'Ernesto, quiero presentar Valdin. This isn't really how I pictured this to happen.' He looks up at me. 'What happened to your phone charger?'

'It can wait. Mucho gusto,' I say to Ernesto. He doesn't say anything, but he nods slightly.

'Ah, Val, Ernesto doesn't talk.'

Lime

G

I follow Thony through his fancy modernist house and out onto the deck, where Casper and my mum are having a serious-looking discussion at the table. The sun has almost finished setting and the trees and shrubs below us are starting to flower in spring colours. It's been unusually warm and unusually sunny for August; my mum has bare legs and red sandals and she sits with her ankles crossed. I assume they're talking about how V went to Argentina and then just never came home and didn't tell anyone. He still hasn't replied to me, but he has posted some photos of trees and flowers and one poorly translated sign in a toilet somewhere.

'Hello, Greta.' Giuseppe puts down a tray of drinks and kisses me on the cheek. I find this embarrassing because he's quite hot and even I know it. He's looking businesslike in grey trousers and a white shirt with a brown leather belt. I wonder what he was doing today in his office where I don't know what he does, but apparently something that means you can afford a house with a window the size of a whole wall.

'Hello, everyone,' I say, and cringe internally.

'Are you by yourself tonight as well?' my mum asks, taking a glass off the tray. If I know my mother, it's Cointreau and orange.

'Yeah, Ell and I had a miscommunication.' I sit at the table opposite her and Casper. 'In that I never told her that she was invited so she assumed she wasn't. She went to a Fashion Week event.'

'Did she?' Thony asks as he sits down, using a voice that indicates that he would not have expected Ell to be at any Fashion Week events.

'They were offered some free tickets at uni; it's a science-themed catwalk or something. She only went because she thought I'd be with you all night anyway.'

'Please let her know that she certainly was invited,' my mum says, and drinks the Cointreau and orange through a metal straw. She's wearing a blue-red-and-white-striped sundress with a square neck and a belted waist and her hair has somehow been folded into an elegant bun.

'Where are your mates?' I ask Casper.

He leans back in his chair with his arms behind his head. 'Greta's at work waiting for the London office to open so they can have an argument over Skype about some questionable branding decisions. Tang's on something called Year 13 Activities Week. Each class picked something to do and every single class that he's in picked escape room. So he's just escaping out of a room every night this week. Freya's here, she's patting a dog through the fence.'

'Don't worry, he's a safe dog,' Thony says. He's drinking something dark. That's unlike him, he's usually partial to a fruity cocktail or a white wine spritzer.

'Greta, what would you like?' Giuseppe asks. I'm taken aback. My family is very big on thrusting into your hands drinks that you definitely never asked for.

'Um, do you have gin and tonic?'

'Of course, what would you like in it? I have lemon, lime, cucumber—'

'Lime, please,' I say quickly. I don't even want to think about cucumber gin.

'Coming right up,' he says and goes back inside the house.

'Where's Dad?' I ask.

Casper looks around, as if he only noticed at this moment that Dad isn't here. He isn't sitting on the other side of the deck hiding behind the barbecue or inside looking at a landscape painting of Xabi's, of his and Giuseppe's hometown, that's hanging above the mantelpiece.

My mum rolls her eyes. 'He went home to have a shower and get some clean clothes.'

'Why, did an octopus explode on him at the lab?' I ask, with a tinge of hope that something dramatic like that might have happened.

She shakes her head. 'We were swimming on Waiheke today, and he dropped his dry clothes in the sea.' I can't believe I've spent my whole day marking truly awful essays by Zoomers who have clearly read not one of *The Canterbury Tales* and my parents have been on an island swimming excursion.

'Like, he dropped them in the sea for a joke?' Casper asks.

'No, he just wasn't paying attention.'

'What was he doing?'

'Oh, we were . . . kissing, a bit.' She looks down at the table, as Giuseppe sets the gin and tonic carefully in front of me. The lime peel forms a delicate spiral as it floats in the glass. It looks almost too pretty.

'Thank you,' I say, and then, remembering, 'Happy birthday.'

'Thank you,' my mum says, looking up at me. She has on her favourite Chanel lipstick, which is an orange-red colour called Vibrante.

Giuseppe sits down at the end of the table next to Thony, and crosses one leg over the other. He has a faraway look in his eyes, and he seems tired. He usually has the complexion of someone who's both ethnically Mediterranean and a liberal user of vitamin C serum. Thony is pale like my dad, and there's nothing to be done about it.

'Giuseppe, have you spoken to Xabi lately?' I ask. Casper

looks across at me. I suppose he wants to know what V's doing as well, having sent some pointed messages to the group chat himself, but I don't think he was expecting me to be this upfront about it.

'Ah, I spoke to him last week,' Giuseppe says. 'Not about anything particularly notable. I look after his money and he wanted some accounting information. I don't know why – I was a little concerned about why he needed it.'

'Why?' asks Thony, incredulously. 'Did you think he was being blackmailed?'

'No, I just . . . worry about him. He doesn't tell me things properly. If he was being blackmailed, I'd find out about it years later by accident.'

'I thought he and V might be together,' I say carefully.

'Why would you think that?' he asks. He puts down his glass, which is short and full of ice. 'I didn't think they'd spoken since Xab left in the first place.'

'V had to go to Buenos Aires for work and he was going to see Xabi, and then he just stopped replying to anyone and didn't come back on the flight with the rest of his work colleagues.'

'What?' He looks genuinely shocked and not especially happy to hear this.

'Greta, stop it,' my mum says shortly.

I whip my head around to look at her. 'Why do I have to stop it! V's the one who's just fucked off without telling anyone anything, thinking he can just do whatever he wants all the time with no consequences!'

She sighs. 'He'll be fine, you don't need to make a big deal about it. Let him live his life.'

I have no idea how she stays so casual. V does so much stupid shit. Once he got locked in a car park building and the parking officer tried to charge him $300 for the call-out, even though he didn't even have a car. His tooth got knocked out during a softball game and he wasn't even playing; he was just walking past on his way home from work. Everywhere he goes, dramatic things happen to him and he can't handle it. We should be keeping track of where he is, or something bad will happen.

'Mum, in what world is Greta in the wrong here? V's the one who literally couldn't even be bothered to message her that he's not coming back to the country any time soon.' Casper shakes his head. 'She deserves a little bit more respect than that. He hasn't replied to Tang either and he's really having a hard time right now.'

'I'm sure Valdin will come back and tell you what he's been doing when he's ready.'

'Oh, come on, that's bullshit.'

She turns her head only slightly to look at him. 'Really, Lavrenti, you want me to agree with you that we should all be mad with your brother for going somewhere without explicitly telling everyone first?'

He doesn't say anything to that.

'I don't even know if I can double-lock the door or if he's going to be stuck outside in the corridor in the middle of the night,' I mutter.

Giuseppe's looking down at his glass in his hands and almost jumps in surprise when Thony puts his hand on his wrist and asks him to take the dinner out of the oven. He looks at him like he'd forgotten he existed, then stands up and takes the empty glasses with him off the table.

'You don't know what it's like,' Casper says, still not looking directly at Mum. 'Having V as your brother. It's hard.'

'I have a brother,' Freya says, having appeared suddenly behind Casper, rubbing his head as if he too is the safe dog. 'His name is Tang Vladisavljevic and he's very cool and friendly, but Dad gets scared when he drives the car.'

'You shouldn't touch people's heads, mate. It's tapu.' He

sighs and looks around at her. 'Did you wash your hands after you played with the dog?'

'Yes, and now I've dried them too.' Freya laughs loudly. I wish I could be more like her. I wish I had the audacity to laugh publicly at my own terrible jokes. V would have loved to see Freya using Casper's hair to dry her hands. I'm starting to think about him as if he's dead. I know he'll come back. I just wish he wouldn't leave me out so much.

I go back inside the house and stand in the half-light of the living room. Giuseppe is speaking in a fast whisper on the phone in the kitchen. The living room doesn't have full walls, so you can't really hide from anyone in here. He's speaking Catalan, which is not a language I can understand. He repeats the same phrases again and again, something about germà and un any. 'Un any, un any, sóc el teu *germà*,' he says.

My dad comes through the front door with damp hair, wearing a light tan trench coat over a dark jumper, and pants the colour of the coat. He looks at me and hugs me.

'Greta, what's wrong?'

I don't know what particularly is wrong, everything's wrong, so I just stand and snivel into his coat, like when I was very young and Annie Zhang said I couldn't come and play Zoo Tycoon on her sister's computer anymore because everyone was calling us lesbians and she didn't want to be one, no offence. 'Neither do I,' I'd said, clinging to a distant memory where a boy had said, 'Cool cape,' to me on a book character dress-up day and I had liked it. I was one of the brothers from *The Singing Bone*. When I got to school it turned out that no one else knew *The Singing Bone*. V went as Rasputin, who he didn't realise wasn't a fictional character. He didn't care; he just went to the library and got a biography of Rasputin to show to anyone who disputed his choice. He's good like that. He doesn't care what everyone thinks all the time, like I do.

G

'I just feel like V doesn't care about me,' I say, and I feel so stupid and melodramatic for letting the words come out of me. 'And I just feel like he was the one who wanted the expensive internet plan because he was mad at the guy on the phone for assuming that he wasn't a big gamer, so I don't think I should have to pay for it.'

'He's been gone for a month, I don't think you should worry about taking him off the broadband contract yet,' my dad says into my hair. 'Have you been worrying about money again? I wish you didn't have this New Zealand attitude of being too proud to ask for help; I know how little you get paid.'

'I don't know. I read too many articles in the *Herald* about how I shouldn't squander my elderly parents' retirement savings.'

He looks down at me and holds me by my elbows. 'Has V not given you any indication of his plans at all?'

'No, he hasn't replied to me even once.'

'He's fine. He's in Medellín in Colombia. With Xabi. I saw in the app. His phone is off a lot, but he usually seems to charge it when it's after midnight there. I messaged him asking if he was on a Pablo Escobar tour and he replied saying no. That was it.'

'How do you know he's with Xabi?'

'Ah, because V once added him to my contacts to show me how the app worked. Xabi's had a very busy year; he's been to Medellín a few times actually, he went to Brazil, he met with Giuseppe in Shanghai in February and they went to a Pizza Hut on Nanjing Road. I thought that was an unusual choice for that area.' He looks at me like it's all fine and normal that he knows where these people are all the time.

'Why do you know where Giuseppe is too?'

'Because Thony wanted to know how the app worked and got me to add him. Thony doesn't use it though, he thinks it's creepy. I think it's okay though, I only really use it to see how far away your mother is when I'm making dinner. It's useful when your son may have been kidnapped by drug lords, but it turns out he's just palling around with his ex at a planetarium. I saw you waiting for a long time at a bus stop in Wellington once, and I was very close to messaging you to ask if you needed me to call you a taxi.'

'Dad. You don't need to worry about me.'

'I mean, I heard on the radio the situation was bad, but I didn't realise people were waiting for buses for hours on end.'

Giuseppe comes into the living room, twisting his watch around his wrist and looking like he wasn't expecting to see us huddled together in the dark like this.

'Oh, Linsh, welcome,' he says. His tone is wrong. He sounds like he's a receptionist at a hotel and he was just about to go on a break and now we've shown up.

'Has something happened?' my dad asks.

'No, no. Just some work stuff.' Giuseppe puts his hands in his pockets. 'Can I offer you anything? Merlot?'

My dad nods and puts his arm around me and I know he doesn't believe him.

After a decadent meal of coq au vin and after having to switch to ginger ale before I expressed my opinions too much, I'm sitting on the closed lid of the toilet, my feet on the edge of the bath, looking at my phone. I needed to have a break from everyone around me and catch up on international trends. I've made a conscious choice to hide in this particular bathroom, because there's another one closer to the action and I figure everyone will go there and leave me well alone.

The bath in here is beautiful – white with gold taps and little green tiles the colour of an alligator in a picture book. I think it reminds me of the bathroom where Zooey analyses himself in the mirror, in *Franny and Zooey*, and then I think maybe I'm just thinking of the colours of the book cover and transposing them over the scene in my mind's eye. I think this set-up would make for quite a nice photo of me, if someone wanted to publish an article about how I'm a young woman with her finger on the pulse.

We didn't talk any more about V or Xabi over dinner. I got the impression that everyone felt it was too controversial to talk about at a birthday event. Freya gave a fairly convincing presentation about why it's her dream to go on holiday to the Gold Coast. I don't know what my dream is. To feel like I really belong somewhere. To have some semblance of success. To be respected by my family and peers. To go on holiday to Bucharest and Athens. I can hear someone loading the dishwasher in the adjoining kitchen. A second person comes walking across the polished wooden floor, clack-clack-clack.

'Hey, you aren't allowed to help,' says a voice, Giuseppe, in his soft amalgamation of accents.

'I can't leave you to clean up by yourself,' says my mother. She clacks along in her Swedish Hasbeens, and the sound of plates being rinsed and transferred continues. 'Are you okay, what happened before?'

The tap is turned off. 'I'm fine. I just . . . I just don't know why with Xabier, I don't know why everything in his life has to be such a big statement. And maybe it wouldn't be like that if he let me in on things a bit earlier. You know, how long has this been going on for? Oh, I'm going to art school in New Zealand. Oh, I'm going back to Spain to paint a thousand kilometres of murals between Costa Brava and Costa del Sol. Oh, you know how I told you I wasn't gay? Well, I am now and I'm moving in with my boyfriend who's twenty-eight years old. Oh, now I'm worried that I'm bad for his mental health so I've bought an abandoned ranch in Argentina.'

'Gep.'

'And now this? This massive thing he just didn't tell me about for a year? Now he's saying he might have to move back to Barcelona, he doesn't know what's best, he doesn't know about visas. I don't want him to be all the way over in Spain, it's literally the furthest you can be from here. What if something happens? Then what?' Giuseppe sounds like he's scrubbing something, possibly a pot with a coconut fibre cloth. 'I want him to be happy, I want him to have a fulfilling life, but I don't know why he has to hold things back from me for so long that by the time I find out everything's already happened, it's too late. Am I being too righteous?'

'No. He knows that it's important to you to feel that you have some connection to what's happening with him. And he's so self-conscious, you know that he's considering what to tell you all the time, and then decided that nothing at all is appropriate.'

'You were too harsh on Greta,' he says, and I feel my heart thud in my chest at the mention of my name. I wish I could say my cheeks flushed but my skin is an unusual shade of pale yellow and it either stays like that or goes brown in the sun like banana cake. I'm panicked. I didn't expect myself to exist in the world of this private conversation I shouldn't be listening to.

'I know,' my mum says. 'I've spent every day of my life worrying about V for the last thirty years. Every time he calls me, I'm afraid something's wrong with his heart, or he's had a panic attack and quit his job, or he's stopped talking again. Not hearing from him the last few weeks and knowing that he's fine on his own, or at least that Xabi's looking after him, it feels like such a relief to not have to carry that fear around with me.'

'I know.'

'I'll tell him, when he comes back, to remember to give his little sister a basic idea of which foreign country he's disappeared off to. He must be a conspicuous absence in that small apartment. And she loves him so much; I don't think he has any idea how much other people care about him.'

'You don't think he'll move to Barcelona with Xabi?'

'No.'

He laughs. 'You're not even going to consider it a possibility?'

'Neither of them is moving to Spain.'

He closes the dishwasher and turns it on. 'Did you have a good birthday?'

'Yes, I had a lovely birthday,' she says. 'I didn't know that Linsh was going to take the whole day off work. You know that I would prefer to be on an island nearly all of the time. And I didn't think you were going to make me coq au vin again. You didn't have to.'

'Oh, so you do remember.'

'Of course I remember.'

'Well, I wanted to. To make up for the first time.'

'You didn't have to do it then either, it wasn't your fault that the ferry tickets blew away and that aggressive vendor pretended he didn't remember selling you them. Even though he saw it all happen.'

'I know he was being an asshole because he thought I was Roman.'

'Gep. Stop it – who cares what the Sicilian ferry ticket salesman thought of you, he probably isn't even alive anymore.'

'The whole day was a mess. Xabier's hacking cough, him refusing to leave the apartment or let me open the curtains, my dad with the car phone, calling the house and telling us about the driving conditions, that guy on the beach who kept asking if you liked Italo-disco clubs even though I was right there, and then I, you know, I cooked you a burnt coq au vin in that tiny holiday apartment kitchen using my keys as a knife—'

'I liked that day. I was happy.'

'Are you happy now?' he asks. I don't know how he's looking at her, how far apart they're standing. I think I'm going to throw my heart up into the beautiful bath and all I can think to do is flush the toilet and press my face against the cold white porcelain of the cistern, so I don't have to hear the answer to that.

Usagi

V

Xabi's tired at lunch. He has ordered the worst drink on the menu, a bottle of Fuze Iced Tea in the flavour 'herbal'. I'm drinking something called Premio, in the flavour 'rojo'. Ernesto thought that was funny, I don't know why. He kept shaking his head when I ordered it. An adult man can have a bright red drink, I think. Ernesto thinks everything I do is funny. He gave us a tour of the school and I hit my head on a doorframe. I'm glad he has an appreciation for physical comedy, because it really hurt.

'Are you okay?' I ask Xabi with my hand on his arm. He is gazing at the mustard bottle on the table.

'What?' He blinks a few times and looks at me like he doesn't know where we are.

'Did you not go back to sleep after Gep called you?'

He shakes his head and eats a chip from its paper cup. I don't know what happened in this conversation that happened at 1:30 this morning, but it didn't seem good. Afterwards, he whispered that he didn't want me to go and then he said he was selfish. I don't like seeing him sad. It's strange. He's so good at pretending not to be. I have to go home tomorrow morning. I have to go back to my own life.

'He's just mad with me because I didn't tell him about any of this,' he says.

I watch Ernesto as he tries to fold his burger wrapper into an origami shape.

'Why didn't you?'

'I thought he might tell me it was a bad idea. I was a dick to him when he told me he was about to become a parent.'

'Those were different circumstances. And it was 1990, I'm sure that tensions were high because of the landslide victory of Jim Bolger's National Party in the New Zealand general election.'

'I don't think my brother was trying to comfort Geneviève because she was upset about economic reform.'

'Yeah, she's not that political. She told Greta she could have her vote at the last election if she stopped complaining about complacent centrism for five minutes.'

He looks at the time on his phone. 'Shit, I have to go and pick up those documents before the office closes. Nes, are you okay to stay with Val or do you want to come with me?'

Ernesto has been enjoying learning English and wants us to speak it to him, despite Xabi's concerns about the international school ruining his mind with their hifalutin approach to education. But because he doesn't talk it's hard to tell if he can understand. He narrows his eyes.

'Voy a un . . . departamento de gobierno,' Xabi says to him.

Ernesto shakes his head firmly.

'¿Seguro?'

Ernesto nods and goes back to his folding. I think it's supposed to be a boat. Or a frog.

'Are you sure it's okay?' Xabi asks me.

'Of course, we'll be fine. We'll use Google Translate if we have to.'

'No, you won't, your phone never has any battery.' He stands up and lingers at the side of the table for a second, then pats us both on the shoulder on his way out.

'Nes, vamos a las tiendas,' I say. 'Necesito un . . . telefono charger.'

He folds his boat frog into a neat square and puts it on the

tray, chuckling at me like a little old man. I wait for him to zip
up his jacket. You can buy phone chargers pretty much anywhere these days, so I don't think it will take long to find a shop
that sells them. We walk side by side and I try to remember
what it was like to go without talking. When I was his age,
every day I felt like I was a balloon filling up with more and
more things I wanted to say, but I couldn't expel my comments
until I got home, when I would make sure the door was locked.
Then I couldn't stop. I would stand in the kitchen talking as
other people went in and out passively hmm-ing and ahh-ing.
Like a soapboxer. I don't know if he feels like that. Xabi says
that Ernesto can talk; he just doesn't. He'll say 'Sí' or 'No' if he
has to, to the social worker or a doctor. I suppose he doesn't
have a home where he feels safe, like I did.

'Tell me if you see a shop that has chargers,' I say, pointing at
the windows of the shops we pass by, as clearly as I can. He
nods.

This is the first time we've been alone together, and I hope he
isn't nervous to be with me. It's been a funny two weeks since
we met. I had some assumptions about what a child who had
been living without parents would be like. A troublemaker, I
thought. Maybe violent, even. He would have abandonment
issues. He would want us to take him to a football game. He'd
wet the bed, things like that. I shouldn't have thought those
things; the agency made an effort to match Xabi with someone
he would be suited to. And people have all sorts of different
reactions to their circumstances.

'Nes, did you know I didn't used to talk either?' He stops
walking and shakes his head.

'Yeah. I was mute. Estaba mudo. Until I was an adult. I only
talked to my family and people I knew very well, and only in
my house usually, somewhere I felt safe.'

He's frowning and he does a *why* sort of gesture. 'Because I had problems with my health. Mi salud, um . . .' I look around and then pull the neck of my T-shirt down to show him the top of my scar. 'I was very sick all the time, when I was a child. I felt like I was a problem. For my parents, for my brother. I thought that if I stayed quiet, everything bad would . . . go away. If I didn't talk to people, they wouldn't think I was sick, and I wouldn't have to go to the hospital anymore. It took me a really long time to change that.'

I don't know how much of that he understands, but he nods slowly and puts his hands in his jacket pockets.

'I thought I should tell you that, before I go—' I hesitate to say 'home', to bring up the idea of my home being somewhere away from here. 'Before I go back to New Zealand.'

He nods again and smiles a very small smile at me before we keep walking. I hope he feels better having heard that, and not worse. He's been in a particularly solemn mood today. The other day at the Planetario, Xabi said he was the happiest he'd ever seen him. I love going to observatories and space museums with people who are interested in listening to what I have to say about my former areas of research, especially my favourite planet Neptune, and Ernesto is very interested in how things work. Xabi has no idea about space. He thinks that it's too big to worry about and it induces a sense of existential dread in him that he says he doesn't have the capacity for. So I found someone who worked there to translate for me instead, a physics student from the university. We had a great chat. Afterwards I bought some chips from a vending machine that I didn't realise were mandarin flavoured and Ernesto nearly died laughing at me attempting to subtly spit them out into a bush. He was walking around with a huge pointy grin for hours. I felt disappointed when we had to deposit him back at his school at the end of the day.

Ernesto points out a shop that looks a bit like a Flying Tiger.

Not as Scandinavian, but with the same colourful plastic-type things. We go inside and there are phone chargers hanging in plastic packaging on a rack against the wall. I wonder if I should get purple, green or a lurid sky blue. I have a sudden sharp memory of people at school saying that purple was the national gay colour, and how I would stringently avoid anything in any shade between lavender and mauve. I take the purple one off the shelf. Then I hear a voice behind me.

'Can I have?'

I turn around and Ernesto has his hand on something in a display container. I can't see what it is, but the sign says 6,000 pesos, about $2. I nod. I put my charger on the counter and Ernesto flashes whatever he has to the girl at the counter and then closes his hand around it again. I pay and say, 'Keep the change,' because I'm leaving anyway and won't need this cash anymore.

'What did you get?' I ask outside the shop, but he shrugs and doesn't show me.

Xabi comes to meet us while we're enjoying some Frappuccinos in a Starbucks, where I'm charging my phone. I would never get something like this at home, because someone might see me, but I don't know anyone here and Xabi's seen me in much more compromising positions. He comes in holding a document folder and has an expression I can't read.

'Val, it's done,' he says.

'What do you mean?'

'I got the papers, it's official.'

I stand up and hug him tightly, something I haven't done in public since we've seen each other again, and almost find it hard to let go.

He sits at the table and takes the documents out of the folder to show Ernesto, speaking very quickly and seriously in Spanish, as Ernesto nods along and runs his fingers over each new page. He'll remember this forever, I think, seeing the pieces of paper that mark the official start of this new part of his life, and I wonder how long the memory will include me. I'm not sure what to say when we leave him at the school gate and I know I'm not coming back, and I'm surprised when he hugs me and whispers very quietly in my ear, 'Goodbye.'

Matau

G

I've left my fucking phone at the party. I message my dad from my laptop, and he proposes the great idea that Giuseppe can bring it into town and I can pick it up from his office. I imagine myself going to some tower building downtown, heading up to the twenty-fourth floor in a fancy wood-panelled elevator, telling the receptionist I'm here to see Mr Alonso, looking at the great view from his desk where he probably just approves international business decisions and texts my mum about how beguiling she is and how best to rid themselves of their pesky Russian husbands. No, I don't want to do that. I ask him to check if Thony's home, and he is, so I take the train to Remuera.

It's bad having to walk from the train station to the house without my phone, because it means I have to engage with my surroundings. Three girls from the private school nearby are talking loudly and laughing on the other side of the street as we all walk past the enormous houses. They think their English teacher is a bitch, that Jeremiah was acting real shady at the food court, and Daisy's only doing School Strike for Climate because she wants to be prefect. I don't know if this is the same Daisy who hates Tang or if that's what they're all called these days.

I run my hand along the azaleas lining the driveway as I walk past, then go up the steps and ring the doorbell. I'm surprised when it's not Thony who opens the door but Geneviève.

'Welcome to my home,' she says, bowing slightly.

'What are you doing here?' I ask.

'Anthon and I are full-time creatives; we spend most of our days sunning ourselves and complaining about up-and-coming young prodigies.'

'I think that's just because you're rich old people.'

Thony is sitting out on the deck wearing shorts, sunglasses and a loose linen shirt, holding a fan. I think it's about 19 degrees. Geneviève sits down and stretches out, undoing a few buttons on her denim shirt.

'Is this what you really do every day?' I ask.

'No, some days it rains,' Thony says, making the slightest effort to turn his face towards me. 'Greta, it's nice to see you again so soon. I put a glass for you there.'

I sit down at the table and fill up my pre-organised glass with whatever's in the jug next to it. It could be Pimm's, but there's a slight chance that it's something more appropriate to drink at 11:30am on a weekday. I sip it and it isn't.

'I need to get myself a deck like this,' Geneviève says with her eyes closed.

'I'll give you my guy's number if you do me up another one like that painting I liked that you sold to someone else,' Thony says, fanning himself. 'I really think we could use more art in the house, to brighten it up, but Giuseppe is so reluctant to hang paintings here. It's like he doesn't want to commit to the house, even though we've been here ten years already. I put up that one there while he was away.'

'I painted the painting you're talking about when I was a young woman who cared about attention to detail. I could never recreate it,' Geneviève says. 'If I did, I would want something more than some guy's phone number in exchange for it.'

'You should wait until after you see the guy, you'll change your mind.'

'I don't care for men these days, I'm . . . Greta, is there a special name for when you used to love nothing more than meeting a man at a bar or a party and spending five minutes seducing him and then leaving your phone off the hook for the next few days so he couldn't call you again, but now you would rather drink in the daytime with your son's stepfather?'

'I think that's still just being straight,' I say. 'Did you hear from Cosmo in the end?'

'The thing with Cosmo is, you hear from him when you hear from him. That's enough for me. He calls me, I have no idea where he is, there's the sounds of motorbikes in the background or whatever, and I say, "Just tell me you're healthy and that's fine."'

'I don't know why Giuseppe can't be like that,' Thony says. 'He takes a very hectic approach when Cosmo calls. He acts like he's speaking to a hostage negotiator. Pacing around, running his hand through his hair, making demands.'

'It's because he loves projecting, he loves channelling all his energy into worrying about someone else's problems. It's so he doesn't have to think about himself. Reflect on his own many, many issues.' Geneviève takes a tube of sunblock off the table and rubs some over the exposed part of her chest.

'Wait, Gen, did Cosmo not go back to Paris? That was, like, six months ago that you said he'd gone away somewhere. Do you still not know where he is?' I think this is actually quite concerning, but I try not to show it in my voice.

'No, he didn't go back. He has a new life somewhere, I think. I don't ask.'

'Giuseppe's less worried about Cosmo at the moment,' Thony says, turning to Geneviève. 'He's fighting with Xabi instead. He's very upset about it.'

'Really? What happened?' she asks.

He shrugs. 'I don't really know.'

'Gep didn't tell you?'

He waves her away. 'Since when does he ever tell anyone how he really feels?'

Geneviève makes a disapproving noise, and my heart aches a little bit. 'He's a fool.'

'A very beautiful fool,' Thony concedes. 'Greta, I'll get your phone for you. You probably have a very busy day with many beautiful fools to see and I'm sure they'll be disappointed if I hold you up.'

He gets up to go inside and squeezes my shoulder as he passes me. I decide to follow him into the house, and we go into the kitchen and he puts his sunglasses up on his head and starts opening drawers. I look at the white granite benchtop and feel like I'm at the scene of a crime. I've been trying my hardest not to think about what I overheard being said here last night, and put it all down to a misunderstanding. Maybe I misconstrued the vibe, the words I heard, the context. My brain has to put in a lot of effort to believe this reinterpretation of events, but I think I can make it happen.

'I know I put it in this drawer so that it wouldn't get lost,' he says, rifling through cardboard boxes of tinfoil and spools of ribbon. 'Huh.' He takes his own phone out of his pocket and starts calling someone, leaning with one hand on the benchtop. 'Giuseppe, I . . . How am I? I'm fine, I'm just having a meeting with Geneviève. Mm. Do you know where Greta's phone is? It's not in the drawer where I left—Oh. Well, that was very thoughtful of you, but completely ineffective because she came over here to pick it up. Okay. Okay. Yes, I'll do that now. Bye, love you, bye.' He ends the call, but he keeps looking at his phone, doing something on it. 'Greta, unfortunately Giuseppe took your phone into the city because he thought he could drop it off to you at lunchtime. He didn't tell me that. But it's okay because I've ordered you an Uber.'

'What?'

'So you can go and meet him and get your phone back. You must have so many messages by now, I'm sure you're desperate to . . . post a status, or something. *Having coffee with my friends. So sick of exams.* Oh look, he's almost here now.' He hugs me and kisses me on the cheek. 'Geneviève, Greta's going now!'

'Goodbye!' she shouts and waves her hand limply in our direction as Thony hustles me out the door. I walk back down the driveway, unsure if I feel worse about being sent to go and see the man who I'm trying very hard to convince myself is not having an affair with my mother, or why Thony thinks my internet presence is that of a teenage Facebook user in 2009.

A man rolls down the window of his Nissan Pulsar. 'Yo, are you An-thone?'

'Uh, yeah, I guess so,' I say, getting into the passenger seat.

Giuseppe Alonso, the well-known beautiful fool, is apologetic. 'Greta, I'm so sorry,' he says, sweeping his hair back from his face and looking genuinely sorry, which doesn't seem necessary. 'I left for work before Anthon was awake and it seemed perfectly logical at the time to bring your phone into the city, since you live and work here.'

When he says it like that it does seem perfectly logical. 'It's okay, I'm the one who left my phone at your house. I didn't have much on today anyway.'

'Please, let me buy you lunch to make up for the inconvenience.'

'Oh.' He's smiling with his palms facing towards me, like an illustration of someone who isn't being deceitful. I feel conflicted, but I also remember the three old pieces of sushi in my fridge waiting for me and I feel actively repelled by the idea of going home to them. 'Okay, sure.'

'Is the food court okay?' he asks, gesturing to the mall behind him.

'Yes,' I say, quietly relieved that we aren't going wherever fancy businesspeople go for lunch. I'm not sure where that would be in town. All my ideas about what it's like to be a high-flying operator in the world of business come from the film *American Psycho*.

We ascend to the second floor by way of several escalators. I pretend I don't love malls when I'm with liberal elite types, which I often am because of the university, but I do. I like the busy people rushing from shop to shop to find one particular thing that they can't order online because they need it right now. I like the tourists with all their shopping bags, and the comings and goings of hundreds of different people as they grab some food and then leave again. There aren't any rules about who's allowed in here and you won't get kicked out unless you're trying to skateboard down the steps or film a viral prank video.

'What do you think you want to get?' he asks.

'Hmm, I'm not sure,' I say, but I know and am embarrassed to ask. 'What are you going to get?'

'Please don't judge me for being a stereotype, but I want to get an empanada. I've been thinking about them all day. And something else as well. I haven't eaten since last night.'

I haven't eaten since last night either. 'What do you think about Korean?'

'Sounds good,' he says, opening his wallet and handing me a black credit card. I feel like the bank might come and arrest me for even touching this. I hold it like my hands might melt it. 'Could you order something for me?' he says. 'I'll go and get my empanada.'

I go and order a beef bulgogi, kimchi fries and some fried chicken as well. I look around at Giuseppe chatting away to the people selling empanadas and paella, and decide it's probably okay if I get a Coke. I feel extravagant. I tap the card and it accepts straight away.

'This looks so good, thank you,' he says when we're sitting at a long wooden table with benches in amongst everyone else with their different lunch companion configurations. I wonder if anyone else is eating with a man who might be cucking their dad. Probably not; probably they're just sitting with the least annoying person from their work. You never know, though.

'How is, um, your day going?' I ask.

'Oh.' He looks thoughtful as he takes some beef and slaw with his chopsticks. 'I haven't really slept. I'm sorry if I seemed a bit off last night, I, um . . . I always feel so stupid when I get upset about my brother not telling me things. I know he isn't obliged to. It just would be nice.'

I nod. 'I feel the same about my brother.'

'We should form a support group.'

'It must be hard. Um, Thony and Geneviève were just saying about how you still don't know what Cosmo's doing.' I open my can of Coke and it feels very cathartic.

'Xabier and Cosmo are my family, so I would prefer if I knew where one of them was, yeah.' He smiles sadly. 'I suppose you can't have everything. I haven't had a disagreement with Gen about parenting for a long time though, so that's a silver lining.'

'I can't even imagine.'

'What, co-parenting with Geneviève? Definitely one of the most unexpected things that's ever happened to me.'

'I kind of thought . . . that was a decision you made? Like, two friends helping each other out.' I pull some fries out from under some kimchi and dip them in the sour cream.

'Oh, God, no, Greta, we didn't even know each other.' He reaches for some fries as well. 'I came over to see Xabier because I was having a bad time working in Brazil, but when I got here . . . well, Xabi was annoyed because I didn't tell him I was coming. Thony and I had dated for a bit before, and now he was with someone else and . . . everyone else was with someone else. There was a party at your parents' house. Xabi thought I should stay home, but I didn't. No one really thought I should be there, except Geneviève, who spoke to me for about five minutes and then asked me if I wanted to leave. Which I really did, at that point. I wasn't expecting to hear from her again; she made it very clear it was a one-time thing. And then I did, and I decided that I had better stay here. Xabi thought I was deliberately trying to ruin the life he had made for himself here. So he moved back to Spain.'

'He moved to Spain because he was mad at you?'

He shrugs. 'We really get to each other.'

'Then you got back together with Thony?'

'Yeah, when he was sick. His other boyfriend couldn't handle how sick he was.'

'Oh.' I wonder if these questions are too intrusive, but he doesn't seem to mind. 'What's your job?'

'What's my job?' He smiles at me. He has a warm smile that makes me feel both welcome in his company and slightly sick. 'I own a refrigeration company. I started selling air conditioners when I was seventeen. Now it's mainly refrigerated shipping containers. It's not interesting at all, sorry.'

'I think shipping is interesting. Ell's brother is in the world of shipping. But what would you do if you weren't doing that?'

'No one's ever asked me that. Do you want half of this?' He gestures to the empanada. I nod and he cuts it in half and gives it to me. 'I used to have a fantasy about being a middle manager. Just having a really average life, two kids, married to a florist, going to the park in the weekends and really phoning it in at work.'

'What's your dream now, though?'

'Are you writing a profile on me for a magazine?'

'No.' I slump a little bit. Maybe I have gone too far. 'I would love to be employed by a magazine to write profiles, though; I would really phone that in.'

He shrugs. 'I can't say I want to retire to spend more time with my family, because they don't want to spend more time with me. I just want to be happy. Maybe see some things I haven't seen before.'

I don't know what to think. Hearing this I really want him to be happy too, but not if that means breaking up my family. But would that be for the greater good? Maybe I shouldn't be thinking about affairs of the heart in such a heavily utilitarian way. I feel even sicker, but not in my stomach; in my brain and in my chest.

'How is Ell?' he asks. 'Did she enjoy the fashion event last night?'

'I don't know, I don't have my phone.'

'Oh, I'm so sorry, I forgot.' He takes it out of his pocket and gives it to me. 'I noticed someone was messaging you a lot about covering their tutorial this afternoon.'

'Oh, don't worry about that.' I put my phone in my bag. 'Sorry I left it behind in the first place.'

He shakes his head. 'I lose my phone all the time. I left it behind at a fish market recently and when I got it back it smelled for days.'

'Did you get a good fish though?'

He takes the cap off the bottle of iced tea he bought. 'Yes, a great kahawai.'

I nod. 'That's my mum's favourite.'

Mint

V

I walk through a desolate Auckland Airport at 5am. It feels strange hearing people say our words again, talking about doing a massive hike in Siem Reap with a broken jandal, how cold it is compared to Raro, whether or not Gary booked the shuttle back down to Waihi. A begrudging Vodafone employee lets me use his tool to change my SIM back to my New Zealand one. By the baggage carousel, a girl in the airport-uniform black polo and trousers asks me if I'm all goods and I say yeah, because I think I am all goods. In a way. When the white-haired customs inspector sees that I've come from Colombia I have to go straight to have my bags checked. I look down at my shoes, which still have dust in the cracks of the soft leather. I felt far away in the desert, and now I feel the same, even though I'm supposed to be home now.

I can't be bothered with the SkyBus so in the arrivals hall I take my phone out to order a Zoomy. But then a hand reaches out and grabs me. Tang is leaning on the metal railing, wearing jeans that are way too tight for this time of the morning and a T-shirt that says 'Girls Rock'.

'What are you doing here?' I clutch him like I haven't seen him for 600 years. 'How did you know I was coming?'

'I saw you were at Santiago Airport and then I looked up the flight schedule and figured you were coming home. I didn't think anyone else would come and pick you up, because my dad's been complaining about you a lot.'

I hold him by the shoulders and look him up and down. 'Because I didn't keep in contact with anyone?'

'Yeah, he says you have no respect for Greta, and he's mad with your mum for not agreeing with him and he's mad with Papa Linsh for calling him a hothead.' Tang looks different. Last time I saw him he was all knees and elbows, and now he looks confident, like someone who's surprised that not everyone knows how to change a flat tyre.

'I could have kept them more informed about my whereabouts,' I say, and push my bag up my shoulder.

'I think it's all good. Dad needs to chill out. He gave me a really long pep talk about recovering from failure the day before my restricted test.' We walk past a huge hobbit statue and out the automatic doors into the cold dark of the too-early morning. Tang zips up his hoodie.

'You didn't fail, though,' I say, pointing to the car keys in his hand.

'No. I don't actually think I'm bad at driving. Waka Kotahi thinks I'm fine. Dad just needs to trust me and stop clinging on to the door. How was your trip?'

'Ah, yeah, no. Good.'

At the parking-ticket machine we wait behind a family with a trolley full of umu packs from Samoa. They'll be having a huge to'ona'i for lunch on Sunday. An older man pulls his polar fleece up over his chin. 'Malulu,' he complains as the woman he's with tries to get the machine to accept a twenty. I slap Tang's hand out of the way when he gets his card out. I don't even know how much money I have left at the moment, but hopefully more than he has. I need to do some invoicing. I think I only have a jar of jalapeños in the fridge. I need to do everything that makes up a functioning life. I need to put the pieces of a functioning life back together again.

I type my PIN on the cold metal buttons of the parking machine – 1939, the year *The Wizard of Oz* came out. When I told it to Xabi, he asked me if I had been supporting Franco in the Spanish Civil War. Then he went to the dairy near my old apartment to get me my heart's desires – a Bubble O'Bill and a bottle of lube. I lay around luxuriously in my Briscoes sale Egyptian cotton sheets, and I thought this was what it meant to be alive.

I'm following Tang through the car park, the ground damp, not thinking which car we're looking for. He stops and unlocks the door of an early-nineties white Corolla.

'Tang, did you buy a car?' I say, peering in the window. It's completely clean and empty, not even an old jumper or XLR cable on the back seat.

'Yeah,' he sighs. 'I know cars are bad, I had a moment of madness on Trade Me. I just really wanted to be able to go to the beach. I want to go to Opononi in the summer and be pulled away by the tide where the two harbours meet.'

'That doesn't sound like a particularly safety-conscious summer plan.'

I try to figure out how to move the seat back as far as it will go, and Tang accidentally turns the windscreen wipers on.

'It will be good to have a car if Plan comes over.'

'Who?'

'My boyfriend. Did you not read any of my messages?'

'Um,' I say, trying to think of an excuse. 'No.'

'That's okay,' he says brightly. 'I have a boyfriend now. His name is Plan, we met last year on my trip. We were just talking before I came to get you. He lives in Munich. He's at Ludwig-Maximilians-Universität, which is, like, so bougie. He thinks everyone's too uptight and he should have gone to Cologne. He keeps saying he's going to throw himself in the river in the Englischer Garten . . . I would say it was more of a creek. It's got these cool rapids, though, and people surf on them – like, right in the city.'

I've never heard someone speak so positively and openly about a relationship that must exist mostly on the internet. I don't think I understand young people.

'Do you have any plans to go there?'

'I could be keen. He wants to come here for a few weeks in the summer, if he can save the money. I have to remind him to be sensible. The first time we talked on the phone it was 4am his time and he was eating ten chocolate croissants he bought at the bakery in the train station because he was sad.' Tang stops the car to feed the ticket into the machine and we drive out onto the empty road.

'What does he study?'

'Politics. He's very passionate about the European Union and very anti-Serbia. Before I told him I still had feelings for him, he said he was planning to go to Serbia and seduce a bunch of guys and then spray-paint the Montenegrin flag on their walls while they slept and then jump out the window.'

'What did you think about that?'

'I thought it would be quite complicated artistically. The flag has a Byzantine two-headed eagle holding a sceptre and a shield with a lion on it.'

I look out the window at all the things I haven't seen for a month. The sky starting to lighten, the Z station, Carl's Jr., Countdown, The Warehouse.

'Would you be worried about committing to going over there when there's a chance it won't work out?'

'No, you have to take a chance. What's the worst that could happen? It doesn't work out with Plan. I cry, I run out of money, I have to learn how to snowboard so I can be a snowboard instructor in Austria. I meet new people. I could always come home.'

We drive past the enormous blue Mainfreight building with its electronic inspirational message all lit up in the gloom: *LIVE EVERY MOMENT*.

'I didn't even know you were into guys.'

'Really? But you always take me to French films and then we both cry at the end and pretend we aren't.'

Xabi cried at the airport. I wasn't expecting that. I hadn't really seen him cry before, except a little bit when we watched a documentary about hard-done-by Australian boys turning their lives around and training dogs. I didn't want to let go of him, not knowing when we would see each other again. I felt so empty on the flight by myself, sitting in Santiago Airport for six hours by myself, watching the LATAM air-safety video for the sixth time in three weeks by myself. Not getting very far through the only English language book Xabi could find me at the airport bookshop, Michelle Obama's autobiography, *Becoming*.

'I just thought you had good taste. I didn't assume you wanted to feel the rough touch of a man.'

'Plan doesn't have much of a rough touch.'

I look through all the messages Tang sent me that I never opened, and I feel ashamed.

'God, Tang, I'm so sorry. I should have looked at these sooner; I didn't know you were trying to reach out to me about something so serious.'

'Oh, it's okay. Don't worry about it,' he says, frowning and shaking his head.

'No, it's not okay. I have to . . . remember that I have a responsibility to people. I can't be unreliable because I have other things going on.'

'I came to your apartment late at night one Saturday because I forgot you weren't there. Greta helped me, though. Greta and Ell helped me tell Dad . . . about the mental health stuff.'

'Is he being okay about it?'

'Yeah, Greta talked it through with him and said he shouldn't blame himself or make a big deal of worrying about it because it would make things worse for me. He took it on board. For once. I think that's why he was being so weird about my driving test. No one told him he wasn't allowed to be super overbearing about it.'

'He just wants to look after you.' I turn my body to look at him when we're stopped at a light. 'I want you to know that you can talk to me about anything. Any time. I won't judge you.'

He nods slowly. 'Anything?'

'Yeah, anything.'

'Is eating ass a real thing or is it something that people just say because it's funny? Is that something you do all the time?'

'Oh.' I close my eyes for a second, wondering why the fuck I said I was happy to speak on any topic directly after thirty-one hours of travel. 'It's a real thing but it's not . . . my fave. Too damp.'

He nods seriously. 'Cool. I'll let you know if I think of anything else.'

I don't want Tang to get stuck in the roadworks for the City Rail Link so he lets me out at Princes Street and I walk down to my building through the park where people are walking their dogs. I go past the café that always smells like sulphur and the florist; I want to buy flowers for Greta but it isn't open yet. I want to buy Greta fresh bread and pastries and when she wakes up, I'll tell her everything, about work and Xabi and Colombia and Ernesto, how pretty the desert is, how sorry I am I didn't tell her sooner. Maybe about Dad and Thony and the sham New Year's concert tour as well. But there's no bakery in the city, just a Starbucks and seven Subways, and when I open the door of the apartment there's no one there at all.

After I attempt to revive myself with a container of Vicks, a body scrub claiming to be made of caffeine and a bathroom so full of steam I feel censored from myself, I go and buy the flowers and the things that Greta likes but she thinks are too extravagant. Feta, orange juice, spinach, limes. Then I walk around the empty apartment like a dog that's been left at home by itself, hoping she might come back and forgive me and react appropriately to all my drama. She doesn't, though, so I call my mum, who's packing in a show at Q Theatre but agrees to meet me for lunch.

I walk over and pick her up and let all the older women from the show tell me how tall I am and how they've heard so much about me, an international man of mystery. One of them asks me about tertiary funding for Māori kids and I have to say, sorry, that's my brother who does all of that; I haven't been doing anything for the kids. When we walk up Mayoral Drive, my mum says that talking about being gay on TV without giving straight people makeovers is doing something for the kids too. I never thought about that before. I never thought that my mum thought I was a good person.

'Of course I think you're a good person,' she says when we sit down at a booth inside the Fed. 'You have a strong moral backbone. You stand up when you think something's unfair, you're not one of those gay men who says awful things about women. You take Tang out all the time, you don't have to do that. You let your sister pay rent proportionate to her income. What more could I want?'

'I could stop calling you and moaning all the time,' I say, taking my coat off.

'You didn't call me and moan for a whole month. I was beginning to miss it.'

A waitress in the mint-green short diner dress comes and takes our order. We get poutine and pastrami which I think is the only thing I can deal with. I pour water into our red plastic tumblers.

'I'm trying to be more responsible. I'm realising that just as many people rely on me as I rely on them.'

'What's brought this on, V?' she asks.

'Did Giuseppe tell you?'

'He was upset with Xabi because he doesn't want him to move back to Spain, but I don't know why he would. I assume you do.'

'Oh. Mum, Xabi adopted an eight-year-old boy. From Colombia. But he was actually born in Ecuador, it turns out. Xabi can't stay in Colombia because he doesn't have a visa. He doesn't want to go back to Argentina permanently. He could get Ernesto a Spanish passport and take him back to Europe, but that isn't what we really want to do.'

'We?'

I look at my mum, so much smaller than me, so much smaller in real life than in my memory. She was thirty-seven when Casper made her a grandmother. I wish that just once I could tell her something that was purely good news. Why is every circumstance I get myself into extenuating?

'Maybe we. That's what I want. I know that Xabi wants to be with me, but he's very wary of pushing me into anything. I don't know how to make it work. I don't want to move to Spain, not at this point in my career. I know it's not ideal timing, but I think sometimes things happen and you just have to go with them.'

Her turquoise pendant earrings sway slightly as she nods along with what I'm saying.

'I'm lucky that I have options,' I say. 'It's just figuring out what they are, and kind of . . . trusting myself that I can do it.'

'That is complicated,' she says.

'How did you feel when you found out you were going to

have Casper? Did you know that you could do it, that you'd be fine?'

'Oh, no,' she says, straightening the salt and pepper shakers. 'I was very ashamed.'

'What? Why?' I ask, embarrassed that I've asked something that would make her say that.

'Because. I thought I was an exception. Everyone knew me as Beatrice, Rangi's daughter with the fancy white name who thought she was too good for gutting fish or farm work, the girl who left the island to go to the flash university in the big smoke. And not to come back and help everyone, just because I wanted to learn. Then I was pregnant before I even turned twenty-one. Just like what was expected of me. I was ashamed that I'd thought that I could be something different. I don't even know how it happened; I had just come back from a trip and I was all . . . out of sorts.'

'What made you go through with it? If that's okay to ask.'

'I was scared of both options. I knew it was hard to get an abortion – I didn't want to have to convince two doctors that I would be an unfit mother. If I did that, I would believe it myself. Your dad said that whether we had the baby or not he would do anything to make sure we had a good life, and he looked so sincere when he said it that I believed him. I don't know if I'd ever trusted anyone before that. It was different, for Linsh. Where he was from, it was normal for people to get married and start having kids at that age. It didn't make you a statistic. He didn't have the fear that I had that someone would take my baby away because of my race. I'd never told him that I felt like that. Then, you know, he got a big grant and invested it and bought the house. He got up for Casper every night and did everything so I could finish my degree. But I was still jealous of the people I'd met at uni, how they were always going out and going overseas and things. Feeling jealous made me feel like I was a bad mother. Then you were really sick, and I felt like it was my fault, that I couldn't keep you alive—'

The waitress puts down the food in front of us and we have a short, pleasant and untimely conversation about it. Then I turn to my mum again.

'Mum, nothing that happened with me was your fault—'

'I don't feel like that now. But it was hard. And it was hard to watch your brother go through similar things with Tang. I saw myself in him, the constant worry that he wasn't doing a good job, and the added guilt that he didn't know his own son, even though it wasn't his fault that he hadn't been allowed to see him before. I'm glad you have more choices than that.' She takes a fork and spears a piece of pastrami. 'Then I couldn't prove to my dad that I had made anything of myself, because he was dead by then. Valdin, I don't want you to feel guilty because you think you get to live a more privileged life than I ever did. You've been through enough for one person. I'm lucky that you're alive.'

I nod, not really able to say anything. I pick up a chip, separating the stretched cheese curds with my fork.

'How mad is Greta with me?' I ask.

She finishes her water. 'She's not angry. She's just sad that you left her out of your life. To her it's as if you've compiled a list of who's most important to you and she's so far down that you don't even tell her which continent you're on. And it didn't help that Casper put the idea in her head that you don't respect her. I thought he was being wholly hypocritical. Greta will get over it though, the same as when you went to robotics camp the whole school holidays and didn't take her to see *Casino Royale*.'

I pour her another glass. 'I only went because a hot boy in my class said he was going. I had no interest in robotics.'

'I know. Greta only wanted to see the film because she

thought the lead actress was hot. She had and continues to have no interest in the exploits of James Bond.'

I wonder how many other things we've both failed at trying to hide from our mother in our lives.

'Do you think I'd be a good dad?' I ask.

She nods, and says, 'Yes.'

Gaze

G

It's not a great day at the university, or in Greta's life in general, I think, pouring myself another plastic cup of mysterious punch from a big bowl in the staff common room. Us low-ranked staff members have been allowed in because there's going to be a panel talk, all invited. None of my students had done the readings today, not even the nerdy one with the posh English accent who went to an international school in Singapore. The discussion was bad because everyone was basing their thoughts on my summaries only, and I didn't know what I was talking about either. I don't give a shit about *The Merry Wives of Windsor*. There are rumours of another department restructuring and I don't think they will be choosing me of all people to stay on for summer school. The only new job listed today on Student Job Search was selling fireworks, but you needed your own 'turf'. I pour the punch a little too exuberantly and it spills on the bench.

'Whoa, calm down,' a guy I don't know in shiny brogues and a paisley shirt says, taking an orange slice. I glare at him, drink half the punch and fill the cup again.

I go and stand by Rashmika, who for some reason is having a good time. She's laughing with a guy in an Oxford sweater and burgundy chinos and a girl in a long abstract print skirt and black suede jacket. They're talking about a show I haven't seen. I partially stand in the circle and look down at my clothes I put on yesterday afternoon. I went out after the lunch, because I didn't want to be alone. I slept on Rashmika's floor because I didn't want to be alone. I just want to see Ell, but I'm embarrassed by the state I'm in: very emotional, not very clean. I said she could come up and hear about diversity in nineteenth-century literature if she was finished with her plants, but she hasn't been receiving my messages; the little Messenger bubble is not filling in. I check my phone again but there's nothing.

'Rash, that guy just told me to calm down, can you believe it?' I say.

She shrugs. 'You kind of seem like you need to at the moment.'

The panel begins and we all sit down on cushioned red and orange metal chairs, the kind that exist in all universities and waiting areas across the country. There isn't enough room for me to sit with Rashmika and the fun television fans, so I have to sit in the back row by myself, which is fine because I'm self-conscious about people not being able to see over me anyway.

The panel is comprised of the kind of people you would expect to see at this sort of thing: people who can sit casually in a line knowing we're all looking at them. A confident man with glasses, about thirty, who when asked if he knows a particular book says that he hasn't got to it yet, as if he has a towering stack in his house of all the books that people talk about. A girl with a sharply cut wavy bob and a silk floral skirt, who speaks like someone from Radio New Zealand, upright consonants piercing her every word. An American lecturer in her forties with spiky red hair and a purple pashmina worn tightly around her neck. I didn't hear what any of these people's names were, but I assume they are things like Patrick Bushell, Emma Kennedy-Staines and Anna Rosenfeld. The moderator is a lecturer I had for an undergrad paper, where I got a B+ despite not going to the lectures or reading the books. They are all white, on this diversity panel. I feel a deep anger bubbling away inside me.

G

The door opens and Holly comes in, late but unapologetic, holding her lanyard so it doesn't jangle. And then she sits next to me. I have to cross my legs the other way so my foot doesn't touch her. I look as if I am suddenly very interested in how men described women in the 1860s, I'm fascinated, enraptured by the subject, I have absolutely no idea who is sitting next to me and how I feel about that. My feet are angled this way because it provides me with the ideal posture for absorbing this pertinent information, not because I'm sitting next to a woman known to have contracted foot fungi in the past.

I feel Holly looking at me. I think of the Barbara Kruger picture *Your gaze hits the side of my face*. She looks at me like we have a special bond. Please turn away, I think. I haven't talked to her since she tried to buy me a juice, but she's still been messaging me trying to get me to cover her tutorials. One time it was because she was skiing. I have never been skiing in my life. Although my parents are quite middle class these days, things like skiing never occur to you when you've grown up poor. My mum once said that skiing is the same as sliding down the Te Paki sand dunes on a real estate sign, except it's cold and wet and expensive. My dad used to say, 'Why pay for ice skating at Paradice when you can skate for free on a pond?' despite the nearest frozen pond to our house probably being in Japan. Maybe if they'd invested more time in ice activities, my mum wouldn't have turned to doing a flirty laugh for the pleasure of a Spanish businessman.

The panel goes on and on about craft as an art form, letter writing, and the stolen artefacts in the British Museum. No matter how hard I try to take in the discussion, I can only think about how I want Holly to be anywhere else except sitting next to me. How much are the people on this panel getting paid? How am I supposed to afford things like pashminas and silk skirts if I don't get any hours? I get zero dollars in student allowance. I just have to rely on the university valuing tutors, which I don't think it does, and on V's man money subsidising my rent. But who knows if he's coming back and if he's going to pay for anything ever again. Maybe he'll just send me a postcard saying, *Hi Gre, loving being so close to the equator, never coming back xo*. Not that he would even write *xo*, probably something like, *your brother in arms, Valdin V Vladis-avljevic*. Fuck him. Fuck capitalism. Fuck being told to calm down. Fuck Holly.

When the discussion ends, I clap along politely with every-one else, all the normal, pretty, clean people not wearing their clothes from last night and who didn't sleep on the floor. I grab my bag and climb over the people on my right so I don't have to ask Holly to move or acknowledge her in any way. I exit the room quickly, figuring I'll have to tell Rashmika that I had to rush off. I speed down the corridor, stopping only at the photo-copier because I remember I've left a book on top of it and everyone will know that it's mine because it's in Russian and I'm the only person still studying that.

'What's going on?' asks Holly, following me into the photo-copying room and closing the door.

'I'm getting my book,' I say, shoving the book in my bag and not looking at her.

'Are you upset about something?'

'No. I'm normal.'

She shakes her head and leans on the door. 'No, you aren't. I know you.'

Mate, you don't know the bloody first thing about me, I think, but I refrain from saying it because I don't want to sound like a farmer in a Sunday Theatre about property inheritance.

'Greta,' she says, in a tired voice as if she's been reasoning with me for hours and hasn't just followed me into the photo-copying room. 'I can't do this anymore.' I turn around and look at her for the first time. She's wearing a very typical Holly out-fit: reddish-brown trousers and a forest green overshirt with a navy T-shirt, her hair shaved at the sides and flicked over in the middle like a Swedish fisherman.

'You can't do what anymore?'

'Have you play with me like this. It's not good, for either of us.'

Every blood cell in my body surges towards my face and I feel like I might actually combust right now.

'What the fuck are you talking about?' I ask and I want to do a face that would demonstrate that I don't care about this conversation at all and have a very busy and full life, but I'm too furious.

'You, being all hot and cold with me, showing up at events you know I'm going to be at, saying you don't want to cover my tutorials anymore. It's too much. You need to tell me how you feel,' she says, like she's being patient with me. Like I'm the one who's deluded.

'Holly, I haven't been doing anything to you! I don't want to do your tutorials because you should do them yourself! I don't owe you anything, least of all an explanation of how I feel when you're the one who led me on, made me do all this shit for you all the time, then told me you had a girlfriend, and now you're mad that I don't want to help you out anymore!'

I'm angry at myself for how angry I am, and how much of a reaction I've given her, and the dumb tears rolling down my face. She calmly shakes her head and exhales slowly.

'Greta, if you want to be with me, just say.'

I'm so mad, I hit my elbow on the photocopier and pretend it didn't hurt.

'I do not want to be with you, I have a girlfriend, for fuck's sake.'

She scoffs. 'Come on.'

I'm incredulous. 'Come on? What the fuck is that supposed to mean?'

'Stop denying that we have something,' she says, folding her arms and standing in front of the door. 'Stop being avoidant.'

'We have nothing. We have zero things. I am not the pitiful person you've made me out to be. I have moved on with my life.' I reach around her and open the door, sliding out into the safety of the non-confrontational corridor. But she doesn't let me go, she follows me out of the room and grabs my wrist.

'Greta—'

'I don't want to be with you anymore!' I shout, embarrassingly tearfully as it echoes down the empty corridor. Except the corridor is not empty.

'What are you doing?' Ell asks, in her burgundy cord jacket with her bag over one shoulder, and a can of the expensive oven cleaner I wanted to try in her hand. Then I do a really dumb thing and wrench my arm out of Holly's grip and run the opposite way down the corridor.

I run down the stairwell, out the automatic doors, through the underpass, past the plaque dedicated to the Ghost of Vaile, past the Michael Parekōwhai security guard statue, along the wall that may or may not have something to do with the Māori Land Wars, past the library, under the tree that smells like weed, through the muddy entrance to Albert Park, past the fountain where people want to take their graduation photos but it's never good weather on graduation day, past the newly blooming daffodils and tulips, under the magnolia trees, over the huge knotted tree roots, past the sculpture that's just a huge white D, down the slippery steps past the art gallery, down the suffragette mural staircase, past the shoe shop where people sit in chairs camped out all night for Yeezys, past the fountain where teenagers always hang out and into my building, up all the stairs, down the corridor, in the door and then I drop my bag on the floor and burst into loud, messy tears because I live alone now and no one can hear me or see me and then I notice the big bunch of white lilies on the table and a whole bag of limes and I close my eyes because I'm crying too much and I feel V's arms around me and smell his stupid fancy cologne and push my face into his dumb soft wool jumper and I dissolve.

Roimata

V

I have to put Greta to bed. She can't stop crying enough to tell me what's wrong or what's happened. She just wails. It makes me think of Hine Hukatere, who cried out Fox Glacier because her boyfriend was shit at mountaineering and died in an avalanche. I don't think Ell has died in an avalanche; it doesn't really go below 14 degrees in Auckland in September. A more logical way to die in Auckland is getting hit by a bus because the driver was yelling at a cyclist.

I hug Greta for a long time and then I put her in the bathroom, turn the shower on, and get her dressing gown and a clean towel and the Aēsop Geranium Body Cleanser that cost me $71 and that I keep under my bed so no one accidentally uses it. She doesn't stop crying but she undoes her hair from its bun and takes her shoes off, so I shut her in the bathroom and make her bed properly, the way she likes it with the sheets very tight. I pace around the living room, still getting used to being by myself again. No more Xabi to halve my problems with anymore. I wonder if he's feeling the same about me. I think about polishing our concrete floor; there must be a machine for that.

Greta emerges from the bathroom securely tied up in her robe, still sniffing, and I turn down the bed for her. She doesn't let go of my arm, so I sit on top of the pale blue linen duvet next to her. I cross my ankles and look at her walls, a seafoam colour. The sheepskin rug on the floor she's had since she was born. I think of the time before that, or what I remember of it, when it was just me and Casper and our parents, going to Rainbow's End and crying when the frog said *Go back!* on the Log Flume because I couldn't. Going to Marineland and watching a dolphin jump through a hoop. That probably wouldn't be allowed now, it doesn't seem like a good thing, but it makes me feel like I've lived quite a life, to remember things that wouldn't be acceptable these days.

How strange it is that there was a time before me, too. Casper went to Aotea Great Barrier, but he doesn't remember. Greta and I have never been. Sometimes people remember my mum is from there and ask me for tips when they go for a wedding, like I might know a tapas place or a microbrewery. I don't know anything about what's happening there. I think there's a shop – sometimes my mum will say *the shop*, which I guess means there's only one. There's no high school; she did correspondence because her family didn't have anyone for her to stay with in Whangārei like other people did. She was going to stay with her great aunt, but her dad got in a fight with the aunt and didn't let her go. The Correspondence School's original mission statement was *For the most isolated children*. Once my mum said she just read any book that anyone on the island would let her borrow. I think of the book Ernesto was reading, *Herejes de Dune,* a Spanish translation of the fifth Dune book, which he found outside the supermarket. He hadn't read the first four.

'Do you want to watch something? Do you want to watch *Mommie Dearest*?' I ask Greta.

She shakes her head. 'She's never coming back,' she says, leaning against me, closing her eyes, a single tear running down her cheek.

'People don't never come back,' I say, hoping Ell hasn't actually died in an avalanche. 'Do you want to talk about it?'

She shakes her head again and keeps her eyes closed. I look at her for a while, and then I don't know what to do anymore so I take my phone out and read over my Spanish vocab. Eventually she falls asleep, gripping my arm so hard I can't move. So, I download the book I have in my room as an e-book – *Small Holes in the Silence*. I can hear the silence now. I feel something in my pocket, although I don't remember putting anything in there. I put my hand in and pull out a rubber ball painted in the colours of Neptune.

Fugitives

G

I wake up because I'm too hot. I'm wearing my dressing gown under my duvet and sunlight is pouring in around the edge of my blind. I don't want to open my eyes because they feel puffed up and awful; I must look like a tree frog or a tarsier. I don't reach for my phone to check the time because I left it in a pile of dirty clothes in the bathroom last night. I remember everything again. V almost having to bathe me like I was a woman in a TV drama whose husband had just died in a horrific car accident, how Holly grabbed my wrist, Ell's face when she saw us. She must think I'm a scheming adulterer and I'm not, just my mum is. Holly is a horrible, manipulative person, it turns out. I got sucked in because I'm the beautiful fool after all. Put me on a list of Auckland's top ten biggest fools, slightly behind the man who runs for mayor every election with an anti-abortion campaign, an issue the mayor has no control over.

I feel so sad. I've let everyone down but most especially myself. Why did I *run away*? Why did I do that? Why did I cling on to V's arm and not let him go, like when I was five and he came to my class to collect the list of absentees and I thought that he had better just stay in the New Entrants with me from then on?

I put my hand out to feel for my kea toy so I can hug it and cry more but my fingers come across something much larger than a regular alpine parrot like a kea, something more like the size of Heracles, the giant extinct parrot from the South Island.

'Hello,' says Ell. I open my eyes as much as they'll allow me to and Ell is there, having at some point replaced V. She is sitting next to me on top of my duvet with her ankles crossed, reading a book.

'What are you reading?' I ask, redirecting her from breaking up with me.

'Oh.' She looks down at the book cover. 'It's a book that V gave me when we switched places. It's short stories; one's called "Doll Woman", which reminded me a bit of you when you were asleep.' She strokes my hair and I think this is the last time this will happen. 'Are you okay?' she asks, maybe judging my mental state before she begins the break-up proceedings.

'I don't know.' I sniff.

'Look, Greta,' she says. This is not the phrase I want to hear. 'I have to tell you something before anyone else does. Assuming you've thrown your phone out the window at some point, I saw you didn't receive any of my messages.'

I've never thrown my phone out the window. Throwing things out the window is V's signature move.

She keeps stroking my hair, and she does the thing I like when she holds her fingers under my chin. 'I hit that woman,' she says.

'What?'

She swallows and looks rueful. 'Yeah, I got in a disagreement with that girl who was grabbing at you and then I smacked her over the head with the can of oven cleaner.'

I feel my eyes go wide. 'You hit Holly with the Glitz BBQ and Oven Cleaner Spray?'

'I don't know what came over me, I didn't like the way she was touching you, and she said you didn't really love me, that I could never understand you, and I got mad and then I just hit her. I'm really sorry, I know that violence isn't the answer.'

'Did anyone else see?'

'Yeah, Rashmika was there; she was coming to help me find you.'

'Then what happened?'

'Rashmika grabbed my arm and we ran and hid in case campus security came and arrested us for assault. We were hiding out in the Arts Tuākana room, but then that seemed too obvious, so we went back to my building. Then we ran into your dad and Rashmika told him we needed a place to hide, so he corralled us into his office, but there was a student who wanted him to be his supervisor next year having an interview. He just said not to mind the fugitives.'

'Did you tell him what happened?'

'No,' she says, and I still like the way it sounds in her accent, as if it's spelt with three Os instead of the half O we have here. 'He asked if you were okay and if there was anything he could do, and Rashmika said that you were . . . fucked as. I believe that's the phrase she used. He hoped you'd feel better when you saw V.'

'And then what?'

'Ehm.' She pauses. 'Then we all went for a kebab.'

'You and Rashmika went for a kebab with my dad?'

'Yeah . . . ? I'm sorry. I kept trying to call you. Rashmika said you'd be fine, and we shouldn't say no to a free chicken shish. I was so worried about you, though. I kept thinking about how disgusted you'd be that I'm an oafish thug going about the place carrying a weapon, on the attack. So I came up here to come clean to you, and V was sat next to you reading a book on his phone and we switched out.'

'I thought you were here to break up with me.'

'Why would I break up with you?' She frowns down at me, backlit from the sunlight coming through the blind, still wearing one of her satin shirts and the dark wide-legged jeans from yesterday. 'I just hit someone over the head with a bloody can of oven cleaner and temporarily became a fugitive from the law because I love you so much. I only want to be with you. If you still want me.'

'Of course I still want you. I hate Holly.' I realise it's true when I say it. It's been so long since I realised that Holly wasn't so great after all, when I was in McDonald's that night with Matthew. I just wanted someone to be in love with. Now Ell loves me. And V probably cares about me too, even though I didn't ask him a single thing about his trip and bawled in his face. 'I should have hit her over the head myself a long time ago. I did say I wanted you to be more Scottish.'

'Oh, that's not a stereotype I'm trying to uphold. I get worried, Gre. I do feel like a hobgoblin sometimes, sitting about covered in pie crumbs while you swan around being beautiful and funny and speaking five languages with your fashionable friends. I know I dress like a seventies record executive and I don't know how to use highlighter.'

'I like your highlighter. You look like te marama.'

'Is that one of your mates?'

'No, it's the moon.' I try to kiss her, but she holds me back with a finger on my chin.

'Greta, I want you to tell me the next time you feel like everything's gone wrong. I know you haven't been eating properly and you're up all hours of the night. I know you were upset with your brother and you haven't got any job security, because other people told me. But it should be you telling me. Before you get into an altercation with a young Hannah Gadsby in a photocopying room.'

I swallow hard and then nod. I really want to do that.

Holes

V

I'm enjoying being home again, eating fresh foods and mumbling and having everyone understand me anyway. I don't so much enjoy being at work, but I get it done. Today I have to go to Casper's house and repent, at my mother's recommendation. She says he doesn't really deserve it, but it will make things a lot easier for everyone. I feel like I'm on *Real Housewives* again, or the one that's like *Real Housewives* except everyone's a real estate agent. I walk over to Casper's because I don't really want to get there, and it's a nice spring day and I like to see the flowers appearing along the way.

My phone rings. I've been having a lot of phone calls recently. A lot of professional calls and also less professional calls with Xabi, where we talk about how Ernesto is doing at school and then, when we get too sad, I get him to recount times when he thought I was being particularly debonair. This time it's someone else calling.

'Hey, V, it's Cosmo Alonso.' I know it is because he's Face-Timed me and I can see him, in a wood cabin with his dark blonde hair in a small bun on top of his head and his glasses on, and he can see me, walking over Grafton Bridge in my navy cable-knit jumper. No coat, that's been safely put away until next year now. Unless I have to go somewhere where the seasons are different.

'Hi, Cosmo, it's Valdin Vladisavljevic.'

'How are you?' he asks. He's wearing an open floral shirt and a grey singlet, and he looks a bit overheated.

'I'm good, I'm walking to Casper's house. Cosmo?'

'Yeah?'

'Where the fuck are you? Why are you in a simple cabin made of batik wood?'

He pushes some hair back from his face. 'I'm in Labuan Bajo, yeah.'

'Why?'

'Ah, Paris was presenting a lot of problems.'

'Right,' I say. Cosmo is very difficult to get any answers out of. He doesn't exhibit his feelings publicly like the rest of us.

'Have you seen my dad?' he asks.

'No? I've only been back in New Zealand a few weeks.'

'Where were you?'

'I was with Xab.'

'I see.'

'How long have you been in Indonesia?' I ask. 'Did you see your dad there?'

'Ah, I'm not sure how long I've been here, maybe three months. I was travelling around before that. But my dad's never been to Indonesia. He was considering opening an office in Surabaya, but he didn't like what was happening politically and he pulled the deal and never came over. Do you know, like . . .' He pauses and looks at something in the distance, maybe a Komodo dragon. 'If there's anything going on with him?'

'Why do you ask?' I definitely remember Thony telling me Gep had gone to Jakarta earlier this year, and I wonder which person is wrong.

'He doesn't seem like he's all right,' Cosmo says. 'He says that he is, but he seems really stressed. He keeps telling me he cares so much about me and he just wants to know where I am, but I feel like it's something else. I tried to talk to my mum about him, but she said some racist stuff about Spanish people and then talked about how it's great being single because you never have to worry about where to scatter your partner's ashes.'

'That sounds like something she would say. Why don't you just tell your dad where you are?'

'I don't know. I don't want him to buy me a ticket back. I don't need that right now.' Cosmo's patting a local Indonesian dog now. I would be scared to do that because of potential disease transmission.

'Will you ever come back?'

'Yeah. I will.'

I sigh. 'I know something's going on with Gep, but I don't know what. Vlad knows and he's coming over soon. I'll find out. Please send me a picture of a Komodo dragon as soon as possible.'

It's Freya who opens the door when I get to the house. She folds her arms and her eyes disappear when she smiles.

'No one told me you were going to be here!'

'No one told me you were going to be here either,' I say.

She laughs. 'I live here!'

'Really? I had no idea.'

'Dad! Uncle V is here and he's being very funny!' she shouts into the house. I wish everyone had such low standards for humour. People could stop commenting on my show's Facebook posts and asking when New Zealand will get some real comedians.

'I'm in the kitchen,' he calls out.

I follow Freya down the hall. The house seems more spacious than I remember; it's not that big as far as houses go, but it still seems nice to have all this room. I think of my apartment as a place to be when I'm not anywhere else.

Casper has made lunch. I didn't know there was going to be food on offer.

'What's all this?' I ask.

Freya points seriously at a big ceramic dish of what looks like an eggplant bake. 'It's Auflauf.'

'Sit down,' Casper says, sort of smiling, maybe a little bit sour at me still. 'No one else is home.'

'Where's Tang?' I ask. I sit down opposite him, with Freya next to me.

'He's driving his friends around illegally. Op-shopping. School holiday stuff. Freya, if you sit all the way over there, I can't reach to help you.'

I take the serving spoon that she's struggling with and ladle eggplant, mozzarella and ajvar onto her plate, then a little bit of salad so that Casper knows I'm responsible.

'I spoke to Cosmo on the way here,' I say.

'Is he missing?' Casper asks. 'Thony said he was missing but he seemed very blasé about it. We went to a Russian market together a couple of weeks ago. That's where I got the ajvar.'

'Ajvar's Serbian, isn't it?'

'I don't think there's a Serbian market. They have to make the sales where they can.'

'Cosmo's only sort of missing,' I say, buttering a piece of bread. 'He's in Indonesia. He's been there for months. Something happened to him in Paris, but he wouldn't say. He just wanted to know if I'd seen Gep, because he thinks something's going on with him.'

Casper shakes his head. 'Of course, he's disappeared into the Sumatran jungle or whatever but it's Gep who's the problem.'

As we eat, I look at the fridge with stuff all stuck to it, time-tables and certificates and letter magnets. My fridge doesn't have anything on it at all. How do you end up with a proper fruit bowl instead of just a normal bowl or an ice-cream container that you shoved some fruit into because it kept rolling off the table onto the floor? Xabi made his own.

'Have you heard about the Gold Coast?' Freya asks me. 'It's very cool and fun. There isn't a better place you can be, than at Surfers Paradise.'

'I didn't know you'd been there,' I say, pushing her fork back onto the table before she knocks it on the floor.

'I haven't, yet.'

'It's good to be optimistic. What are your plans for your holidays?'

'Become a detective,' she says with her mouth full.

'I thought we were going to Te Hāwere-a-Maki with Papa Linsh,' says Casper. 'He was going to teach you how to snorkel.'

'If it rains, though.'

He leans back in his chair and smiles at her, with her crooked bowl cut and a plaster in the middle of her forehead. 'It wouldn't rain if we were on the Gold Coast, would it?'

On the deck after lunch, Casper leans on the railing and watches Freya dig for worms with a small trowel. I stand next to him drinking Coke from a mug. Freya isn't allowed any. She thinks all mugs contain coffee anyway, which she thinks is gross. Children sometimes know things that adults don't.

'How's Tang?' I ask.

'He's a bit better than he was before, I think,' Casper says. He's wearing old jeans and a fisherman's jumper. I don't know where he gets all these good dad looks, if there's a special shop or a mail-order catalogue. 'It's hard to tell because he hides it so well, which freaks me out. Even when he was a little kid he was afraid of so many things, but I never knew unless there were tears rolling down his cheeks or he said point-blank, "I'm very scared right now." He's seeing a counsellor, and he says it's going well. I don't know what else I can do really, except be around for him.'

'It's really good that he wants to talk about it. I . . . felt incredibly guilty when I saw he'd tried to reach out to me, and I hadn't noticed.'

'That's why you need more than one person to be there for you.'

'What about the queer stuff?'

Casper turns around and leans back on the railing, running his hand through his hair. I pay a lot of attention to his hair as a forecast for my own and I'm pleased to note that it all appears to still be there.

'That didn't go as I expected it to,' he says. 'I always had in the back of my mind what I would say if it came up, and I imagined he would cry and I would say I accepted him and maybe something about how there are a lot of things that I don't understand in this crazy world but I know I love my son. Then I would put up a poster fundraising for Rainbow Youth at work. He just asked me if we could leave it until the afternoon to swim laps so he could call his boyfriend first. Then later he said that pansexual memes were dry and he showed me some and they were all dry.'

'I know it's good that it's not a big deal to be gay anymore, at least in some circles, but it really takes the drama out of it, doesn't it?'

He smiles. 'Yeah, I could have used some theatrics.'

'Is that why you told him he was going to fail his driving test?'

'Oh God, did he tell you that?'

'Yeah. Why did you do that? Why didn't you say that he was a great driver and if it didn't work out he could easily resit?'

He narrows his eyes. 'Because sometimes I do dumb stuff, V. I think I'm being a good dad and then the next day I wake up and think, Why the fuck did I tell my son he's shit at driving when he's actually not too bad? I watched a show that came on after the news about teenagers in Darwin sitting their tests and a lot of them were awful but none of their parents told them that they were. They said, "Get out there and give it your best shot." Freya has that plaster because her mum sliced her forehead open cutting her fringe with the kitchen scissors. Over the sink, because she didn't want to clean up afterwards. It just happens. But we love them, and we don't let them go hungry, so it's fine. That's what we tell ourselves.'

I nod. My chest feels tight. I want that. I want a house with a fridge with stuff stuck to it. I want to be shown memes. I want to be shown up by Australians on TV. I want my dad to teach Ernesto how to snorkel. He's never seen the sea before.

Casper looks up at me, sipping Coke from his own mug, which has a picture of Peppa Pig on it. 'Where have you been, V?'

'With Xabi.'

'Are you okay? What's happening with you two?'

I pause. 'Cas, can I ask you something?'

'Yeah, of course.'

I look down at the decking. I've seen so many ads about men varnishing decks in my life, and I've never thought that it would ever have anything to do with me. 'How did your Greta adopt Tang?'

'Oh. We'd been together for a few years and Tang told her he didn't like explaining why his last name wasn't the same as either of ours, and that kids would say she wasn't his real mum, just his dad's girlfriend. We were fine with our relationship as it was, but she asked me how I would feel if we got married and she adopted Tang. It seemed like a good idea in a legal sense if anything happened to me. We thought it would be good for Tang to have a more cohesive family, and you can change your name for free at the same time. That's when

Tang wanted his name to change to Yellow Tang Lavrentivich Vladisavljevic. We thought that was too far. There was a boy at our school called Gandalf Merlin because his mum let him pick his own name. I really thought Tang was just a phase, but it's been ten years and he's still going by the name of a fish.'

'Indiana Jones named himself after a dog and he did pretty well.'

'That's true.' We both watch Freya trying to keep the worms she's found from wriggling away by telling them not to. 'It wasn't that difficult with the paperwork, but it was a bit hard emotionally. I had to get his biological mother's consent and we hadn't spoken for a really long time. Even with the custody stuff, it was all through lawyers and she didn't come to court. I found her on Facebook and sent her a message. It was so uncomfortable. She said it was fine, that it was difficult to live with being the legal parent of a child who doesn't feel like yours.'

'That must have been hard.'

'Then there were a couple of meetings with Oranga Tamariki, to make sure we knew what we were doing, and that Tang understood what was happening. He took it very seriously and asked if he had the right to remain silent and whether he would have to swear on a Bible. We filled out a lot of forms and then that was it.'

'Does that mean that theoretically Greta could pass on her German citizenship to him?'

He nods. 'Yeah, there's no difference between her legal relationship with Tang and Freya. It's a pain to become a German citizen, though; you have to prove why you'd be a useful asset to the Fatherland.'

'Then you could all live in Germany.'

'Yeah. We don't want to do that though. I wouldn't want the kids growing up without family around.' He drums his fingers on the railing. 'I worry that one day Tang's going to ask me about his mother or want to get in contact with her. I don't think she would want to see him. I wouldn't want to see him go through that.'

'He may never want to. Dad never got in contact with his mother.'

Casper's gazing down at the deck. 'I don't know how you could, though. How you could not feel like you have a huge hole in your whakapapa and know that there are answers out there somewhere.'

'I don't feel like that. I think sometimes there are things you don't know about where you came from and that's just the way it is. You have the relationships you have, and you have to make the most of them. I want to go to Aotea, but I wouldn't feel right without Mum taking me and I know it would be really hard for her to go back there after so long.'

He still isn't looking at me. 'Mum's right.'

'What, about not wanting to go back there?'

'I am a hypocrite.'

'Oh, Cas, we all say stupid shit. She didn't mean it seriously. I was being a dick not telling anyone where I was, I upset our Greta and she's been having her own problems.'

'You've never done anything as bad as I have.'

I don't know what that's supposed to mean. He stays silent and then sniffs and holds his hand up to his eye. I look at Freya back on the lawn, trying to do a cartwheel but not really pulling it off. I reach into my pocket, pull out an old serviette from Esquires and straighten it out to give to him.

'I feel so guilty, I never told you, I . . .' he trails off and looks at his hands and I move forward to hug him.

'It doesn't matter what happened, Cas; you don't have to tell me. Sometimes you don't have to tell people everything, you just have to trust them. And I trust you.'

'You shouldn't.'
'I do.'

In the evening I sit on my windowsill in the apartment with my back against the cool glass, rolling the Neptune ball between my fingers and listening to people as they walk past on the street below. Then I call Xabi and ask him when he can come over.

Agenda

G

It's after midnight when V asks me if we can talk, and I go back out to the living room. He sits on the cane chair and I sit on the couch in front of him. The curtains are open and the lights from the bars and restaurants beneath us reflect on the window. V's all dressed in black, like my favourite Shangri-Las song. I don't think anyone's parents are warning them not to go out with him, though. He's not that exciting. He crosses his legs and then uncrosses them and then puts his elbows on his knees and holds his head up, looking at me.

'Greta, I'm really sorry that I haven't been keeping you in the loop recently.'

'Oh. Well, that's okay. You had your own stuff going on. Probably. You didn't tell me.'

'Not really. Sometimes people give me too much leeway because they're just glad I'm not dead.' He keeps looking at me and it's a bit too intense; he looks like an enormous black vulture. 'Xabi's coming to see me next month. Just for a couple of weeks. He has a festival to go to in Melbourne.'

'If you're just asking if your boyfriend can stay at our flat, you're being very serious about it.'

'I'm going to ask him to marry me.'

'Why?' I blurt out.

'Oh.' He sits up and folds his hands in his lap. 'As a symbolic gesture of commitment.'

'I thought you said that marriage was inherently queerphobic and that the only gay people who do it are buying into the monotony of the straight agenda and a proscriptive society that stipulates that the only ideal life is one where you're committed to one person, own a house and work forty hours a week for one employer.'

He tilts his head to one side. 'I still think that. But I have to buy into it a bit.'

'How come?' I feel like he's being unnecessarily obtuse, but he might just be thinking things through before he says them.

'For bureaucratic reasons. I want to form a family with Xabi and his dependant but none of us are currently citizens of the same country.'

'His dependant?'

'Sorry, I've been reading a lot of legal nonsense and government websites. Nes. His child. He adopted him. And I want to adopt him too, so we can live here together.'

Everything V is saying to me is blowing me backwards a little bit, in the style of an industrial fan. 'Can I see a picture?'

'Um, yeah.' He lurches forward to sit next to me on the couch and then holds his phone so I can't see it while he scrolls through it.

'Gross, I don't need it implied that you've been expressing your desire for commitment through a series of intimate portraits.'

'No, I haven't been doing that actually, I just have a lot of ruthless screenshots of other people's awkward online interactions and posts that were quickly deleted, you know . . . I don't care if you see me naked, but I don't want you to think I'm a bitch.'

'I don't want to see you naked. I've seen you hanging out on your bed with Slava like a Calvin Klein campaign. That was enough.'

'Hmm. I need to update him that that's never happening again.' V hands me his phone. I look at the photo.

G

'Why are you throwing up in this picture?'

'I'm not throwing up. I'm just spitting out some mandarin-flavoured chips.'

I look at it for a long time. 'To me this is a photo of my brother throwing up and a kid I don't know laughing at him, but to him it's a photo of him and his dad.'

I turn my head back to V, who nods slowly. 'Maybe. It depends what Xab says.'

'He'll say yes. I hear the way he talks to you; you always put his calls on speaker and tell him no one's home.'

'I don't like holding the phone, it makes my face oily.'

I look through all the photos and they're all really bad – poorly framed, bad lighting, someone about to fall over – like all of our family photos are.

Lemon

V

The first time Xabi referred to me as his boyfriend was during a filmed interview at the Venice Biennale. The interviewer asked if he felt a duty to produce art that represented the struggles of the Catalonian people and he said that he didn't know how well he was doing with that, but he would really like to go to Sitges with his boyfriend. He didn't answer any of the questions that followed; he just stared into space, fanned himself with a brochure and said, 'Could you repeat that, please,' not in English but in Catalan, which I can't understand but I could read the subtitles, far away on my phone under a tree outside my old work. It was November and exams were ending at the university. People younger than me were lying on the grass with their friends, holding hands, waving goodbye, shouting, 'Have a good break!'

It's strange for me to think that people can know about me without me having met them, to remember me when I'm not there, to know I exist when I'm not standing in front of them. It seems even more strange for someone to want me to be with them when I'm not, and the most strange for someone to need me, to depend on me, to love me. But I suppose this is what is happening. I put my keys on the counter. I don't want my hands to smell like metal. Everything has to go perfectly today.

My mother comes into the kitchen. 'Valdin, what are you doing here?' She stands on the opposite side of the counter, resting her hands on it. She has her hair up and is wearing an orange and yellow floral dress with a tie at the waist, no shoes.

'Do you know when you make a cake, it tastes better if you bake it a couple of days before and not on the day that you serve it?'

She considers for a second. 'It depends what sort of cake.'

'A lemon-and-poppyseed cake. The kind that's made with yoghurt.'

'Okay.'

I scrunch up my face. 'I need to make the cake today.'

My mother sighs lightly and goes to look in the pantry. 'I have a bag of lemons. What else do you need . . . oil, flour, eggs, yoghurt, caster sugar, baking powder, poppy seeds of course.'

'When will Vlad be here?'

'Tomorrow. He's in Singapore now but he doesn't leave until nine tonight. He had a lovely day at the Gardens by the Bay.'

'So he'll still be here on Saturday?'

'Of course he'll be here on Saturday: tomorrow is Friday.'

'Is he staying here?'

'Yes. I've made up the room for him downstairs.'

'What if other people want to come and stay?'

'Which people?' She peers at me from around the pantry door.

'I don't know. Different people.' She looks at me without saying anything. I just look at the keys on the counter.

'Whose are those?' she asks, noticing the keys.

'Mine. I bought a car.'

'Okay. Which model did you go for?'

'I don't know, a black one. A Toyota.'

She starts putting all the ingredients for the cake on the counter in front of me, stopping to get a bowl out from a low cupboard and measuring spoons and cups from a drawer behind me. 'Isn't Xabi supposed to be arriving today?' she asks.

'I don't know.'

'What do you mean you don't know?'

'Sorry, yeah, he is. Not until later. My phone kept going flat so I left it at home. Does Dad have a wedding ring?'

'Yes. Have you never seen the hands of your own father?'

'Did you give it to him at your wedding?'

'Yes. I didn't have a pocket so Geneviève put it in her bra. It was very warm when she gave it back to me. Linsh had to try not to laugh.'

'What else do you need at a wedding?'

'You don't need anything at a wedding, though I suppose it's just nice to have some things. Flowers, friends, food. A location. Music. A marriage licence.'

I breathe in sharply. 'Fuck, a licence. How long does it take to get one of those?'

She stands very still on the burnt-umber tiles of the kitchen floor, her arms folded, her expression vaguely bemused. 'I really couldn't say, V. I've never decided on a Thursday morning that I might want to get married on Saturday.'

She takes her phone out of her pocket and slides it across the kitchen counter.

'You look up what you need to do, and I'll start making the cake.'

Pez

G

I walk through my parents' house, calling, 'Hello?' I'm worried that something bad has happened, even if my mum said in the message that no one's dead. There are other bad things that can happen. I'm expecting to see people speaking in hushed tones or sitting silently around a box of tissues, but it's just V and my mum in the kitchen, taking a cake out of a tin.

'Greta, don't breathe,' says V, as if they're performing a risky and complicated surgical procedure. The cake comes cleanly out of the tin and they both sigh with relief.

'Did you summon us here to watch you take a cake out of a tin?' I ask.

'No, I'm going to get married this Saturday,' V says in the same tone I imagine he would have used if the answer had been yes, I just wanted you to see me take this cake out of the tin. 'You can ask your friends to come. Fereshteh, Rashmika, and who's that white boy? Emmitt Rhodes?'

'Elliot Stokes.'

I don't know what to do with myself. I put my keys on the counter. The cake smells really good, but I suppose we can't eat it until my brother's wedding in two days.

My dad comes hurrying in with his briefcase and papers in both hands, which he puts on the desk in the corner that serves no purpose other than having things put on it.

'What's going on? Do I need to call an underhanded coroner?' he asks, standing next to my mum, his arm around her waist.

'I said no one was dead,' she says.

'Sometimes you have to lie to protect the ones you love,' he says.

'I'm getting married on Saturday,' V repeats.

'Oh, Valdin,' Dad says. 'I never thought I'd live to see you have a shotgun wedding; not since your mother found out she was going to be a grandmother at thirty-seven and said pointedly, "At least we don't have to worry about that with V." Pust' budet krepkim vash soyuz.' He hugs V so hard I think he might complain, but he doesn't.

I sit at the table, overwhelmed. How has my dumb brother, who once managed to fall over while his Year 9 class photo was being taken and appeared as a blur that all the other boys were leaning away from, become someone's dad? It's been four weeks since V told me about Nes, and I'm still not used to the idea. V seems so different, talking on the phone to Xabi about school fees and vaccinations, Skyping Nes at his school to ask how his day was. Enquiring about his friends and enemies by name. Explaining the water cycle in his careful Spanish. Last week Nes was sick in bed and V told him all about Māui y el sol, Māui y sus hermanos, and Māui y el gran pez. He loves him. I can't believe it all happened without me knowing.

Casper comes running in, adds his keys to the pile on the counter and hugs Dad, ignoring all the rest of us.

'I told you I'm not dying,' he says.

'I was worried anyway,' Casper says. 'I thought you might have had a fall.'

'A fall? I'm not an eighty-year-old woman trying to hang on to independent living.'

'You're right. If anyone had fallen over it would have been V.'

V makes a loud indignant noise. 'In 2003, who was the one who nearly smashed the glass in the Hundertwasser toilets with their own thick head because they slipped in their Etnies skate shoes—'

'Valdin, who fell over in the middle of the school production of *Grease* and tried to act like it was a part of the choreography, I don't even know why they let you in the play anyway when you didn't even talk—'

'I had anxiety, Lavrenti! That would have been discriminatory if they hadn't included me!'

They keep arguing and my mum comes and sits next to me. I don't know the last time it was all five of us and no one else. It used to be like this every night. In those days someone would always announce they were going to consult the *World Book*.

'Are you okay?' she asks me.

'I think so.'

'Casper, I'm getting married in two days,' V says. Casper turns around too fast and knocks him into the cabinet.

'Oh my God, V, I'm sorry.'

'Watch out! I don't want my wedding photos to be all depressing and concerning like Priscilla Presley's,' he screeches. 'Dad!'

'What do you want me to do, send him to his room?' my dad asks.

'No. I need everyone to help me organise,' V says, his hand to his face like a man scorned. 'I've compiled a list.'

I see the list on the table and take it. 'What is this? Why is the first thing *plates*?'

'What are people going to eat off if there aren't any plates?'

'Why did you write *food*, and then in brackets, *kai*? Where is the venue? Why are Dad and I listed under *music*?'

'We can have it here,' V says. 'I thought we could drag the piano outside, and you could play and sing, like at a party in a classic film.'

'I'm not a human jukebox,' I say, even though I am.

'You can have creative control.'

I decide I'm quite happy with this. I imagine how many eighties pop hits I can sing as piano ballads. My dad can play by ear; he's fine.

'Who is *white boy, not sure name*? How has he made the guest list?'

'Tang's friend. The blonde one who looks like he's in an ad for Danish raincoats.'

'His name is Tristan,' Casper says, leaning on the bench. 'I'm so sorry I knocked into you. Your face looks fine.'

My mum moves closer to me and puts her arm around the back of my chair. 'Why have you crossed out *ribbon*?'

'Ignore that,' he says. 'I thought we'd need to cut a ribbon but it's not the opening of a mall. Then I thought, I could paint my nails something that went with the ribbon, but now I don't know.'

'What are you going to wear?' I ask.

His mouth gets smaller and smaller and his eyes get squinty. 'Where the fuck am I going to get suit pants from in two days when I'm 18 centimetres taller than the average New Zealand man?'

'Casper, go and get the smelling salts,' says my dad. He gets his laptop, puts his glasses on and turns to my mum. 'What's been done so far?'

'We made the cake and I asked him to look up how to get the licence and then he read out an explanation of when to spell *licence* with an S, then he made this list that includes . . . *photos, can use phone (all good)*.'

'Dad, why do you want salt?' Casper asks, holding a grinder of Himalayan salt. 'Is it a Russian thing?'

'It's only midday on Thursday,' my dad says. 'We can get some pants adjusted for you in time. If we go to the registry office in Manukau, we can line up and get the licence in person. I think that will be less busy than the city one.'

'Who's going to pick up Vlad, though?' V asks, almost hysterically.

'Someone can pick him up,' my mum says. 'Don't worry about that. Maybe you should call Slava to come and help; wasn't he in events before he got his marketing job?'

'Have some water,' Casper says, but he turns the tap on too hard and splashes it on himself.

My mum looks at this happening and shakes her head. 'Linsh, why don't you take V to get the suit and the licence and the rest of us can stay here and organise other things. How many guests are you expecting V? I'll need to figure out how many fish to smoke.'

'Is there a colour scheme?' Casper asks, texting. 'I'll have to get something for Freya to wear, she's growing like a weed at the moment, and Tang will want something new as well.'

'Should we get some trestle tables?' my dad asks. 'How many guests does Xabi have?'

'Where is Xabi?' I ask. 'Did he arrive already? Is he organising something? Can I cross it off the list?'

V sits on a stool at the counter and puts both his hands on his face, which has gone very red. 'I didn't ask him.'

'What do you mean you didn't ask him?' I ask.

'I didn't ask him if he wanted to get married.'

'You *didn't ask him*, V!' Casper shouts. 'What the fuck? Tang and his friends are already on their way to SaveMart – what if someone messages Xabi about his wedding that he *doesn't know about*!'

'I don't know. It just felt right to do it this weekend and I kind of felt like it would be nice if I talked to Giuseppe first, but I forgot, and my phone went flat and then I just freaked out and started baking. Xabi's supposed to be here at five.'

'Ah, that's okay, you only need one person to sign for a marriage licence,' my dad says, not looking up from his laptop. 'No one tell Thony before Xabi finds out, he's a terrible liar.'

My mum stands up and gives V her phone. 'Call Gep now.'

V nods and takes the phone, looking through the contacts. 'You don't have his number.'

I glance at her quickly. 'It's under Joseph Allen,' she says as if she has nothing to worry about. He puts the phone to his ear. 'Hey, it's—No, I don't want to go to Perth with you, it's Valdin. I actually thought I was going to Perth earlier this year for work and then we went to Argentina instead because the airline deals the marketing team at my work make dictate the course of my life apparently.' He looks at us all looking at him, and goes and stands in the hall. 'Maybe I should go. Have you ever seen the Indian Ocean?'

I look at my dad who hasn't seemed to notice anything happening. My mum stands with her hands on her hips, looking at the door that V's just closed. I message Ell, suggesting she order the suit she wanted to be express shipped right now.

V re-emerges. 'Giuseppe was very touched that I asked him for his blessing to marry his brother. He's coming over now. Mum, he said you can talk about Western Australia later.'

'Okay,' says my dad, closing the laptop. 'Get in the car, let's go to 7 Ronwood Ave, Manukau. I'll pay the $150 licence fee so you're not out of pocket if he says no.'

V stops walking. 'Do you think he'll say no?'

'No.' My dad puts his hand on his shoulder. 'He's the only person I've ever seen laugh at your Archangel Gabriel García Márquez joke. He'll definitely say yes.'

By late afternoon, things have escalated. People are constantly coming in and out of the house. V and my dad are back from the registry office. The woman there was very friendly and thought they wanted to marry each other. Slava is here, wearing a beret and snakeskin-print pants, making phone calls and using a special voice for getting what he wants. There are a lot of things that Slava knew were necessary for a wedding that V certainly did not put on his list. Ice. A marriage celebrant. A dress code. Forks.

There have been some minor limits placed on my creative control. V says I'm not allowed to sing any songs about old men in love with younger women, such as 'Sixteen Going on Seventeen' from *The Sound of Music*, which I had not at all thought of singing at my brother's wedding. He also said not to sing a song I'd never heard of called 'Gayby' because it was 'too on the nose'.

V is so stressed out that he's not even complaining about how much Slava is flirting with our dad, which he usually hates. My mum, Gep and I are doing some organising. I don't like seeing them together, so I keep looking at the ceiling. Casper forgot the other Greta is in Sydney for a conference, but she'll be back tomorrow night. I've added this and what time Freya needs picking up from school to a chart I've been put in charge of. V shouts that I'm not allowed to sing 'But I'm a Top' by a band called The Ballet. Noted.

I look at my phone for the first time in a while and I have a message from Xabi. 'V, Xabi's already at the airport; he's wondering where you are and wants to know if he should take a taxi here. A taxi? How old is this man?'

He looks at me in utter panic.

'Tell him I'm dead.'

'Absolutely don't do that,' my mum says. 'Are you sure he said five, V?'

'He might have said fifteen, sometimes he uses twenty-four-hour time because he's foreign but I forgot about that and just assumed he meant five.'

'He messaged me too,' says Gep, looking at his phone. 'Oh, shit, Thony told him I was here and—'

'Tell him just . . . fuck off,' says V.

Gep answers his phone. 'Xabier, com estás? . . . Guai.' He starts saying a lot of stuff very quickly and I don't understand any of it because I don't speak Catalan. Then he says my name. He takes his keys out of his pocket and slides them across the table to me.

'What's happening?' I ask.

'I told him you would come and pick him up from the airport.'

I take the keys. Gep thinks it's okay for me to drive his fancy businessman car. I stand up. 'What do you want me to do with him, just drive around indefinitely?'

V looks down at the bench, making the serious face he usually only uses when he's figuring out a complicated mathematical problem. 'Go and pick him up and drive him back to the apartment. Tell him to go and get my phone from inside, it's charging by the bed. Then come back here. Yeah, I'll meet him inside.' He takes his own keys from the pile on the counter. 'Can you give me about an hour? I need to wash my hair and . . . decide what I'm going to say.'

I nod. 'I can do that.'

'Don't come back,' my mum says to him. 'We'll see you tomorrow.'

He looks pained. 'No, there's so much to do.'

'We're fine. You aren't going to have any time to yourselves until after this is all over: take it now.' She gives him a look that means this is the end of the conversation. He's seen it before at Video Ezy when he wanted to get out *Emmanuelle* for our family Friday-night movie, and one time when he wanted our holiday to be to the Egyptian resort town of Sharm El Sheikh, even though tourists kept being murdered there. Except this time I won't end up watching *The Parent Trap* or going on a trip to Tauranga. I will be as dependable as two strong boys.

Lila

V

I stare at myself in the mirror in the bathroom and think about my hair, just like the first page of *Fifty Shades of Grey*. I don't think my life is heading in the same direction. What am I going to say? How do I start?

> Hello.
> Hi, this is Valdin speaking.
> Excuse me, sir.
> Keen, oi?
> I was wondering if you had a few moments to chat.
> Kia ora.
> Hey team,
> I just want to take a second to tautoko your mahi.
> Wuu2 ;-)
>
> Would you like to hear about an exciting new opportunity in your area now?
>
> Ngā mihi,
> Valdin Vladisavljevic

Should I ask him how his flight was? Maybe I could read a speech off my phone. Maybe I could type it up in Word and get Microsoft Sam to read it out. Maybe I could do a pre-recorded message like the winners at the Silver Scrolls who are too important to come back to New Zealand and collect their award.

I take my phone out to check where Greta is but then just look at my reflection in the black screen. What will I say if he says no? I would like to think I could be casual and say, 'Nah, all g, man, fair enough, at the end of the day it's your call.' In reality I would probably put on 'Not Pretty Enough' and start crying. I look in the mirror again and think how funny it is that we only get one face, and this is mine. I rub some concealer under my eyes. Greta has some body glitter; would that be good or . . . ?

I hear the door open and I shut the bathroom drawer.

'Val, are you here?' Xabi asks.

I don't say anything. All of my planned greetings fly out of my head. I march into the living room.

'Hey,' he says, looking me up and down. 'You look nice.'

I stand slightly away from him so he can't distract me with any gentle but focused kissing or anything like that. He looks nice. It's very good to see him. I fold my arms and then I unfold them because I think it looks too confrontational.

'Have you got your phone? Greta's waiting in the car outside. It took us so long to get here, she said there was no point trying the motorway at this time of day and then we got stuck in the roadworks for the CRL.'

'She isn't waiting. It's all lies. It's a litany of lies.' I stand very still with my arms stiffly by my sides.

He smiles. 'Have you been reading about communist Albania again? She's not an informant.'

'Lots of people's sisters were informants. Xabi, my life changed when I met you,' I blurt out. I expect him to be taken aback but he only nods slowly and waits for me to go on. 'I had never spoken in public before. I had never said, "Just these, thanks," or, "The council should really do something about this tree." I wasn't good to people I dated. I never talked about my feelings and I never told anyone I loved them even when they really wanted me to. I was obsessed with controlling everything because I felt out of control with my body. Words and . . . expression were a really big deal to me. Then I met you and—' I have to stop and close my eyes for a second because they're stinging. 'I just wanted you to like me so much. I thought I could be someone else. When I called and asked you out, I'd never done any of those things before. I'd never ordered a coffee. I don't even like coffee.'

'I know,' he says very quietly.

'I'd never asked a bus driver if I could tag on two people or told someone I really enjoyed their set. I couldn't believe how easy everything felt. But then I started to feel worse about the rest of my life. It had all been set up to avoid these things. I didn't want to sit at my desk looking at equations all day anymore. I wanted to go out and meet people and experience things, but I felt so conflicted because I had spent so much time and money acquiring this life I didn't want. I could feel myself falling apart over it, and I wasn't in a place where I knew how to explain that to you. I understand why you thought that it was your fault. And I was sad that I had changed so much but it still wasn't enough. I didn't know how to be this new version of myself without you. But I learned. I needed to do that, I needed to be alone to do that. It was only when I had figured things out and I had this new job and money and friends and this really nice apartment, that I started wondering about you again. Then I lost my mind a bit because I missed a package delivery and I thought you were trying to send me my book back—'

'*Summerhouse, Later.*'

'—but it was just this stupid book about fungi someone sent to me instead of my dad. I started thinking about you all the time. I didn't think there was any way you would be thinking about me too. I thought you would have found someone age-appropriate, with proportionate features. I thought I needed to see you so that I could see that things were different now and you had moved on. But it wasn't like that. Things were different, but the way I felt about you was still the same. I thought maybe you felt the same way.'

'I do.'

I shake my head. 'I love lilacs so much. I love Albania. I never thought I would feel like this. I never thought the happiest I could feel would be with my head on your chest watching dash cam videos of people all over the world lying on the ground in front of cars pretending they got hit for the insurance money. I love you so much. All I want in my life is for us to be together with Nes and maybe a turtle, if he wants, and maybe a dog, if you want, because you should have what you want and I hope that what you want is me and I hope you want me to be the father of your child because that's what I really want. Xabi. Will you marry me?'

'Valdin—' He's standing close in front of me, holding my upper arm.

'Because all good if not, that's chill.' I put my hand up to my jaw to stop a tear running down my neck.

'Yes.'

'Are you sure?'

'Val, I carried that book around with me for months because I knew I should send it back to you, but I couldn't let go of it. I love you. Yes, I want to marry you.'

'I want to adopt Nes so we can live here – do you want that?'

'Yes, that's what I wanted, but I didn't know how to ask.'

'Okay, sweet as.'

He has his hands on my shoulders. 'Why are you talking to me like you did to the guy at the bagel shop when he said they weren't doing the one you liked anymore?'

'Because I only prepared for if you said no.'

'You were going to say, "Okay, sweet as," if I said I didn't want to marry you?'

'No, I was going to say, "All good, man." '

V

He looks like he's going to say something, and then something interesting happens and he picks me up instead. Thank God for high ceilings and Xabi's exercise regime that I don't know the exact details of because it always happens when I'm still asleep. I think this is one of the sexiest things that's ever happened to me, then I forget what I'm thinking because he's kissing me, and I feel like my teenage dream of becoming Rita Hayworth is coming true.

'Xabi,' I say, as I watch the living room disappear and I'm carried off to bed. 'How do you feel about getting married this Saturday?'

Tōrangapū Māori

G

It is the day before the wedding. We have all been rushing around arguing with each other about chairs, borrowing shoes, contemplating whether we should dig up the backyard for a hāngī pit or turn the garage into a smokehouse. The idea of having a 'Russian party' tonight has been aired throughout the day. It began in the morning, when Thony, furious that he was the last to know about the wedding, put down the mango he was scoring and said that we should have a Russian party. My dad kept humming Tchaikovsky as he painted the trellis, a job my mum said was definitely not a priority. Then Giuseppe asked if he could come to the Russian party, and Thony told him to go and fill up a bucket with red wine and oranges and play a song off someone's phone. So, it has been decided that there will be a Spanish party tonight as well. I suppose this circumvents the discussion of stag and hen parties, dividing everyone up along racial lines. No one has pointed out that V doesn't really identify as Russian and Xabi doesn't really identify as Spanish. I guess there were enough things going on already. My mum is invited to both parties, but says she'll see how she feels later on. Thony has texted Vlad to buy vodka and cigarettes at duty-free.

I have an unexpected new role in wedding organisation: being V's publicist. This is because the episode of his show in Queenstown aired on national television last night. None of us remembered it was on, so we didn't watch it, but other people did. A lot of people did. There have been think pieces.

Journalists calling and asking for a comment. I have to look after his phone now. He seems very calm about the whole thing. I messaged Ell asking if she felt closer to being Russian or Spanish, and she sent me back a screenshot that said *Vladisavlje-vic could not be reached for comment as he was 'at the nail salon', a representative confirmed.* Casper wanted to be V's representative instead, but he was too shouty and someone had to take Freya to get new shoes. She's been taken out of school for the day and keeps peeking out the window to see if the police are coming to get her.

Xabi comes downstairs with my dad's laptop. It's just me, him and my mum here at the moment. This is the quietest the house has been for twenty-four hours.

'What did he do?' my mum asks.

Xabi sighs. 'He met with a real estate developer who showed him some incredibly expensive properties, which were all foreign-owned, and then they got him to interview a man who owned this enormous golf course. He'd even flat-tened out a whole hill for it. And then V said, "Do you know how many Māori children are living in poverty in this coun-try?" Then they had an argument about whether it was possible to work your way up when you exist in a system that doesn't want you to succeed. Then V looked right into the camera and said he didn't want to talk to the Pākehā anymore. He left the golf course and gave a speech about the commodi-fication of land that I don't think he knew was being filmed.' My mum pours Xabi a glass of water, which he drinks. 'Then he walked around asking people if they knew whose land this was and what it was really called, and none of them knew. He ended up meeting a woman called Whaea T who was working in a souvenir shop, and they went and got a cream bun together and she told him the story of Hine Hukatere. At the end he walked past the queue of people lining up for burgers and said, "You'll never get a better burger than one from Big J's Mt Wellington."'

'Auē.' My mum sits down at the table. 'What did the people have to say about that?'

'They're saying a whole lot of things,' I say, flicking through the open tabs on the two phones and V's laptop. 'They're saying it's racist to even use the word *Pākehā*, they are confused as to why someone was talking about Māori problems on the normal channels, they think Māori should go back to being funny like Billy T. James. Some stuff about the Moriori. Someone says Aucklanders should go back to . . . drinking lattes and sucking themselves off. Obviously, some people think it's about time someone said it and they stan a brown fag who knows land back is the only option. There is some discussion over whether V is hot or looks like a broom, and if he's single.'

'No, he's my broom,' Xabi says. 'I suppose I'll need to find somewhere secluded to take my celebrity husband on honeymoon now.'

'As long as you don't take him back to the island,' my mum says. 'I want to.'

She doesn't let anyone help her dig the hāngī pit.

When Vlad arrives from the airport in his camel coat, carrying his leather travelling case, he hugs me first. It's time for the Russian party to begin. I flick through the Stefan Zweig book Vlad has brought me from Vienna, as Xabi, Giuseppe and my mum look for their jackets and keys.

Vlad kisses my mum on both cheeks and asks, 'Aren't you staying for our party, Beatrice?'

'The Spanish need her to make up the numbers,' my dad says. 'Thony was running a smear campaign against them; he kept talking about a medical show he saw about how many venereal diseases people get in Ibiza.'

G

'No one's going to get a disease,' Giuseppe says. 'We're going to order dinner and talk about old times.'

I find it hard not to stare when he and Xabi are together, to try and see how they're the same and different. They don't move the same way and they have different ways of speaking, but they can't help having almost the same face. Giuseppe might have broken his nose at some point. I look at my book until after they've left.

The Russian party in the downstairs room has descended into a mess of empty glasses and playing cards thrown in a rage after four lost games of durak in a row. It's hard to do a shot out of a wine glass, it turns out. My parents were not equipped with the correct glassware for the occasion. They do have an adequate space for the occasion, though: a funny wood-panelled room under the rest of the house, with couches and a TV. When I was at school and I brought Pākehā friends over, they would call it a rumpus room.

'Should I deal another round?' Vlad asks, shuffling the cards as he sits on the floor in front of the coffee table. Geneviève is sitting on the floor across from him. She came over thinking my mum would be here and was vehemently opposed to joining the Spanish party.

'Don't deal me in,' Casper says, putting down a cup we got from the Valentines buffet in around 1999. 'I'm going to say goodnight to Freya.' The other Greta took her up to bed some minutes ago after she started feeling sick. Too many Raro shots.

Ell is leaning on me. She came straight from a meeting she had but we didn't end up talking about it because the party was already in full swing. She's been very quiet but it's probably because everyone has been shouting at each other in Russian for hours. My dad is sitting on the couch behind us with his arm around Thony, who's quiet as well.

'If you love her, you should get married, too,' my dad says in Russian. 'I'll give you the money.'

'Don't be weird,' I say in English. Ell looks up at me and smiles, blankly.

'She's too young to get married,' Vlad says, in Russian as well. 'Stop telling her what to do.'

'What do you know about romance, Papa? You haven't had a girlfriend for fifty years. In modern times you have to say how you feel before it's too late.'

'What on earth do you mean, fifty years?' Vlad says. 'Do you think your father is a monk?'

'What?' my dad asks, sitting up straighter. 'Do you have a girlfriend?'

'Not right now, but I haven't been alone since your mother left. Why would you think that?'

He starts dealing the cards. Geneviève concentrates hard on what he's doing. She can't understand what anyone's saying either. She's wearing a black velvet dress and I hope she isn't disappointed by how decidedly not classy this party is.

'You've never introduced us to anyone,' my dad says.

'It's not very seductive to introduce a woman to your elderly son who can't lose a card game more than three times before he throws the deck across the room.'

'You were cheating.'

'No, I wasn't, you were trying to cheat, and you were doing a bad job of it.'

Thony stands up quickly and goes back up the stairs. Vlad and my dad look at each other and then my dad gets up and follows him.

'Just deal three,' I say to Vlad, and kiss Ell on the head before going upstairs too. I'm on my way to the bathroom when V leans out into the hallway on his wooden desk chair.

'Gre, you have a way with words – come and help me.'

Our parents have never converted his room to anything else. They probably want to keep V's options open in case he has a breakdown again. I stand next to him at the desk and look at a faded Mint Chicks poster.

'Do you need me to help you with a statement to the press?'

'No.' He's staring at the grid-ruled notebook he's writing in. 'I'm trying to write my wedding speech, so I don't go off on a tangent and start listing my favourite Arnold Schwarzenegger movies. I was thinking I could write an acrostic poem, but I've made the foolish decision of marrying someone whose name begins with X. What begins with X? Xtreme Entertainment, the bowling place?'

'I don't know, X-Ray Spex? Thony's upset, by the way.'

He stops and looks at me. 'Did Dad throw the cards at him again?'

'No, I think it's about something else.' I look at him carefully, to see if maybe he knows something I don't know.

'Oh.' He looks back at his notebook. 'The elephant in the room.'

'What do you mean?'

There's a knock on the wall. The wall has a dent in one side from a knocking fight that occurred around the turn of the century.

'What are you doing?' calls Casper through the wall.

'Gre's helping me write my wedding speech.'

There are some shuffling sounds and a muffled conversation before Casper appears in the doorway.

'Tēnā kōrua i tēnei ahiahi,' he says, combing his fingers through his hair and tucking his shirt in.

V pushes his glasses up his nose. 'Who visits their parents' house to have sex in their childhood room?'

'We were just enjoying being somewhere with a door that locks.'

'You're lucky to have one.'

'V, I broke your lock because you stole our advent calendars because you wanted to control when we ate the chocolate, like you were a prison pharmacist,' says Casper.

V frowns. 'Well, I'm glad to know that the sex doesn't always completely go after marriage. Can you think of something beginning with X?'

'Xi'an Food Bar,'

'I'm trying to write my wedding speech about my love for Xabi, not hand-pulled noodles. Or . . . maybe that's a good metaphor, actually.'

'What's going on downstairs?' Casper asks me.

'Thony's upset.'

'Oh.' He looks at V. 'It was his idea in the first place.'

'He didn't think it through.'

'What are you talking about?' I ask.

V folds his arms. 'Thony essentially goaded Gep into spending tonight with Mum, and now he's worried about what they're doing.'

'They're with Xabi though,' Casper says.

I look between them and feel a deep sense of unease. 'Is this something everyone knows about?'

Casper looks at the floor. 'I wish they would just end things.'

V stares at him blankly. 'Why would they do that now, after all this time? Don't you want Mum to be happy?'

'No, not them,' Casper says, shaking his head. 'Thony and Gep. Did you hear what happened?'

'No, I know something happened but I don't know what. I went to Thony's house one day and he was crying and said Gep had gone to Indonesia, which I know now isn't true, and then he distracted me from asking any questions by telling me a really dark story about Dad's childhood.' He turns to look at me from his desk chair that's too small for him and was probably too small for him when he got it as a teenager as well. 'Greta, Vlad didn't bring Dad and Thony here on a work visa. They were refugees. I'm sorry, I should have told you.'

Casper takes on an expression of extreme vexation. 'What the fuck, V, of course they were refugees! The Iron Curtain was very much in force. Do you think Greta's never figured that out? She's doing an MA in Cold War literature, and she's not stupid.'

'Well, I didn't know. It's not stupid to not have put every little puzzle piece together so you have a complete picture of everything your parents have ever done. God.' V turns back to his desk. 'Help me write my vows or get out.'

'I have to go to the bathroom,' I mutter as I leave, still feeling like I am the stupid one.

My dad is outside on the small balcony, drinking a glass of water. I go out and stand in the dark next to him, looking out at the quiet backyard with its freshly painted trellis and hāngī pit.

'What's going on?' he asks, but I just shake my head. He considers me and then says, 'I'm feeling very foolish that Vlad has been . . . socialising with women my whole life, and I never noticed.'

'Did Thony know?'

'Yes, we were just talking about it. He said he'd known about it since 1979, when he came home early after sneaking out of youth group because they were doing trânta. What is that in English, upright wrestling?'

'Is he okay?'

He looks at me and doesn't say anything for a second. 'He'll be fine.'

'Aren't you afraid?'

'Of what?'

'Of Mum leaving you.'

He shakes his head. 'Your mother and I tell each other how we feel.'

'What about what you're doing though? Where you are? Who you're with? How can you really know what anyone else is thinking?'

'You can't. There's no way of knowing. When you love someone you have to trust them and you have to believe that they wouldn't make choices that would intentionally harm you. If you can't, that's when issues arise.'

'You don't worry that she's a snake?'

'No, she's more like a bird. A kūaka.' He looks at something out of the corner of his eye. 'Greta, I think we should go inside.'

'Why?'

He smiles a funny half-smile. 'There's something in our line of sight that we shouldn't be privy to. I know I have a hard time accepting when I'm wrong, but I don't need anyone to rub it in my face. Especially my own father.'

As he moves me along inside, I catch a tiny glimpse of Vlad and Geneviève, no longer concerned with the duty-free cigarettes between their fingers, slowly dripping ash onto the patio below.

Braut

V

I wake up alone in my childhood room and consider my situation. I've become a controversial figure in race relations. It looks like it's going to be sunny. I'm getting married today. I put on my robe and knock on the wall once. I hear the muffled sounds of Casper telling me to fuck off, and make my way downstairs.

In the kitchen, my dad is frying bacon and halloumi and talking on the phone. Freya is sitting in front of him at the counter, eating a bowl of almonds and dates.

'Do you need me to come and pick you up, or can you make your own way back?' he asks the person on the phone. 'You don't need cash to pay for a taxi these days, you can order one on your phone . . . Well, that's the perk of a younger woman, she can show you how to do it. Absolutely don't ask her for cash . . . Okay, see you soon; don't do anything I wouldn't do.'

I steal an almond from Freya's bowl. 'Who on earth was that? Have you become a pimp?'

'No, certainly not. Good morning, Valdin. Happy wedding day. Have you changed your mind? Should I be expecting a runaway bride situation?'

'Nope. Freya, did anyone tell you you're going to have a cousin?'

'Nope,' she says.

'His name is Ernesto and he's eight years old. He'll be moving here from Colombia and it will be hard for him and he doesn't understand much English yet. I hope you can be a nice friend to him.'

She looks at me with two dates in her mouth. 'Bonjour, mon ami.'

'Valdin, I saw a nice gif of you rolling your eyes about white people this morning,' my dad says, flipping over the halloumi.

'I muted my own name,' I say. 'Why are you frying that? Couldn't you cook it on the barbecue?'

'It's just your wedding, it's not Christmas.' He takes some bacon out of the pan and puts it on a plate.

'Dad,' I say, looking at the bacon. 'Should you be eating that? Aren't you here as a Jewish refugee?'

He opens his mouth in surprise and promptly tips the bacon down the waste disposal.

There's a knock at the door and Freya jumps down from her stool and runs to open it. We hear her turn the lock, and then she gasps loudly and says, 'Xabi, why have you got a black eye!'

Tang

Casper

'Are you okay?' Tang asks, leaning around the trellis. Then he looks at the paint on his hands. 'Why is this wet?'

'I'm fine,' I say, wiping my eyes. I didn't think that I'd be so emotional all day. I'm not the sort of person who cries at weddings, but V has really done a number on me. 'My dad just painted that yesterday. I don't really know why.'

'Mum said you were being a Heulsuse and I should come and talk to you.'

'Go back and dance with your friends.'

He straightens out the knees of his peach suit pants. Tang and his two friends found three matching peach suits in SaveMart and presented them to me this morning, as if they'd found the treasures of Tutankhamun.

'We're having a dance break. Luce did too many spins and didn't want to be the first person to throw up.'

I look over at my sister lying on top of the piano singing 'Graceland'. I don't know if it's the best song to dance to, but V's dancing anyway, slowly, with his arms loosely around Xabi's neck, looking the happiest I've ever seen him. Happier even than when he got a flip phone for Christmas. He has no idea what he's in for.

'Tang, I'm sorry I told you that you're shit at driving,' I say.

'Oh, it's fine. It was pretty crack-up.'

I turn to look at him. We're the same height these days and I'm still surprised every time we meet each other's eyes. 'I know I'm not always good at dealing with things, but I would always rather know than have you try to spare my feelings. Even when it's hard.'

He leans his head on my shoulder. 'I'm not going to do anything really dramatic and not tell you.'

'Sometimes you think you aren't and then you just do anyway.'

He inhales. 'Dad, I've read all the court documents. I don't need to meet my other family. I don't feel bad that they didn't want me, they didn't even know me. The family I have is enough. And I'll like . . . I'll tell you if I decide to go to Germany to be with Plan. I'm not just going to buy a ticket and disappear. And it won't be forever.'

I kiss his head. 'You do what you want to do. Go and have fun.' The song ends and Greta, looking exhausted, announces a short break. Tang slopes off to join his friends lying on the lawn and I don't tell him to stand up straight because who cares.

'What are you doing, hiding back here?' My dad touches the trellis and grimaces when he sees that it's still wet. 'That was a real moment of madness, painting this.'

'Dad.'

'Mm?' He looks around for something to wipe the wet paint off his hand and settles on a leaf from the hedge.

'I'm really sorry.'

'About what?'

'That when I was twenty, I felt so alone in Moscow and I was so mad that you didn't want to come and see where I lived because I didn't understand why you—'

'Oh, are you referring to your secret rendezvous with my mother?'

I feel as if time stops momentarily. 'How long have you known?'

'I've known the whole time. She told Vlad as soon as you came to see her in Sochi, and he told me.'

'Why didn't you say anything? Why weren't you mad at me?'

He shakes his head. 'She's your grandmother. That's not my relationship, it belongs to you. Your mother knows your relationship with the whenua is yours too, but she wishes you would let her know the next time you're planning a four-and-a-half-hour ferry trip, because she'll spring for the flights. And you should invite your siblings, too.' He pauses and squeezes my shoulder. 'Ya lyublyu tebya, Lavrenti. You're not the bad person you think you are. I have to go and wash my hands.'

As he goes back into the house, Freya emerges from behind the trellis. 'Will you stop crying if I give you this little piece of cake?' I pick her up while I still can, and she puts the cake in my mouth and says, 'Sorry, I already licked all the icing off.'

Greta

Ell

Everyone at the wedding is impressed with V's beautiful sister, who has been lying on the piano in an emerald brocade dress for most of the night, even though a lot of her song choices aren't really appropriate for a wedding. I keep turning around and telling people she's my girlfriend. More often since I got into the punch. Even when people aren't talking about her. Hello, I'm Ell, don't talk to me about Brexit but have you seen my very attractive girlfriend?

She's gone off somewhere now, explaining that she had to take a break because she was gearing up to sing 'One Week' by Barenaked Ladies and it's got a lot of words. I go and look for her. I need to tell her something important. I walk around the garden searching, in my new slippery brogues, my treat after my interview. I find her by the hedge with Fereshteh and Elliot. I'm sure that's his name but everyone seems to have been calling him Greg all day.

'Elizabeth,' she says as she comes over. She leans down and inspects me. Her eyelashes are so long I don't know how she can see anything. Her lips are a glossy red and I want to kiss her but I don't want to mess it up. 'You're looking quite crooked. I might have to take that away from you.'

'No, ahm no,' I shout soberly, but she takes the cup out of my hand anyway and drinks it herself. 'I need tae tell ye a wee . . . factoid.'

'A factoid?' she asks, raising one pointed eyebrow.

'Yeah, see, while ye were havin ya wee sulk because ye don't know whether ye mam's gettin' off with some Mediterranean bloke with an Audi, I had me interview and in actual fact it went really well, and I just wanted tae ask ye, have I ever said aboot how I lost me marrow at the school fête?'

Her eyes move from side to side like when she's trying to translate something, and then says, 'No, you haven't told me any stories about marrows. Where is this going?'

'When I was a wee lass, or whatever, I think ahm somethin' else these days, anyway, me and me dad grew a fuck-off enormous marrow and we both knew we was gonna be winnin' that blue ribbon, he looked at me dead in the eye and said, "Ellie, this here marrow is a winner." Nowadays they don't want tae talk to me so much because it turns oot I'm great at shaggin' birds but nae bother.' The corner of Greta's mouth is twitching, but I keep going. 'I dinny know why yer laughin', tis a very sad story about prize-winnin' vegetables and homophobia.'

'I'm sorry, please continue.'

'Thank you. We cleaned up the marrow all nice and brought it down the school and we just knew we had the competition, but when we was all let back inty the hall, me marrow no was there.'

'It was gone?'

'Aye! We was lookin' all over, people were sayin', "Where's that lovely huge marrow of Ellie Livingstone's got to, maybe a wee dog's got in here and nicked it, but what the fuck would a wee dog want with a feckin' massive marrow?" Ye know what I'm tryna say here?'

'Um, sort of,' she says. She looks over at her mates by the hedge who are just stood about looking as bewildered as she does.

'Well, I could hardly enjoy myself after that, I couldny stop think aboot me marrow. Me mam said I could have the ten quid she won at tombola but I couldny give two shits about the feckin tombola, where's me marrow? But we didn't find it. I think maybe Simon McGilvery nicked off with it, the wee prick. Aye, he's a cunt in actual fact, but I know ye don't like it when I say that, ye think it's only awryt tae say cunt if ye bein' nice aboot a lad, dusny make no sense, ahm tellin' ye.'

'Is that the end of the story?'

'No. So I just kept thinking aboot the marrow for years and years, it was a right mystery plaguing me mind all the time. But one day I woke up an' realised it's nae bother tae me where the marrow went no more. Because I have you. Yer the marrow.'

She screws up her face. 'That's very sweet, I think.'

'So basically I want tae know if ye want tae come tae Rakiura with me for the summer so I can watch feckin' grass grow and tae be honest with ye they want tae give me lots of money so we can probably be doin' that wee trip ye want tae be doin'. Budapest.'

'Bucharest.'

'Yeah, that lot. Do ye want tae? It could be dead borin' but ye can look at ye books and sing ya wee tunes tae the birds an' all, I know ye've never seen a kiwi oot an' aboot.'

She puts her arms over my shoulders. 'Yes, Ell, I'll come with you to Stewart Island and watch grass grow and . . . see if I can sing a song to a kiwi who's out and about. I love you more than any vegetable I've ever seen.'

'Is that true? Have seen ye go a bit mad fer an eggplant parmigiana—'

I have more things to say after that, but she doesn't want to hear them.

Cosmo

V

I have a moment to myself on the garden ledge. Then I feel something warm and heavy on my back.

'I can't believe you married my uncle,' Cosmo says into my neck.

'I can't believe your mum went home with my granddad,' I tell him.

He laughs and sits next to me. 'I couldn't believe it when I asked her where Etienne was, and she said they broke up over a year ago.'

'I'm so glad you came,' I say, and he leans on me.

'My dad called me up and said I had to,' he says. 'Despite everything else, when my dad calls me and starts shouting in Spanish, I know I have to do what he says.'

'You're such a jerk to him usually. He worries about you.'

'I worry about him too. And I don't know how to express it without just being a jerk. I watched your show on the plane. Why did they think it was okay to put you in a situation you were so obviously uncomfortable in?'

'Because they don't understand what it's like to be a minority in this country.'

'Are you going to talk to them about it?'

'I quit.'

'What?' Cosmo undoes his hair from its bun and shakes it out.

'I got a better offer. I'm going to make a new show, something more political. But it will be fun. I'm going to ask Greta to come on board.'

'And work with you?'

'Yeah, she'd be amazing. Everyone knows she's funnier than me and people really like her. And she'll tell me if I'm being a dickhead.'

'I used to be so jealous of you, that you had a sister,' he says.

'Really?'

'Yeah. Do you remember that time my dad and your mum took us to see *2 Fast 2 Furious*?'

'Yeah, we went to the Burger King in Newmarket afterwards and Casper tried to get me to drink all the drinks mixed together.'

'That was the best day of my childhood,' he says. 'I thought it would be so nice, to have straight, married parents and siblings to hang out with. I felt like a real piece of shit when we went home. Thony is the nicest stepdad. I just . . .'

'I get it.' I squeeze his arm. 'What happened in Paris?'

'I nearly cheated on my girlfriend because I was in love with a guy from work and then I had a big crisis that I was turning into my dad. Then it turned out she was cheating on me anyway. I freaked out and booked a ticket to Bali like some gross white person who can't handle themselves. Now I'm alone but I feel much better about it.'

'Have you met Casper's friend, Ben? Over there, talking to those people from my lab. In the blue suit, with the nice hair.'

'No, I haven't.'

'I kissed him this morning.'

'What?'

'Yeah, he came and apologised to me because he tried to ask me out earlier this year and he'd thought I was offended. I just didn't realise at the time. I had low self-esteem. Then I didn't know what to do, so I kissed him. Xabi thought it was funny. It was nice though. You should go over.'

He shrugs and gets up. 'I'll give it a go. In front of both my parents, why not.'

'They won't notice, they've been smoking whole packets of duty-free cigarettes around the side of the house all night. Cosmo.'

He turns round and stands in front of me in the borrowed shirt and pants he's wearing. He still looks like a model.

'I'm glad you're home.'

'I'm glad to be here.'

'And you have to call me Uncle V now.'

He leans over and kisses me on the head. 'I can't believe I ever wished you were my brother.'

Geneviève

Giuseppe

Geneviève comes back outside with a new cigarette already in her mouth and I light it for her. 'Is that a menthol? Where'd you get that?'

'I confiscated it from a child,' she says, leaning against the weatherboard side of the house. 'One of Greta's friends, couldn't be older than seventeen.'

'Greta turned twenty-six in September.' I watch Cosmo cross the lawn to where a guy with nice hair is deciding which beer to take from a flexible tub full of ice. I wonder how long he'll stay for this time. If it will be long enough for us to talk properly.

'Should we have another one?' I look across at Geneviève and she's already cackling.

'One is enough,' I say. I watch Xabi sit down next to V on the ledge with a plate of hāngī. I don't think I've ever looked as happy as he does tonight.

'What did you do, Giuseppe?'

'To who?'

Geneviève exhales. 'That says a lot. How did Xabi get a black eye? Did you hit him?'

Xabi's black eye is barely visible now. V spent a good hour this morning covering it up, calmly explaining how colour theory comes into make-up while I sat on the side of the bath and felt guilty about it.

'It was a reflex: I thought he was going to hit me,' I say.

'Why would you think that? When has Xabi ever hit anyone?' Geneviève says.

'He really looked like he was going to; Betty thought so.'

'What led to that happening?'

I shrug. I can't see Betty now, she was here before in her red dress. She doesn't like it when I smoke but she didn't say anything about it. Not tonight.

'Well, I'm glad I didn't go to the Spanish party then, if it was all people punching each other and listening to "La Bamba",' Geneviève says.

' "La Bamba" is Mexican,' I tell her. 'If you came to the Spanish party you wouldn't have been able to go home with my father-in-law.'

'How long is he going to be your father-in-law for?'

'I couldn't say.' Thony's talking to Tang, getting him to take off his peach suit jacket so he can see the lining of it. He looks good tonight. I haven't seen him happy like this in a long time either. 'Did Thony tell you what happened?' I ask Geneviève.

She nods. 'I'm sorry. He felt so bad about it. You should have told Xabi, though. I don't want you to tell me that you're too proud to admit to your own brother that you were cheated on.'

'No, I just . . . I'm not innocent. I wasn't the one who met a nice Romanian photographer at the Melbourne airport and went back to his hotel room with him, but I was the one who created the environment in which it was bound to happen.'

'You're not innocent but neither is Thony. Neither is anyone else. Xabi wouldn't have tried to fight you if he knew that.' She shakes her head and flicks some ash onto the tiles of the patio. 'You should have told me.'

'I feel like I owe it to Thony not to tell anyone.'

'No, you should have told me you were in love with her in the first place. I don't wish for a different life, but I wouldn't have gone anywhere with you if I had known that. She's my best friend.'

'I'm sorry.'

'It was a long time ago. Thank you.'

'For what?'

'Bringing Cosmo back. I missed him.'

Space

G

I walk into the house through the French doors and into the kitchen, looking for my mum. I need to tell her about my trip. I need to tell her that I love her and that we should go to learn te reo together, even though I'm really scared it will be the one language I'm bad at. I need to find my dad and tell him I would like to sing 'Words' by F. R. David, if he knows that one. Of course he knows that one, it's a classic.

I think I can hear my parents talking in the laundry room, very quietly, what sounds like very close to each other. I stand by hesitantly. I hope that something terrible hasn't happened and they're hiding it from us so that V can have a nice wedding day. It's been such a nice day. I don't think anyone's done anything weird at all, except Casper managed to call Elliot Johnny three times in one conversation about the summer football season. Rashmika thought it was so funny that she spat her cake all over the ground.

'When's the flight?' I hear my dad ask.

'Next Friday night,' my mum says.

'He doesn't have a house there, does he?'

'No, we'll stay at the hotel we stayed at before. He just has the house in Wellington; he was going to move there, but now he doesn't know because he wants to be here for Xabi.'

'You should go to Broome when you're there, the beaches are so beautiful. Send me pictures. Let me know where you are.'

'I will or you'll just track me down anyway like you're the KGB.'

'Does he know how much you like it when—'

She breathes in sharply. 'No, that's only for you.'

I walk outside hastily and find V by one of the tables, eating green grapes in his almost metallic teal suit, smelling great, his skin glowing.

'You look like you've seen a ghost,' he says, cheerfully.

'V, do you get off on the idea of Xabi with another man?'

'No. I don't always like to follow the example of my parents.' He sees my expression and almost laughs, the light of the candles reflecting brightly in his eyes, hugging me tightly. 'If you want to go back to not finding out about things, please let me know. But I can't keep things bottled up until I burst into tears in the supermarket anymore, I'm a third-rate New Zealand celebrity now. Someone might write about it in the magazines.'

I think I don't want him to let me go, but when he does and there's space between us, I can see how happy he really is.

Dear Ernesto,

I hope that you're reading this letter because you've turned 21 and I've given it to you to read the morning of your birthday, not because you've found it in a drawer somewhere while you're looking for bus money, or spitefully because I said you can't go to the hop, after having watched too many fifties horror movies. I actually hope that by the time you read this, they won't be allowing cash on the bus anymore, because it really holds things up. Also, hopefully the world hasn't ended because of climate change; fingers crossed.

I'm writing you this letter because I'm marrying your dad today. I wish so much that you could be here with us, but at least we will be together very soon, hopefully before Christmas. It's a beautiful day; it's 22 degrees and there isn't one cloud in the sky, which is unusual for Tāmaki Makaurau. All our family is here; your grandfather and aunty are practising a song called

'Skandal im Sperrbezirk', which I get the feeling might be inappropriate for a wedding, and your grandmother is smoking fish on the patio. Xabi has a black eye, which we don't need to talk about. It was a wild and unbelievable series of events at a Spanish party that led to it. He still looks great, anyway. Everyone is really looking forward to meeting you and I want you to know that you will always be very loved here, no matter what happens.

I am afraid of being your parent, worried that I'll do something wrong, or that we won't understand each other or that we're doing the wrong thing by taking you so far away from your home and everything you know. Although I know it will be hard and that there will be many difficulties we need to overcome, it's my sincerest hope that you'll think it's worth it in the end. I would do anything for you, and I know that Xabi would too. You are our top priority, and you will be for the rest of our lives. It's a kind of love I've never known before but now that I do, I don't think I could have it any other way.

I love you so very much,
Your father,
Valdin V. Vladisavljevic

P.S. If you're reading this and for some reason I'm not around anymore (maybe run over by a self-driving car), please buy your dad some pink carnations and tell him I love him – I know they're old-fashioned, but they're his favourite.

Acknowledgements

I wrote this book in 2019, existing on one eggplant and a packet of pizza bases per week, and as an unwilling participant in a student rivalry with a man in his fifties who slept on a beanbag and had his velvet scarf stolen by an amateur burlesque performer. Many things have happened since then, in the world and with this book. I can now, on occasion, pay a local takeaway to make a pizza for me and to the people who made that happen, I am thankful.

Thank you to everyone at Hutchinson Heinemann for publishing this UK and Commonwealth edition of this book, especially the marketing and publicity team, Charlotte Cray, and my first editor Ansa Khan Khattak; to my agent Martha Perotto-Wills who plucked me from obscurity and made this happen; to all the people who posted about the book from New Zealand enough for it to reach the other side of the world; and to all the booksellers who sold it to them.

Thank you to my personal friends and their aggressive support of the book – Amelia who thought she should be in the book as 'comic relief'; Grelj, Michael and Hannah who were prepared to learn accents to 'perform' it; Vondy who investigated my professional contacts and their sisters on LinkedIn; Stacey who printed a T-shirt; Mitchell who had a car; and especially Mikee who threw up when I didn't win the New Zealand Book Award.

This is for the colonised, queer, trans, ace, and intersex people, and the hot autistic community. He hono tangata e kore e motu; ka pa he taura waka e motu – he rā ki tua.

Barking (BLC)	8724 8725	Rectory	8270 6233
Castle Green	8270 4166	Robert Jeyes	8270 4305
Fanshawe	8270 4244	Rush Green	8270 4304
Marks Gate	8270 4165	Thames View	8270 4164
Markyate	8270 4137	Valence	8270 6864
		Wantz	8270 4169

MCT

1 5 APR 2008	1 0 SEP 2011	2 9 MAY 2014
	2 1 OCT 2011	
− 5 AUG 2008		RESTELL
− 4 OCT 2008		THOMPSON
	− 2 FEB 2012	KARSTADT.
2 0 DEC 2008		23
− 3 AUG 2009	1 0 APR 2012	
2 7 AUG 2009	1 2 OCT 2013	
2 4 SEP 2009	− 7 NOV 2013	
2 9 MAR 2010	5 DEC	
1 1 MAY 2010	9 JAN	T4